"As with all literature, it's the questions that matter and in SF they are often the big ones. These are perhaps the biggest questions of all. What is life? What is intelligence? Is there a God? Is there such a thing as soul, or a personality? Are they different? Of what do they consist? Can you manufacture emotions?" - Dave Luckett, author and reviewer for The West Australian newspaper

"*Eclipse* is an intelligent novel that will leave readers with much to think about." - Victoria Strauss, Sf Site

"Bedford also raises some serious issues, using the interplay between disposables, synthetic minds, augmented animals, and a woman artificially enabled to live beyond her death to intelligently explore questions of free will, humanity, and the existence or non-existence of the soul." - Victoria Strauss, SFsite.com

"*Eclipse* works in all the ways that matter. It kept me turning pages way past bedtime. It has an edge of barely contained terror through-out; it has love, (sort of); it has mysterious, very alien aliens. It has a big picture that gets bigger as the story ends. It left me eager for more." - Terry Baker, Eternal Night

"*Eclipse*... is a good read - very intense in parts, violent in others - and had me staying way too late in the evening when I had to get up early for work the next morning... I couldn't just put it down to finish tomorrow." - Lisa Ramaglia, scribesworld.com

"This book has a delightfully strange feel to it, even though the setting and plot seem normal enough, as if any science-fictional world can be considered truly 'normal,' in line with a reader's actual experience." - Lucy Schmeidler, sfrevu.com

"Bedford does an admirable job of world building and moving the at-times gory story along." - Timothy Capehart. VOYA

"Finally, probably the best of the three is Australian author Bedford's *Eclipse*, a dark, brutal sci-fi tale that alternately recalls *Platoon*, *Lord of the Flies* and the aforementioned Dick. The novel follows the exploits of James Dunne, newly graduated from the brutal Royal Interstellar Service Academy, whose first flight into space turns out to be a violent nightmare. Dunne's battles with corruption read like a space-age memoir, offering enough vulgarity and blood-spray to satisfy more than just sci-fi fans." - Bryn Evans, Fast Forward News

Books by K. A. Bedford

Orbital Burn
Eclipse
Hydrogen Steel
Time Machines Repaired While-U-Wait

Time Machines
Repaired
While-U-Wait

by
K. A. Bedford

EDGE SCIENCE FICTION AND FANTASY PUBLISHING
AN IMPRINT OF HADES PUBLICATIONS, INC.
CALGARY

Time Machines Repaired While-U-Wait
Copyright © 2008 by K. A. Bedford

Released: August, 2008

Edge Science Fiction and Fantasy Publishing
An Imprint of Hades Publications Inc.
P.O. Box 1714, Calgary, Alberta, T2P 2L7, Canada

In house editing by Matt Hughes
Interior design by Brian Hades
Cover Illustration by Rachel Haupt
ISBN-13: 978-1-894063-42-5

EDGE Science Fiction and Fantasy Publishing and Hades Publications, Inc.
acknowledges the ongoing support of the Alberta Foundation for the Arts and
the Australian Council for the Arts for our publishing programme.

Library and Archives Canada Cataloguing in Publication

Bedford, K. A. (K. Adrian), 1963-
    Time machines repaired while-u-wait / K. A. Bedford.

ISBN-13: 978-1-894063-42-5

CIP Data on file with the National Library of Canada

FIRST EDITION
(z-20080625)
Printed in Canada
www.edgewebsite.com

Dedication

To Brian and Anita — for everything

CHAPTER 1

"If it's another dead cat," said Aloysius "Spider" Webb, senior time machine technician, "you're buying the next round." Spider was driving the company van, a big fuel cell-powered behemoth, with the words *TIME MACHINES REPAIRED WHILE-U-WAIT* emblazoned on its side. In the shotgun seat was his coworker, mechanic Charlie Stuart, a young guy, very capable, lost inside a white lab coat at least a size too big for his scrawny frame.

"If it's another dead cat," Charlie replied, "I'll eat my bloody lab coat."

Spider shot him an amused glance. "I'll hold you to that."

The last time Spider and Charlie had been called out to look over a broken machine — yet another Tempo — it turned out that a cat had gotten trapped in the unit's engine compartment and died. The deceased cat's bodily fluids had then leaked into the translation engine and complicated things needlessly. Cats had a way of turning up inside broken time machines. They were a royal pain. Spider remembered how the owner freaked out when he was told. "It's not even my bloody cat!"

Today Spider and Charlie had been called out to look over a twelve-year-old second-hand Tempo 300 whose owner reported that it was "acting funny." The Tempo was the world's most popular time machine model, far outstripping its nearest rival, the more up-market Boron. The Tempus Corporation, headquartered in Nairobi, was pumping out Tempos at such a prodigious rate that market experts were always predicting the end of the "time-travel bubble," but so far demand remained high.

The owner of this Tempo, according to the work order, was a certain Mr. Vincent, who lived in a huge house, close to the coast but not too close, up in one of the more northern exurbs of Perth, Western Australia. At least, Spider thought, the guy wouldn't have to worry about his expensive abode falling into the hungry sea anytime soon

Spider pulled into Mr. Vincent's sweeping driveway and parked behind an immense, black hydrogen-powered SUV.

Spider said, "Get the gear."

"On it, boss." replied Charlie as he got out and went around to the back of the van.

Spider shut down the van and climbed out. He took a moment to take in the sheer monstrosity of Mr. Vincent's house and thought about what you could do with the amount of credit it must have taken to fund the damn thing. *You could do a lot*, he thought. *Buy your own artificial island, maybe.*

The entrance of the house swept open, and a tall, thin guy emerged. "Hey!" the man said cheerily, and made his way down the driveway to Spider and Charlie. "How's it hangin'?"

He was younger than Spider, and wore fashionable camo shorts and a Bali tee-shirt that played gamelan music. Most worrying to Spider, though: both of his eyes had been re-placed by the eye-plugs favored by people working in the information business. They made Mr. Vincent look as if he had the eyes of a fly, all black, circular and studded with wireless transponders. It gave Spider a chill, but he ad-justed his white lab coat and went up to the client.

"Mr. Vincent, I presume?"

"Geez," Vincent said, grinning, flashing big teeth — which appeared to feature animated images — and pointing his eye-plugs at Spider. "You guys took your *time* getting out here, huh?" He laughed. Because, surely, time machine technicians would turn up even before you called, right? Right?

Mr. Vincent led Spider over to the time machine in question. This type of unit looked something like a heli-copter, minus the tail boom and overhead rotors: it was an all enclosed cockpit with an engine compartment on the back. It rested on a carbon-fiber trailer, parked on the other side of the SUV. Vincent made nervous small talk of the sort that Spider hated. When he asked what footy team Spider supported, Spider said, "None of them."

Mr. Vincent said, "Uh, okay, um," and moved on to the Tempo. Spider asked him if it was true that Mr. Vincent had bought the unit second-hand, from a classified ad.

"Yeah. Going for a bloody steal, too. God, it would've been a crime not to buy it, you know?" He laughed again, and Spider once more had to look at the guy's disturbing face. He shuddered discreetly.

"Hmm, okay," Spider said, looking the unit over, "when you bought the unit, did you ask — or did the vendor provide — any documentation for it?"

"Um, what kind of documentation?"

Spider felt his blood pressure starting to rise, and he looked back at where Charlie was getting everything set up. His assistant was a good kid, didn't require much supervision, and knew time machines in a way Spider found a bit spooky. Spider turned back to Mr. Vincent. "Yeah, documentation. You know, service manuals, travel logs, warranty papers, evidence that the vendor had actually bought the unit from an authorized reseller. Anything like that?"

Mr. Vincent shut his mouth and looked a little troubled. He stared up at the Tempo on its trailer, as if seeing it for the first time, and not liking what he saw. "Um, no, actually. None of that. S'pose there should've been something, huh?"

"So you bought a used time machine in a private sale with no support papers," Spider said.

"Not so bright, huh?" Mr. Vincent said, flashing a *God, I'm stupid* nervous grin.

"You have no way of knowing, for example, if the unit is stolen, do you?"

"Stolen?"

"Wouldn't be the first hot time machine that got sold like that, sir."

"The guy didn't look like a criminal," he said.

Spider said, "Okay, then," perhaps too brightly, "maybe I'll just have a first peek at the beast itself. How's that sound?"

As if grateful for the change of subject, Mr. Vincent grinned. "Yeah, okay. I've already unlocked it. Knock yourself out."

Spider nodded, climbed up on the trailer, and — tensing a little — pulled open the driver's side door. He took a cautious sniff. No dead cat smell. That was a relief. *So far*, he thought, *so good. Just the usual faint waft of electricity and lost time.* The interior of the Tempo *looked* okay, more or less the way you'd expect a twelve-year-old, used time machine to look, with lots of custom mods and duct tape and epoxy. He closed the door. Externally the Tempo looked as if it had been through quite a few time jumps. The bodywork was dented and some of the hull panels no longer fit together as snugly as they had when the unit was still in the show room. He shivered, and jumped down to the ground.

Spider said to Mr. Vincent, "Before you gave the vendor any money did you at least, um, try it out to make sure it worked okay?"

"He offered, actually," he said, smiling. "Took me and my girlfriend for a spin. Yeah, it was great."

"So the unit did work correctly at that time?"

"Oh yeah. He took us back to — oh God, what was it? 1974? Something like that. Anyway, that part of town was still just wilderness back then. Scared some local bird life, and the girlfriend got bitten by some kind of bug. God, was she pissed!"

Spider nodded, trying hard not to imagine how the picturesque moment must have played out. "Okay, so it's started acting up since you got it home, yes?"

"Yeah, you're not wrong."

Vincent started telling Spider all about his exciting adventures in time and space. "It was bloody fantastic, you know? So cool, I mean, the first thing I did, the very first thing, I went back to when I was in high school, right? I thought it'd be fun to hang out with my past self, and, you know, give me some advice about 'the ladies.'" The way he said "the ladies" creeped Spider out all over again.

"And let me guess," Spider said, "your former self either didn't believe you were really him, or he did but none of your advice made him change his ways, or he couldn't actually see or hear you?"

"Uh, yeah. That last one. It was kinda puzzling."

"Ghost mode, Mr. Vincent. It's a toggle switch on the control panel. I'm guessing you accidentally switched it on at some point."

"Yeah, okay, that makes sense, yeah. God, do I feel dense!"

Spider said, "So when did it start acting up?"

"You probably get to hear a lot of stories about people doing dumb things with their time machines, huh?"

"One or two, Mr. Vincent, one or two. Now—"

"Right. Yeah. Um, to answer your question. Let me think. Yeah, it was last week sometime, Saturday? Yeah. Thought it'd be a hoot to take the girlfriend and go and see the *Titanic*, right? The actual ship?" He paused a moment, waiting for Spider to laugh or at least smile.

Spider stared at him, not interested in playing along. "And that was when the problem manifested, is that right?" To say nothing of the fact that a Tempo model like this one couldn't travel in space the way it could travel in time. Yes, idiot Mr. Vincent here could certainly go back to the date of the *Titanic's* departure from Southampton, but he would still be in this particular part of Western Australia, in fact stuck in the middle of what at the time was very nasty outback desert. He would have had to make his own way, using available transportation, to Southampton. Spider had heard of plenty of idiots who had tried something similar, arrived in the middle of the desert where moments ago exurbia had sprawled around them, and rather than cut their losses and come back to the welcome embrace of the modern world, they'd chosen to set out, on foot, in the desert, in search of someone with a truck who could give them a lift to the nearest big town. It was amazing how many of these idiots met very bad ends, baffling the police of those periods very much. The federal government's Department of Time and Space was threatening to mandate nationwide pilot training and licensing for time machine operators, which always met with enormous protests and opposition.

Charlie was finished preparing the gear. Spider asked him to take some preliminary readings and poke around a little. "Gotcha," Charlie said. He opened his toolbox and pulled out a wireless scanning device. He switched it on, loaded a suite of analytic software, hoisted himself up onto the trailer and set about climbing his way around the unit, taking readings, all the while swearing quietly to himself. After he finished the external inspection, he opened the driver's-side door and got inside.

Mr. Vincent was still talking, "Yeah, I'm sitting there in the driver's seat, right? And I punch in the date and the time and everything, and hit the go button, and, well, nothing. So I tried again, and still nothing. Must have tried like twenty times. Then I noticed, and you won't believe this, I noticed the TPS was on the blink—"

This got Spider's attention. "The Temporal Positioning System? On the blink how, exactly?"

"Look, it's easier if I just show you, okay?"

"Uh, no, sir. I am not setting foot inside that cabin until my assistant tells me it's safe to do so."

"But it's—"

"You want to show me what happens, that's fine. But I'm not climbing into this unit until I know I'm not going to end up three hundred years in the future, okay?"

"What about your assistant?"

"He gets paid to do that. I get paid to talk to you."

"Really?"

"Yes. Really."

"Has that ever happened to you, though? Suddenly flung off into the far future by mistake while fixing one of these?"

Spider allowed a small smile. "Uh, no, not to me personally. Now then, we'll just see how Charlie's doing." Spider went around to the driver's side. "How's it look in there?"

Charlie opened the door, and the first thing Spider noticed was that Charlie was unusually pale, even for him. He said, "Something is *so* not right in here, boss."

"How do you mean?"

Mr. Vincent piped up, "Actually, that's one of the things I wanted to tell you about. If you sit in the cabin for any length of time, even with everything powered down—"

Charlie leaned out of the unit and sat there, taking deep breaths, feeling woozy. "Oh God," he said.

Spider helped Charlie down, took the scanner off him, and got him to go sit in the van. He asked Mr. Vincent to get Charlie a glass of water, and the guy hurried off. Spider leaned against the unit's trailer and scrolled back through Charlie's scans. The readings were strange: in many ways, even though the unit was powered down, it was reading as if it was in fact powered up and ready to launch. And, yes, the Temporal Positioning System, which was supposed to tell you the unit's current location in its own timeline, and which should have given a straightforward reading of time since leaving the factory, was indeed on the blink. The numbers were a flickering whirl, a blur. The unit had no idea when the hell it was located; as far as it was concerned, it was lost in time.

Spider saw this, freaked out a little, and sprang away from the trailer, swearing under his breath. He stood there, hands on hips, staring up at the thing, feeling nervous in a way he never usually felt. He went and found Charlie, sitting sideways on his side of the van, the door open, his legs dangling outside. "Feeling any better, mate?"

He did look a little less pale. "Sort of, boss. It's just, I don't know, maybe a touch of food poisoning. Had some Chinese takeaway last night after work, and you know what that's like, bloody salmonella roulette..."

Spider nodded. "Look, if you want to take the rest of the day off—"

"No way. I'll be right."

"You think maybe the unit made you sick?"

Charlie looked him in the eye. "Soon as I sat down in there, I started feeling clammy, but I ignored that and kept looking around, doing my thing, checking everything like you said. But after a bit I did start feeling really crappy, and I just figured it was last night's Chinese, but—"

"It's not you, Charlie. Something's spooky wrong with that thing."

Mr. Vincent found them, and handed Charlie a glass of cold water. "There you go, straight from the tank to you. Fresh as," he said.

Charlie lifted the glass, said, "Cheers, mate," and took a long drink. "Oh, that's just magic. Thank you!"

"No worries. I'm just sorry you—"

Charlie waved off his concern. "Quite all right. Quite all right."

Spider looked at Mr. Vincent. "Have you ever felt sick inside the machine?"

"Well, yes, now you mention it. A couple of times. I never thought too much about it, and figured it was just, you know, too much fast food. I don't do much cooking here at home, and I'm always working late..." He was looking at his time machine now. "You think it made me sick?"

"Could be," Spider said. "It's not unheard-of, but it *is* rare."

"Not a good sign?" Mr. Vincent said.

"No. Not a good sign," Spider said.

"What's it mean, though?"

Spider scratched his chin. "Most likely thing is just that the unit is not fully here in this spot in space-time."

Mr. Vincent stared at Spider. "What?"

Spider left Charlie to rest while he took Mr. Vincent back to the unit. "Look here," he said, holding the scanner in front of the guy. "See this graph? The way that line curves way the hell up there like that?"

"Yeah, what does it mean?"

"The whole unit is powered down, isn't it?"

"Yes, of course it is. You could see that for yourself. Just look at it."

"I know. The unit looks powered down. This says it's powered up. Mr. Vincent, what you've got here is a bloody death trap. You're damn lucky you and your girlfriend weren't killed!"

"We could have been killed?"

"Or worse, yeah."

"What's worse than being killed?"

"Worse than being killed, sir, is being lost. As in no-where, and nowhen."

Mr. Vincent thought Spider was kidding, so he smiled to go along with the gag. "Like that ever happens, yeah, right!"

Spider paused a moment, staring at Mr. Vincent's horrible bug-eyes, wondering which of the vast number of things he could say at this moment would prove most effective in convincing Vincent that he had the luck of the truly stupid, and which would also be very satisfying to say in a very loud voice. He waited for his heart-rate to settle, and then said, "It would be tempting to tell you to drop your Tempo into one of those car compactors they have at the salvage yard, and turn the thing into a nice cube of dead matter — but, sadly, that wouldn't be safe. There could be so much energy still running through the unit that you would end up wiping out a large swath of the metroplex, and the local coppers would understandably take a dim view of that outcome."

"So what do I do with it?"

Spider couldn't believe he was about to say this. "Give it to me. I'll see what I can do. It might be fixable."

"You just said it might explode!"

"I didn't get my qualifications from a box of corn flakes, Mr. Vincent. There are things we can try that might help."

"And if not? What if you get killed?"

"You'll be among the first to know."

"Holy crap," he said, now starting to understand. "I could have killed my girlfriend."

"This is what you get for buying a used time machine off a classified ad, if you'll pardon me saying so. No warranty. No service contract. No protection of any kind. You've gone and bought yourself a bloody bomb!"

"Right," said Vincent. "Right."

"I'll need the name and contact details of the guy you bought it from, too."

Vincent stared at Spider, all anxious. "I'm not sure if I still have those. We did a big clean-out recently, going through all the accumulated crap on the household network, old bills, bank statements, receipts, business cards, share dividends, bits and pieces, you know, a real purge."

"You don't keep backups, just in case?"

"Not for stuff like that. Takes up too much space."

It baffled Spider that, in an age when computational storage capacity was nearly free and limitless, most people persisted in behaving as if it was terribly expensive and scarce. It was strange. He really didn't understand it.

"Hmm. Too much space. I see." Spider was feeling that, at this rate, he might have a stroke. "Look. Mr. Vincent, listen to me. We're going to take your Tempo back to the shop. We'll do what we can. Meanwhile, you are going to find out for me exactly who you bought this thing from. Odds are he's still selling them. Look on eBay, too. I can't tell you how many dud time machines get sold on eBay. Find the guy. When you do, give me his details. We'll have a chat. All right?"

"Okay. Right."

"Right. Now then..."

Mr. Vincent piped up. "Oh, wait a minute. Can you give me some kind of a quote for what all this might set me back? Just so I know."

Spider was tempted to give him a quote from something bleak by Shakespeare, but instead told the guy that just for openers he'd be looking at about one thousand dollars, and probably more.

"But I only paid two thousand for the thing itself."

"Sir," Spider said, "we're risking our lives by working on this death trap of yours. Do you have any idea what our public liability insurance is like? Huh? If it blows, and takes me, Charlie, and most of the rest of Malaga with it, the insurance company will come looking for you, Mr. Vincent. It's your choice."

"And if I just say forget about fixing it, I'll sell it on to someone else..."

"In that case I will personally report you to DOTAS. You could, and this is the funny part, you could do time. You see how that would be funny?" Spider wasn't smiling.

Mr. Vincent, not happy, beamed his details into Spider's watchtop.

Spider reciprocated, sending a quote, a receipt (1 x Time Machine, Personal, Tempo 300, Non-Functioning), and a business card to Vincent's own watchtop.

That all done, Spider got the guy to move his SUV out of the way, so he and Charlie could hook the unit's trailer up to their van.

Ten minutes later, the trailer attached, Spider and Charlie took off back to the workshop, trailing what Spider was certain was a bloody great huge bomb that could go off at any moment.

Charlie, feeling a little better, though still uneasy about the unit behind them, said, "You know what you're doing, right?"

"Sure I do," Spider said, being careful to take the very long way back to Malaga, following obscure back roads wherever possible.

"And if it kills us?"

"If it kills us, we'll be dead, and we won't ever have to piss about with bloody time machines ever again, Charlie. It's practically the best outcome we could ask for, really, if you think about it."

"I hadn't thought of it that way."

"Stick with me, kid, you'll do all right."

CHAPTER 2

The workshop was one of countless, ugly, concrete tilt-up structures built in the Malaga area over the past few decades. There was a small and fairly tidy reception area out front, and a huge, echoing workshop behind. The sign above the door, in a large bold font, read *TIME MACHINES REPAIRED WHILE-U-WAIT, Established 2015. ALL MAKES AND MODELS. GUARANTEED. TEMPUS CERTIFIED SERVICE ENGINEERS.*

Spider and Charlie pulled into the driveway and went around to the parking area behind the workshop. They unhooked the Tempo's trailer from the van then rolled the trailer and its load into one of the few available bays in the workshop. There was a strong odor of electricity, grease and existential bitterness. The time machine repair business was good; no shortage of people with malfunctioning time machines that happened to be out of warranty, or who didn't want to pay the ludicrous prices charged by the official dealerships. The thing that impressed customers the most was the way, once their machines were fixed, no matter how long it took to actually do the work, the technicians could time-travel the unit back to the client, returning it mere moments after said client had watched Spider and Charlie take it away. It made for very happy customers, good word-of-mouth, and plenty of repeat business.

Spider left Charlie to supervise things as the workshop became aware of the new arrival and interrogated it for its details. Spider went to the office in search of badly needed strong coffee. The new receptionist, Malaria —

her real name, to Spider's surprise and her apparent lifelong dismay — was on the phone with a potential client. She looked to be having a bad day. "Ah, and here's the boss, just walked through the door. Just a moment, I'll put him on..."

Spider was trying to wave her off, or indicate that he wasn't really there, or was much too busy to come to the phone, but Malaria was insistent. She was a towering young woman nearly two meters tall, all gawky and angular, dressed in black. He checked to make sure he was wearing a fresh phone patch under his ear. "This is Webb," he said, dreading whatever might come next.

"Oh, thank bloody God," a frustrated older woman said, "I'm in a real pickle here and I can't get anybody anywhere to give me the time of day, let alone some help—"

He gestured to Malaria that he needed coffee, and she made a production out of ignoring him. To the caller, he said, "You've got a problem with your time machine, is that right, ma'am?"

"Time machine? What did you say?"

"I asked if you're having a problem with your time machine. Which would be why you'd decided to call a time machine repair shop."

"I haven't got a time machine," she said. "I'm calling about my car."

Spider stared at Malaria, still hoping to get her to organize some coffee. She continued to ignore him. "This is a time machine repair shop, ma'am. We don't fix cars, I'm sorry."

"I'll have you know I got this number from one of your advertisements," she said.

This was starting to get amusing. "You found an ad for 'Time Machines Repaired While-U-Wait', and decided we were a likely source of help with your car troubles?"

"Time machines?"

He rubbed his forehead. "We fix time machines, yes, ma'am."

"How did you get this number?" she asked, indignant.

"Um, you called us?"

"Call this number again and I'll set my lawyers on you. Good day, sir." She killed the connection.

Spider touched his phone patch to hang up. "That was different," he said.

"She was on the phone with me for half an hour before you got here. Bloody nutters, the world's full of 'em."

Spider politely ignored the opportunity to ask about Malaria's parents, and said instead, "Any other calls? Genuine inquiries, preferably?"

"Usual assortment. You realize most of what I do here is low-level tech support, right? I mean, I get people phoning up who don't know how to start their time machines. I get people who get all upset that they can't visit ancient Rome, or go to the Crucifixion. I—"

Spider listened patiently, only too familiar with such complaints. People loved having time machines — but hated the government-imposed restrictions on what they could do at certain key events in history, and the Crucifixion was perhaps the most controversial. Yes, you could go there, but only in ghost mode.

"Yeah, the number of people who complain to me because they can't save the Lord, or take His place, or who want to give Mary a hug or a biscuit. How do you stand it?" Malaria had only recently started working at the shop.

"Maintain a sense of humor, Malaria. It's your best defense."

"You mean I'm allowed to laugh at them?"

"Not out loud, no, sadly."

"Pity."

"Any other calls?"

"There was a Ms. Pollit, asking about her unit, and if she'd have to pay extra to have the interior carpeting cleaned. Apparently someone here told her something about hideous extra charges for having stains removed?"

Spider sighed. "I'll call her back. What else?"

"Just the usual blather. Oh, and your wife called, said it was, and I quote, 'urgent.' You'll note the irony quotes I put around her use of the word 'urgent,' sir."

"Quotes logged and noted, Malaria. And, point of information, she and I are..." He sighed, worn out from trying and failing to make Molly happy. "We're doing one of those trial separation thingies."

"Is that why she calls so often?" Why doesn't she just call you direct?"

Spider said, "I try not to give her my personal number."

"Ah," she said.

It was true. Spider had heard from Molly far more often, sometimes several times per day, since they started the trial separation, than he had ever heard from her when they were together. And, as Malaria had indicated, when Molly called it was always something "urgent."

"So what's the problem this time? Did she say?"

"Something to do with the home network? Router on the blink, I think. Oh, I made a rhyme!"

"You're a poet, Malaria."

"Oh yes. Bob from the wreckers called to say a 'cryo coil' for Mr. Tan's unit, should be in tomorrow. Having some problems getting a good one, apparently, and also wanted to know how you'd feel about a reconditioned one." Mr. Tan's time machine, a high-end Boron, needed special care.

"Okay, that sounds fine. Now, I need you to call James at DOTAS. Let him know we've just picked up a unit with what looks like a Section Three situation, and—"

Malaria was frowning at him, her left hand wrapped around a stylus in a grip of death, waiting to make a note. "A Section Three situation? Um, what?"

Spider was sure he had specified to the job agency that all candidates for this position had to have at least a *Time Machines for Dummies* level of familiarity with the business in order to get the job. He said, trying to keep calm, "Looks like bad manifold-displacement problems."

"Oh," she said, hunched over, scribbling on a screen, writing, apparently, upside-down. "Of course."

Spider ignored her sarcasm. "Basically, it's possible the thing could blow up on us, so you need to tell James that we need the Bat Cave."

Malaria froze, straightened up, blinked three times, and stared up at Spider. "Bat. Cave. I see."

Spider gnawed at his lip for a moment. "Hmm. Bat Cave. How to explain..." He looked around the office, noting all the glossy posters advertising high-end time machines, as well as the dire animated motivational posters Dickhead McMahon — Spider's boss, and owner of the company — insisted they had to have. To Malaria, he said, "The 'Bat Cave' is a portable, self-enclosed, man-made universe, you might say. The idea is—"

"Man-made universe, you say?" she said, chewing on the end of her stylus. Spider tried not to notice the way her fingernails flickered with tiny videos.

"Yeah. Otherwise, the unit might explode, you see, when we try to take it apart."

Malaria stared at him, wide-eyed. "It might what?"

"Yeah. Sort of dangerous. Need to let the government know, that kind of thing."

"Nobody at the job office told me I could get blown up!"

"That's why we need the Bat Cave. We put the unit in there, and we stand outside, teleoperating various tools, and if the thing does explode, nobody gets hurt."

"'If the thing does explode,' you say," she said, clearly disturbed but trying to act cool about it.

"The glamorous world of time machine repair, Malaria." He forced a jolly smile he didn't feel. "Always something exciting going on!"

"All right," she said, trying to manage her breathing, "keep calm, keep calm. Um, if the thing is going to explode, how much warning will there be?"

"Warning?"

"Yeah, as in—"

"No warning. It's basically a live bomb. We have to defuse it."

Malaria was unhappy to hear this. "Holy shit. Uh, sir."

"Nothing to worry about, Malaria. See, the Bat Cave is a self-enclosed—"

"You're saying it's like a portable hole in D&D, right?"

Spider had spent far too much of his youth and early adulthood gaming, and knew what she meant. "Yeah.

Like that. Put time machine inside. Fiddle with it from outside. If time machine goes boom, no damage outside. Everybody happy. Well, except the owner, depending on his insurance."

Malaria nodded, tapping the end of her stylus against her jaw. "All right, then. One Bat Cave, coming right up."

"Thanks. It's really no big deal. Mostly."

"I didn't hear that, sir. I really didn't."

"Hey, you get to sit out here, with all these solid concrete walls between you and the bomb. Spare a thought for me and Charlie."

"You just said you'll be fine. I believe you used the word 'teleoperate' in a meaningful way."

"We still have to put the unit inside the Bat Cave and get it set up. That could be a bit iffy."

"It doesn't bother you?"

"Yes, it bothers me. It bothers me lots."

"You look pretty calm about the whole thing."

"What choice do we have?"

"What choice?" she said. "What about the choice to not take the bloody thing?"

"And leave the 'bloody thing' with its idiot owner? You think that's a good plan?"

"I think it might be time for my annual vacation, sir."

"You haven't been here long enough for annual vacation."

"Shit. I really need this job, too."

"Yeah," Spider said. "Me, too."

They reached one of those moments when there was nothing further to say. "Well," Malaria said eventually. "Best get to calling this James guy, huh? One Bat Cave, please. Hold the fries."

Spider nodded encouragingly. "How long ago did my wife call?"

"Um, the last time was, let's see, nineteen minutes. She sounded kind of all worked up."

Spider muttered under his breath. "I'll be in my office. Thanks. You're doing a good job."

The phone went off again. "Time Machines Repaired While-U-Wait. Malaria speaking." There was a pause.

Spider had a feeling he'd best hang around. Sure enough, Malaria waved him back. She whispered to him, her hand over her phone patch, "It's her again."

"I'll take it in my office."

"Check," she said, and then to Mrs. Webb, "Just putting you through now."

§ § §

In his office at last he felt, for the first time today, that he could relax for a moment and decompress a little. Instead of a fixed desk he had a nifty bit of intelligent furniture that, depending on what you needed it for, could be configured as a desk, or as a bed, or a couch, or some interesting combination of all three. Theoretically, and according to the sales pitch you got when you were thinking of buying one, you could make the thing transform into all these different configurations using nothing more than a wireless remote. In practice you actually had to manhandle various panels and sections. This was so annoying that Spider generally only swapped it between desk mode and bed mode. Right now it was a bed, and he collapsed into it with the sort of loud, grunting sigh that men start to make once they reach middle age. He lay there a moment in the blissful silence, trying not to think about how much he hated time machines. Such thinking was a pathway to madness and stomach ulcers.

He touched his phone patch. "Molly, hi—"

"Oh, finally! Where the hell have you been all day?"

"Lovely to hear from you, too, dear," he said — and the sad thing was that it actually was good to hear from her. Her voice, he loved her voice. It had a sort of lilting, even musical quality to it, even when she was yelling at him. It was one of the things that had attracted him to her, years ago. He sighed.

"The bloody system's on the fritz again, can you pop round and have a look at it?"

"The upgrade didn't go so well?"

"Upgrade?" She laughed caustically. "At this point in time the thing won't even boot, for God's sake. I'm doing what I can on my watchtop, but it's not the same. I need bandwidth and I need it now."

He remembered buying her that watch. It was engraved on the back, *Forever yours, love, Al*. That in itself showed how much he'd loved her. Nobody ever called Spider "Al," except Molly. It was short for "Aloysius." He let her get away with it, even though he hated that name perhaps even more than he hated time travel. It was the kind of name that got a kid beaten up at school every day, that made a kid want to quit school — and he had been that kid. He could have killed his parents. They told him it was a lovely, traditional family name. Not that he was bitter, of course.

"Okay, it's just, I'm a bit tied up at work right now," he said, checking his watch. It was nearly three p.m. "I can get over to you by, I suppose, maybe six? If the traffic gods are kind?"

"And what am I supposed to do for the next three hours until you get here?"

"It's the best I can do. I'm busy."

Molly swore at him and hung up loudly. He winced and touched his patch. Rubbing his face, trying to manage his breathing and his blood pressure, let alone the stupid time machine out in the workshop, he felt as if he might explode at any minute. Molly had always been the kind of woman who exasperated him, and then charmed him, and made him believe all the exasperating behavior was just "the magic that was her," and not at all something toxic and manipulative. He didn't care. He was still in love with her. The trial separation had been her idea. He'd gone along with it because it had seemed better than a divorce, less final. From a trial separation, he thought, he could still try to bring her around, negotiate, and have some semblance of a relationship with her. He was well aware that he was being an idiot. He knew she was bad for him, and that he should draw a line under the whole sorry mess and move on, maybe find someone actually compatible.

Even if he did all that, even if he did find someone "compatible," he knew that in his heart he would always be comparing the new, compatible woman with Molly, and that Molly, for all her vexatious ways, would always seem more exciting, more passionate, more alive. He'd never be able to leave her alone. It was a hopeless thought. Maybe, he'd even thought here and there, he should get some help. Wasn't there a word for this kind of thing? Codependency? Something like that. It wasn't healthy, of that he was sure.

Molly was an artist, a sculptor. He'd met her at university: he was doing an English and communications degree; she'd been doing fine arts. They hated each other on sight, and kept hating each other, sometimes to an alarming degree, for over a year before they realized it was just too exhausting. These days Molly worked with semi-intelligent 3-D fabricators, producing articulated, moving "sculptures" that looked distressingly like living things, the products of complex genetic algorithms given millions of generations to develop and refine themselves. The results were definitely unearthly. *Alien beings from a world that could never exist in our reality*, was a description Spider remembered from a gallery catalog. She called it "HyperFlesh." It gave him the creeps.

Not that any of this rumination was helping his blood pressure. He forced himself up, tapped on the face of his watch, causing it to unfold several lightweight panel segments which, when the arrangement was complete, formed an eight-centimeter-square flat screen no thicker than a stiff sheet of paper. He found all the pending calls he ought to return in the phone interface, and started to return them. Most were "simple question" calls. He knew what to expect. "It's just a simple question... a quick question... not meaning to bother you, but just one more question." Thank God he had the answers. Not, he knew, that they would do any good. Most people, no matter how often you explained things to them, simply couldn't be made to understand. There was also the problem that time travel itself was a downright spooky subject. Many never quite felt comfortable with the thought that their personal time machine was being hauled away by Spider and Charlie only to be delivered moments later by the same but future versions of the two technicians! There were times when even Spider himself forgot about this aspect of things, and unexpectedly saw his future self driving the same vehicle, going the other way. So, he did his best, when delivering fixed units, to take different routes back to the customer's home from the routes he'd taken the first time.

Malaria knocked on his office door. "James at DOTAS said to tell you he can't get the Bat Cave out here until tomorrow a.m. Is that okay?"

"That's just fine. Thanks."

She went back to her desk, and Spider went out into the workshop to see what Charlie was up to. With a little luck he'd have a problem that really needed a fresh pair of eyes to sort out, something that might call for a lot of overtime. He knew Molly, when she heard, would want to jam a grenade in his head, but, as he had often told her, the life of a time machine technician is, by its very nature, unpredictable. Or at least he certainly hoped so.

CHAPTER 3

Much later that night, sometime past one a.m., Spider parked his recumbent bicycle in the locked garage next to his current home, The Lucky Happy Moon Motel. He'd been living here — no, wait, "living" was too strong. He'd been sleeping and bathing here for nearly a year. The management did their surly best to ignore any wild stories about "cleanliness" and "hygiene" they might have heard about, but it was cheap and not far from the workshop. Less pleasing, it was also only a few minutes from the airport, where flights to and from Southeast Asia flew over every five minutes. Spider logged himself in at the door, which buzzed open, and a great waft of the nasty stink of the place washed over him. The odor of hundreds of lonely, broke, and nearly homeless people, most of them men, plus a distinct undersmell of stale instant noodles and another, more elusive reek that Spider had always assumed was the stench of personal failure. He went in, nodded to old Mrs. Ng, who was hunched behind the reception desk. She was knitting, she once told him, a model of a hyperspace manifold. In bright, festive colors. The thing was really coming along. "Any messages for Webb?" he asked her.

Not missing a stitch, Mrs. Ng glanced at a screen and shook her head. "Sorry, Spider."

"Thanks," he said, patting the ceramic Buddha on the desk.

The elevators, still not working, were now entering their third month of being broken, he noted. Muttering, he started up the six flights of stairs, watching out in the dim and flickering lights for deposits of human refuse left behind by residents too lazy to use the washrooms on each level. It was, he was sort of pleased to note, getting easier to make the climb to his level. When he had first moved in here these stairs had just about killed him. He'd thought he'd have to be medivac'd out. Now, even though he was puffing and sweating, he was doing better. His pulse felt merely very fast and hard.

He'd spent several hours trying to fix Molly's network so she could send her construction scripts to The Queen's Gallery, in Bangkok, where huge 3-D printers would start building her latest HyperFlesh creations. The Gallery's exhibit of her work started in three days, and she planned to be there for the opening.

Spider spent much of the evening doing his best to diagnose the problem, even while several of Molly's creations writhed and stretched and moaned quietly around him. It was unnerving, the way they looked so organic, so biological, and so uncannily alive, while at the same time appearing utterly alien. He was sure they were all looking at him with their unnatural eyes; it made the hairs on the back of his neck prick up. Molly herself started the evening being very nice, and even made him an actual cup of reasonable coffee without his having to ask her, but as progress proved elusive she started to release her inner monster, screaming — yes, screaming! — at him that she needed bandwidth and she needed it yesterday! Spider tried suggesting that she take her script to a commercial bandwidth rental shop — there were plenty around, including many that operated twenty-four hours a day — where they would be happy to shoot the bloody thing off to wherever she might want to send it, for a low, low price. This, Molly told him, was an "unhelpful" suggestion. Yes, she could go to some grubby little shopfront run by sleep-deprived uni students or worse, and trust them to upload her delicate and complex script to the correct destinations, and, maybe, hope for the best. But the designs needed to be available to the printers right now! Only she could supervise the upload process to the degree she felt was necessary for the integrity of the work. "And you do want me to be a success, don't you, Al?"

Spider, depressed and staring hopelessly at the interior components of a router, looked up at her and dead-panned, "Oh my, yes. Your success is the most important motivator in my entire life. I practically live for your success, Molly."

She told him he could go fuck himself, but only after he'd sorted out the network.

At length, worn out, and fed up, Spider had a brainwave, the kind of blinding flash of inspiration he would have had much earlier, if he hadn't been so fried with fatigue. He said, "Look, you've got a time machine. Why don't you just pop back in time to before your system here packed it in, and upload your creepy thingies to your black, black heart's content?"

She'd nearly kissed him, she was so pleased with this idea. "I should have thought of that myself," she said, manifesting a genuine smile for his benefit.

So that was something, he reflected as he climbed the stairs. He yawned, dead on his feet, dodged around gray-faced shiftworkers, people coming and going from the filthy washrooms, and even some sullen kids sitting around with their heads plugged into cheap, portable game servers, lost to the world. Spider's capsule was number 639. Each level of the motel featured racks and racks of these plastic sleeping capsules, three rows per level. And it looked as if most were occupied. The rent was cheap, providing you didn't mind not having any space for storage, other than for toiletries and a few items of clothing. Spider kept the rest of his stuff in a self-storage unit in Osborne Park.

Once crammed into his capsule, Spider thrashed about, trying to squeeze his considerable bulk into a sleeping bag. He wished he could afford decent accommodations, but this was an age when modest and tiny mass-produced concrete tower-block apartments, modelled on those in Hong Kong and Singapore, required sixty-year mortgages. He was giving serious thought to the idea of maybe trying to find a second job. The pittance he got for fixing busted time machines, it seemed, was barely enough to buy decent meals.

Long ago, Spider had been a police officer, a detective senior sergeant, on the Major Crimes Squad. It had been a reasonable job, at first, before all the trouble started. His days as a copper were one of the many things Spider didn't like to think about these days.

He lay there quietly sweating in his capsule for hours. Noise from nearby capsule occupants didn't help; many of them appeared to have no concept that the thin plastic walls did nothing to block sound. Planes roared overhead, making the whole building shake. Spider tried folding the pillow around his head, to block his ears, without success. He knew he needed, at minimum, some noise-canceling ear-buds, but couldn't afford them.

Meanwhile, his evening at Molly's place — he had to try to not think about how that house had once been his, too — kept swirling round and round in his head, the way she drove him absolutely crazy, but somehow kept him coming back for more. That wasn't right. And then there was the business with that idiot's weird time machine today, the way it was neither here nor there, now nor then. Yes, it sat there looking very much part of "now," but it wasn't. It was flickering up and down its own timeline so fast you couldn't see it moving. Even so, Spider thought as he lay there, there was no reason why Charlie should have felt so ill just from sitting inside it. And what was with its being somehow powered up while looking exactly like an inert, powered-down unit? How could that be possible? It wasn't simply that the unit's own internal sensors were wonky; their initial tests would have revealed something as simple as that. No, there was something very spooky going on with this one, and it bothered Spider more than he was prepared to let on. He was very pleased he'd arranged for the Bat Cave. That would be a big help.

Bloody time machines. What the hell are they good for? He often found himself thinking this. No good came of them, none at all. Yes, you could do what Molly was planning, and use them for just bopping about in your local timeline, but every time you did something in the past that hadn't previously happened, so to speak, you wound up creating divergent timelines: one where that change did happen, and left the original one without the change. Both went forward, for good or ill. And it was mostly ill. For every story you heard about some clown wanting to go back in time to save his father from dying in an accident, you heard plenty of other stories about said clown succeeding, only to inadvertently cause his father's death from something else!

People had this stupid idea that a time machine was a magic wand they could just wave about and it would fix all the bad stuff that ever happened in the world; or even worse, they would take a reasonable, okay sort of life, and try to tweak it to make it better. The number of tragic stories Spider had heard about that kind of thing, and how it never worked out the way it was supposed to. Time travel was notorious for biting you when you least expected it.

And somehow it always turned out to be Spider's problem. These sad idiots would turn up at the shop, complaining that fiddling with their personal timelines had wound up making things worse, or caused all kinds of other trouble, and nothing they tried could fix it, so clearly the machine itself was the problem, and Spider had to fix it. It was the kind of thing that could make a grown man weep.

The bitter truth was that the only good thing you could do with a time machine was to visit historical events, just to watch. For most historical events given a DOTAS Historical Significance Rating of more than 2.0, you could only go in so-called "ghost mode," where you could watch everything, but you would not be visible, and would not be able to interact with the locals, even if you could speak their language.

Fortunately for the manufacturers of time machines, time tourism was enormously popular, far more so than anybody had ever previously suspected. Travel agents had to open separate businesses to cater for people with a passion for the past. There were companies operating luxurious time cruisers, catering for hundreds, or even thousands, of people at a time, conducting guided tours of history. As a consequence of this, these days the online world was choked with uploaded videos of historical events shot by tourists, often with commentary alluding to the fact that history was always so different from how they thought it would be. Not that personal access to history settled anything for the world's academic historians. On the contrary: even when following in the footsteps of the great men and women of the past, observers still tended to see what they wanted to see, or interpret what they saw through the filters of their own preconceptions.

It also frequently turned out that what everyone thought of as capital-H "History," and about which people had worried so much in the early days of mass time travel, was itself the way it was because of extensive manipulation by mischievous time hackers from the future who'd found ways of getting around the extensive and supposedly secure firmware blocks that DOTAS and their various international analogs bolted onto time machine translation engines to keep them from doing exactly that, and who always proclaimed that they only hacked history to "draw attention to its vulnerabilities." Never mind that this also meant that many unfortunate developments turned out to be a consequence of some harmless-seeming time meddling that proved impossible to "fix." This was referred to as the "Third Reich Problem," after the most notable example of harmless tampering leading to dreadful outcomes. History, everyone was learning these days, was nothing more than an astonishing series of kludgy fixes, with one fix leading to terrible problems that in turn needed fixing, and so on. Time was frustratingly fluid and slippery, a truth known only too well to those poor bastards in charge of trying to fix everybody else's meddling.

§ § §

The next morning Spider pedaled through heavy bike traffic and cold, drizzling rain to the shop. Even while he was drinking his first double espresso of the day Malaria was telling him about all the people wanting to talk to him about how their time machines had screwed up this time, and how it was somehow his fault, or at least would soon be his fault. Malaria also said, "And, by the way, Mr. McMahon is coming by later this morning for a meeting."

"Oh shit, that's bloody perfect. What's Dickhead want now?"

"Something about your key-point indicators not shaping up too well, I think. Let me check. Ah. Yes, indeed. You're well under the curve for this quarter. Mr. McMahon said—"

"Look. Malaria, you can call him Dickhead. Even to his face. Honest. Even his own wife calls him Dickhead — I am not lying about this."

"I can't call him Dickhead!" she said, horrified.

"You haven't met him yet, have you?"

"Well, no. I've—"

"Trust me. Dickhead by name, dickhead by nature."

"I see," she said. "Oh, and Charlie wants a word about the, er, Bat Cave thing."

"Problems?"

"Not sure. You'll have to talk to him."

Spider went out to the workshop, nodded at Charlie, who was on the phone with DOTAS, then went to look at the unit while he waited. It was baffling, he thought, it looked perfectly ordinary, perfectly inert. About as interesting as a dead car up on blocks in somebody's front yard. It occurred to Spider that maybe their testing gear needed recalibrating, and he made a mental note to get Charlie onto that later. Then again, what was he to make of Charlie's getting sick inside the thing? Since Charlie was showing no sign of getting off the phone anytime soon — when Spider got his attention, Charlie just rolled his eyes and clutched at his forehead — Spider thought he might just test the "makes you feel sick" observation. It was possible that it was indeed as a result of something Charlie had eaten, rather than something to do with the unit.

Spider hoisted himself up onto the unit's trailer, popped the passenger side door, and hesitated for a moment. *Do I really want to do this? The machine could explode, right?* That was why they were getting the Bat Cave. All the same, Spider felt a strong need to get on with investigating it. He wanted to find out all its secrets — and then get the thing the hell off his property!

Taking a calming breath, Spider swung into the cockpit and sank down into the seat. Nothing bad happened. There was an iffy smell, as they'd noticed before, but nothing dramatically wrong. He saw that all the instruments were in the off position. The unit's power plant was properly shut down.

He frowned, baffled, as he inspected the entire cockpit, the storage bins, the system-access panels.

"It's a dead parrot," Charlie said, right behind him.

Spider jumped and let out an embarrassing squeak.

"Oh, God, sorry. You okay?"

Spider sat there, a hand pressed to his chest, feeling the booming of his heart. "Never better. Never better."

"It's just — I finished with the phone, and I saw you were having a look round."

"I'm fine, Charlie. Just fine. You just—"

"It is kinda spooky, huh?"

And then Spider began to feel it. "Oh," he said, suddenly feeling not at all right. "Oh, no." He put a hand to his forehead, and discovered he was clammy. He asked Charlie to move out of the way so he could get out before he spewed everywhere. Cleaning vomit out of time machine interiors was deeply unpleasant, and Spider had done more than his share over the years.

He jumped down from the trailer and stood, leaning against a bench for a long moment, breathing carefully, feeling awful.

Charlie said, "It's not just me, then?"

"No, mate. Not just you." He turned and stared at the unit. "Bloody thing's haunted, I reckon."

Charlie said, "That was James on the phone."

"Let me guess. Problem getting the Bat Cave here on time?"

"Stuck in traffic somewhere in North Perth."

"Shit," Spider said, still monitoring his stomach.

"And there's something else, too."

"There's more?"

"It's probably nothing, okay? Looks like there was a guy in a car sitting outside for a few hours last night."

"What?"

"It's true. Malaria noticed it when she checked the shop's surveillance video this morning."

They moved into the office and Malaria cued up and played the file.

Charlie fiddled with the video controls, hoping to get a better look at the face of the guy, but no amount of photoshopping helped.

"If he starts making a pest of himself," Spider said to Malaria, "it might be worth letting the coppers know."

"Got it," she said, scribbling a note on her screen.

Spider knew that the trade in stolen time machines was driven by: (a), people too cheap to buy one legitimately: (b), would-be time hackers; and (c), folks who just wanted to strip the units for parts. The most valuable component of a time machine was its translation engine, the thing that actually made the unit move from point A to point B in space-time.

He wondered if he was possibly looking at a member of group (c). A broken time machine still had at least some working parts, after all.

It was too hard to say. There was something disconcerting about it, though. Something that bothered the part of him that had once been, and would always be, a policeman.

CHAPTER 4

The Bat Cave was a large, inflatable structure which looked, when it wasn't inflated, like a sinister, black hot-air balloon. It came with a support van, an air compressor, and a pair of technicians in charge of setting it up and monitoring its operation. Spider and Charlie left them to their work while they chatted with James, who was very interested in the spooky Tempo.

James Rutherford, a worn-down guy in his late 50s who looked like someone had killed his favorite dog, was a chronosystems engineer with DOTAS Perth. Spider liked him. Or maybe he just felt sorry for him: six years ago James's wife Sky had killed herself. It wasn't something he and Spider talked about, if Spider could avoid it. God, he always thought, what do you say to someone in that situation?

James took some readings with his own handheld diagnostic gadget, and even though he'd been fully briefed about the unit, he still stopped dead, staring at the readings. "That's just not right," he said. "Look at the bloody Fenniak Transform!" he said, pointing at an alarming curve with a pinky finger that bore a gold signet ring.

"Uh-huh," Spider said, not grinning at all.

"It's gone asymptotic!" James was staring at that curve as if it was the most surprising thing he'd seen in years.

"We did say," Charlie said.

"And this, look, the Leong Standard Curvature is an error message — one I've never seen before, lads."

Spider looked at the error message. "Oh. I see. Shit." The situation was worse than Spider had first thought.

At length, James pulled his astonished eyes away from the meter, and he stood looking up at the unit, in a kind of religious awe. "What the hell have you got here?"

"We'd like to know," Spider said.

"But you can see why we wanted the Bat Cave, huh?" Charlie added.

"Oh my, yes," James said, nodding.

The Bat Cave techs came over and told James the Cave was finally ready. James thanked them, and led Spider and Charlie out into the parking lot to have a look at it. Considering that the Bat Cave, once fully activated, would create its very own universe, its appearance was hugely disappointing. Spider always thought it really needed to have some cool mad scientist-type gadgets all over it, complete with great arcs of brilliant, eye-searing electricity and so forth. Instead, it was a big black bag with an opening just large enough to let them wheel in the unit and its trailer. James gave Spider and Charlie a hand with it, telling them, "Just don't tell the union I'm doing this, okay? They'd fry my nuts if they knew." There were all kinds of byzantine rules imposed by the Public Service Union governing what public servants were allowed and not allowed to do, and moving "third-party" machinery around was strictly forbidden, on pain of serious penalty.

Inside the Bat Cave there was a faint smell of ozone and outgassing of complex non-rational plastics. The sense of immense power just waiting to manifest itself was palpable, and deeply worrying. Spider and Charlie couldn't get out of there fast enough. Once outside, James signaled the techs that the opening could be sealed, and the device enabled. Spider watched the techs working their screens, checking the cables connecting the Bat Cave to the van, and carrying on as if they did this kind of thing — creating a tiny pocket universe — every day and it was no big deal. They worked through a checklist, calling to each other, confirming that they had green lights on each major and minor subsystem. Spider felt his guts clench with apprehension.

When the moment of activation came, it was so quiet and undramatic that Spider almost missed it. Suddenly the Bat Cave was a big sealed plastic shell, like a strangely menacing black beach ball, and the technicians, watching their screens, called out, "All systems nominal."

Charlie said, "Oh, God."

Spider said, "No time like the present," and they went over to the technicians.

James ran a hand over the outer surface of the shell. It was cold, terribly cold, and rigid. "So you've got separation?" he asked the lead technician, who told him the system was indeed ready. A tiny, self-contained, and entirely separate region of space-time existed inside the shell, cut off from the universe outside.

Spider, feeling extremely nervous around such energy and weirdness, cleared his throat and said, "Better get to work, then, huh?"

"Er, yeah," Charlie said. "You first."

The pair of technicians gave Spider and Charlie a quick briefing on how to operate the manipulator arms and the various toolsets from their screens. Then it was time to get to work.

James said, "Hope you don't mind if I just lurk here next to you, just to keep an eye on the government's very expensive property."

"Yeah, sure," Spider said, concentrating on the screen. "Go nuts."

They started by removing the Tempo's doors and external hull panels, which they stacked on either side of the unit. The seats came out next, then Charlie started stripping the interior while Spider concentrated on removing the engines and power plant. He was sweating, taking his time over every wire, every connection, wishing he'd taken more training on this gear. More difficult was shutting out that part of his brain that found the whole idea of quantum entanglement — the way his interface out here was connected to the tools in there — fundamentally hard to accept. When he'd first been told about the Bat Cave and its uses, Spider had just stared at the guy, and said, "That's bullshit!" The guy had explained again and again that quantum stuff was like this. Action at a distance. It made no bloody sense, and here, again, Spider was seeing that for himself. He fiddled with a joystick here, and inside the Cave, which might as well have been light-years away, robotic arms and power-tools did the rest. Then, as he worked on the screws holding down an access panel on the engine compartment, his sweaty hands on the joystick caused the tool head to slip off the screw and skitter away. He managed, with his thumping heart in his mouth, to save the tool from dropping down into the guts of the engine compartment where he'd never find it. He swore under his breath, paused, and wiped his forehead with a sleeve.

It took more than an hour, and a lot of sweat and swearing, but eventually Spider was able to separate the seemingly billions of cables linking the scanning engine to the translation engine. Disconnecting both of these components from the power plant was another story. Surely, he thought, it's all just electronics and machinery and hardware and crap. It shouldn't be this hard, and normally it wasn't hard. It was simply the thought of the Bat Cave itself looming huge and black and unearthly next to him, and the conviction that if the unit inside did explode, the Cave would not save them. It would all turn out to be a big hoax, and they'd all be fried in a white-hot blast of unthinkable energies.

Slowly, with enormous care, he and Charlie worked the controls together to lift out each component from the engine compartment and set them down next to the unit. He didn't know about Charlie, but he felt like his guts were knotted up tight; the pain was distracting.

Then it was time to confront the power plant. Spider and Charlie, when they had talked about this job, agreed that it was likely that the power plant would be the thing to give them trouble, if there was going to be trouble at all. And they were not disappointed.

The power plant, a monster fuel cell squeezed into a casing as big as two archival boxes, sat at the bottom of the engine compartment. Any number of cables, and any number of types of cable, spread out from its white shell to all parts of the time machine. Many of these cables had already been neutralized. There were still other cables linking the thing into the frame of the unit, to the control interface, and elsewhere. Disconnecting each one would take time and great patience. James offered to stand in for Spider, to help spread the tension around. Spider told him DOTAS or the PSU would be bound to find out, and he'd be out of a job.

So, one at a time, and working in sequence, Spider and Charlie started unplugging the power-plant from the rest of the machine. It was at this point that a time machine mechanic typically felt most weirded out, even in situations where the machine was not expected to explode. There were so many cables disappearing into the guts of the unit, and you could trace them all down to where they connected to this and that, but the next time you looked, half of those connection points were no longer there. There were certain parts in the guts of a time machine that appeared only sometimes to exist, and which appeared subject to Heisenberg's Uncertainty Principle. Cats were notorious for disappearing inside units this way. You could smell the unique odor of the dead cat, but you could never find the actual corpse, no matter what. You could strip the entire machine down to bare metal and carbon fiber, but it wouldn't help. Your co-worker, on the other hand, would find the dead cat without any trouble, in a place you were pretty sure you had checked, and had found nothing. This was one of the many things Spider hated about time machines. At a certain level, they just stopped making any bloody sense.

At last, with sweat dripping from their faces, Spider and Charlie succeeded in removing the last cables from the fuel cell.

They paused, and looked at each other.

Nothing happened.

Spider let out his breath. Charlie started to smile. They turned back to their screens, switched tools and went to undo the screws fastening the fuel cell to the frame of the unit. There were six such Phillips-head screws. With the last one removed and set aside, they were able to begin to contemplate lifting out the power plant.

"No pressure, then," Charlie said.

"I think, if it was going to blow, it would've—"

It blew. The screens went to static. The joysticks went loose and useless, all haptics lost.

There was no sound from within the Bat Cave. Spider felt sick. Charlie said, "What happened?"

The technicians eased Spider and Charlie aside and ran diagnostic routines. This took longer than either Spider, Charlie or even James expected. One of the techs suggested they might like to go and have a break, and maybe a coffee.

"Excellent plan!" James said, smiling, not looking all that creeped out. Spider and Charlie stared at him, then stared at the Bat Cave, silent and black and cold.

Spider shivered. "Coffee sounds good."

They went inside. Malaria ducked under a doorframe to tell Spider that the phones were going nuts. People experiencing weird problems with their time machines.

"Uh-huh," Spider said, trying to persuade the coffee droid to produce the brew he wanted. "Tell 'em I'll call them back first chance I get."

"If we're not dead," Charlie said, giggling.

Spider giggled, too, and the two of them stood there, giggling away, and their giggles turned to laughter. James finished organizing the coffees, but said over his shoulder, "Aren't you glad I let you use the Bat Cave?"

"Oh, yeah, do please thank the government for us," Spider said, still laughing.

James handed round the coffees. "You know," he said, deadpanning, "if there's any damage in there, you guys are liable, right?"

Spider grinned, but Charlie did a spit-take, spraying coffee at the floor. "Oh God, I've got coffee coming out my nose now. Shit!"

One of the technicians appeared at the doorway, out of breath, wide-eyed. "Uh, you guys really ought to come and have a look at something."

"Let me guess," Spider said, "we've discovered a gateway to another universe?"

"No," the tech said, rather pale. "Kind of worse than that."

James said, "We haven't woken up Great Cthulhu, have we?"

Spider said, "No, that's Thursday."

James nodded, but kept looking at the tech. "So what's the trouble?"

"It'd be best if you'd just come and..." He trailed off.

"You've got picture back?"

"Yeah. Just. The radiation's died down quite a bit."

Charlie was fixing himself a new coffee, and glanced up at that. "Radiation?"

"That's not right," Spider said, heading for the door.

They went back outside. It was starting to rain again; thunder rumbled in the black and forbidding cloudscape to the west. The Bat Cave looked no different. The other tech was walking around it, holding a wireless handheld device, watching the screen intently. He turned to talk to the first tech when he came over, and showed him her readings. "Oh," he said, pointing at something. To Spider he said, "Looks like we can power down the Cave."

"Let's just see what's going on in there first," Spider said, going to the screens, and working the in-Cave cameras that were still intermittently working. Then he saw the problem. "Damn," he said in a reasonable tone, and invited Charlie and James to have a look, too.

They crowded round, and Spider pointed out the problem.

"That's not right," Charlie said at last.

Inside the Bat Cave, the original time machine, its hull panels and interior components, its trailer and the articulated tool-arms lay in scorched and twisted bits and pieces on the floor. The tires from the trailer were still burning, filling the universe in there with thick, black smoke. Where that unit had stood, however, there was now another time machine. It looked to be in reasonable condition, considering.

"I've seen a lot of weird shit in this time machine repair caper over the years," Spider said, "but I've never seen that."

James stood there, staring at the image on the screen. He'd gone even more pale than usual. "Good God", he said, shaken.

Charlie asked, "Could someone have sent a unit into the Bat Cave from out here?"

James shook his head. "Not possible. Not remotely possible."

Charlie said, pointing at the image of the new machine, "There's something in the passenger seat."

James bit his lip, and leaned in for a better look. "It looks like blue plastic."

Spider, too astonished to say much of anything, zoomed in on the blue plastic object in the passenger seat. It was large, and bent over. He felt a wave of shivers up and down his spine. He knew what it looked like, but that made even less sense than everything else. Attempting to stay calm, he pointed. "Is that duct tape?"

Charlie nodded. "Think so, boss."

James said, "I think I need to sit down for a minute."

Spider, concerned at how James looked, and a little surprised — but then, he thought, this development was not exactly routine — ducked into the office and grabbed a chair for James, who sank into it gratefully.

Spider went back to scrutinizing the screens, checking readings inside the Cave. Everything was returning to normal, he was amazed to see.

"So it's safe in there now?" Charlie asked. "What about the radiation?"

James consulted with the technicians, who nodded in agreement and then politely asked Spider and Charlie to move away from the screen, so they could start shutting down the Bat Cave.

Charlie said to Spider, "How is that even possible?"

Spider just looked at him. "You're asking me?"

"You're the expert!"

"I'm just a guy who fixes busted time machines," he said. "You want an expert's opinion, ask James. Though I'm guessing, looking at him there, he's as baffled as we are, and he's a bloody engineer!" James was ashen, his face drawn. It worried Spider, and made him wonder if

what was happening here was even more freaky than
he had previously thought. But then, did he really want
to know just how incredibly freaky this was? Curiosity
and fear warred within him for a moment, and then decided it was somebody else's problem. That felt better.

"So you're saying we've got nothing to go on here."

"We've got bugger-all to go on, Charlie."

"James," said Charlie, "Where — or when — did it
come from?"

James got up and came over to join them. Spider could
see he was sweating. James said, "If I knew I'd tell you,
that's for bloody sure. Right now, all I can say is the
universe inside the Bat Cave had a zero point — when
we powered up the Cave — and an end point, just now,
when we powered it down. Total existence time of maybe
a few hours. No other time machine could be in there,
or we'd know about it, simply because it would have been
there, or at least have been detectable, from when we
powered up. And it couldn't have bopped in from out
here, the cave is a hole in our reality. The universe as we
know it has a temporary Bat Cave-shaped boundary right
there. It's a discontinuity. It's—"

Spider said, "Look, I don't mean to interrupt, but are
you quite all right there, James? You look like shit."

James flashed an unconvincing smile. "Thanks for the
concern, but I'm okay. Really. Just busy lately. Not much
sleep."

"Right," Spider said, thinking about James' home life
these days: it was just him and his daughter Electra. Even
after all this time, things had to be difficult between them,
and he could believe James was putting in long hours
at work.

"Yeah." A sad smile. "So," he said. "About all this…"

Spider said, suddenly inspired, "You know what it
might be?"

James watched the techs working their controls. Slowly
the Bat Cave-shaped hole in reality was turning back into
a big black balloon. He said, "I've had one or two ideas.
You go first." Spider noted that James was avoiding looking at the screens if he could help it.

Spider said, "What if it's a sandwich?"

Charlie stared at him. "Um, what?"

James mopped his brow with a handkerchief. "No," he said, breathing hard. "Not so much a sandwich," he illustrated with his hands, "as a *superpositioning*. Two time machines—"

Spider saw where he was going. "Occupying the same space-time." His mind lit up as he started to see how it might work, and how it might lead to the Tempo's odd symptoms. "You'd have to have a way of folding space-time to do it, or something, anyway. But that'd be why we were getting all those crazy readings. It'd be why Charlie and I both felt sick inside the thing, and why it behaved so erratically for the owner."

One of the techs came over. "Okay, the Cave's been safed. You can go inside if you want."

Spider and Charlie exchanged apprehensive looks. "You want to go first?" Spider said.

Charlie said, "This is one of those invitations which superficially look like the kind of thing I could say, 'Oh, no, I'm good. Why don't you go first?' — only it's really more like the Army asking recruits who'd like to volunteer, right?"

Spider clapped him on the shoulder. "The kid's quick, I'll give him that."

James said, "It should be perfectly safe. Now, anyway. Look, I'll go first." He went over to the gaping opening. Very hot, thick black smoke billowed out of the Cave. James stood there, coughing, waiting for them. "Might be wise to put out the tires first, though."

Later, the fires extinguished and the smoke cleared, Spider, Charlie and James ventured inside the structure. The stink of fire, smoke and something nasty and unexpected was almost disabling. Coughing, careful where they stepped in the small space, they went up to the "new" time machine. It was a Dolphin, nearly as old as the Tempo had been, and, like the Tempo, it was in poor condition. It rested on the floor, its small rubber wheels deployed.

Spider, who was pretty sure what he was going to find, went up to the Dolphin's passenger door and opened it, being careful to avoid contaminating what he was pretty sure was a crime scene. The thing in the blue plastic wrapping folded over, slumped out of the unit and fell in a big disgusting lump onto the floor. Even with all the duct tape to keep it sealed, a surprising amount of blood started to pool at Spider's feet.

Charlie had to step outside suddenly, and could be heard retching. James was just staring, pale and speechless. Spider covered the lower part of his face, and bent down, his knees shaking with adrenaline — and carefully tried to open the plastic near what he thought must be the head. With the opening, a new wave of malignant odor wafted out, warm and sickening. He felt his guts protesting, but he saw some hair, dark blonde, longish, and part of an ear. It was so pale it was almost bluish.

"You never get used to the smell," he said to nobody.

CHAPTER 5

They had to give customary statements and biometric samples to the uniformed police who responded to the emergency call. *Easy enough*, thought Spider, noting how young and fresh-faced they were and how *that* made him feel old and useless. Had it really been that long since he'd left the service? At least the two uniforms wouldn't recognize him, so that was something.

Later, when the unmarked car from the Major Crime Squad turned up, and he saw Inspector Iris Street get out, he swore out loud.

"Boss?" Charlie said, looking at the detective. She was middle-aged, looked like she'd had a long day already and didn't appreciate getting called out in lousy weather over some damn thing to do with a time machine. "You know her?"

"Yeah, you could say that," Spider said, watching her. It had been many years. *In fact, not nearly enough years*, he thought. "Guys, we are probably screwed."

James, who was hanging around because DOTAS would want to be involved in the unfolding investigation and would require detailed first-hand reports of what had happened this afternoon, said, "She's bent?"

"Let's just say you hear things, over time," Spider said, not wanting to go into it. He could feel the old anger building, deep in the back of his brain. His blood pressure, if that steady hammering at his temples was anything to go by, was already getting out of hand.

Inspector Street was talking to her partner, a detective constable most probably. Very tall, very thin and black like a silhouette, the guy listened to Street and took notes as she told him what to do. Spider didn't recognize the kid, which wasn't that surprising. He really had been out of the Service for a long time. Spider watched the pair of them as they went over to the Bat Cave, where they spoke to the two DOTAS technicians, and then went inside the inert device to inspect the body and talk to the crime-scene guys. That done, he watched Street working her handheld to review their initial statements. It looked as if she was doing a thorough job, reading and re-reading, making a lot of annotations. Then she left the detective constable to supervise the crime scene work, while she came over to the workshop to talk to Charlie, James and himself. Malaria had also stayed behind, claiming they would need her moral support if not copious quantities of her coffee.

Inspector Street ducked through the workshop door, made some disarming comments about the rain, smiled, and came over. She engaged in some light banter with Charlie and James, and then she came to Spider. He found he was seething with suppressed anger, far more than he had ever suspected he might feel in such a circumstance. He'd been extremely careful, all these years, deliberately trying to stay the hell out of police trouble. Street looked at him, smiled a little goofily, even self-consciously, and shook his hand. "Hello, Spider, long time."

His mouth was dry; his tongue stuck to his palate. It was difficult to speak, there were so many conflicting emotions boiling away in his head right now. "Iris," he said at last; not sure whether to fake a smile for the sake of politeness, or just to keep it simple, he wound up looking nervous and self-conscious. It occurred to him that she might feel much the same way about meeting him as he felt about meeting her, but knowing that didn't help.

"Congratulations," he said, not meaning it, "you've done well for yourself." Getting that out was harder work than he'd expected. He watched her carefully to see if she could tell what was really going through his mind.

She shrugged, thanked him, and flashed a quick self-deprecating smile. "You know, work hard, keep your head down..."

He managed to say, "Anyway, good on you." The words nearly choked him.

"Time machines, huh?" she said, looking around the workshop.

He felt embarrassed, watching her taking everything in. "Someone's gotta fix 'em."

"Good line of work?"

"Not bad, not bad. Always some idiot doing something stupid."

"You have to go to university to qualify?"

"Nah. Did three years at TAFE, then an apprenticeship."

"So you're the owner?" she asked.

"Oh no. Just the senior tech. You'll probably want to talk to the company owner, Mr. McMahon."

Street looked at her handheld. "Ah yes. McMahon. We've got an appointment with him first thing tomorrow."

"Right," Spider said, nodding, sweating, seething.

Street was looking at Spider now, noting the way he looked, the way he was vibrating with suppressed anger. He remembered her from the old days, when they were both lowly detective constables. At the time, during a bad time with Molly, he and Iris Street had had a bit of an affair — before they discovered they had nothing in common, other than their line of work. That and the fact that she had been ambitious, far more so than he had been. His ambition had been to be a good copper. He saw it as a public-service kind of thing. Helping the community. She didn't want to be a good copper; she'd wanted to be the top copper. She'd wanted Superintendent Sharp's job, and she made sure he knew it. There had always been rumors that she was sleeping with him, but Spider had never believed it.

Inspector Street said, softly so Charlie and James wouldn't hear, "I'm sorry how things turned out for you, Spider."

He nearly spat. Instead he said, "Gee, thanks."

She bristled a moment, staring up at him, thinking about how to handle him. "What happened to you should never have happened."

He entirely agreed, but said nothing. After a moment he said, "So you'll be wanting me to go over my account, right?"

It looked to him very much as if she was going to say something at that point that she might come to regret, but instead she said, "Yes. Yes, if you would."

He nodded, but took a few moments to breathe, to try to get his screaming mind back under control. Street produced her handheld and he spoke into it, taking his time, describing as best he could the events surrounding what had happened today, from getting the initial call yesterday morning from Mr. Vincent to the discovery of the second time machine and the body inside the Bat Cave today. Keeping his mind focused on this account helped him regain his composure. It also helped to know the kind of detail that policework required, which with any luck would keep him from having to repeat the story too many more times. He was careful to think about any possible ambiguities, contradictions or other problems that might somehow get him into trouble. He was worried about finding himself on the hook for this murder. He knew that even though Superintendent Sharp was gone, many of his minions had risen to great heights in the Police Service, and they would remember Spider. Indeed, one of the things he had learned in those days, often the hard way, was the amazing, dismaying, habit that these people had of never forgetting a slight, never forgetting any kind of attack. Spider had spent a lot of the last ten years waiting for the hammer to fall on him — and right now, with that body in the time machine outside, he believed he could feel the blow coming at last.

Inspector Street read back his statement on her handheld, nodding here and there, then showed it to him, and asked him to read it through carefully. He noticed that she was going out of her way to show him she was being professional. Once he finished reading his statement, and shaking his head at the way he "sounded" in print being so different from how he sounded to himself, Street gave him her plastic stylus and he signed in the verification panel. The handheld chirped to indicate it had successfully authenticated his statement and signature, and that it was on file there in the handheld and in a database back at CIB headquarters. *For better or worse*, he thought, his stomach aching with tension. *For better or worse.*

That done, Street should have moved on to talk to Charlie, James and Malaria. Instead, and to Spider's great discomfort, she stood looking at him for a moment, clearly wanting to say something to him, but in the end decided against it. "Thank you, Spider," she said at last, and moved on to Charlie.

Spider went to get a coffee from the tiny break room behind his office. When he tried working the controls on the machine, he found his hands were shaking too much. "Fuck!" he said. "Fuck!" He sat down on a chair, worried he would start crying.

Malaria came in a while later. "You okay there, Spider?"

He should go home, but the prospect of cycling in the rain twice in one day was less than appealing. "Never better, Malaria. Never better."

She nodded, uncomfortable. She had to be aware of the hot-anger radiation pouring off him. "You and the Inspector. You and she go back a bit."

"Your point?" he said, and immediately regretted the harshness in his voice, and the startled look on her face. "Sorry, Malaria." It felt as if it had cost him a year of his life to make such an apology, the way he was feeling just then.

Malaria nodded, looked away. She went to the fridge, and stood there a while, staring into its interior, apparently trying to decide what she wanted. There was a modest collection of fizzy beverages, some cheap imported mineral waters, a few chocolate bars, and a collection of instant-noodle cups.

Spider felt like shit, wanting to keep apologizing to Malaria. He said to her, "The inspector and I knew each other years ago, we were junior coppers together."

Malaria was still staring into the fridge, as if it would provide the answer to the mystery of existence. Without turning to look at him, she said, "The way you guys were looking at each other, I figured you must have slept together and regretted it."

Spider actually laughed, but not the happy kind of laughing. "I wish it was that simple." All the same, he was thinking, now that he had time to think, one of the things that made that bit with Iris Street just now so horribly difficult was this: he thought she still looked all right. He clapped his forehead. "No bloody way," he muttered under his breath.

Malaria grabbed one of the tiny bottles of mineral water, and spent a few moments trying to pronounce the words on the Italian side of the label. She came and sat down next to Spider, and quietly sipped at the water.

"I really am sorry, Malaria. I had no business taking it out on you. I—"

She looked him in the eye, and he knew that she saw that he was in danger of breaking down in tears at any moment. "It's okay, sir. We all have bad shit in our histories. It's part of life. You go along, you do dumb shit, dumb shit happens to you because of other people, it all piles up, and makes a big shitty mess everywhere."

"Maybe I should borrow a time machine," Spider said, voicing a thought he'd often entertained, "go back to back then, and have a quiet word with my former self about getting along with people."

"You haven't got a time machine?" Malaria said, surprised.

"I wouldn't have one if you bloody-well paid me a squillion dollars and draped it with supermodels covered in whipped cream and chocolate toppings. No way."

"But—"

"Time machines don't solve anything, they never do."

Malaria finished her bottle. "It was nice the times I've gone back to see my parents."

He would like to have been left alone to brood about the past and his crappy present, but Malaria's last remark distracted him. "Sorry, what?"

"My mum and dad? They were killed in this stupid car accident when I was a kid."

"Oh," he said, surprised and uncomfortable in a different way, "I didn't know. I'm—"

"Yeah, you're sorry. I know. It's okay. They didn't suffer. I've gone back to see them all these times. First it was to warn them about the accident, right? But to start with they never believed me, didn't believe it was me, their daughter, even when I took my birth certificate to show them. Then one time I tried to get my earlier self to stop them going out that night, and that kinda worked — but they ended up getting killed later from something else."

Spider nodded. Yup, it was always like that. It was like some things wanted to happen.

"So now, when I go back, I just go back to hang out with them. They know it's me, now, and that we've got these time machines and all that. I took them for a spin this one time into the future."

"You went to the future?"

"Yeah, it was something like the 22nd century?"

"But nobody goes to the future." It was true. The only people who even thought about visiting the future were grizzled old science fiction fans and writers, and they were generally disappointed with what they found. Polls taken to discover the reason for the general lack of interest in the future as a destination showed that nobody expected there to be much future to speak of. One way or another, the results showed, people imagined the future as being just a black void of nothingness, the Earth long since wrecked beyond habitation, and humanity either wiped out somehow, or existing in such a miserable state it would not be worth visiting. The future was too depressing to contemplate.

Malaria got up. "You want a coffee? I'm getting one, and you look like you could use one, if you'll excuse me saying."

"Um, sure. Yeah. Thanks," he said, and told her how he liked his coffee.

Then Charlie and James came in, talking about football. James, Spider thought, sounded somehow too bright and cheery. Strange. Malaria offered to make them coffees, too, if they wanted. "It's been a pretty bad night, huh?" she said.

Charlie sat on the table, stretching his neck. "They've just taken the body."

James, pulling up a chair, said, "Stabbed something like twenty times, the Inspector said. A woman, wrapped in plastic. Very Laura Palmer."

Charlie looked blank for a moment. Spider explained about *Twin Peaks*. Charlie said he kept meaning to download that show.

James said, "Skip the second season."

They talked idly about *Twin Peaks*, and classic pre-millennium TV generally, for a while. It helped defuse some of the tension Spider had been feeling. He started to relax a little. Considering the coffee droid Malaria had to work with, her coffee was sublime. "Where did you learn to make coffee like that?" he said, amazed.

James and Charlie were likewise astonished. Charlie said, "We paid a hundred and fifty bucks for that piece of crap, and its never made anything but crap coffee."

Malaria bashfully owned up to having been trained as a barista, but then she added in stern tones, "Don't you think this means I'm making coffee for you all the time, either. This is just a favor, 'cause of tonight, and all the..." She waved her hands. "All the fuss."

Spider said he really appreciated it. Especially tonight. His head was hurting less. He felt as if he could breathe again, and the rock-hard tension in his guts was easing.

Charlie said, "So what's the skinny with you and Inspector Street, boss?"

"There's no skinny. No scuttlebutt. No loose talk, no rumors, no idle stories or tales told out of school, Charlie. We knew each other way back when, and that's it."

Charlie said, "The way you guys looked at each other, though—"

James, who was starting to look better under the healing influence of good coffee, observed, "I thought you could power a small city with that much juice."

Spider rubbed his face, wanting to change the subject. "That woman was stabbed how many times?"

James and Charlie exchanged amused looks, and decided to play along. Charlie said, "Maybe twenty times or so. It was pretty bad. Lots of blood."

"Who'd hide a murder victim like that?" Spider said, thinking aloud.

Charlie said, "Somebody bloody clever, I reckon."

Spider asked, "How clever?"

Charlie, who hung out on tech exploits forums on the tubes, reading about crazy things people did with time machines, said, "Genius clever, I'd say. I mean, it's not meant to be possible, for starters. You have to align the two machines' time fields, just so."

James, who had been very quiet, said, "So, a criminal mastermind, yes?"

Charlie said, "Cool!"

Spider, staring into his coffee, trying to think his way around the whole thing, said, "A woman was brutally murdered, Charlie. It's not 'cool'."

"Sorry, boss. I was just thinking about the way—"

"I know, I get it. It's devilishly clever. She could have been hidden away like that indefinitely."

"The explosion in the Bat Cave, by the way," James said, looking at Spider. "Roughly equivalent to about two hundred kilos of high explosive."

Spider blinked, stunned. "Two hundred kilos?"

Charlie swore. Malaria, listening closely, said, "I don't mean to sound stupid here, but what exactly is high explosive?"

"Bad news on a stick," Spider said. "Military-level explosive. Packs a massive wallop. The upshot is that these two time machines, stuck together in the same space and time like that, were a touch unstable."

Malaria said, "A touch?"

Spider was thinking as he sipped his coffee. "The second time machine," he said, staring at the floor. "It wasn't damaged, or at least not that much."

James said, "Yeah, I'd noticed that, too. Odd. Makes you wonder where all the explosive energy went to."

"Could it be that the second machine was stuck inside its own private little bubble of space-time, and the first machine, the Tempo, was superposed around it?"

"Could be. We won't know for sure until DOTAS finishes giving the whole thing a good going over. Maybe by the end of the week?"

"Any chance you could get me a copy of their report?"

James smiled. "You know that's really not kosher, don't you?"

"Yeah, but could you do it?"

"No chance, mate. No chance in hell."

Spider bit his lip and nodded. "Damn," he said.

Once they finished with their coffee, Malaria announced that she'd better get home or it'd be time to get up again before she went to sleep. She rose to her full gangly height, grabbed her coat and bag, and headed out. This cued the others, too.

James took Spider aside once Charlie and Malaria had left the room. "I can get you a copy of the report by Friday at the latest."

"I don't want you compromising your job there, James."

"It'll be fine," he said.

"You're sure?"

"Sure as eggs. Sure as eggs."

Spider did want to see that report. He knew it was technically illegal, and that James would be taking a serious risk by making a copy of it and letting Spider read it. He wanted to know what the hell was going on with this dead woman, and how she came to be stuck like that, maybe in her own tiny bubble of space-time, or whatever the hell it would turn out to be. A murdered woman on his turf, such as it was, was something that spoke to his hindbrain, and stirred up entire old ways of thinking about things. But he'd hate himself if James wound up losing his job over it — or worse, if he, Spider, wound up losing his own job, and prosecuted by the DOTAS Time Crime Unit.

He said, "It's all right, mate. Don't do it. It's okay."

"It's no trouble," James said, sounding utterly reasonable.

"It bloody is trouble, James. It's too much risk."

James looked at him for a long moment, then nodded. "Fair enough. Fair enough."

Spider managed a smile. "Hope you understand."

"Oh yeah. Sure. No worries."

"You've got a family and all."

"Appreciate the thought," James said.

"Well. Better go."

James clapped him on the shoulder, turned and left. After a bit Spider heard James's car starting up, pulling out, driving off into the dismal night.

Spider walked around his tiny fiefdom, torn up inside. In the workshop he looked at the three other time machines in their service bays, each waiting on some damn thing or other to get them going again. Tomorrow morning, bright and early, he'd be back here, fixing them, just like any other day. He and Charlie would swap jokes and try not to think about just what a shitty job this really was.

He stood at the workshop entrance, looking out into the parking lot where the Bat Cave had been set up. It was all gone now, taken as evidence, as if it had never been. *Something deeply strange happened out there today*, he thought. *Something puzzling*. It called to him; he could feel it, like a tidal pull. He hated puzzles. Puzzles needed solving. He was helpless against them, and always had been.

Standing here, feeling the buzzing in his head from the coffee, and from the sheer weirdness of the day in general, he knew that even when he got back to the capsule motel he wouldn't be able to sleep. The dead woman in the hidden time machine was going to call to him all night long, wanting him to help her.

Resigned to the prospect of a sleepless night, and to riding home in the rain, he pulled his still-damp wet-weather gear on and went out to where his bike was parked. Damn, it was cold. He could hear the rain spattering on his hood. Folded down into his recumbent bike, the canopy pulled down tight overhead, he set off, pedaling steadily, out through the main gate and onto Inverness Road.

Then he spotted the small nondescript car, a late-model Sony, parked just up the road. "What?" he muttered, and remembered the images of this very car. "Two nights running?" Once was a random occurrence. Twice was starting to look like a pattern. He thought about riding past the car, to get a better look at the occupant, but decided against it, and instead he rode off the other way, into the wind and rain.

CHAPTER 6

Dickhead McMahon was a big man who managed to take up more room than the space he actually occupied. Spider was always reminded of the old wargaming concept of "zone-of-control." Dickhead McMahon physically occupied his own hex on the map, but he somehow managed to dominate all six hexes around him, and stopped anyone or anything else from passing him. Whenever Spider had to talk to his boss, which he was thankful wasn't too often, he always did his best to stand well back, as far away as he could get, just to keep out of Dickhead's zone of control. It wasn't that the man lacked hygiene, or even that he was all that obnoxious. He was just the kind of large man who filled entire rooms, squeezing people out, by his sheer presence. He had a loud voice, and he had a great many opinions, all of which he was only too keen to tell you about at length and in detail, without any regard for your interest in said opinions. Spider had heard, he thought, all of them.

Dickhead McMahon was not pleased to have the federal government bothering him about the whole "dead woman in the time machine" thing. "What you should have done, Spider, and mark my words this is gold, this is, pure gold, what you should have done in the first instance, when you met the client, is refuse to take his machine. First sign of any fruity weirdness in the machine, you say, 'I'm sorry, sir, but we're absolutely snowed under with work right now.' Right? Easy to do, it's not rude, and it's only slightly lying.

"Then, when the guy says the usual, 'Oh, but what do I do now?' you tell him you'd be delighted to recommend another reputable time machine repair firm. Nothing but polite and friendly, right? It's not brain science, Spider, and we're not a charity. We do quick, simple straightforward repair work. Component out, component in, give everything a nice polish, and get the unit out the door so we can take another unit.

"Your key-point indicators, Spider, your key-point indicators are in the absolute toilet lately, you know that? And this business yesterday, that's not going to help. We can't have that kind of thing getting in the way and taking up valuable company resources, now can we?"

Spider said, "Yes, Dickhead. How wrong I was to get all concerned about a dead person."

Dickhead beamed, even his smile seemed to take up a lot of room. It was as if he hadn't heard a word of Spider's remark. Spider found this fascinating. You could say anything at all to Dickhead McMahon, and if it wasn't a response he was expecting, he'd somehow pretend that it was. Spider had a theory that this was because Dickhead believed that he was the only real human being in the world, and everyone else, including Spider, was a machine of some sort. Anything that appeared to conflict with this view of things was discarded without Dickhead's having to think about it. Spider thought it must be a marvelous way to live your life.

"Good. Excellent," Dickhead said. "You're a top bloke, Spider. One of my best. I've got big plans for you, my boy. Big plans."

"Is that right?" Spider said, not that interested, but playing along.

"Oh yes, Spider. The biggest." A strange gleam shone in Dickhead's eyes. He said, apropos of not much, "Listen, what's your thinking about angels, hmm?"

"Um, what?"

"You heard me. Angels. Thoughts? Views?"

Spider stared and stared at his boss, deeply troubled. This wasn't the first time Dickhead had talked to him about angels. Even that night, years ago now, when Spider first met Dickhead in a pub in Northbridge, a night when Spider had been at rock bottom, even then, now he thought about it, Dickhead had talked about angels, describing himself as an "angel of redemption". At the time Spider thought the big bastard was crazy, but since he was being friendly, and buying him a drink, he didn't mention it. He glanced around the front office, looking at the huge motivational posters — and noticed for the first time that they all featured angels, looking all luminous and fierce, performing great deeds, smiting heathens left and right. *Why have I never noticed this before?* he asked himself. Feeling more than a little uncertain, a little anxious, he looked back at his boss, and said, "You know, angels good. Real good. Why?"

Dickhead, perhaps seeing that Spider wasn't reacting quite as favorably as he might wish, nodded and smiled, clapped his hands together, as if breaking a spell, and changed the subject, saying, "Now then, I could murder a coffee. Where's your new receptionist, what did you say her name was?"

"Malaria doesn't make coffee, Dickhead," Spider said, distracted from all of Dickhead's angel nonsense as his mind filled with the rapturous memory of the coffee Malaria made last night with their crap little coffee droid.

"Of course she makes coffee. Don't be foolish, Spider. Now where is the little minx?"

It was currently Malaria's lunch break. She'd taken off to wherever it was she went — Spider didn't know, and didn't think it was his business to know — and would be back in due course. He could imagine what Malaria might say on being referred to as a "little minx," and decided it was a good thing she was out at the moment.

Dickhead, seeing that Malaria was out, turned to Spider. "Well, you're not doing anything important right now..." he said, a suggestive curl to his lip.

"You want coffee, Dickhead, you make it yourself. I've got three units needing work." When Dickhead shot him a sour look, Spider added, "And you did tell me my KPIs were in the toilet, right?"

And yet, even as he said this, he was aware that Dickhead was using his eerie zone-of-control powers to force Spider into the break room. He swore under his breath, hated himself, and decided it was easier to go along with Dickhead, make him a bloody coffee, and then get back to work, where he could seethe all afternoon about his spinelessness. While it was true that you could tell Dickhead he was a dickhead to his face, and he would hardly notice, it was also true that if he didn't get what he wanted, he could fire you.

He tried to get the coffee droid to produce the same caffeinated miracles Malaria had coaxed out of it last night, without success. It was making a worrying buzzing, gurgling sound, and the only liquid he could get it to produce was a nasty thick sludge that did not resemble coffee. "Fuck-a-bloody-duck!" he muttered under his breath, wishing Malaria would hurry back, so she could at least tell him what to do.

"Problems, Spider?"

Spider ignored him.

Dickhead said, "Listen. About that whole 'dead woman' business."

"What about it?" Spider was reading the prompts on the droid's screen, but he wasn't getting the predicted results. What had Malaria done last night? he wondered.

Dickhead said, "Yeah. Had a bit of a word this morning with that detective lady, what's-her-name, Street? Is that it?" He checked the screen of his watch for verification. "Yeah, that's it. Bit of all right, she is, I thought. A go-getter. Very Type-A — do people still talk about Type-A personalities these days? I get so caught up in running things I lose track of all the management voodoo. Anyway. Inspector Street."

Spider had a bad feeling about where this might be going. He focused on the animated instructions the droid showed him, but it wasn't helping. "Yeah, what about her?"

Dickhead said, "Mmm, yeah. So just what did you tell her last night, Spider?"

He sighed and felt his neck muscles starting to bunch up. His stomach hurt, and he wondered if he wasn't getting another ulcer. "I just told her what happened. Why, what did she tell you?" Spider, fed up with the coffee droid's nonsense, decided to start fresh, and for good measure he ran a cycle of clean, bottled water through the machine to try to clean it out. He'd heard that that was sometimes a good idea.

"Not much, actually. Wanted to know all about you."

"Is that right?" he said, trying to remain calm.

"She seemed to think it very odd that a murder victim should turn up on the premises of a former copper."

Grinding his teeth now, Spider tried to concentrate on operating the coffee droid. Even with cutesy animated instructions, he knew he was somehow getting it wrong, and Dickhead, typically, wasn't helping. *Concentrate*, he told himself.

"Right. Step One. Grind the damn beans. How hard can it be to grind beans?" he said, as if his life depended on it, and dumped fresh beans in the grinding hopper. The automatic grinder started up with a loud shriek, which was over almost as soon as it started. Spider thought he must have done something wrong, but no. The beans were done. They smelled wonderful. "What else did she have to say?"

He glanced behind him to look at Dickhead, and just as he expected, the idiot was enjoying Spider's discomfiture. He was also rocking back on his chair. These chairs were cheap plastic lawn furniture, all the office budget could afford, and Spider knew from his own embarrassing experience that they would crumple under you without any warning and leave you sprawled on the floor. So far Dickhead, as huge as he was, had managed to find some magical balance point that supported his entire mass without collapsing. It was the luck of the oblivious.

Spider followed the onscreen help, triggered the next stage in the cycle, and hoped for the best. He thought he might be on the right track this time.

Dickhead said, "She wanted to know where I found you, what you were doing at the time."

"Where you found me? What am I, a lost kitten?"

"Worry not, son. I've told her nothing but the truth, and the truth is good."

"The truth? You told her the truth?" This was not good news.

Dickhead laughed, and his great bulk jiggled. "No, not the actual, you know, biblical truth. God, no, Spider. I bullshitted her, told her what she wanted to hear, and you mark my words, you won't have any more trouble from her, you can take it from me. I told her you're my ace technician, that you have a unique gift for fixing busted time machines, and that I should probably pay you more than I do."

"You really did bullshit her," Spider said, surprised at this unexpected loyalty from his boss. The coffee droid produced a cardboard cup and slotted it under the nozzle. A peculiar whirring occurred deep within the machine, followed by a very wet sound, and plumes of steam rose from vents. The steam smelled good.

"Reading between the lines, Spider, I kind of had the feeling she was thinking about you as maybe a suspect, or at least a person of interest, as they say. That kind of thing *de rigeur* with your lot?"

"I wouldn't know, Dickhead," he said, not wanting to talk about it.

§   §   §

Spider's career in the Western Australian Police Service had not gone the way he wanted. The first decade, as he worked his way up from constable to senior constable to sergeant, had been fine. His evaluations stated that he was well regarded by his peers, that he had a good attitude, and that he was detail-oriented. It was an interesting life, with a fair amount of variety, and, once he entered the realm of merit-based promotions, he found himself doing well. He made detective senior sergeant at thirty-seven years of age, and was seen as a capable officer with a bright future.

But his competence led him into the problem: two officers from the Internal Affairs Center approached him one day with a job offer — they were mounting an operation investigating the unauthorized use of the then-new technology of time travel by certain members of the WAPOL. Was he interested? Spider was interested — in those days the idea of time travel seemed very exciting and interesting, even a bit glamorous. They told him that he had been recommended for this job by his current boss, Inspector Christopher "Dracula" Lee, who spoke highly of Spider's abilities, particularly his capacity for impartial investigation.

Flattered, Spider had asked what he would have to do. The job involved following designated target personnel in what was known as "ghost mode." The officers in question, informants had told them, were conducting various activities via time travel, and it was now time to see if these claims were true. The idea was not to arrest these officers so much as to document their activities. All Spider had to do was follow along, invisible, armed with high-tech vid recording gear, going wherever — and whenever — his targets went.

In the course of this work, Spider had learned the following things:

(a) that he had to follow his boss's boss, Superintendent Sharp;

(b) Superintendent Sharp was traveling back in time to various points around the turn of the nineteenth-to-twentieth centuries, and meeting up with certain fellow officers;

(c) these senior officers, in period costume, and not in any way pretending to be police officers, were molesting small children.

Spider got it all on video. It was hideous, terrifying, sickening work. He nearly quit the investigation. Molly told him that no matter what he'd learned, he had a duty to keep going, so he did.

Soon enough, the Internal Affairs officers told him they could let him go back to regular duties, but that he had done well enough that if an opening should appear in IAC, Spider should consider applying. More important, though, no one would ever know it had been Detective Senior Sergeant Webb who had followed Sharp and his mates around with a camera. Spider asked about this a lot. While the Service had a stated policy of protecting whistleblowers, and a determination to investigate all claims of corruption and impropriety by its officers in a thorough fashion, Spider was still terrified that his role in the operation would leak out. Molly told him he was being silly and paranoid.

His name leaked. He never found out who leaked it, but the whole thing became public knowledge within the WAPOL. Superintendent Sharp and his buddies resigned in disgrace, were put on trial, were convicted, and were sent to prison for their crimes. They did not do well in prison. Spider started getting letters in the mail. They were not direct threats, but they felt like threats. One contained a detailed breakdown of Molly's movements over one day, with photos. Another contained photos of Spider's mum and dad going about their daily business. It turned out, one letter told him, that Superintendent Sharp was appealing his conviction. Spider should think about his priorities, the letter said.

He talked to Inspector Lee, who sent him back to the Internal Affairs Center. They told him he should hold firm. His work on the operation was first-rate, as they told him before. If he resigned over these veiled threats, Sharp would likely win his appeal, and might even consider suing Spider for anything Sharp's high-powered lawyer could think of. He'd be ruined. So Spider hung on. It wasn't easy. His marriage got a bit rocky. Nobody touched Molly or his parents, but he worried himself into an ulcer. He slept poorly. Every odd sound outside, every unusual observation his parents reported, made him jumpy and fearful.

The crisis passed in time. Sharp's conviction was upheld. He died in prison; it was messy.

Spider was sent to work in the Traffic Warden State Management Unit. They told him he was the man best qualified for the position, but nobody there wanted him, he could tell from the distinctly chilly manner of every single person he met. Spider resolved to tough it out, to do the best damn job he could do, and if that meant making sure the state's traffic-warden-controlled crosswalks were as safe as humanly possible, then that's what he would do. Yet nothing he tried, no initiatives, no ideas, no suggestions, ever made it into policy. It was frustrating, knowing he was being punished, but unable to prove it. Everyone treated him professionally, but no one wanted to be his friend. No one wanted to have lunch together, or to have a drink after work on Friday evenings. They destroyed Spider slowly, bit by bit, the death of a thousand small cuts. He never rose higher than his current rank, no matter how well he performed.

"But I did the right thing!" he told Molly.

"Maybe you should have said no, did you think of that?" she said to him.

He resigned from the Service six months later. The only written references he could get were the sort that stated Spider had worked in the following capacities and positions at these times. There was never any comment about how well he had performed, the quality of his character, no recommendations to future employers that Spider would make a model employee.

A year later, unemployed and unemployable, as if the entire city of Perth somehow knew that Spider was a traitor, a rat, just waiting to screw over anyone who hired him, he found himself in that Northbridge pub one night, nursing the one beer he could afford that day. He was a wreck, and looked it. He met a guy who insisted Spider call him "Dickhead," and who offered him a job. It would mean going to TAFE to get qualified, but Dickhead would pay for that. Spider would just have to do the three years, then a year as an apprentice. It was good work, technical, well-paying, and plenty of it. Spider asked this strange man, "Doing what exactly?"

"Time machines, Spider. Time machines are the future."

"Cool," he said, and that was that.

It was the kind of thing, he often reflected these days, that anybody else would try to fix using a time machine. All he'd have to do was go back to when those two Internal Affairs guys approached him, and make sure his earlier, eager-beaver self refused the offer. "Just tell them you're very happy working homicides, but thanks for the offer." It would be easy. Except, of course, nothing about time travel is easy. Worse, Spider knew that all of Superintendent Sharp's former minions — and yes, he did have minions, men and women who did what Sharp told them to do, who had looked the other way while he and his mates had jaunted about in the past, destroying children's lives — now also had access to time machines. If Spider even thought about trying to give his earlier self a little help, he could quite possibly be erased from history, all of history.

§ § §

Meanwhile, back in the present, quite outside Spider's awareness, actual, good coffee was quietly dripping into the cup. He'd done it. He'd really done it! "Oh," he said, surprised, finding himself back in the break room, standing in front of a coffee machine. This was a triumphant moment, and at any other time it would have been something to celebrate, but not right now. The memory of his final days in the Police Service, even after all this time, was still bitter, so bitter he could hardly talk about it.

Dickhead, drawn by the heavenly vapors, got up and came over to the coffee droid to inspect Spider's handiwork. "Good man," he said, squeezing Spider aside.

Spider raged and stopped short of hitting the man. Instead he left the room, and walked out of the workshop and filled his lungs with fresh air. It felt good. He would not go back in there. Dealing with Dickhead was too much to ask, at least right now. He wasn't up to it.

Dickhead, who was called that for a reason, appeared at the front door behind Spider, and called out. "Hey, this is fucking decaf! You trying to poison me, Spider?"

At that very moment Malaria pulled up on her electric scooter. Her towering frame made the scooter look tiny, a toy, something a clown in a circus would ride for laughs. Dickhead spotted Malaria, said, "Oooh," tipped out his coffee and went to put the moves on her. "Well, hello!" he said in the tone he used on "the ladies."

He said to her, "We've not previously met. I'm Dickhead McMahon, kind of the big cheese around here, you might say. I take it you're Malaria, is that right?"

Spider, meanwhile, felt wretched. He wanted to call Iris Street and find out just what the hell was going on, and if he was indeed a suspect in the dead woman's murder.

He wanted to tell her a few choice things, some home truths, things he knew but was forbidden to talk about. Maybe she should watch her own back, he thought.

He reached into his pocket for his packet of phone patches; he was down to his last three. It would be the easiest thing in the world to stick one under his ear and call Street, and have a quiet word. His hand curled around the packet, and he pulled it out. There they were, the three adhesive patches, each no bigger than a ten-cent coin, and each bristling with more computing power than the big desktop computers he remembered from his childhood. He peeled one off, stuck it under his ear, got a dial tone, then popped his watchtop open and found Street's phone address. Spider could hardly stand, he was so nervous and angry. With a stylus in his shaking hand he touched Street's address on the screen of his watch, and heard her phone ringing. A voice in his head was screaming at him to hang up, hang up now, this won't get you anywhere, it'll only make you look guilty — and then that same voice saying that maybe he wanted to be guilty, maybe he'd had enough, maybe—

Street picked up, "Street, hello." Her voice was brisk, all-business, no time to waste chatting. He could hear jingling bike traffic and car horns blaring in the background. She was outside, walking somewhere.

He closed his eyes, but said nothing, hating himself.

Street said, "Hello? Is that you, Spider?" She sounded astonished.

He'd forgotten that she would know who was calling. He flapped his mouth, dumbstruck.

"Spider, is that you? Are you okay?"

It was like a kick in the guts. She sounded actually concerned, as if she cared how he might be doing.

He killed the link, and stood there, breathing hard.

Behind him, Dickhead had employed his zone-of-control powers again to block Malaria from going into the office. He was trying to get her to agree to a date.

Malaria told him, "No, I don't think so, I'm sorry, um, sir." She managed to squeeze past him into the office. Spider saw her through a window, shuddering in disgust.

Dickhead laughed, genuinely amused, and followed her inside. Spider watched them. Malaria had done well in her first encounter with him, but he had a hunch he would have to keep an eye on his boss.

Spider went around to the rear of the workshop where Charlie was stripping the engine compartment from a Tempo that belonged to a certain Mr. Thwait. "Need a hand?" Spider said.

"Nah, I think I got it. Looks like blown circuit-breakers, after all that."

"You're kidding," Spider said, amazed despite himself.

"We can probably send her back this afternoon. What do you reckon?"

Spider did not relish the prospect. It would mean either time-traveling the unit back to just after Spider and Charlie had towed it away, and then driving it to Mr. Thwaite's home, or driving it there first, and then time-traveling it while sitting in his driveway or his garage. Either way, it meant a jump of, he thought, eight days there and eight days back again. It would be great if he could just get Charlie to handle it, but he knew Dickhead's policy: it made a better impression on the client if the senior technician brought the unit back. It was good for repeat business, and good word-of-mouth. Even better if Spider wore his official monogrammed white lab coat. Dickhead told him to think of the lab coat as a theatrical costume, that it was all part of delivering the right user experience to the client.

Spider didn't see why Mr. Thwaite couldn't come and pick up his own bloody time machine, but he knew what Dickhead would say.

He chatted with Charlie a while, and told him about Dickhead being a dickhead. Charlie said, grinning, "Better you than me, boss."

Spider was starting to feel a bit better. In that respect, Charlie was a great guy to have around.

Charlie said at one point as he was rebuilding the circuit-breaker panel, "You going to call that Vincent guy about how we blew up his Tempo?"

Spider muttered under his breath, but he knew Charlie was right. He'd been putting it off. The thing was, though, now that he thought about it, the way the police had taken everything away with them for forensic examination and so forth, they would almost certainly have already called Mr. Vincent to tell him about the state of his time machine, the technical term being "smithereens." In a logical universe, Spider thought, pursuing a dangerous line of thought, that meant that Mr. Vincent should have been on the phone to him already, furious about his smithereened Tempo, and threatening not to pay up. But Malaria had told him of no such calls.

So, the thing's a significant financial investment for the guy, and he's not hopping mad about it blowing up? Sure, he might have insurance, which would ease the sting a little — assuming the insurance company would pay up over such unique circumstances — hell, the more he thought about it, the more he came to believe that any insurance company worth their weight in policy jargon would say that what had been done with that particular Tempo was very much in the realm of "not covered by this policy." Spider imagined Mr. Vincent's grinning-idiot face on learning about all of this.

Hmm. Spider certainly knew how he would feel if told that his many-thousand-dollar time machine had been smithereened and his insurance would not cover it.

So why had Mr. Vincent not called? Where was the threat of a lawsuit? For that matter, where was the shoebox full of dogshit?

Charlie noticed Spider looking troubled. "Okay there, boss?"

"I need to call a man about a time machine."

CHAPTER 7

The rest of that week at the workshop dragged on like a toothache. Every morning when Spider arrived at the workshop, he stood there in the doorway, looking at the service bays, each one occupied by a time machine needing some damn thing done with it, and he felt himself die a little. There was no satisfaction in this line of work, no glory, no real sense of accomplishment, as if you were making some kind of difference to things. Busted time machines came in, and fixed ones went out. Average workshop time-per-unit was eight working days. Bouncing back and forth through time, delivering fixed units, apparently immediately after taking them away, gave Spider headaches and weird dreams that freaked him out in the depths of the night. Too many times, he'd woken up screaming with frustration. Too many times, guys in adjacent capsules would bang on the sides or yell at him to *Shut the fuck up we're trying to sleep over here*! and he'd yell back that he was sorry, and he was sorry, though he could never remember a single detail about those dreams. That was time travel bullshit all over, though, wasn't it? Stuff happened, and then it didn't happen, or something else happened instead. Your memories were constantly sorting and re-sorting themselves behind your consciousness. What you remembered and believed about your past on Tuesday you no longer believed on Wednesday, and you had no memory of believing anything else.

§ § §

A few years ago, apparently, Spider had started keeping a diary, using an old-fashioned pen and paper, jotting down things each day. Nothing important, just random details, things he heard, or read in the media. It was strange, reading back through previous pages, recognizing his handwriting, such as it was, but often not remembering writing down those things. Once, he discovered he'd written, "I've always been at war with Eastasia," and only later did he remember that he had once read *1984*.

§ § §

There was no news about the dead woman. He'd tried to call James at DOTAS every day, and found that James was always away from his desk, or out in the field, or in a meeting, or consulting with colleagues from the future, and so on. Nobody would ever put him through to James's personal phone. Nobody would ever pass on a message. Okay, he thought. He and James weren't close friends. They were colleagues in related lines of work who got on very well. They'd had drinks together on Friday nights. One time Spider picked James up at the airport. A couple of times they'd tried to play time-travel chess, but James had a galling way of winning without Spider having moved a single piece, and he'd be left sputtering, "What? What just happened?" while James just laughed and told him how he'd used the time-travel dice like so, and Spider decided time-travel chess wasn't such a fun game. Mostly it was just nice getting together and bullshitting about their troubles.

All the same, Spider thought James should have returned at least one of his calls. He wanted to know what was going on with the investigation. Sometimes Spider would go and stand out in the parking lot on the spot where the Bat Cave had stood, remembering his first sight of the body in the second time machine, the Dolphin — a bizarre sensation, both blank puzzlement giving way to gasping horror, and then an electric shock sizzling through his hindbrain as he realized what this was: a case, an actual case!

It was disgusting, he knew it was, getting excited because a woman had been murdered. *It's just*, he told himself, *it's been so long. I miss it.*

He told Charlie at one point about the difficulty of getting hold of James for a chat about the investigation. Charlie said, "You could call Inspector Street."

Yes, yes, he could indeed call Iris Street, he told himself, remembering that day last week when he actually had called her, then hung up immediately. She hadn't called him back, either, and that was good, he thought. If they were interested in fitting him up as the guilty party in the case, they would have been in touch by now, right? They wouldn't just leave him dangling in the breeze, would they?

And then there was the puzzling matter of Mr. Vincent, who still had not called about his smithereened Tempo, and who Spider had not gotten around to calling to ask why he, Vincent, hadn't called. Spider commented on this to Charlie every day, and Charlie told him not to worry so much about it. The guy was obviously prepared to cut his losses, and was probably just keeping his own head down in case the cops decided to take a nice long look at him as a possible murderer. Spider thought the kid had a point, but all the same the question ate at him, particularly on those long, long afternoons in the workshop, up to his waist in bits of some malfunctioning unit, only too aware that someone had thrown up on one of the seats and it hadn't been cleaned up too well. Why had Vincent gone so quiet? It made no sense. None of it made any sense at all.

So that Friday afternoon, not long before close of business, Spider got Malaria to give Mr. Vincent a call, just a courtesy thing, a follow-up, you might say. She asked him, "What if he asks about his unit?"

"At the moment I just want to know if he's even still alive," he said to her, telling more of the truth than he had meant to. Maybe the guy hadn't been bitching at them about his machine because he was dead.

Malaria called, and got no response. Vincent didn't have his phone switched on, but she was free to leave a message. "What should I tell it?"

"Just ask him to give us a call during business hours next week," Spider said, scowling. He chewed at his lip.

I should go over there and have a look around, he thought. *After work, of course. Completely unofficial, just stopping by, seeing if the lights were on, that kind of thing. That wouldn't be so bad, would it? Nobody could say anything. I was just riding along that street, right?*

Spider's guts were in knots, just thinking about it. If the guy was still in the land of the living, but was merely, for example, away from home on business, surely he'd have his messaging system explain about that. *That's what he would do*, Spider thought, telling himself he was being entirely reasonable. Telling himself that he was simply concerned about customer follow-up. He could hear Dickhead telling him that customer care was number one!

"Hmm," he said, and went back out into the workshop.

By close of business, Spider had decided he would take a spin out past Mr. Vincent's place. He had no intention of actually stopping and looking around, or even getting out of his bike at all. Just a straightforward ride-by.

Until, just as he was pulling on his wet-weather gear, his phone rang.

It was Molly. Spider stared at his watchtop, seeing her flashing name. "Now what?" He was tempted to shunt her call through to his messaging service. He stood there, eyes closed, trying to breathe slowly. He answered. "Molly. What a lovely surprise," he said.

"Al?"

"What's happened, Molly?"

"The toilet's stopped talking to me. God, I cannot believe I just actually said that."

Spider sighed. "It's broken down again?"

"No. Not 'again.' This time it's something different. It won't recognize me, won't open. Nothing but bloody error messages. Can you come by and have a look?"

He winced, and looked outside. The forecast rain was going strong; he shivered, just thinking about how much fun it would be pedaling all the way over to Molly's place, and then back to the motel. "Can't you get an on-call plumber?"

"You, of all people," Molly said, voice dripping contempt, "should know what plumbers cost these days."

"Yeah, true," he admitted. "Okay, so how long's it been?"

"Al, I need the toilet now," she said, biting off each word. She sounded as if she was in a lot of pain.

"I take it the neighbors are no help?"

"After last time, do you blame them?"

He remembered. The case was still working its way through the courts. "It's just, I had plans for tonight—"

"Al! I *neeeeeeeeeeeeeeeed* you now!"

He swore to himself, knowing he was going to cave. "Okay. I'll be right there. Uh, sit tight." He killed the link, swore out loud, and kicked a chair across the room. He made sure his wet-weather gear was correctly sealed up, told the building alarms to arm themselves, and left. The door clunked closed behind him, and he heard the alarms chime. It was nearly seven p.m., fully dark, and the rain was bucketing down. It looked like it had settled in for the foreseeable future. Thinking dark thoughts about Molly, he splashed his way out to where his bike was parked, got in, and headed out into the night.

As he left the property, he glanced both ways along the road to see if the Sony was parked anywhere nearby, and didn't see it.

Almost an hour later he pulled into the driveway of Molly's place. He got out of the bike and carried it up to the porch.

"Spider! Spider — wait!" called a male voice.

That was odd. The bike slung over his shoulder, he turned to peer out into the wet darkness. "What?"

A familiar-looking figure appeared at the end of the path leading to the mailbox. Draped in shadows and rain, the guy wore regular clothes rather than wet-weather gear, his hair plastered down over his head and face. He looked awful, and not because of the weather. He looked grievously upset. Taking a few steps closer, so Spider could get a better look at him, he called out, "Get back on your bike and leave right now!"

Spider stared at him, puzzled but feeling all tingly-weird about it. Something was deeply not right here. The figure looked familiar, but he couldn't place him. Spider said, "Come and get out of the rain, you'll catch your bloody death out there like that."

He came closer, and Spider could see more of him. The man said, "Forget about me, Spider. Just get on your bike and go. Don't come back. Stay here and you'll — look, just go. Go now, while you can."

Spider was intrigued despite himself. "It's just, I have to fix my wife's toilet."

The man came closer still, and pulled sodden hair out of his eyes. In the light spilling from Molly's porch, Spider could see who it was. "Oh, crap," he said. Ever since the advent of time machines, and despite his own deep reservations about using the things, he'd always imagined that one day, in some circumstance, something like this would happen to him. It seemed you couldn't have a world with ubiquitous time travel and not have a situation where you met some other version of yourself. It was like a rule, he thought. And, sure enough, on this wretched evening, here was his double. "Oh, ah, well," he said, not at all sure what to say. He was distracted, too, by how fat and old his other self looked. "Do I really look like that?" he said.

Then the other Spider was there, on the porch with him, looking him up and down. "I'm telling you, Spider. In about one minute, the cops will be here. They're already on their way."

"What?" This was making no sense. "What's going on?" He turned to look at Molly's door — and saw that it stood ajar, light spilling out. He could hear her media wall going full blast, and that in itself was strange. Molly liked to work in silence — and she was always working. He started feeling cold inside. He put the bike down and glanced at his other self. "What's wrong?"

"Spider, it's—" He stared off into the dark, looking pale and wretched. "We have to go, right now." He tried to grab Spider's arm to drag him away.

Spider pulled free. "I have to see her!"

"If you go in there, you'll wind up as me!"

Spider protested. "I can't just take your word for it!"

"I told you, we have to go right now."

He stood there, staring — first at his other self, then at Molly's door — and tried to imagine the scene, and imagined nothing but the worst. "She's dead?"

The other Spider grabbed for Spider's bike in one hand, and hauled him down the steps and along the path with his other hand. Spider went along, starting to feel numb, unaware of the cold rain beating down on his wet-weather gear and trickling down his back. He needed to see her. This other guy must be lying, surely, but the other guy was obviously himself, and why would he lie to himself?

The other Spider had a car with a big cargo space at the back. He popped the back door, flung the bike in there and shut the door. "Get in. It's open."

Spider stared at him as his other self went around to the driver's side and climbed in. He stood there in the dark, in the rain, cold all the way through, confused, thinking that somewhere along the way his life had broken, and he was only now becoming aware of it. The light from Molly's porch, and the booming music coming from inside the house, seemed to call him back. The other Spider was already in the car and powering it up, and he was just standing here. He could go back, he thought. He could see her, see for himself. She couldn't be dead. She was that kind of person, someone who'd outlive everybody she knew, if for no other reason than just because she was cussed, because it would piss people off. Because, most of all, it would piss him off.

Then someone appeared out of the darkness and clobbered Spider in the face, and he collapsed into a more private darkness.

Later, when he woke, he was in a lot of pain, had lost a lot of blood from his broken nose and missing teeth, and he was in the other Spider's car. They were going somewhere. He recognized the area: it was one of the sprawling northern enclaves, all towering apartment complexes and monster homes and malls so big they had their own weather, permanent residents, and airfields on their roofs.

His face — his whole head — hurt like hell, and for a while he just sat there, holding himself, breathing through his mouth while blood dripped down the back of his throat.

The other Spider, watching the head-up display, keeping an eye on the autopilot as the car wove through flocks of cyclists, said, "Ah, you're back."

"Did you have to fucking hit me?"

"Yeah, about that. Sorry."

"So it was you." Spider was trying not to let his tongue touch his teeth on the side of his face where he'd been hit.

"I had to get you out of there. Another thirty—"

"Yeah," Spider said, clutching his aching face, "I heard."

They drove in silence a long while, the rain beating on the shell of the car, the wipers squeegeeing back and forth, back and forth.

At length, clearly upset, the other Spider produced a handheld with a luminous screen, and handed it to him. "Here. I took photos."

Spider took the unit, frowned for a moment, confused, then realized what he was seeing. He gave an involuntary moan of pain and shock, but then flipped to the next image, and this was worse than the previous, like a knife to his own heart.

§   §   §

Later, much later, that night, when Spider thought he might at last be able to speak without pain, and while he and his future self sat in the car outside a garishly lit fast-food place, he said to him, "How do I know you didn't kill her?" He'd been rehearsing the question in his head for some time, thinking that the most likely situation here was that he was sitting next to his wife's murderer. Why he — or at least this future version of himself — would kill Molly, he couldn't say. Yes, she was infuriating. Yes, she took him for granted. Yes, she expected things of him he could never provide, and yes, their relationship was and had always been deeply messed up. But why would he kill her? He had always thought that one day they'd get back together somehow, that she'd finally see that he was, if not the man of her dreams, then at least a good man in his own right.

"You don't know, Spider — but I didn't do it."

Spider said nothing. Inside his head, he was still screaming. He thought he would be screaming the rest of his life.

The other Spider said, "Yeah, I know. I still feel that way."

"Don't you fucking tell me you know how I feel," he said.

His other self went to say something, then looked at Spider, and thought better of it. He nodded. They sat there a long while, saying nothing, listening to the rain, watching kids coming and going from the fast-food place. It was well after two in the morning.

"Have you ever heard," his future self said, "of an organization called 'Zeropoint?'"

He had not. He shook his head, gently. The combination of facial trauma and acute shock was making him wish he were dead.

"Right. Okay. Where to start?" He looked stricken, lost for words for a long moment. "Um, Zeropoint is an organization deeply interested in the End of Time."

"Of course they are," Spider said, humoring the guy.

"No. Seriously. Listen to me. This is important."

"Sorry. I'm all ears."

His future self was irritated, but kept at it. "You will be tested on this later, so listen to me. It's all about the End of Time, okay? It's about being the last man standing at the end of the universe."

"Mmmm," Spider said, barely interested.

"Okay, fine," he said. "I have to admit, when I was you, I felt the same way you do now, only I got my butt kicked later on. You'll enjoy that."

Spider looked at the other guy. "Hmm, okay, and I suppose, somehow, you're going to segue from all this 'End of Time' bullshit to Molly's death, and that it's all connected up somehow, right?"

"I think so, yes."

Spider slumped against the closed window. "Uh-huh."

"If you'd gone inside at Molly's place, you'd never have gotten out before the cops turned up."

"Let me guess. They caught you?"

"I did fifteen years, Spider."

This got his attention. "Fifteen years?"

"Hard time."

"Shit," he said.

"When I got out, I wanted to save her."

"What happened?"

"I couldn't. The fix was in." I was framed.

Thinking about frame jobs, Spider asked, "What about the woman in the Dolphin?"

"Yeah, exactly."

Spider glared at him. "Meaning?"

"Meaning that woman, the dead woman, worked for Zeropoint."

"So what the hell was she doing—?"

"No idea."

"What, you come back in time all this way to save me from your wretched fate," he said, speaking as carefully as he could to avoid aggravating his loosened teeth, "and you can't even tell me that?"

"I had to do something, Spider."

He was exhausted but knew he'd never sleep even if he went "home" now. Another thought bothered him. "Okay," he said, "you saved me from your horrible fate. Woo. So why are you still here? Why haven't you—?"

"New timeline. Old timelines never die, Spider. They just spawn new ones. Like bloody rabbits that way."

"Okay. Fine," he said, his whole face throbbing with pain. "Whatever." But this Future Spider told him he had a lot of stuff to tell him, and he only had a limited time to do it. Spider sagged in his seat, feeling wretched in so many ways, and let it all wash over him.

"So," Spider managed to say, "how did you find out about this Zeropoint outfit in the first place?"

"They came to me, while I was inside."

"What, just like that? They just walk in and tell you they're, what? Crypto-spooks from the far, far future?"

"Not at first, no. No, at first they led me to believe they were lawyers from DOTAS. Said they were concerned about my case, that there was an ambiguity in the evidence against me. Was I interested in appealing the verdict?"

"Were you?"

"What do you think?"

Spider, his whole head wracked with pain, nodded minutely. "Listen, you wouldn't have any painkillers, would you?"

Future Spider had been looking out the side window as he talked, keeping an eye on the kids out front of the fast-food place. Now he turned and looked at Spider and he swore. "Yeah, sorry. I had to get you the hell away from Molly's as quick as I could."

"It's just," Spider said, "you know, ow!"

§ § §

The other Spider powered up the car and told it to find the nearest all-night pharmacy. The car swept out of the parking area and back onto the road. The head-up display said they should reach a pharmacy in two minutes. The other Spider apologized profusely. Spider, his eyes pressed shut, let him go on in this vein.

Soon they pulled into the pharmacy parking area and Future Spider went into the shop and came out with, he said, "The most heavy-duty shit they had." He also had a small bottle of water. Spider took the water, and used it to wash out his mouth as best he could. The coldness of the water on exposed nerve tissue made him jump and cry out involuntarily. He took a handful of the caplets, and hoped for the best. The drugs took their time kicking in — and then there was a strange tingling, burning sensation in his injured teeth.

"What the hell?" he said, looking at the box. The label indicated that the caplets contained reconstructor agents for minor tissue damage. Spider stared, astonished. He knew very well that you needed a doctor's prescription to access drugs like this. You didn't just pop into a pharmacy in the middle of the night and buy it over the counter. Meanwhile, his mouth felt alive, full of activity. He imagined tiny builder ants erecting giant skyscrapers in the bloody ruins of his teeth.

Future Spider said, "Least I could do. Sorry."

He didn't want to say anything, lest he somehow damage the rebuilding effort in his mouth, so he sat in silence.

The other Spider got the car to take them to the beach, and they wound up in the parking area adjacent to a Surf Life Saving Club building, with a dim view of Trigg Beach. Spider could see kids wearing psychedelic and glowing wetsuits on surfboards out there in the churning water — at this hour, in the rain. *Mad buggers*, he thought.

§ § §

By the time the sun started to rise behind them in the east, Spider's mouth was feeling better, even if the long night had left him feeling like he'd been awake three days. The images showing what had happened to Molly would not leave the front of his mind. It was as if he was living in an old-fashioned movie house, with those images blown up to unthinkable size and clarity on the screen, while he tried to go about his business down in the stalls, lit by the glare of all that blood and horror.

They found a place open for breakfast not far from the beach. Future Spider was paying. Spider ordered a giant-sized, all-day breakfast, with sausages, bacon, eggs, mushrooms, tomatoes, hashbrowns, toast and coffee. He sipped the coffee, and felt weak and a little dizzy from hunger and exhaustion. There had been something very surreal about this endless night on the road with his future self. He wondered if he wasn't dreaming. Molly would still be alive. She might still have a problem with her toilet.

But thinking that only reminded Spider that he was living in that theater, with Molly's death lit up behind him, a million times larger than life. He drank a lot of coffee but, faced with all that food, didn't think he could keep anything down, even if he was now prepared to risk his brand new teeth.

In hesitant blurts between mouthfuls, Future Spider tried to explain about Zeropoint. "They got my sentence reduced, which was great, but not the verdict itself, which was bullshit." He paused a moment, staring out to sea. "But then one day one of them, let's call him 'Mr. O'Brien,' took me aside and said that while DOTAS was very pleased to help me out the way it had done, there was such a thing as, as he called it, 'mutual obligation.' They were looking for me to help them."

That breakfast smelled fantastic, Spider was thinking dreamily, only half-awake. He was tempted to try a bit of toast, and if his teeth didn't like it, he could take some more reconstructor agents, right?

Then, Future Spider was saying, "And all this time, you're thinking, what the hell does DOTAS have to do with a straightforward murder, right? To say nothing of all the other stuff, you know, the—"

"'The End of Tiiiiiiiiiiiiiiiiiiiiiiiiiime!'" Spider said, in a comically spooky voice.

"You really are gonna get your butt handed to you, Spider."

Spider slumped in his chair, holding his bristling face up with one hand, realized his other self was still speaking to him. He nodded. "Mmmm," he said. "You were saying this is all to do with..."

He couldn't quite bring himself to say Molly's name. He thought his brain might burst if he said it, as if saying it would make it real, would make it more than just a couple of gigantic shining images on a screen — and if it was real, and she was really dead, well... It was a point beyond which he could not think. Not right now, anyway. He remembered Molly's voice on the phone yesterday afternoon, just as he was planning to head home for the evening. So long ago. It felt as if — as if it had never happened, as if he had always been out tooling around with his shadow self. Maybe he was crazy, he thought. It would explain everything. Insanity was good that way.

"Yes," his future self was trying to explain, doing his best to be patient with his former self. "It's like this, now listen up, all right?"

Spider did his best to keep up. He felt himself drifting off.

§ § §

"Sir? Excuse me, sir?" It was a woman's voice.

Startled awake, he jumped a little, blinking, sitting up straight, looking around. The light was very bright, and hurt his eyes for a bit while he tried to get used to it. "Oh," he said, squinting at the waitress.

"Oh, I'm sorry. Can I get you some fresh coffee?"

"Uh, wha — ?" He was in a café near the beach. He could smell the sea. Before him stood a half-full cup of cold coffee. Looking around, taking in the aromatic wafts of breakfast around him, he saw that he was alone.

He said, "What happened to my friend?"

The waitress smiled but looked puzzled. "I'm sorry?"

Spider stared at her for a moment, then said yes, he would like a fresh coffee. He checked his teeth; they felt fine. He clacked his jaws together; his teeth appeared as solid as they ever did. His nose was sore, but that could just be the way he'd been sprawled across the table. Getting up, he felt very stiff and achy, but he stretched and took some steps across the polished floorboards, attracting a few odd looks from the handful of people who weren't hard at work on their screens, taking care of business.

Outside, Spider checked the parking lot, and saw no trace of Future Spider's car.

He did, however, find his recumbent bike, chained to a bike rack.

Back inside, he resumed his seat just as the waitress came back with a fresh mug of coffee for him, and left the bill. When he checked it, the bill was for seven cups of coffee, which cost thirty-five dollars. Even without checking his pockets, Spider knew he did not have that kind of money on him.

Confused, frightened, and now suddenly in debt, he tried not to panic. After a few minutes he got up, went to the counter, and asked to speak to the manager. The manager, who looked like he was having a bad day even though it was still very early, listened to Spider as he recounted his problem.

"So you're saying that you've consumed seven coffees, but now you can't pay? Is that the gist of it?"

Spider felt tiny and vulnerable. He said, "That is indeed the gist. Um, can you help me out?"

The manager stared down at him, then looked out the windows at the morning ocean. He turned back to Spider. "You know, you should have thought of this little problem before you decided to guzzle down all that coffee."

"I thought my, um, my friend was paying."

"Right," the manager said. "The friend who was never there. Okay."

If he ever ran into Future Spider again, he was going to kill the bastard for dropping him in this situation. "Look, take my bike. It's—"

"I don't want your fucking bike, mate. Just pay the bloody bill."

"I can come back with the money, okay? Just take my bike as collateral."

Then the manager said, glancing at Spider's wrist. "I'll take your watch as collateral."

Spider had never been offline before. The thought was terrifying. But he could see this was his only chance to avoid running into the police. He took off the watch and handed it over. "Thank you," he said.

"Yeah, yeah. Just be back here before midday or I'll be hocking the thing."

"Okay. I'll—"

"What, you're still here?"

Furious, humiliated and ashamed, Spider left. He discovered he did still have the key to his bike's security chain, climbed into the bike and took off, heading for Malaga, swearing loudly the whole way.

CHAPTER 8

Spider got his watch back and the coffee bill sorted out in time, but while he was pedaling back to work — for the second time that day — his mind was a storm of confusion, trying to figure out what was going on in his life.

He tried calling Molly, just to check; her phone told him she was in Bangkok, attending to her HyperFlesh exhibition. "What?" More surprising, her phone asked him if he'd like to contact her. Bewildered, wondering what the hell was going on, he said, "Yeah, put me through." Soon he heard her voice in his ear. "Spider? What on Earth are you calling me here for?" He could hear a noisy engine, traffic, bicycle bells, and someone talking to her in what he guessed was Thai. Spider checked the screen to see if there was a video option, but there wasn't.

"Molly?" His throat was tight; he could hardly speak. It was getting difficult to keep an eye on traffic conditions, so he pulled over to the breakdown lane.

"Spider, what is it? This is not a good time."

He was starting to feel the effects of much too much coffee. He was getting jittery and feeling ill and strange and woozy, and there were thousands of thoughts in his head trying to get out all at once and his mouth wasn't big enough — but most of all, it was Molly's voice in his ear!

Like an idiot, he blurted, "You're alive!"

That voice in the background was speaking to Molly in very urgent tones, and she was speaking back to him in what sounded like the same baffling language, in a mollifying sort of tone. At least it sounded that way to Spider, whose knowledge of foreign languages did not extend to Thai. He listened to Molly and the other guy going back and forth, then Molly said, "Look, I'll call you later from my hotel, okay? Bye."

And then she was gone, just like that. He peeled the phone patch from under his ear and looked at it, as if to see some faint remaining trace of Molly's presence on it. Right this moment, he thought, his sort-of ex-wife was riding what sounded like a tuk-tuk through the streets of Bangkok, arguing with some local guy about who knew what.

So why would Future Spider tell him she was dead? That she had in fact been murdered by some shadowy outfit from the future?

He'd shown him photos, photos he now found he could only barely remember. He had a faint recollection of lots of blood on the body and on the floor, but he could not be sure the woman shown in the photos was in fact Molly.

Had any of last night really happened? He felt his face all over for signs of the hit he'd taken, but found nothing. His head felt, well, not exactly fine, but all right. He sat there watching traffic whizzing by, feeling cold and damp, and trying not to think about the unpaid overtime he was going to have to put in to recompense Dickhead McMahon for all this time away from the workshop, and for the thirty-five dollars. Dickhead had told him to take the money out of petty cash. That wasn't a problem. But Spider would absolutely have to pay it back, out of his own wages. And, if that wasn't enough, he'd have to put up with Dickhead telling him off about it, telling him it was a "black mark" on his personal file, that he'd have a hard time finding an employer willing to take him on if he were ever to leave Dickhead's zone-of-control. Not that Dickhead put it quite like that; he was quite unaware of his own zone-of-control, but Spider immediately saw it that way. Dickhead, he knew, was protecting him.

If last night had not happened, Spider was thinking, then how did I get stuck at that café? Then again, the café staff had no recollection of Spider's "friend" being there. Could he have somehow sleepwalked — sleepcycled? — all the way from the workshop out to this café and sat there all night drinking coffee after coffee, alone? To the best of his knowledge he was not prone to sleepwalking. Molly had never commented on it, back when they had still lived together. Nobody at the capsule motel had ever pointed it out to him. Could this be a new thing? Should he now be worried that some nights he would get up in the wee small hours and go off tooling around the metroplex?

Had he dreamed that encounter with Future Spider? His memory of the whole thing was vivid enough. He remembered all that business about this so-called "Zeropoint" outfit, and how they had supposedly murdered Molly, and that the dead woman in the time machine the other day allegedly worked for Zeropoint.

Why on Earth, he thought, would he make up stuff as specific, and as obviously nuts, as that?

He hunkered back down into his bike and eased out into the flow of traffic, being sure to stay in the bicycle lane. He made his way back to work, not sure what to believe — except that if he did run into his future self again, he'd bloody-well punch his head in.

The rest of the day dragged on miserably. He felt sick and weak and "fluttery" in his chest. Charlie asked him if he was all right, and Spider told him he was okay, just maybe coming down with the flu or something. Charlie nodded and said there was a lot of that going around at the moment, and Spider had better watch out. He'd heard it was a bad one this time. Spider nodded and got back to work on a Boron II unit that belonged to a certain Mr. Lee, who had brought the thing in two days ago, saying, "It just won't go."

When Spider asked Mr. Lee for a more specific description of the problem, Mr. Lee told him, with great irritation, that he "didn't bloody know," that the machine was "fucked," and that Spider had better fix it for less than the five hundred dollars he'd been quoted by the Boron dealership where he'd bought the unit in the first place.

Spider would have told Mr. Lee to get stuffed, but he remembered what Dickhead McMahon had told him about his drooping key-point indicators, and how he had to pick up the pace. If this meant taking on annoying assignments like this, well, so be it. So he spent the whole day stripping the Boron down, testing everything, and eventually traced the fault to a circuit board in the translation engine. No longer preoccupied by mysterious visitors from the future, Spider inspected and tested each and every chip, module and component in the translation engine. After all, the fault might not be in the hardware but possibly in the control software that drove the hardware. Anything could be the case. But, of all the parts of a time machine likely to cause trouble, the translation engine was most often the problem. The translation engine took the quantum data gathered by the scanning engine, data reflecting not only the machine itself but also its passengers, and performed the necessary multidimensional "editing" of that data, specifically the data reflecting a specific location in the space-time manifold. When it worked, machine and passengers shifted seamlessly from wherever and whenever they were to where and when they were going. When it didn't work, the typical failure mode was to simply prevent the machine from doing anything, rather than risk transporting anyone to some random location and time.

Spider had been on this one repair for a long time. On five occasions he'd thought he was done, reassembled the unit, powered it up and attempted a dry run, going through the scanning process and letting the translation engine set up the coordinates for the jump. At which point the unit showed a red light, announced it was not going anywhere, and fed a bunch of annoying error messages into Spider's handheld. Five times. Mr. Lee's Boron II was a big, humming paperweight. So he had to take it apart and go through the entire process again. It was doing nothing for his mood.

Towards close of business with no end in sight to the Boron's problems, Malaria came out to the workshop, all nervous and apologetic. "Phone call, Spider." When he sighed and glared at her, she said, "It's that Inspector Street lady. She wants a word."

Spider sagged against the frame of the Boron II and dropped his digital multi-tool into his toolbox. He wiped his hands on a rag and threw it to one side. Looking up at Malaria, he said, "Thanks. I'll take it out here." She nodded and said something into her headset as he tapped his phone patch.

It was indeed Inspector Street. "Spider," she said, "I hope I'm not interrupting anything."

"What's up, Iris?"

There was a pause at her end as she registered his tone. He could hear phones ringing, people talking loudly. She said, "Look. Are you free this evening?"

He sat on the Boron's fuel cell, closed his eyes, and rubbed his face. "Why?"

"We need to talk."

"Talk to me now."

"Right now is a non-optimal situation, Spider. I need to see you."

"Shit."

"Wait a moment." She put him on hold. A recorded voice started telling him about the amazing range of helpful community-based programs provided by today's modern Police Service. Spider clutched his forehead, a headache pounding away at him. He wanted to go get some sleep, but knew he was still so hopped up on caffeine he could be awake for days.

Then Iris was back. "Sorry. Had to get away. Can you hear me okay?" Her voice echoed a little, but there was no other background noise.

"Come on, Iris. Spill your guts."

"I had a visitor last night, Spider."

Something about the tone of her voice as she said this touched a nerve. "Oh?"

"He said he was you, basically, but—"

"From the future?" He was sitting upright, leaning forward, staring at the floor, heart banging hard, feeling scared all over again.

"Yeah, but he looked a real mess, and he said he'd had a very fruitful meeting with you, too."

"This is what you wanted to talk about?"

"You might say that, yes."

He squeezed the bridge of his nose. "Okay. Where and when?"

They settled on a quiet spot in the middle of Kings Park, at eight p.m.

Charlie Stuart came by Spider's service bay. "That sounded intriguing."

"It's nothing," Spider said, grabbing his multi-tool and trying to focus again on the Boron's problems, which was no easy task after a conversation like that, particularly with it so close to closing time. Key-point indicators be damned, he thought, and decided to wrap it up for the night.

Charlie said, "That was Inspector Street on the phone, though, right?"

"Yeah," Spider admitted. "Just a follow-up. Strictly a formality." He made a show out of securing all the loose parts of the translation engine for the night, but one tiny system module caught his eye, and he picked it up. After peering at it for a moment, he lowered his magnifier over his right eye and took a closer look. Something was different about it. He showed it to Charlie. "This look blown to you?"

Charlie took the part and stared at it. "Have you checked the 'scope?" They had a cheap Nigerian quantum microscope in the back of the workshop. It worked most of the time. Needless to say, Dickhead McMahon refused to buy something newer, something that might work more reliably, until that one failed utterly.

"Yeah," Spider said. "Yesterday I had a look at it, and it looked all right, right down to the atomic level."

Charlie asked to have a look at the component; Spider handed it over. Charlie was still wearing his antistatic gloves. He scowled and went cross-eyed as he looked at it. "So it was okay yesterday, but today it looks funny?"

"Mmmm," Spider said, secretly glad for the distraction from talking about Inspector Street.

Charlie pulled down his own magnifier and studied the piece all over. "Looks okay to me, boss." He handed it back.

Spider held it in the palm of his hand while he grabbed his multi-tool with the other. He was dialing in the unit-integrity mode when Charlie said, "Say g'day to the Inspector for me, huh?" He grinned at Spider. Spider shot him a foul look, annoyed, wishing he didn't feel the need to keep secrets. The fact that Iris Street had called him and proposed a get-together in an out-of-the-way location was giving Spider chills. It reminded him altogether too much of the old days, with secret meetings going on all the time, and it was hard to keep track of who was in league with whom without elaborate charts. Even after all these years, secrecy was a tough habit to break.

"I'll be sure to convey to the Inspector your kind regards, Charlie."

Charlie grinned, enjoying seeing his boss discomfited. "So, what's on the cards, then, huh? Hot date with an old flame?"

Spider found himself coughing out bitter laughter. "Yeah, that's what it is all right. Yeah, absolutely."

Then Charlie's tone shifted, and his voice dropped. He said, "You think she knows who the dead woman is?"

Spider was still looking at the module, determined not to get drawn into Charlie's teasing. As to his actual question, he said, "We'll have to wait and see, I guess."

Spider plugged the suspect component into his multi-tool and hit the grimy scan key. After a moment, the tool came back with its verdict: *positive*. Yesterday, when Spider had tried this same test, it had come up negative. He was sure of it. Pulling out his handheld, he scrolled back through his work logs, looking for a record of performing the test, and found it. "That's odd," he said, staring at the handheld, and then at the component.

"Boss?"

Spider set down that component and started grabbing others from the same section of the engine and systematically trying each one in the multi-tool, then checking his logs from yesterday. The results were consistent: components that, according to the logs, had tested one way yesterday were testing the same way today, even though he clearly remembered their testing the other way yesterday. Or, at least, he thought he remembered it that way. The more he tried to concentrate on it, the less sure he felt. He looked at Charlie, and told him what he was finding.

Charlie told him he must be misreading either his logs or the multi-tool. Spider showed him what he was seeing.

Charlie took a little longer to go through the same tests and checks, but got the same results. Even as the sun was setting outside, and crows began cawing mockingly at them, Charlie failed to see the problem. "You're saying this part tested positive yesterday, and it tested positive again today."

"Yeah," Spider said, frowning, trying to think, "and that's wrong. Yesterday it was negative, I'm sure it was bloody negative!"

"Boss, maybe you're just tired."

"Oh, thanks," he said, irritated, looking at the exposed guts of the translation engine, and contemplating testing every single component, no matter how long it took.

Charlie said, "You look like shit."

The kid was almost certainly right. He was tired, bone tired, but Spider was also feeling cold all the way through. An idea had occurred to him that would explain the discrepancy between his now-fuzzy memories and the results he was getting from his tools. It was a crazy idea, but it would explain what was going on, even if it did piss him off. "Hmm," he said, wondering how he could prove his hypothesis if he had to.

"Maybe you should look and see if the firmware in the multi needs upgrading," Charlie suggested. "How long's it been since you updated?"

Spider thought Charlie had a point. He should try to exhaust all rational possibilities before leaping to crazy conclusions. He picked up the multi-tool again and hit the update key. It went online for a few moments, scanned for updates, and reported back that it was up to date. He did the same for the logging software in his handheld, and that came back also showing it was up-to-date, and all its checksums were good. Spider's tools weren't the problem.

Charlie said, "Things don't just change overnight."

Spider said, looking at him, "Well, that depends on what happened overnight, I'd say."

Charlie, not aware of Spider's adventures the previous evening, was puzzled. "Um, what?"

"Suppose, for a moment, that we've been shunted into an adjacent timeline."

"Hmm," Charlie said, stroking his chin, "suppose for a moment your boss has just lost his bloody mind!"

"Further suppose," Spider said, annoyed, "that your boss has earned the right to formulate such an opinion, and would not formulate such an opinion just for the sheer overwhelming joy it gives him." He paused for a moment, chewing his lip. "I realize it sounds nuts. I'm comparing these test results with the contents of my memory — never the most reliable source of information," he conceded, and looked about at everything before him. It all looked and smelled and felt exactly the way it should — and that was the proof, because in his memory, everything was minutely different. If he didn't have a good head for small technical details he would never even have noticed the change.

The thing was, it made a certain kind of sense. In this timeline, Molly was alive and tooling around in Bangkok on a tuk-tuk and tending to her exhibition, but in the other timeline she was dead. Could Future Spider, in coming back to talk to him have either deliberately or accidentally disrupted or fractured things?

So it was possible that he had been up all night driving around with his future self, just as it was possible that none of that had happened. Sort of. And then there was Iris Street's claim that she had met Future Spider as well last night. What was that crazy bastard up to?

"Yeah," he said to Charlie, putting away his tools and closing the service bay for the night. "Yeah, you're probably right. I just need to get a good night's sleep and have another look at all this tomorrow, right?"

Charlie smiled warily. "Yeah. Bet you wish you could take a couple of days off."

"You're not wrong, Charles," Spider said, thinking about what bliss that would be, actual time off, holidays. It was a sweet idea — and, under Dickhead's rules, out of the question, unless Spider was gravely ill. Work for Dickhead McMahon, you agreed to work six days a week, and be available for emergencies on Sunday, no penalty rates, and no vacation time. "You want to be treated like children, go and work for the bloody government," McMahon would say.

Once the shop had been secured for the night, Charlie
wished him goodnight and jumped into his fuel cell-powered jeep, telling him, "Be a good boy for the inspector!"

Spider waved him off, smiling for a moment, but then
plunged back into a gloom of speculation. What the hell
was going on? He had no idea, and wasn't sure he wanted
to know.

CHAPTER 9

Spider wanted to duck back home to change clothes before meeting Iris Street later that night. He parked his bike in one of the few available slots in the crowded locker at The Lucky Happy Moon Motel, got out and secured his ride. He went up to the motel entrance, passed through the outer door and logged in — or tried to. His key was refused. Surprised, he tried again, and again his key was refused. "Now that's looking a bit odd," he said. Meanwhile, a small crowd of other residents was accumulating outside, waiting for him to either go through the inner door or come back outside. And there was no going through the inner door without the system accepting his key.

So he stood there, trying his key again and again. Each time he got the same frustrating result. "This is bloody nuts!" he said, even as residents outside, most of whom had that same beaten-down doomed look, started pounding on the outer door. He yelled back at them that he just needed a minute. The banging and mocking continued, only louder and more insistent. Starting to panic, Spider tried cleaning his key (no help), inspecting the key-reader mechanism for bits of dirt or other problems which might be causing the system to reject his key (no help), and he even tried yelling to the guys outside, some of whom he knew vaguely by first name or nickname, and asking — as politely as he could — if he could inspect their keys to see in what ineffable way his key could possibly read as different or suspect. There were no volunteers. In the end, swearing loudly as another aging Singapore Air A380-800 rumbled overhead, he went back outside, copped a lot of verbal abuse and shoulder-shoving, and considered his options.

The best of these was to go up to the after-hours intercom screen, hit the big red talk button, and try to plead his case with Mrs. Ng. She peered at him with great surprise as he explained his predicament, then said, "But Spider, you're already here, aren't you?"

He was confused for a moment. "Um, what was that?"

Mrs. Ng leaned into the camera, the better to talk to him. "I said you're already here. Look." She grabbed another screen and held it up for him so he could see. "There, see? Six-fifty-two this evening, your key, containing your bio-metrics, accepted by the system." She pointed at the relevant entry, in case he couldn't see for himself. Spider stared and stared. He had indeed turned up a while ago. Then she peered at him more closely, and asked, "How did you get out without me seeing?"

Then he started to see what might be going on. "Mrs. Ng, he's a future version of me. What did he look like?" Spider asked, doing his best to look bemused, aware of how absurd this situation appeared — and starting to get deeply annoyed at his Future Self.

"That's the thing. He looked quite a bit like you, well, not exactly, you know a bit down and out, sorry. I just get used to seeing guys like that."

Spider nodded. "Seems like I fell on some hard times. He's up there now?"

Mrs. Ng sighed. "A future version of you, Spider? Really?" She was not amused. "Did you not read Paragraph Four of the Conditions of Service?"

"It's just, I—"

Mrs. Ng cut him off. "Paragraph Four," she said, reciting from memory, in aggravated tones, 'The client will refrain from the use of any chronotechnology (time travel) device for the purpose of subverting this Agreement'! Did you not read this, Spider?"

It was true. He had not read Paragraph Four. He hadn't read any of the Conditions of Service. At the time he'd just been pathetically grateful for some cheap accommodation, and would have signed almost anything, quite possibly including a document allowing unsavoury doctors to remove his 'spare' organs. "I'm sorry, Mrs. Ng I screwed up. Well, not me, exactly, my future self—" Mrs. Ng cut him off again, scolded at him again, and ultimately let him in. "Last chance, Spider! Last chance!"

Once inside, he thanked Mrs. Ng, patted the Buddha on the counter and decided it was time he had a quiet word with his future self. The elevators were still under repair, according to a sign, so he puffed his way up to his level and found his way to his capsule.

"Uh-oh," he said, tingles going up and down his spine. The flap on the front of the capsule looked much as it would if he was in there. The occupied light was on. But something about it looked all wrong, and he could not say why. *Well*, he reasoned, *it might have to do with the whole bloody time paradox bullshit, meeting your own future self, and so forth*. Then he thought, *No, it's not that*. He wished he were still a cop, and that he had a gun.

Spider approached the flap. He knocked on the front of the capsule. "Hey numbnuts!" he said. "Get your ugly mug out here!"

There was no answer. And, this close, there was a very familiar, very bad smell. "Fuck," he said, tense. Standing to one side, he pulled the flap open.

Nothing happened, but the smell got worse. Some of the guys nearby gave him nasty looks. One told him to "Clean up your shit, man. What's wrong with you?"

Gritting his teeth, knowing what he was going to find, he leaned over and looked inside — and immediately pulled away, revolted, spooked, gasping for breath, his heart booming. He stood there, his legs threatening to give way at any moment, and tried to think through his options. It wasn't easy. For one thing, the cops would have to get involved. No doubt they would be fascinated to see what had happened to Spider's future self. He checked himself for any possible forensic traces that might conceivably tie him to what had happened, and found none. Which meant nothing, of course. As best he could tell, forensics should only show that he was here, stand-

ing outside his capsule. He had not been inside interfering with the scene. All the same, his DNA and so forth
would be all over the inside of the capsule, simply because that was indeed himself in there, and it was the
place where he lived, such as it was, day to day. He swore
under his breath and rubbed at his face. He felt weak and
dizzy and cold.

He forced himself to take another look inside, trying
to distance himself, as if it were any other crime scene.
It wasn't easy. It was too much like seeing his own future,
which he supposed it was, or at least might be.

The victim, he thought, forcing himself to see the scene
professionally, had clearly been knifed, by the look of
it, several times, primarily in the gut and chest. The quantity of blood sprayed across the inside walls of the capsule
and pooling next to the narrow mattress suggested
strongly that the heart had been punctured. There were
few signs of a struggle: possibly the victim had been
asleep at the time of the attack, or otherwise subdued,
or caught by surprise.

It felt strange. He was the observer of his own messy
death and yet remained detached from the fact it was
himself. He used his watch to take some photos, just in
case he might need them later.

How had the murderer got in here, without disturbing
the victim? The capsule was barely large enough for one
person. Surely Mrs. Ng would remember a blood-soaked
killer leaving the premises. Everybody would notice
something like that. Or, he thought, would they? He
looked around at his fellow residents. There were few
residential options lower than this, other than getting
yourself a refrigerator box and finding a quiet bit of city
sidewalk. Guys living here were hanging on by their
fingernails. So, one day, as you go about your business,
doing your best not to disturb the other residents because
you've seen how disturbing the wrong guy at the wrong
time could go all kinds of bad, you spot this guy, carrying a blood-soaked knife, and he's covered in blood,
too. You're not going to make trouble for this guy, are
you? You're not going to report him to the coppers, or

raise any kind of alarm, because you might wind up dead, just like the guy's last victim.

Spider could see how that could work out in the killer's favor, but he still could not see how he could escape Mrs. Ng's notice. She, unlike the residents, would make a stink about it. She would call the cops, and lock down the building until they arrived, and she'd have surveillance footage.

Interesting, he thought, still detached and doing his best not to think about the victim as his own future self — yet he realized that he himself had this very same appointment with the very same murderer. Which future had this guy, this future version of himself, come from? From this point in time, he knew, millions, billions of alternate futures spread out before him. The dead Spider could have come from any one of them. He, Spider here and now, could, through his choices and the choices of other people, avoid this fate — but how would he know?

He thought, *this guy might have been knifed by some bastard he pissed off in prison during his fifteen years for killing Molly.* Who right now wasn't dead, and he hadn't killed her. If he stayed out of prison, he could avoid meeting whoever it was, avoid pissing him off, and maybe avoid getting stuck like a pig in his capsule tonight. Future Spider came back here in a time machine, so what would stop this other guy, the murderer, from doing the same thing?

Or it could be something entirely else.

He made his way downstairs to the lobby, clutching the hand rail for support, wiping sweat out of his eyes with his free hand. Once there, he sat in the uncomfortable lobby chair and forced himself to have a look through the photos he'd taken.

Viewed this way, the scene was easier to take. There was none of the visceral, up-your-nose, sphincter-tightening horror. It was just pictures. And in some of the photos, he could see that there was sketchy, fingerpainting-in-blood writing along one wall of the capsule. This surprised him; he hadn't noticed that when he was up there. He zoomed the image and read the message.

THE VORES ARE COMING

Who the hell are the Vores? he thought, reviewing the images. Was that "vores" as in, say, carnivores? Cannibals from the future? Had they killed Future Spider? He didn't know.

A couple of guys asked if he was okay; he just nodded weakly. This, he knew, was going to get bad very fast. He'd have to call Iris. It was all related — it had to be related — to the dead woman in the time machine. Vaguely, as he tried to regain his composure, he remembered that he still needed to find an explanation for Mr. Vincent's weird silence. Or maybe, he thought, thinking about what he'd just found, he didn't want to get involved. Something bad was going on. He could see that. Anybody could see that. And it was something big. Murder was, probably, the least of it, he thought, but at that moment he could not have said just why he thought so. There was something ominous about that enigmatic message on the capsule wall, *THE VORES ARE COMING.* He got his watch to do a tube search on "Vores", but he didn't find anything helpful.

At great length, feeling a little better, he knew what he had to do, and called Iris. She answered almost immediately. "Spider? This is unexpected. I was just—"

"Iris, change of plan. Listen. I need you to bring your team out to The Lucky Happy Moon Motel, in Midland."

She was quick. "Isn't that your current domicile?"

"No flies on you," he said, taking refuge in banter so he didn't have to think about what he'd seen, and what he could still smell. "Just bring your guys out here. Without sounding all cliché or anything, I need to report a murder, of a sort."

"You don't sound good," Iris said.

"Just get over here pronto."

"Okay," she said, recognizing his tone. "We'll be right there."

"One thing I should tell you."

"Yeah?"

"The dead guy is me."

"God," Iris said, and Spider could tell that she was seeing where he was going, and what must have happened. "I bloody hate time travel."

"Who doesn't?"

He quietly informed Mrs. Ng what was going on. From her screen she could lock shut Spider's capsule. "And it's actually you?" she said, astonished. "Up there? All dead?"

"Future me, yeah."

"Oh," she said, disturbed for a moment. Then she said, smiling, "My grandson, Chris, he's just a baby now, but he comes to visit me sometimes as an old man from the future. He tells me the most amazing things."

"I bet he does," Spider said, trying not to visualize the scene inside his capsule. After a moment's effort to try to clear his head, he said, "Oh, and yeah. I'm gonna need another capsule."

§   §   §

Later, once Iris had inspected the scene and left her team to deal with it, she came back downstairs to talk to Spider. They sat in a nook near Mrs. Ng's desk. Mrs. Ng gave Spider a huge mug of impossibly sweet tea, and draped a colorful crocheted rug that smelled of dogs and incense around his shoulders. Iris recorded as he narrated the whole thing, doing his best to keep his voice steady, to speak only in facts, knowing that the number-one thought in Iris's mind would be that Spider himself had killed his future self (and somehow got himself completely clean without drawing any attention, of course). It was too coincidental that the dead woman in the time machine incident should occur within a few days of this latest murder. He was the only common factor, he knew that, and fully expected to be taken in for questioning, and possibly even charged. Iris listened to his account, looking very serious and intense, making notes in her recorder, and asking for clarification here and there. When he finished, and verified his statement, Iris ran it back, listening again, nodding, biting her lip, making more notes. She said, "You know how bad this looks, don't you?"

"You can't seriously think I did it," he said.

"You know," she said, putting the recorder away, "to be perfectly frank with you, I actually don't think it was you."

"You don't?" This surprised him. He wondered if she was toying with him. Would she do that? He remembered the Iris Street he'd known years ago, the one who was only too prepared to play along with departmental politics in order to get ahead, the one who wanted it all. Now, years later, she looked different. This Iris had a hard, lined, and weary look to her features, but she did seem genuine. A ruse? At this point, with so much on his mind, and no reason to imagine the Police Service would do the right thing by him, he doubted her, and imagined he'd be in a holding cell by the end of the night, and to hell with the lack of evidence.

Instead, she surprised him. "God no, Spider."

"No? You don't think all this looks rather suggestive? You don't think there are guys still in the Service who'd be quite happy to see me do some hard time?"

She glared at him. "Yes, there very likely are some guys like that. Sure. There are probably quite a few who'd like to see the end of me, too, for that matter. That's just the way it is. People are people. We're petty. And what happened to you, that was rotten, that was. Bloody rotten. You did the right thing, at enormous cost to yourself. It was a bloody scandal!"

Spider was stunned. He stared at her. She still looked genuine. It was hard to take. Every cell in his body wanted to doubt her. Surely, she was just trying to get him off-balance, to make him drop his guard, so he'd say something incriminating. Surely, in other words, at some level, she was still "One of Them." And yet, as she sat there, looking for all the world like a cop who wanted to help him, to do the right thing by him, he felt confused and angry and helpless. Some weird and nasty shit was going down around him, for no good reason that he understood, and he didn't know what to do or whom to trust. In the end, though, worn out, and tired of doubting, he found himself saying, "Thanks, Iris. Means a lot to hear you say it."

"You're welcome," she said. "Things have changed in the Service, or haven't you heard?"

"To be honest, after I left, I didn't hear much of anything for ages. Didn't watch news, didn't read the paper, certainly didn't hang out online. It was all I could do just, you know, getting through each day. Probably had a bloody breakdown and didn't even know it, I was so far gone." Why he was telling her this he did not know, but it didn't feel like a mistake. Maybe, it occurred to him, she wasn't an enemy.

"God," she said. "I didn't know."

He nodded and sipped at his tea. It was so sweet it was vile, but the warmth was good. Spider doubted he'd ever feel warm again.

Iris said, glancing through some crime scene images on her handheld, "So who do you reckon these 'Vore' bastards might be?"

"You saw that?"

"Hard to miss," she said, allowing a small, wry smile.

"No idea," he said. "You'll have to talk to Mrs. Ng, find out who's been in and out all day."

"Yup, got that in hand."

"Sorry. Old habits."

She nodded, not unkindly. "So, how are you doing now? Feeling any better?"

He still felt shivery and strange and upset. "Okay, I s'pose. Not exactly what I had in mind for this evening."

She nodded. "Yes, well."

Spider said, "So you really met, uh, 'him' last night, too?" It was difficult to figure out what to call Future Spider, without feeling ridiculous.

"I did, yes." She avoided his eyes, saying this, he noticed. She went on, "Perhaps you could describe your own meeting with the deceased last night?"

Already, in his head, his memory of last night, driving around the burbs with Future Spider, was fraying. He felt as if he was trying to remember a dream he'd had a couple of nights before, as if he was leaving out important parts. Nothing made sense, but he did his best to sketch in what he could of the encounter — and how today none of it appeared to have happened at all, leading to his idea that his timeline had been shuffled around somehow, possibly to protect him. "On the one hand I was trying to deal with what happened to Molly, but then I'm talking to Molly on the phone, and she's in Bangkok, for God's sake."

"There were no reports last night of a situation at her address."

"The whole thing was probably faked, now that I think about it."

"Spider," Iris said after a thoughtful moment. "Did he mention, this future version of you..." She looked a little uncomfortable saying this. "Something called 'Zeropoint?'"

For reasons he did not fully grasp at the time, on hearing that name Spider felt a sudden jolt of panic shoot through him. He wanted to get going, get away, leave, hide, keep his head down. Nothing good could be attached to that name, he believed, as if it was the sort of bad magic that reacts poorly on hearing its own name invoked. Surprised at this sudden flash of anxiety, he actually said to Iris, "I don't know if we should be discussing that here." Having said it, hearing himself, he felt ridiculous, but the fear was there. Something about the name was *wrong*; it was bad juju. He caught himself glancing about, trying to read closed faces, looking for hidden menace.

She pressed her point. "Do you know what it means?"

He was keen to change the subject, but the fact of his strange fear of that name was disturbing. On the one hand he wished they could talk about anything else, anything at all, even his future self's death; but on the other, Spider had a tense, visceral feeling that he needed to know as much as he possibly could about Zeropoint, regardless of the consequences, even if it meant he'd wind up dead upstairs inside his capsule. It was as if, he was surprised to realize, his life — indeed, his entire existence — might depend on it. He remembered what Future Spider told him about Zeropoint, not that he had said much — but the idea that there were some kind of spooky bad guys off in the future, messing with timelines and histories, was gravely unsettling. It had certainly crossed his mind that these Zeropoint people might well have killed his future self, possibly for talking about them. "Not really, no. You?"

Iris looked as troubled as he felt, looked like she wanted to talk about it, get everything out in the open. "I got a call last night. I was getting ready to head home for the night. Long day. Frustration Central. Dead ends galore. So I'm putting on my coat and checking my stuff, and my phone goes off. I answer, and at first it sounds like you, and you need to see me right away."

Spider was thinking about his own encounter with Future Spider, as he had stood on Molly's front porch. "Go on," he said.

"So anyway, it sounds like you, and for reasons I can't disclose I explain that I can't actually see you, not at the moment."

"What?"

She rolled her eyes, looking dead tired. "Long story. Listen. I try to explain to you, er, Future You, that I can't be talking to you. Word's come down from head office. If I hear from you, I'm supposed to just cut you off, ignore anything and everything you might say."

He thought about the empty days that followed the discovery of the dead woman in the time machine. "This is to do with the dead woman, or the other business?" The "other business" being his history with the Police Service.

"Look. Shut up. I'm trying to tell you what I know, and maybe getting myself in a whole bunch of shit for doing so, okay, so just bear with me."

There were too many deep and messed-up emotions swirling around him right now. It was hard to sit still. "Sorry," he said, "it's just—"

"Yeah. I get it, Spider. I do."

"You going to catch shit for talking to me now, about the business upstairs?"

She sighed, looking away. "Yeah, probably. I don't know. I mean, you're a material witness, at the very least, and certainly a person of interest. The fact that it's your future self, for God's sake — I pretty much have to talk to you. It's just, there's complicated stuff going on in the upper reaches of things, wheels within wheels, okay?" She sighed, shook her head and looked back at him, and flashed a weary smile. "God," she said, "who'd be a bloody cop, huh?"

This made him smile. He was starting to feel that he might be able to trust her. She went on. "So you — shit, sorry, 'Future You' — ring up again, and this time I don't even answer. All I wanna do is just go home, microwave some soup, and sit on my butt watching bad TV all night. One of those days. Too much politics, not enough chasing about catching bad guys, you know? The slightest thing you do, you have to complete an 'Ethical Awareness Breakdown,' and you have to work out the 'Cost-Benefit Index Assessment,' and you have to be always thinking about 'PR Downsides,' and let's not forget the bloody 'key-point indicators'—"

Spider blinked, surprised. "You have to deal with KPIs, too?"

"I think these days even God has to worry about his KPIs, frankly," she said.

He nodded. "I wouldn't be God for any amount of money, would you?"

"Too depressing," she said. "Anyway, like I say, we've only got so many resources, and the city and metroplex is such a vast place, we have to make priorities and it just makes me crazy and I want to scream."

"I had no idea it was like that these days."

"You've got no bloody idea, Spider."

"I can see that."

"So I'm home, I've fed the bloody cat, I've had a shower — you know how you always felt like you wanted a shower when you got home? You remember that?"

He closed his eyes, and tried to control his breathing. "Oh yeah."

"That part hasn't changed. So I'm heating up some lamb korma, and my phone is just going nuts. Guess who? Yeah. I kill the link. He phones back. I kill the link. I take the phone off, screw it up, stomp it under my shoe — and guess what?"

"Turns up at your door?"

"Turns up at my door. Scares the shit out of the cat. I'm sitting there, eating my soup, I'm wearing my ratty old pajamas and my Cthulhu slippers—"

Despite everything, Spider had to laugh at this image of Iris.

"Oh yeah, don't you mock Great Cthulhu. He'll come and eat your brain, he will." She smiled, and it looked like a genuine sharing-a-laugh-with-a-mate smile, not like a politeness.

He laughed some more. "I never saw you as the monster-slipper type, Iris."

She nodded, smiled, and said, "Anyway, so there's you at the door, banging away, yelling that you have to see me, and how it's all important, and lives are at stake, and all this."

"Future Spider was busy last night," he said, absently.

"So I go to the door, and I'm yelling through it, telling him to fuck off or I'll call my mates to take him away. He won't budge. He says he needs to talk to me tonight. He says it's about you, only he calls you his 'past self.' I say 'what?' and he gets me to switch on the security cam, and sure enough, it *is* you, but it's really *not* you. This is an old and seedy version of you — sorry..."

"He told me he'd done fifteen years for the murder of Molly. Which he said he didn't actually do."

"That's what he told me, too — but I was also thinking maybe it was just regular you, and you were pulling some ridiculous stunt."

"Why would I do something like that?"

"I don't know. It was a weird situation."

"So," he said, "what'd you do?"

"I let him in."

"Was that wise?"

"See previous comment: it was a weird situation. It was you, sort of. I trust you."

This was also news to Spider, but he wasn't sure if he believed it. "Thanks," he said, "anyway...?"

"So we talked. A lot. He was definitely you: he remembered all kinds of stuff from, well, before, you know."

Spider felt himself starting to blush a little, thinking about what things his future self might remember about Iris from "before." "And at some point he told you about Zeropoint."

She nodded. "He said they're some kind of security service-type outfit, only they exist, he said, in the remote future, and there's this war on for control of all of history. I'm all, 'What the fuck?'"

"Go on," Spider said, amazed. This was more than he had got from his own run-in with Future Spider.

"There was a lot of stuff he said, too much — and would you believe it never occurred to me to record any of it?"

He clapped his hand over his forehead, exasperated. "What about notes? Did you make any notes?"

"It was late, I was out of my head on sheer weirdness, and I knew I was risking all kinds of bad shit from work just talking to him. And then, this morning, when I got up—"

"He was all gone, and you weren't sure he'd even been there?"

Iris blushed, and glanced away for a moment, then looked back, concentrating on her hands. Spider was baffled, and stared at her, wondering what the hell was going on, but then in a great rush of understanding he saw what must have happened.

She hung her head and sighed. "It was... it was weird—"

"Weird? Well, thanks very much!"

Acutely embarrassed, her face bright pink, she said, "Sorry, bad choice of words—"

"Weird!?"

"Look. It was one of those things. It got late, we'd been talking all night. I offered him the couch. It's just, he was all kind of sad and pathetic—"

Spider thought his head might explode from shock. "Pity sex? You had pity sex with him?" He took a minute or two to try to think his way past it.

"I didn't say I was proud of it, Spider."

"Not helping your case there, Iris."

Nearby, two guys from the Medical Examiner's office were carrying a sealed temporary casket containing the dead man's body down the stairs. When they reached the lobby, Iris took the welcome opportunity to escape from Spider, and went over to have a quick word with the two guys, who nodded and took the body outside to the waiting van. Uniformed officers and equipment-laden forensic techs wearing bug-like black eye-plugs, like the ones Spider had seen on Mr. Vincent, followed the ME guys. Iris's partner, Sergeant Aboulela, looking very tired, came over and briefed her about the preliminary findings. Iris brought him over to meet Spider.

Spider got to his feet, and was relieved that he could actually stand up without feeling as if his legs would collapse. It was hard not to keep staring at Iris: the thought of his future self having sex with her — it was freaky yet also strangely appealing, and yes, "strangely" was the right word.

Sergeant Aboulela, a tall thin Sudanese-Australian, on meeting this version of Spider, was visibly taken aback. His handshake was weak and cold. "Pleased to meet you, Mr. Webb," he said, very politely. "Must be a strange situation for you."

He shot a glance at Iris. "I've known stranger, believe me."

Iris glared back at him, then said to Aboulela, "Spider met with the deceased last night."

The sergeant was surprised, but interested. "Did he give you any indication that someone—"

"I've already taken Mr. Webb's statement," Iris said.

Spider, ignoring Iris, said, "I met him last night. We had a very odd encounter." Unconsciously he touched his tongue against the healed teeth; again there was no way to tell, from touch, that anything had ever happened to them.

Aboulela turned to Iris. "I believe you said you met with the deceased last night as well."

"It was a big night for all of us," she said, trying to finesse her way clear. Before he could ask her anything further, she told him to take a statement from Mrs. Ng, and to get a copy of all of the manageress's security data from today.

"Yes, boss," he said, nodding. Then, to Spider he said, "Pleased to have met you, Mr. Webb." He went over to talk to Mrs. Ng.

Spider tried to focus on what was important. "We were talking about Zeropoint."

Iris sagged, "Yes."

"What else did he tell you about them? What do they want?"

She was rubbing the back of her neck, her eyes closed. "It had to do with the woman, the dead woman the other day, in the time machine."

This got his attention. "What about her?"

She leaned in close to him. He could smell the coffee on her breath. "That's just it. When I got back to the office this morning, these guys from DOTAS Section Ten were waiting for me, and they told me I was off the case, the whole thing was a DOTAS matter now, and I had to sign a bunch of paperwork, and hand over all our records and evidence, the whole thing."

"You couldn't protest?" Spider asked.

"Who to?" she said, looking at him. "The minister? The prime minister?"

"Good point," he said, understanding. He wondered if the same guys might have gone around to visit Mr. Vincent in the middle of the night and had a quiet word with him, too. "Hmm, okay."

"Back to your future self," Iris said. "He gave me a name."

"What name?"

"Clea Fassbinder."

"Is that her name? The dead woman?" Spider was wiped out, he just wanted to sleep for three days, and he was pissed off about time travel intrigue generally, but the part of his brain that still cared about murder was hanging on tight.

"She supposedly works — well, worked — for Zeropoint."

Spider sat down. "So who killed her?"

"Future Spider didn't know. Just finding out her name was hard enough, he said. If, of course, that is her real name."

His mind raced, thinking it all through. "Who else knows this?"

"Dunno," she said, yawning behind her hand. "Not my guys, that's for sure."

"You didn't tell them?"

Iris looked deeply uncomfortable. "He told me only to tell you."

"What the fuck am I supposed to do with a name that doesn't connect to anybody?"

"He seemed to think it might help."

"Help what?"

"Beats me. I've already done a tube search, not that that was much help."

"And?"

"And nothing. She doesn't exist."

Spider was rubbing his face; he needed a shave. Sandgrains of gunk were crusting up the corners of his eyes. "So we've got spooks from the future, a dead woman who doesn't exist, some bad guys called 'Vores,' and... what?"

"And a murderer with a taste for gore and cheap drama, who can slip through this place's security without a trace, and without drawing attention. I mean, we talked to nearly everybody who was around at the time, and nobody remembers seeing anything odd," Iris said. She yawned again and stretched her arms over her head.

"Oh good, an invisible assassin. My favorite!" Spider muttered. He thought about his own hypothesis involving a killer who looked so much like trouble everybody ignored him — except the imperturbable Mrs. Ng. She was the flaw in that whole idea.

Iris nodded, but added, "My own impression was that Future Spider was trying to save your life, in his own blundering, shambling way."

He tried not to think of Future Spider shambling and blundering into Iris's bed, and then felt he needed to scrub out the inside of his brain to get rid of the image. "You think he knew they were going to kill him?"

"'They?'" she said.

"Whoever wanted him dead," he said, then added, without thinking, "wanted *me* dead." For the first time he could begin to see the possibility that Future Spider had allowed himself to be killed in order to save him. The idea was bizarre, but he could see a certain crazy sense to it.

"This is the point in the proceedings," Iris said, "where I offer you official police protection."

"Yeah," he said, bitterly amused, "and this is the point where I laugh in your face and (a), remind you that I have no reason to trust any police officer other than you, and (b), ask what makes you think a killer like the one you just described could be stopped by mere police protection?"

Iris, slumped in the chair, was rubbing her eyes. "You are, of course, right. Or, at least, you have a point."

"Thank you," he said, all magnanimous.

"Yes, which is why I feel like I should at least make you the following offer..." She took a deep breath and looked him in the eye. It looked to Spider as if she was trying not to laugh, and not to blush. "Come and stay at my place."

Spider laughed so much he started coughing, and found it hard to stop.

Iris got him some water and pounded his back until he waved for her to stop. At length, he looked up at her. "You are a beggar for punishment, aren't you?"

"In for a penny," she said, pulling out her keys. "So, you coming or what?"

"Got room in your car for my bike?"

CHAPTER 10

Spider was in his office at the shop the next day when Malaria told him she had James Rutherford on the phone, wanting to talk to Spider about a time machine not working right. He'd been sipping a well-deserved coffee at the time, taking five minutes after a dizzying backwards time-jump to deliver a fixed unit to its satisfied owner, and trying not to brood about his troubles. It didn't help that last night at Iris's apartment, trying to get comfortable on her couch, he hardly slept. Not because Iris was keeping him up, but because of the sheer, mindbending weirdness of what was happening in his life just at the moment. The thought that Iris and his future self had actually slept together the previous night, presumably in her bedroom, just through that door over there, did not help. It bothered him more than a little, but only because, when he thought about it (and he had a lot of time in which to think about it), he wished it had been him, Present Spider.

Malaria's news surprised him. He nearly choked on his coffee. "James Rutherford? DOTAS James Rutherford?"

"Sounds like him, yeah," Malaria said, chewing on the end of her stylus.

Amazed, but also far enough into the continuing strangeness of his recent life to feel suspicious about James's timing, he said, "Put him through, by all means!" He made himself comfortable in his office, behind his desk, the one place in his life where he felt at least nominally in control of things. If James Rutherford was indeed on the phone, it could be a very welcome development. At last, he thought, here was someone who might know something, who could maybe fill in some of the gaping blanks.

Then again, he thought, didn't Malaria just say that James wanted help with a time machine? What? James Rutherford, senior chronosystems engineer, time machine geek extraordinaire, needed help with a time machine?

Spider tapped his phone patch, and said, "James?"

"Spider, hey."

Right away, Spider was frowning, listening to the tone in James's voice. The man sounded tired, beaten down. He remembered the way James had been during the initial examination of the crime scene. Spider, wondering where this was going, said, "Hi yourself. Good to hear from you. Been wondering where you'd gotten to. Been trying to call you for ages now. What's up? Am I *persona non grata* with DOTAS all of a sudden?" Spider wasn't sure where that question came from, but it was something he wanted to know. It was also something with which he had some previous experience.

"What? You — what? Um, no. No, you're fine. Everything's fine. It's just, I've been on personal leave for a while now. Didn't want to be disturbed."

Personal leave? Spider thought. "James, is everything okay?"

There was a long pause, and he could hear James breathing hard. "Define okay," he said, only a little dismissive.

Spider knew enough not to pry. "Right, yeah, okay."

"You do know why I'm calling, right?" James asked.

"Malaria said something about you want some help with a faulty time machine? Really? What the hell kind of problem could you possibly have with a faulty time machine?"

"Look. Spider. It's Electra's. It's on the blink. She wants it fixed, and I told her I know just the guy. Is that a problem?"

"No, no, of course not. It's just, you—"

"Do you mind if I bring it round to show you?"

Spider's mind was spinning like mad, trying to think what the hell might be going on here. "Sure. You bet. I'll be happy to give it my full attention."

"Great. See you shortly." And then he was gone.

Spider yelled out to Malaria that James would be turning up at some point this afternoon, and to show him through to Spider's office when he arrived. Malaria yelled back to confirm.

Sitting there in his office, fiddling with paper clips, full of both curiosity and dread about James's visit, Spider thought he should probably do something useful to fill in the time, so he went through to the workshop and got busy helping Charlie sort through some baffling technical problems. It felt like a wonderful holiday, for a while, anyway.

When James turned up, a big backpack slung over his shoulder, Malaria sent him through to the workshop where Spider was soldering new contacts on a scanning engine motherboard. James called out, "Hey, can a guy get a coffee around here or what?"

Spider, startled, glanced up, saw James, and saw that James was doing his best to act all jaunty — and not doing a very convincing job of it. "You know where the coffee droid is."

He smiled. "Got a minute?"

Spider gave some instructions to Charlie, and said he'd be back a bit later. He took James back to his office, got him a coffee, and moved his chair around to the front of the desk. "So," he said, waiting for his coffee to cool.

"Thanks for making time to see me," James said.

That was an odd thing to say, Spider thought. Since when did James feel the need to thank him for "making time" to see him? "No worries," Spider said. "So, that's the offending unit in the backpack there?"

James set his coffee on the front of Spider's desk and hauled the pack around in front of him, opened it, and pulled out a roughly conical device about the size of a vacuum cleaner, sheathed in translucent matte-black plastic. He sat the unit on his lap and smiled. "One Toshiba Umbra base-station unit. The latest thing."

This was true. The industry was moving on from the large-scale units epitomized by the Tempo and its many imitators, in favor of smaller machines like this. The idea was that instead of travelling about in a big bulky time machine, you placed the base-station somewhere near the geographical spot you were aiming for, then used the unit's remote to operate the unit. This way you could move about in time however you pleased, while the base-station remained back in your present. It was a popular idea and so far looked like it was sweeping in a new era of consumer time travel enthusiasm. Spider was less than enthused about the prospect.

"What seems to be the trouble, then?" he asked James.

James produced a note on black paper, written in white ink. "Darling daughter left this on the dining room table this morning before she went out for the day."

"How is Electra?" he asked.

"The same," James said, and sighed a little, closing his eyes for a moment. He looked exhausted, just thinking about her.

Spider nodded. "Right." He read the message. "Oh," he said.

The message read: "Time machine won't go. Make time machine go. NOW!" The handwriting was heavy, with big loops. The I's were dotted with tiny death's-head skulls.

"I see what you mean," Spider said, a little afraid. "Such a subtle girl."

"That's Electra all over, sadly."

"No other diagnostic detail?"

"That's it."

"Okay, then. You want to fire it up, see what happens?"

James fished the remote out of the backpack and handed it to Spider. The remote, like the base-station, was cased in translucent matte-black plastic, only this was sculpted to fit the hand, the colored buttons ergonomically styled and arranged. If you peered close, you could see tiny mechanical clockwork mechanisms hidden inside; they were not part of the unit's functionality, but they looked very cool, Spider thought, despite himself. When he switched on the remote, the clockwork came to life, and he could hear it ticking faintly, like a heavy grandfather clock.

Pointing the remote at the base-station, he hit the "on" button, and waited for the "power" light on the unit to come on. It did not. The unit sat there as if nothing had happened. Spider nodded. "Let's have a look at the system maintenance panel."

James placed the unit on the desk and rotated it slightly until the system maintenance panel cover was facing Spider. Spider opened the panel and had a good look. Inside were a row of status LEDs, now showing red; some input transponders for diagnostic tools; and a very small screen. He squinted, trying to read the small type. "Well, now that's interesting."

"I thought you'd appreciate that," James said.

"I did not know there even were Y-series error codes."

"I did, but I'd never seen one on a consumer time machine."

Spider grabbed a screen off his desk and tubed across to the Toshiba Australia Chrono Solutions site, and dived into the relevant Knowledge Base for this specific model. He soon found the solution to the mystery. "'Translation stack integrity self-check failure'," Spider said. "Is that all?"

James said, "Darling daughter was right."

"Time machine won't go," Spider said.

"You can fix it, though, right?"

"Now I know what it is, yeah, no worries. Swap out the bad DCA module, swap in a new one. Should be fine."

"Great," James said, and took a sip of his coffee. "That's great." He sounded less than enthusiastic.

Spider was watching him. "What really brings you out here today?"

James did his best to feign bafflement. "Er, darling daughter. Time machine won't go? Wants to go shopping in the Fifties. Expects me to organize everything, get the period currency, make an appointment for her to get the shots, the whole ball of wax."

"No, that's not what I mean. I mean, here you are, by far the brainiest guy in the room just at the moment. What you don't know about time machines isn't worth knowing. But you bring me this thing, nice as it is, and you want me to look at it."

"You're the best, I told you that."

"Yeah, thanks, appreciate it. But the fact is, this thing is still under warranty, right? You could have just taken it into the dealer. God, you could have just looked up the answer yourself!"

James listened to all this, nodded at all the right places, and agreed with everything Spider said. "All true."

"More to the point, aren't you, as part of DOTAS, not exactly allowed to talk to me because of the embargo on the murder of the woman in the time machine business? Are you, somehow, for whatever reason, asking for trouble here?"

"The embargo is down to Section Ten. It's their problem, not mine." James looked strangely unconcerned by the very serious possible consequences of his actions. It gave Spider the chills.

"Why are you here, James?"

"I—"

"Don't bullshit a bullshitter, James. Okay? What's wrong?"

"Nothing's wrong," James said, putting the Umbra on the floor. "It's just, I'm not made of money, Spider. You know what the Toshiba dealership wanted to charge me to fix this thing? It's bloody criminal! So can you blame me for wanting to send a bit of business to a mate, and avoid paying through the nose into the bargain?"

Spider wasn't buying it. "What's wrong?"

"Nothing's wrong."

"Bullshit."

James stared at Spider, hesitated a long moment, thinking hard, then looked away. He said, "What do you know about the Kronos Project?"

This was unexpected, and all the more disturbing for it. He thought for a moment, then hit the tubes and looked it up. "Oh, right. The time probe thing. Is that still going?"

"I consulted on the mission nav package. This was years ago. Very hush-hush."

"Didn't know that," Spider said, wondering how this fit in with everything else, and almost not wanting to find out. Almost.

James nodded. "Yeah. And it is still going. The latest time-fix from it said it was more than three hundred thousand years off in the future. In cruise mode. Going well."

Spider was amazed at the vast gulf of years. "Found anything interesting?"

James shifted in his seat, his face darkened, and began to look deeply troubled. "I, um, I can't actually say, Spider."

Spider felt tingles up his spine; the hairs on the back of his neck stood up straight. "I see," he said. "The Umbra thing here. That was just an excuse, like I said, right?"

James hunched forward, his eyes closed, his mouth closed tight, and nodded. "Sorry," he said, mumbling, and stared at the Umbra on the floor as if it were the source of all his troubles. "Things right now... It's difficult. Really difficult. You have no idea."

This was a side of James Spider had never seen, and in some ways hoped never to see. He had been comfortable with the way their relationship had been. Not close, but friendly. Mates, but not really friends. It was hard to think about, let alone explain. Still, all that had changed, apparently. Now he found himself sitting with a man who looked like the most troubled man Spider had ever seen. Spider knew James had spent some time in a private psychiatric hospital in the wake of his wife's death. James had mentioned it once, a long time ago, when they were first getting to know each other. It had been a jarring thing to learn about the man — and so very surprising, too: somehow Spider had always assumed that if you were incredibly smart and capable, an expert in your chosen field, then you were protected, somehow, from mental disorder. Spider's father had had a history of mental illness; Spider had always worried that he would inherit it. Sometimes, like during those years after he lost everything, he wondered if it had turned up and he never noticed, what with all the other misery in his life.

He wondered what to say to James. "It's okay, James. If you want to talk..."

"That's just it," he said to Spider, and now he showed his true face, a mask of anguish and fear. "I *can't* talk about it!"

"Okay," Spider said, at a loss, worried, wondering what to do. "Can I get you another coffee, maybe?"

"How about just some water?"

Spider was up out of his chair, out of his office, into the break room, in the fridge, grabbing a bottle of cold water, and back in his office again so fast it surprised him. He handed the water to James, who sighed and set it to one side, unopened. Spider sank back into his seat, breathing hard. He offered to open the water for him, and James handed it over, more, Spider thought, to give Spider something to do, to help him feel useful in a confounding situation. As he opened the bottle and handed it back to James, Spider felt a strange urge to thank him.

"So. James."

He was slumped down in the chair, staring at the Umbra, wretched. "Spider."

Spider had thousands of questions, but did he dare ask any of them? Did he have any business asking James anything other than, well, would you like me to call you a taxi to go home? There was, after all, no "case". James was not a suspect, and Spider was not a cop, or an investigator of any kind. Yet the urges, the patterns of thought, the approaches to dealing with people in situations like this, were hard to fight. It was hard, in the end, to simply be a civilian. "Is there, um, anything I can do for you?" he ended up asking.

James said, "I thought, I've been thinking, these past few days, I needed to talk to someone. Someone who'd understand. There's a doctor I see every few months, he's pretty good, but I can't talk about work at all. It's difficult, to say the least. Things at work are, well, you could say they're a bit tense right now. They've got a bit of a witch-hunt going on, the proverbial search for the guilty, a scapegoat, someone whose fault it all is. There are meetings, and meetings about meetings, and quiet, informal 'chats', one on one, trying to tease out chains of events, clarifying who did what and when. The whole department, Spider, all of DOTAS, across the country, is caught up in a mad whirl of recrimination, desperately seeking the one officer at whose feet the whole mess can be laid, like a vast electrical storm looking for a good place to discharge. Nothing's getting done. It's a madhouse, do you see?"

Stunned, but increasingly worried, Spider took all this in, put it together with the way James looked, the way he was talking, and didn't like the possible answer. "Are they looking for you, James?" His voice the merest whisper.

James nodded minutely, and his face seemed to crumple, as if under a heavy impact. His eyes filled with tears.

"What did you do?"

There was a long, shuddering silence. Spider felt like he was intruding. James said, "A tiny piece of code, it looked innocent enough, a minor software patch, got included in the Kronos flight management subsystem. It went unnoticed."

"Oh God, James. What did you do?"

"The probe moves in jumps. Five hundred to a thousand years per jump."

"So it can spend time at each point, gathering data, making observations. I've seen stuff about it on the news."

James nodded. "Exactly."

"What does the code do?"

"In the original timeline, Kronos stumbled on something after a particular jump."

"It *found* something?" Spider's pulse quickened.

He nodded. "Something that didn't want to be found."

"Shit. What happened?"

James shook his head, not wanting to go any further. He covered his face, took several big gulping breaths. "The timeline had to be altered. The probe's course had to be changed. It was a simple thing, like I said."

"The software update patch you mentioned."

"That's right."

"So someone told you to do this?"

"Mmm."

"And this someone gave you the code?"

James said nothing. He sat there, face in his hands, weeping silently. "I'm so sorry," he said, over and over, and it sounded like he meant it.

Spider said, "Look, I'll call your daughter, she can come and—"

At this, James stared at Spider. "No. Absolutely not. I'm fine."

"You're a mess, James. Look at you!"

"Leave Electra out of it. I have no desire for her to see me like this. She's been through enough."

Spider leaned back in his chair, his hands up, and said, "Okay. No worries. Sorry. I was just—"

"I'll be fine, Spider."

Yeah, sure you will, he thought. "Right. Sorry."

"Listen," James said, sniffing and mopping his eyes and face, "there was talk of a fresh coffee?"

"Absolutely. Give me a minute." He got up and left James to it, which was probably James's plan all along, the poor bastard. He went into the break room and started up the coffee droid. He called out to Malaria to see if she wanted anything, but she said she was good, thanks.

Fumbling absently with the coffee droid, Spider thought about his options. It appeared James was confessing to sabotaging the Kronos probe's mission, in order to make it avoid whatever it was it had stumbled across somewhere out in the future, in a "previous timeline". Someone told him to do it, and gave him the means to make it happen. Suppose for a moment, he thought, that James was telling the truth. This was huge. James had to go to the authorities. At minimum he would have to tell DOTAS.

And yet, Spider was also thinking, it was all pretty far-fetched. James, he was sorry to think, might not be telling the truth. Maybe he wasn't aware he was lying. Could this be attention-seeking behavior? Was he trying to overcome the grim reality that for all his engineering prowess and expertise in the field of time machines, these days he was a boring public servant in a government department? He hated thinking about James this way.

Then again, he thought, we are living in strange times. All manner of weird stuff does go on. Spider could testify to that personally.

So what Spider needed, he thought, was a way to verify James's extraordinary story. He did know a few other people at the Perth DOTAS office. He could make some calls.

At this point Spider stopped himself. *You're not a copper anymore, Spider,* he told himself, again. *It's not your job to find out whether James is or isn't lying, or whether he's a saboteur. The fact is that James has a bulletproof reputation for integrity. For God's sake, the man was in on the legendary construction of Time Machine 2.0, nearly twenty years ago! So what makes more sense: that James sabotaged the Kronos Project at the behest of mysterious others from the future, or that the man's still messed up, years after his wife killed herself?* Spider had heard about families where one parent had taken their own life; the rest of the family, confused, hurt, shocked, and angry, sometimes never recovered.

Spider finished making the coffees. These ones turned out far better than he expected. Maybe, he thought, he was getting the hang of the damn thing.

Then Spider heard something happening just outside. He caught a glimpse of James through the break room doorway, on the move. He heard Malaria call out to him, "Mr. Rutherford?" Spider went out to the front office, saw James outside, getting into his car. Spider went after him. "James!" James shot him a stricken look through the windscreen of his car, then drove off, tires squealing. "James!"

Malaria joined Spider outside. "What happened?"

Spider checked his phone patch, popped his watchtop, and called James's number. Nothing. No reply. "Shit!"

"Spider?" Malaria asked. "Is everything…"

He shook his head, feeling tired and sad, wishing he could help his friend. "I wish I knew," he said.

CHAPTER 11

All the rest of that day, Spider tried to concentrate on work — doing his best to lift those droopy KPIs — but all he could think about was that meeting with James. He'd tried now several times to reach him by phone without result. He'd left messages on the system at James's apartment. Once, late in the day, he got a call back from Electra, James's daughter. "Dad's not in. Take the bloody hint." That was all she said, and went away.

"That was odd," Spider said, more to himself than to anybody else.

Charlie, working in the next service bay, called over to him, "What's up?"

Spider had told Charlie an edited version of James's visit — that James wasn't well. Work troubles. Charlie had nodded his head, understanding, and commented that James had looked "pretty rough" the other day, when they were taking the Tempo apart in the Bat Cave.

"Just trying to reach James again. Got his daughter instead. Strange girl."

"Never had the pleasure," Charlie said.

"I've only met her a few times. Years ago you would have called her a goth, but even that wouldn't cover the full catastrophe that is Electra Rutherford."

"My mum used to be a goth," Charlie said, laughing. "I've seen pictures. Very moody, all in black. Now she laughs and says she has no idea what she was thinking at the time."

Spider only half-heard what Charlie said. He was going over and over the things James had told him, trying to see if at any point he, Spider, could have handled things better.

As a policeman, years ago, he'd been expected to help people in distress if necessary, if no other more qualified personnel were around. It was tough work, and he'd always felt out of his depth, trying to talk to guys wasted on meth beating up their girlfriends or wives, or depressed kids trying to kill themselves. What do you say to someone who just wants you to go away so they can get on with their self-destruction? James wasn't quite like that: Spider had a clear sense that James wanted to tell Spider everything, that he'd been carrying this awful burden around for so long he was exhausted, and just wanted to put it down, or better, give it to someone, and Spider looked like just the guy.

Spider had had one crazy thought, during the course of the afternoon, as he tried to make sense of James's confessions. The man had gone to some trouble to wrap the whole confession in passive voice, to leave out all trace of responsibility and agency, of who did what when and to whom, but as far as Spider could see, at some point during the pre-launch phase of the Kronos Project, James had met someone — Spider was betting it had been a woman — who had convinced him to do this one little favor for her, in return for, what? Sex? Money? Good times? All so the probe would not stumble across something or someone way off in the future getting up to, he was guessing, no good.

Spider wondered what the name "Zeropoint" might mean to James. Even standing there, up to his waist in disassembled time machine componentry, tools, and system manuals, Spider felt chills up and down his spine at the mere thought of that name. It was spooky, irrational. How could a name evoke such a reaction? Particularly a name he'd never heard before that night with his ill-fated Future Self.

Yeah, and you saw what happened to him, didn't you, Spider? he thought, shuddering.

Spider was so preoccupied with his concerns that he never noticed when close of business arrived for the day. When Charlie knocked off and said good night, Spider hardly heard him. In the end, Malaria had to come down to his service bay and tap him on the shoulder — which caused Spider to jump, startled, his heart racing, and drop his multi-tool. "Oh, Malaria, hi."

"Hi yourself, boss. Thought you'd like to know it's time to go home?"

Home? Spider thought, then remembered he was staying at Iris's apartment. The prospect of another restless, sleepless night stretched before him. "Right," he said to Malaria, and started packing up his tools and gear, securing all the bits and pieces of this particular time machine. "Thanks. God, I've been away with the fairies today!" He shook his head, smiling ruefully. "Need to get some decent sleep."

Malaria nodded, shrugged, and said good night, see you tomorrow, and was off. Soon he heard her electric scooter boot up and she was gone, leaving him to lock up for the night.

§   §   §

Later, full of nasty indigestion after something cheap and crappy he'd eaten for dinner on the way home, Spider let himself into Iris's apartment. A video message on the wall informed him that she was out at another incident, and didn't know what time she'd be back. He wondered if even now she still remembered Clea Fassbinder. There was another video message, autoforwarded from the shop, from Dickhead McMahon, who in typical fashion managed to fill the entire wall with his face. McMahon was in his enormous SUV, tooling along a freeway somewhere, talking to the camera on the dashboard. "Spider, ah, something's come up, we need to talk ASAP, when you've got a moment. Um, oh yeah, it's not your key-point indicator thing. Something else. Kinda worried about you, mate. Police asking all kinds of weird questions — can you do something about that since you're sleeping with that inspector woman? That'd be great. Okay, thanks. Cheers!" The message ended, to be replaced by the service logo, which then vanished also, and was replaced by the usual clutter of Iris's display wall.

Spider was furious. "I'm not sleeping with Iris Street!" he shouted at the wall, too late. He muttered and ranted and kicked the couch — Iris's couch, he remembered, again, too late. The couch survived, but Spider was still pissed off. He put in a call to Dickhead. The boss was unavailable, but if Spider would like to leave a message...

Spider left a message. It took several minutes. When he ran it back on preview, he thought he looked like a crazy person ranting about UFOs or some damn thing, so he deleted it and tried again, more calmly. "Hey Dickhead. Look, um, I'm not actually, er, contrary to your suggestion, I'm not actually sleeping with Inspector Street, all right? Have you got that? She's just letting me crash here 'cause my own place, well, you know about that, huh? My future self got killed the other night? Anyway, I'll be at the shop tomorrow. Any time you want to stop by for a chat, fine. See you then." He signed off and sent the message, still angry. The idea that he and Iris were involved, and that Dickhead could somehow use that relationship to subvert some investigation? He shook his head, trying to clear it. It had been a long, strange day. He went to bed early, feeling tired.

§   §   §

Next morning, when he was out of the shower, he heard Iris doing something in the kitchen. He hadn't heard her come in last night. Once dressed — in yesterday's undies and overalls since he hadn't done any laundry — he emerged from the washroom in time to find Iris sitting in the tiny breakfast nook, next to a window which offered a fabulous view of another apartment complex, eating a bowl of hot porridge, and sipping a steaming cup of tea. She was dressed for the day and, other than the fact that she looked tired, appeared pleased to see him.

"Morning, stranger," she said, flashing a smile. "What's new?"

Spider was unsure what to say. He found he didn't want to get into the whole thing about yesterday with James, which would take ages to explain, so he went with

Option B. "Same old, same old," he said, smiling back. "Is there fresh coffee, maybe?"

"Droid's busted," she said.

He went to look at the coffee droid, thinking he could maybe do something about it. While he tinkered with the machine, Iris called out to him, "By the way, some good news."

"Yeah, what?"

"We think we've got a lead on who killed your, um, future self?"

Astonished, and not certain he had heard Iris correctly, Spider shot back to the breakfast nook. "You what?"

"Yeah, like I said, we went over all the motel's surveillance footage — you have no idea how much of that shit there was to go through, it was bloody epic — and we found what looks like a time-splice."

Spider stood there, opening and closing his mouth, but nothing came out. "And you determined this how exactly?"

"Well," she said, sipping her tea, "there's no trace of anybody entering the motel other than through the main entrance. The rear service door only opens from the inside, and showed no signs of tampering in any case. None of the residents — and we tracked an awful lot of their movements around the place — showed any interest in your capsule during the entire day. The only person, other than yourself accessing your capsule, was the hotel's maid. She changed the linen and left long before the attack. We've got footage of Future You arriving and going up to your capsule and climbing in. All his biometrics checked out, obviously."

"If you've got no indication of anybody entering who shouldn't have been there—"

"I know what you're thinking. There's evidence of a chrono incursion, and, like I said, a splice."

Someone in the future had used time travel to turn up inside the motel, inside his capsule? He thought about it for a moment. "What about the camera inside the capsule?"

Iris finished the last spoonful of porridge. "That's where we found evidence of the splice. The footage shows 'you' lying there on your bunk, then there's a bit of a jump in the signal, after which, well, it's blood everywhere and you — I mean, Future You—"

"I'm dead?"

Iris frowned, not sure how to put it. "No, not quite dead, not yet. The footage shows you trying to write that message. It's—" She took a breath. "It's hard to watch, frankly. You're bleeding out at a rate of knots..." She trailed off, staring at the floor, avoiding his gaze.

It was a hard thing to hear about. He tried to focus on the idea that Future Spider was someone else, from a different timeline. He, Present Spider, was not necessarily locked into that outcome. The fact that he didn't get busted for murdering Molly — that Molly was still alive — showed that whatever else his future self wanted to accomplish, he had prevented that. Which meant he, Present Spider, wouldn't end up murdered in that capsule, right? He tried telling himself this, and he believed it, up to a point, in his head, but that was all.

"So couldn't the killer just have disabled the camera for a few minutes?"

Iris got up to take her porridge bowl and teacup to the kitchen. Spider followed her. She was saying, "The camera showed no signs of tampering, and the monitoring system itself was okay." She ran a little water into the bowl to rinse it, then paused, looking out the small window. "Somebody went to a lot of trouble to kill that guy."

Leaning in the kitchen doorway, Spider was troubled, thinking that the only people who might pull such a stunt were likely to be agents from Zeropoint. He wondered how the hell he would go about talking to them, assuming they would even tell him anything. Spider said, "So, any chance you can get something out of the break in the footage?"

"Working on it, but..." She glanced at him and waggled her hand, looking glum. As she squeezed past him on her way back to the breakfast nook, their eyes met for a moment. She scowled and shook her head and kept going, found her coat hanging over a chair and went to put it on. Spider tried to help, but made a mess of it. "Let go!" Iris said, shrugging into the coat.

He let go, hands in the air, and watched Iris grab keys, handheld, and bag. He wanted to tell her how grateful he was for putting him up like this, and for potentially drawing the fire of whoever killed Future Spider, but everything he put together in his head to try to express this gratitude sounded, to him, stupid. In the end, he just managed to say, "Well, I just wanted to say, Iris, um—"

"You're welcome," she said, anticipating potential awkwardness and wanting to get through it as fast as possible. "So, what's on for today?"

"The usual. Broken time machines in one door, fixed ones out the other. Oh, and Dickhead wants to see me. That should be big fun."

"Fair enough. See you." She gave him a brief wave, and left, shutting the door behind her.

When Spider arrived at the shop, Malaria told him the phones had been going nuts with customers wanting their time machines looked at. She'd taken the liberty of arranging a schedule of appointments so he and Charlie could head out to see them all, find out what was what, and decide what would happen from there.

"Fine," he said, heading for the break room for an early jolt of coffee.

Malaria then told him the truly bad news. "Um, the coffee droid's actually on the blink, I'm sorry."

Spider was already in the break room, and now he stood staring at the recalcitrant machine. "Not working?" Iris's coffee droid had been broken, too. He started thinking there was a pattern here, or maybe the universe was plotting to keep him caffeine-free. It made as much sense as everything else going on.

"Maybe you could fix it?" she said.

"You're the coffee whiz, though, right?" he said, trying to sound reasonable.

Malaria shrugged elaborately, her head tilted over on one side. "Sorry. I only make brilliant coffee with working machinery."

"Crap," Spider said, thinking it was going to be one of those days.

"Oh, and Dickhead's coming by at lunchtime for a word."

"Yeah, I got a message last night. Any idea what he wants to talk about?"

More shrugging. "Dunno. D'you think you could get him to leave me alone, though?"

Startled, he looked at her. Spider knew Dickhead was quite taken with Malaria, and had tried to chat her up the other day. "He hasn't done anything, uh—?"

Seeing what Spider was thinking, she smiled and flapped her hands at him. "No, no, it's all right. It's nothing like that," she said. "It's just, he's always calling me up, and it's always supposedly about something to do with the shop, some bit of info he needs or some stupid thing, but he's always really chatty, asking me how my day's going, what I'm doing on the weekend, and all this, and it just... it kind of wigs me out a bit."

"It makes you uncomfortable?" Spider felt himself slipping into cop mode, and tried to stop it.

"A bit, yeah, I don't think he means anything by it. It's just, I don't know, it's hard to tell him to bugger off."

"You want me to have a quiet word in his pink and shell-like ear?"

"Would you mind?" She looked embarrassed at imposing on Spider's goodwill like this.

Spider dropped into a deep, dark and airy vocal impression. "Leave it to me," he said, doing his best to look sinister.

Malaria stared at him, surprised and puzzled.

Spider said, "Darth Vader?"

"Oh, *Star Wars*!" she said, getting it. "I've never seen it."

"How can you not have seen *Star Wars*?"

"I was homeschooled?"

"Oh, Malaria." He shook his head. "This weekend, when you're avoiding my boss, download yourself some *Star Wars* goodness. You won't regret it."

"Oooookay," she said, fobbing him off.

Spider could see he was not exactly making a convert. "Anyway..." he said, trailing off.

"Yeah, if you could get Dickhead off my back?"

"Consider it done. No bastard hassles my best reception-ist ever."

She grinned. "Thanks. Sorry I can't help with the coffee droid."

He shrugged. "Think nothing of it. I'll have a look at it."

"If you do get it to work," she said, "could you make me a latte?"

So, one busted coffee droid, he thought. *How hard could it be to fix something like this? After all, I fix time machines for a living.* There was no way a coffee droid could be harder to fix than a time machine, surely. Then again, he reflected, time machines were the only machines he knew how to fix. And it sounded as if he was set for a big day exam-ining the bloody things, and with that many potential clients, the odds that one of them would involve a dead cat in the works were damn good. His talk with Iris had left him feeling like she was starting to regret having him staying with her. Not that she'd said anything, of course. There was just a certain chill in the air this morning that he felt only too acutely. Maybe it was that moment in the hallway when they squeezed past each other and their eyes met, and she'd looked away, like he reminded her of some-thing disgusting. He knew she was already getting flak at work for even knowing him, let alone for helping him. Knowing the way gossip worked in the Police Service, probably everybody imagined she was sleeping with him — *if only!* He swore, pissed off, trying to keep the past in the past instead of stinking up the present.

This left him staring once more at the machine. He sighed and called out, "Malaria?"

She appeared in the doorway. "Can you fix it?"

"Take some money out of petty cash, go to the bloody shops, and get us some instant coffee."

She saw the look on his face. "Okay," she said, and hurried out again.

Spider went into his office, which was a mess, and slumped behind his desk, rubbing his face.

Charlie appeared in the doorway. He had his oversized white lab coat on, and looked lost in it, as always. "Boss, all set?"

Time to hit the road, he thought. "Yeah, whatever," he said, got up and grabbed his own lab coat. With a little luck, Dickhead would turn up while they were out. He stopped himself at that point. No, he wanted to talk to the idiot. On the way to the van, he told Malaria to have Dickhead call him if he turned up while they were out.

"Check!" she said, saluting ironically.

The morning ground along, one stupid time machine after another. Again and again, clueless owners told him they never even thought to read the owner's manuals that came with their units, and they only wanted to — for example — visit the near-future to find out the winning Lotto numbers, or — God, the cliché of it — the results of horse races or football matches so they could, and this is how they almost all phrased it, "Make a killing!" There were guys — and they were nearly always guys, he noticed as the day went along — who fancied their chances speculating on the financial markets, and who complained to him that the machine was obviously busted because for some stupid reason it wouldn't let them find out such information. A few geniuses, faced with such frustration, attempted to find information about this phenomenon online, visited some tech-support forums, and learned that the DOTAS firmware in every time machine sold in Australia actively prevented operators from acquiring information that might be used for illegal gain.

The more advanced tech-support forums contained detailed advice for illegally subverting this firmware, or indeed, removing it entirely, even though removing it would render the unit inoperable. Spider had met these clowns so many times since he started working on time machines that it was like he could smell them coming, that whiff of magical thinking, the thought process that made you think, "If only I had a time machine, I could be incredibly bloody rich!" The firmware was not a perfect solution. Sometimes a user genuinely wanted to visit the near future in order to find out something other than sports or financial results. The firmware would also prevent people going back to the stock market crash of 1929 with the intent of buying up crashed stocks and making a killing that way. "How's it know what I'm trying to do?" these frustrated would-be moguls always complained. "How can it possibly know?"

Spider understood, up to a point, how the firmware worked, but he preferred to tell people, "The machine can smell your greed." This was not strictly acceptable under the Mission Statement of Time Machines Repaired While-U-Wait, which was all about customer satisfaction and courtesy and so forth. Then again, nobody ever complained to Dickhead about it, because they'd have to admit they were up to no good.

So, it was a typical day inspecting machines and talking to idiot owners. After the last visit, Spider had an idea. He said, "I don't know about you, Charlie, I think we need a break."

Charlie nodded. "Yeah, know what you mean. Ideas?"

"As it happens," he said, "I have had this one idea. You remember that guy, Mr. Vincent, with the Tempo and the—"

"Oh, Mr. Bug-Eyes, yeah." He mimed to indicate the ugly eye-plug memory prostheses Vincent wore that day. "Yeah. What a wanker."

"I feel like dropping by for a visit."

"You do? What about your meeting with the boss?"

"Malaria will call if he shows. In the meantime we can get the details of who Vincent bought that Tempo from."

"He did say he probably erased the info, boss."

"He did. But who knows?" Spider said. He was thinking that probably the same DOTAS unit that took command of everything to do with the dead woman had also been to see Mr. Vincent and put the fear of God into him and then trashed his entire house searching for that same information. But maybe not, he thought. "So, you up for it?" he asked Charlie.

"Beats talking to these other dropkicks, boss."

"Lay in a course for Mr. Vincent's residence, Mr. Stuart," Spider said, starting to feel more upbeat.

CHAPTER 12

Mr. Vincent, still with the horrifying eye-plugs, was home when Spider and Charlie turned up. He invited them into his huge and obnoxious house, which was nearly empty. Enormous, high-ceilinged rooms, huge media walls, but very little furniture. Spider felt furious, seeing such casually displayed luxury — all this space — wasted on a twit like Vincent.

"I've been meaning to call you," Vincent said, grinning, a little embarrassed, working his watchtop, where he located a file, which he sent to Spider's watchtop. "That's the receipt I got from the guy I bought the Tempo from."

Spider was reading. There wasn't much to it, just a handwritten note on a bit of ordinary notepaper, indicating that Mr. Simon Vincent had fully paid Mr. Ian Fry for a second-hand Tempus Tempo 300 time travel device, including its trailer. Mr. Fry's signature was an unreadable scribble along the bottom of the page. Fortunately, though, it did list the man's address and contact details.

All of which was very good, Spider thought, standing there looking at Vincent and then at Charlie. Maybe a little too good. Vincent had been pretty certain when asked previously if he had this document, and had told Spider how he'd recently purged a lot of useless crap from his household systems, possibly including this very thing. Now here it was, easy to find, no trouble at all.

"Well, then," Charlie said, grinning but looking anxious to get away. In the cavernous room his voice echoed a little.

Vincent said, "The guy said I could call him any time if I needed any help with the Tempo, but I never did, even when I started having problems. Kind of embarrassed, you know how it is. You don't want to look like a twit, huh?" He laughed, too loud, a little nervously. He rubbed the back of his neck.

The sight of his grinning mouth combined with those big, black, faceted plugs where his eyes should be was hard to take. He knew Vincent could *see* him and Charlie just fine. The harder thing to accept was that those plugs were also antennas which allowed Vincent to see great, white-water torrents of ambient data. It made Spider anxious and made him think about the way things changed much too quickly. And how only a few years ago people fretted about the arrival of something called the "singularity," an un-stoppable, inconceivable rush of technological change that would transform everything. And Spider was still waiting! This was not the world of the future he'd been promised when he was a kid. This wasn't even the future he'd been promised in the early years of the twenty-first century. This was something entirely else, and he wanted to give it back, like something shop-soiled or the wrong size, and get some-thing more to his liking. This future he was living in was too much like the past he knew so well. Yes, there were time machines, and people like Mr. Vincent who put out his own eyes so he could have ghastly fly's-eye implants instead, but the world around Spider, at least in Perth, was very much like he had always known it, only bigger and more exhausting.

Charlie nudged him, and he blinked, startled for a moment. He looked around, saw again this immensity of empty space with which Vincent surrounded himself. He hated that he felt so envious, that he wished, at some embarrassing level, that he could go back to school and learn the things Vincent had learned that let him make this kind of money — except even going back to technical col-lege would cost him money he didn't have, short of begging Molly for a loan.

"Is there anything else?" Vincent asked, keen to get back to whatever he'd been doing.

Spider was about to shake his head and say no, thanks, the receipt was all they needed — but then he stopped, and remembered something. He said, "Listen, the day we came to pick up your Tempo—"

Vincent laughed, "Yeah, didn't that go well, huh?"

Surprised, Spider said, "You know the unit was destroyed?"

"Yeah, you told me that night."

"I never told you that. This is the first time—"

"No, not you. I meant, someone from your shop?"

Spider and Charlie exchanged looks. "Someone from the shop came out here and told you what had happened?"

"Yeah. That night. Offered me a thousand bucks compensation, cash, if I didn't say anything, and signed this gag-order thing."

"Which you signed?"

"Shit, yes! Some bastard turns up wanting to give me a thousand bucks, yeah you bet I said yes! You said yourself the machine was a dud, so what the hell? Didn't matter to me."

Spider thought about this. "I said the machine was a potential bomb, that there was something really spooky going on with it."

"You thought it was a dud, I know you did. And you were right, too, probably. I mean, that's why you get the big bucks, right?" He grinned, not trying to be mean about it.

Spider didn't take it that way. He could only see Mr. Vincent lording his wealth over him, how losing an expensive, though second-hand, time machine was no great loss. Spider kept thinking that if he'd lost something that had cost that kind of money, it would bloody-well hurt, because it had taken so long to save up all that money, or it had cost so much to get a loan for it, or whatever. He took a breath, trying to calm himself. "Yeah. Right."

It fell to Charlie to ask the obvious question. "So, Mr. Vincent, the fellow who came out to tell you about your machine: did he leave a card or anything?"

Vincent smiled, nodded. "Oh yeah. Hang on." He popped his watch, sorted through a bunch of files, found the card, and beamed it over to Charlie. "There you go." When Charlie indicated he'd received it on his watch,

Vincent said to them both, now looking a bit wary, "Are you guys trying to tell me he isn't with you?"

Charlie shot Spider the card. Spider had to admit, looking at it on his own watch, it certainly looked legitimate. Spider closed his watch-screen and said to Vincent, "The fellow you spoke to, could you maybe describe him?"

"He wasn't from your shop?"

"No."

Vincent stared at the floor and rubbed his neck some more. "I'm sure they said they were from Malaga. He knew all about my Tempo."

Charlie reminded him, "Could you give us some kind of rough description?"

"But why would he do that? Why would he pretend like that?"

Spider was getting impatient, so he tried changing tack. "This guy, did he tell you anything about what destroyed your Tempo?"

"Nah, he just said it blew up when you tried to fix it — that nobody was hurt, which was good, 'cause for a moment there, I was worried sick, thinking, God, I'm responsible! It was horrible. But he said it was fine, no harm done, other than my machine being toast."

"He didn't say what they found inside it?"

"No, why? What was inside it?"

Charlie looked at Spider. Spider shrugged, and said to Vincent, "Another time machine, and a woman, a dead woman."

Mr. Vincent paused a moment, then stared at them both with his eye-plugs. "*No shit!* Really?"

"Really," Spider said. "Now, if you could just give us that description?"

"So how'd she die?"

"That description, if you wouldn't mind?"

"No, you gotta tell me, I mean, you've told me all this other stuff, you've gotta tell me that. C'mon!"

Spider stared at the floor and tried to get his breathing to settle down. He gave Mr. Vincent the bare-bones version of what he knew about Clea Fassbinder's demise, which wasn't much, but it appeared to satisfy Mr. Vincent, who, clearly still amazed at the whole thing, gave them a rough description of his own visitor that night.

"You're sure about this, Mr. Vincent?"

"Pretty sure," he said. Spider could tell he didn't give half a shit about it, that he was much more amazed to learn about his old time machine's unlikely cargo. "God, if I'd only known. Wait'll I tell my girlfriend!" He was grinning happily, glad to have a bit of tragic violence enter his life, if only indirectly.

Spider and Charlie could not wait to leave. Once they were back on the road, with Charlie driving once more, Charlie said, "That description mean anything to you, boss?"

Spider had been thinking about the description, trying to match it against people he knew, but was coming up blank. "Charlie, I think we just stumbled across an actual Section Ten spook going about a bit of clean-up."

"Shit," Charlie said, genuinely shocked.

Spider was looking at the image of the business card Vincent had given them. It looked exactly right. Not that it was in any way difficult to fake up a business card; what bothered Spider was the gnawing thought that somehow those Section Ten guys might have figured out *who* Clea Fassbinder was and what was going on in the bigger picture. He assumed the Section Ten spooks also had probably figured out who'd killed her, and that they wouldn't tell anyone. It would be their little secret. Spider figured they would keep the details to themselves in case they ever needed the killer to do something for them, in which case they would have tremendous leverage to use against him.

Spider idly fantasized that it would be cool if James Rutherford could help him sneak into Section Ten so he could access the Fassbinder file and make a copy. It would absolutely work in a cheesy spy movie, but in this world, it could never happen. James did have high-level DOTAS access, but that would cut no ice with Section Ten. What Spider needed was a buddy in Section Ten. He wondered, for a moment, if James knew anybody like that.

Just stop, he told himself, sitting back in his seat, taking some calming breaths. *You're not a cop, and you're not investigating anything. You're just some poor bastard fixing time machines. Nothing more, nothing less. However Clea Fassbinder met her death, it's not your business. You do not need to know.*

But he *did* need to know. From the first time he had seen Clea Fassbinder's pale and lifeless body, awash in drying blood, right there in the parking lot of his time machine repair shop, he knew he was bound to her. She was "on his patch," as they used to say — on his turf. He owed it to her to find out what happened, and who was responsible. He'd done his best all these years to shut away all of that part of him that loved being a policeman. But that night, faced with that woman's blood-smeared face, he'd felt something snap deep inside him. He'd told himself, right up until that moment, that he could more or less manage with just being a time machine repairman, where the greatest, most compelling mysteries at hand were figuring out what was making some time machine make that strange rattling sound when it was idling, or where that bad smell was coming from. It wasn't much, and it didn't pay much, but he could be his own boss, to some extent. Dickhead was a pain, but not a huge pain. Dickhead was just doing his own job. It was simple, honest work, even if ninety percent of time machine owners turned out to be inattentive idiots who had no business going anywhere near such things. It was a living, and all things considered, particularly the way his police career had turned out, probably more than he deserved.

It was a little after 4:00 pm when they pulled into the shop's parking area. Charlie asked Spider if he was all right; he'd gone quiet. Spider nodded absently, waved him off, and headed inside; he didn't respond when Malaria told him she'd gone to get the instant coffee, and that she could only get a small jar because she only had twenty dollars on her. He nodded, waved again, and closed his office door. It took a few moments to convert his desk into a bed, and he lay down, his eyes closed, trying to take everything in, the way his mind was blasting memories and ideas and faces and voices at him. The look in Clea Fassbinder's eyes. The smell of her death.

He wished he was in on it. He hated the idea that something juicy and interesting was going on and he was stuck on the outside, frustrated. He hated even more this feeling of needing to be involved, as if finding out the circumstances surrounding a tragic death was somehow secondary to the real issue. It felt horribly like a narcotic craving. All these years he'd been straight and clean, getting through each day, one day at a time, but the craving had never gone away. He knew he missed investigating the awful things people did to one another, finding out what drove people, cleaning up after them. It was appalling, filthy, dispiriting work most times, quite lacking in glamor or even excitement — but it didn't matter. He was helping to straighten things out, to solve hideous, blood-soaked puzzles. He had always missed that part of it. God, how he'd missed it!

He found himself staring at the note Mr. Vincent had sent to his watchtop, the copy of the receipt he'd gotten from Ian Fry. Fry's contact details were right there. The phone number had been automagically turned into a clickable link. He tapped his phone patch, got dial tone, then touched Fry's number. It connected, and started ringing.

Spider said to himself, *I can quit anytime!*

Fry answered. "Speak now or forever hold your peace," he said.

They talked a few minutes. Spider told Mr. Fry that he was trying to trace the original owner of the Tempo 300 Mr. Fry had sold to Mr. Vincent. Fry gave Spider a first name, Jules, and a phone number, and said that was all he had. "He told me that he'd only owned the thing a few weeks and was selling it because he'd just taken a full-time job up north."

"That's a shame," Spider said, "nice new machine like that."

"Rules," Fry said. "No time machines around mining sites. Bad for business."

It was true, for the same reason you didn't want people with time machines going to 1929 to pick up bargain stocks.

"Did this Jules fellow mention if he bought the machine new?"

"No, he got it from a used time machine dealer in Cannington."

"Which one?" There were several, many of them former used car dealers who had branched out into the exciting new world of chronotechnology. Spider suddenly realized that Dickhead owned a share in one such used time machine dealership. *That would be way too circular*, he said to himself.

Mr. Fry heard him. "What was that?"

"Sorry. Um, so, you don't have the name of the dealer this Jules bought his machine from?"

"Nah, sorry, mate."

"Okay, no worries."

Fry said, "Cheers!" and was gone.

Spider was thinking. He had the dodgy Tempo's DOTAS registration code. And there were only so many used time machine dealers in Cannington. He wondered if he could get Malaria to track down which of those dealerships sold it. It was in no way official business. It was even, it could be argued, a waste of her valuable time. To say nothing, as noted previously, of it being in so many ways none of Spider's business.

"Yeah, but how long could it take?" he said to himself, sounding, he thought, very reasonable. Maybe if he told Malaria there was no rush on the info. Just something she could chase up when she wasn't busy fielding calls from idiots.

He sighed, thinking: *Spider, you are one sick puppy. Get some help. Now. You're not a policeman anymore. Just stop it. Stop it now.*

Nodding, feeling a little ashamed, he said to himself, *But I just want to know. That's all. I just... want... to know.*

His phone rang, and he nearly jumped out of his bed with shock.

It was Dickhead. "Sorry I've been delayed. On my way now. Should be there in twenty minutes or so, depending on traffic."

Bloody Dickhead, Spider thought, surprisingly glad for the interruption. A sort-of welcome reminder of Spider's actual responsibilities, like those damned key-point indicators, and the all-important need to achieve higher throughput, higher turnover, higher cash flow, and the endless, often bitter debate over whether to concentrate on simple, quick jobs which would pay modestly but often, or focus on big, expensive jobs that would take a long time, but pay very well. How many times over the years had he had this argument with Dickhead? How many times had he told the bastard that if he'd just give Spider some more staff they could maybe do a "dynamic mix" — a phrase Dickhead had quite admired — of simple and complex jobs, depending on what they had in the workshop at any given time.

Dickhead had always insisted, though, that he had this algorithm that specified just how many staff Spider could have and still maintain profitability, and the bad news was that Spider had the correct number already. More staff meant more overhead, and that meant he'd miss those key-point indicators, fail to hit quarterly targets, and so on, and that wouldn't do. He didn't want to have to close the Malaga branch, and break up the great team of Spider and Charlie. They just had to work harder, and work smarter, he told Spider. That's all there was to it. After all, the Cannington shop managed a higher turnover of jobs with only one full-time service technician and two part-time guys. Why couldn't Spider and Charlie do the same?

There were times when arguing with Dickhead McMahon made Spider want to slash his wrists open and have a nice hot bath. It was like arguing with a machine: McMahon never tired, never got flustered, never lost his temper. He could argue anyone to a standstill. And always, when you were finished arguing with the man, he would leave you with the impression that somehow you'd won the debate, by agreeing with his position. It was a strange sensation. And now he was coming in to go another few rounds with Spider on a day when, quite honestly, that warm bath looked very attractive.

Dickhead arrived a few minutes later. Spider intercepted him at the entrance to the shop, and before the boss could harass Malaria, Spider guided him through to his office. Exactly how he would get Dickhead to leave Malaria alone, or at least to keep his interactions with her on a professional basis, he did not know. Dickhead, after all, would say he was only being friendly, not grasping that there was a difference between "friendly" and "polite." Spider sighed, and followed his boss into the office, and shut the door.

"What, no coffee?" Dickhead asked as he parked himself in one of the guest chairs.

"We have instant," Spider said, warily.

"Good fucking God, Spider! What kind of operation are you running here?"

"The droid's out of commission."

Dickhead listened, nodded very seriously, making a show of calculating complex numbers in his head, and said, "And? I was under the impression that you were in the 'repairing things that are busted' line of work."

"We are in that line of work, for values of 'things' limited strictly to time machines. Nobody here has time to fix a stupid coffee machine. Perhaps you might lend your own considerable skills to the task?"

"You do realize that hospitality to one's employer is an important part of your responsibilities here, don't you?"

"And do you realize, Dickhead, that you're keeping me from actually working on my backlog of jobs, right?"

Here Dickhead smiled in a way that appeared to take up more room than his large face allowed. Even his smile had a zone-of-control. He said, glancing about, as if to make sure nobody was listening, "Forget the bloody coffee, Spider. I'm here regarding another matter, something rather more important, if you take my meaning?" The old bastard looked sly, saying this.

Spider knew he was going to regret what he was about to say, but he said, "Oh?"

"You're not exactly happy in this job, are you, Spider?"

Uh-oh, Spider thought. *Where's he going with this?* "I wouldn't say that, Dickhead."

McMahon shrugged a little, leaned back in his chair, hands folded across his considerable belly. Spider was sure he was going to fall over backwards if he kept that up, but knew not to say anything. His boss said, "In any case, an opportunity has come up, you might say."

Spider sat down. "I'm pretty comfortable right where I am, you know." The last time Spider had expressed eagerness at one of Dickhead's suggestions, he'd wound up in this line of work. If he was indeed being offered something new, he could only assume that whatever it was, it would also be a miserable experience and he'd still be plagued with demands that he keep up his KPIs and turnover and all the rest of the tedious, busywork management shit he had to put up with now.

"You're comfortable where you are now, are you?" Dickhead said, not buying it. "Have you looked at yourself in a mirror lately? You look like you're sitting on sharpened nails. You look like you think eating raw shit from an open sewer might offer you greater job satisfaction. You look, in short, like you want a change, Spider, and — and hear me out here, son — I'm here to offer you just what you want." He smiled slightly, looking mischievous.

Spider reflected for a moment. Would it do any harm to at least hear what he had to say? He could still say no. He hadn't signed anything.

Then again, he thought, he had very few workplace rights in this job. It was within Dickhead's power to make acceptance of this new "opportunity" a condition of keeping any kind of job with him. Accept the opportunity, or lose your current job. Unemployment was no way to try to live. He'd never get Molly back without some kind of income, without prospects. And even Mrs. Ng, who offered the cheapest rent in Perth, wouldn't have him, either.

"All right, then," Spider said, watching Dickhead as if his boss were a bomb that might explode in his face at any moment, "tell me more."

At that moment a figure in black flashed into existence right behind Dickhead's chair.

Spider froze for a moment, panicking — the figure had a gun — but then he recognized him, and swore. "Oh fuck-a-bloody-duck," he said.

Dickhead, surprised at Spider's sudden outburst, looked around behind him, and saw an old man with buzzcut silver hair in a black commando outfit, and then he saw the gun, which was pointed at his head. This, the way Spider saw it, appeared perfectly fine with Dickhead, who said to the old man, "Is that the best you could do, Spider?"

Surprised, Spider said, "What?" He had, from time to time, faced people with guns during his police career, but not often, and he had never had to fire a shot in anger. But that was then, and the visceral terror he felt right now, the fear that at any moment things could go very bad indeed and both he and Dickhead could die, was all he could think about. He wanted, he was embarrassed to realize, to dive under his desk and hide, but he couldn't, not with Dickhead there as well.

This left Spider staring at the new guy, and shaking his head with disappointment. Yes, the new guy was another future version of himself. This one, much older than the last visitor from the future Spider had met, looked like a veteran special-operations commando; you could see it in the way he carried the gun, the look in his eyes, even the way he *stood*, Spider noticed, spoke of long and bitter experience in some kind of warfare.

Less obvious, and more frankly terrifying, was the way Dickhead sat there looking hugely amused at the whole scene — and the fact, Spider now remembered, that he had called the old soldier, "Spider." As if he knew this soldier version of Spider very well. He closed his eyes, wishing he were anywhere else. Why couldn't he be left alone, left in peace? What was it about the bloody future that made these latter-day versions of himself think they needed to come back and bother him? More to the point, he thought, staring at this old, military version of himself, since when was he likely to become some kind of hardcore commando? Yes, he'd once been a cop, but that was different. *I mean*, he said to himself, *look at him! He could cut your throat before you even had time to blink! How the hell do I wind up turning into that?*

"All right, then," he said to his two visitors. "You, put the gun away."

"Uh, no," Soldier Spider said. "You're coming with me."

Then Dickhead, who still looked like he was having a fine time, said to the soldier while staring calmly at Spider, "No, I'm afraid he's coming with me. It's his destiny."

Spider stared between them, starting to panic. "My destiny? My fucking destiny? Who the hell are you and what have you done with the real Dickhead McMahon, for God's sake?"

Dickhead told Spider, "It's time, Spider, for you to learn the Final Secret of the Cosmos. It's—"

Spider was starting to panic. "I, what? You—"

Soldier Spider said to Dickhead, "Again with that messianic bullshit, Dickhead?"

"But--" Spider said, staring from one to the other, and then back to the muzzle of Soldier Spider's gun.

Soldier Spider shook his head, disgusted, and said to Spider, "Look. I don't have time for this shit."

Dickhead, a weird gleam in his eyes, turned to look up at the intruder. "Oh, so what are you going to do, Spider, shoot me? You know that won't—"

Soldier Spider shot Dickhead in the back of his head, which burst apart. There was a lot of blood.

Spider, spattered with gore, sat stunned, not breathing, hardly able to hear anything.

The office door swung open. Charlie burst in, took in the scene, went pale, and said something Spider couldn't hear properly.

Soldier Spider turned and said something to Charlie. He backed out and closed the door behind him. Faintly, Spider heard a high-pitched scream, probably from Malaria.

The gun in Soldier Spider's hand swung around to face Spider. "Can. You. Hear. Me. Now?" he said.

Blinking, aware of his heart booming hard in his throat, Spider nodded. "Sort of. I'm..." He indicated his ears, that they weren't working.

"I. Need. You. To. Come. With. Me., Spider."

"No. No fucking way."

Soldier Spider sighed and shook his head.

Present Spider, trembling with shock and rage, got up from his seat, glanced around at the walls, took in the way Dickhead's annoying motivational posters — DETERMINATION; DISCIPLINE; WILLPOWER — all featuring luminous angelic beings and spectacular cloud-scapes — were now spattered with blood and gore. Spider felt things in his head starting to shift around, starting to maybe understand.

Soldier Spider brought up the gun. "Don't. Just don't."

Spider approached the soldier. "I'm not going with you. I want no part of it. So fuck off."

"Shit," Soldier Spider said.

Spider boiled over. Screaming, he lunged at Soldier Spider until Soldier Spider brought the gun back up and aimed it at Spider's head, and Spider stopped in his tracks, just a meter from the gun's muzzle, breathing huge gulps. His heart either stopped entirely or was going so fast he couldn't feel it anymore, and he stood there, staring at the gun, smelling gore and gunsmoke, only too aware that he was covered in hot and stinking bits of Dickhead—

"Now, then," Soldier Spider said. "You and me, we have to talk."

CHAPTER 13

Spider managed to say, "No."

"No?" Soldier Spider asked, then paused a moment, thinking, then said, "Oh yeah. I said no. Right."

Spider became aware that warm, stinking urine was running down his leg, and he swore to himself. "Great, now I'm pissing my pants. Thanks ever so much," he said.

Soldier Spider nodded, looking a little chagrined. "Hmm. Let's see. When this was me, future me said something that made me go along with him. What the hell was it?"

"Damned if I know." The whole universe had come down to the muzzle of that gun, black and forbidding. Poised there, watching the gun, only too aware that his future self still had his finger on the trigger, as if he was still anticipating having to maybe shoot his way out of the situation if things didn't work out. Spider could hardly hear anything, but he could feel his whole head vibrating with the throb of his pulse, and he was very hot, yet shivery, sweating, alive with tension.

"Oh, the hell with it," Soldier Spider said, the gun still leveled at Spider, as he reached into his pocket for what proved to be some sort of key ring. He touched a control—

And Spider was back in his office, alone, waiting for Dickhead to show up, and thinking about razor blades and warm baths when the man in black showed up, gun already drawn, next to Spider's chair. For a moment Spider remained unaware anything had happened, but then noticed a dark shape next to him where none had been before. He turned, saw the gun, saw the old soldier attached to the gun, and saw him reach for a key ring—

And Spider's office flashed away, to be replaced by a gray cell. There was a sturdy metal table in the middle of the room, and two chairs, one on either side, and Spider was there with this soldier fellow. It was cold, smelled bad, and Spider knew he was in huge trouble.

His captor sat in the opposite chair, and put his gun on the table in front of him. He smiled wearily. "Welcome to the End of Bloody Time, Spider."

"Oh shit," Spider said, recognizing the phrase from his meeting with the first Future Spider, and feeling utterly screwed, just like Future Spider had promised. Looking around, sniffing the air, it occurred to him that this was not exactly what he pictured when he thought about the "End of Time."

"It took some doing, getting you here."

Spider, only too aware of that gun, did his best to keep calm. He sat back in the chair, crossed his arms, and looked at the figure in black. The guy looked familiar, maybe a bit like his dad, if his dad had ever gone into the military. He said, "Look. Take me home. I don't know what you're up to, or why you've brought me here, but I'm guessing it's something to do with Zeropoint, and I've gotta tell you, mate, I'm just not interested. Not. Interested."

"Is that right, Spider?"

"Not interested, even a tiny bit."

"You don't even know why—"

"I know it's bad, whatever it is. I know it's trouble."

"How could you possibly know that?"

"I dunno. Maybe the whole kidnapping thing rubbed me the wrong way."

"You wouldn't have come if we'd just asked you politely, maybe sent you an engraved invitation, all RSVP, and dress smart casual, now would you?"

The idea tickled Spider's sense of humor. "Actually, that might have got my attention."

"So here we are, then," the guy said.

"We are indeed. I'm guessing this place is nowhere good."

He took in his surroundings. They were in a very small room with what looked to be steel walls, painted gray. There were a great many exposed pipes and conduit bundles. In one wall was a hatch that looked far too small for a normal-sized man to get through. The air, now that Spider stopped to notice, tasted metallic, and thin, as if it was being rationed. And, if he listened, there was a quiet background hum, and he could hear other people moving about and talking outside.

"So," Spider said, "this is some kind of ship?"

The older man nodded, but looked nonplused. "Yup, 'fraid so. She's a timeship, and our last redoubt. We call her the *Masada*."

"*Masada*? As in the siege of...?"

"The very one, yeah."

"Hope things go better for you guys than they did for those guys."

"Us, too, Spider, believe me."

"Well, then," he said, taking it in. "Gosh. An actual timeship." He folded his arms.

"Not much to look at, I know," the soldier said. "I brought you here for two reasons. One, the ship is mostly flux-proof, so—"

Spider was surprised that he more or less understood what the guy might mean by this term. He said, sure he was probably wrong, but maybe not, "Causality attacks can't inadvertently delete your whole existence, right?"

"More or less, yeah."

"So how does that work?"

The guy looked pained for a moment, trying to remain calm and affable. "Like I say, there are things I can and can't tell you. Thing is, I just needed somewhere I could talk to you in peace, without being disturbed. Nobody can bop in from some other time to try and rescue you. It's a bit like the Bat Cave. Creates a temporary bubble of space-time separate from the manifold, more or less. Takes a whole shitload of energy to run it, but it's worthwhile for the sake of not being interrupted by well-meaning idiots trying to come and save you from our eeeeeeeeeevil clutches." He mimed cartoonishly evil clutches, the sort of thing Spider would have done, and that made Spider laugh — and then hated himself for laughing, for relaxing his guard.

"Well, you wouldn't want that, would you?" Spider said, making a show of "understanding," while still completely pissed off at getting shanghaied here in the first place.

The old man, acknowledging Spider's response, carried on with the briefing. "I'm only authorized to show you certain parts of the ship, at least at this point."

"Uh-huh," Spider said, refusing to engage with the whole thing — though he was, despite his best efforts, intrigued by the idea of a flux-proof timeship.

"Must admit," the man in black said, "I'm a little hurt that you haven't realized who I am yet. The previous times, you—"

"Previous times?"

"Like I said, it took some doing getting you here."

Spider scratched his nose, and took a closer look at his captor. Definite resemblance to his dad, but only up to a point. The eyes were the wrong color, and the nose — he peered at the man's nose from each side, and noticed a familiar scar, almost hidden by age. All at once Spider realized who this man was. He stared, wide-eyed, touching his own face, and sagged, feeling defeated, into his chair. "Shit," he said, matter-of-factly.

"Hello, Spider," his future self said.

"Hello, your treacherous self."

"You think so little of your own future choices?"

"I'm just disappointed in myself. At some point, for some reason, and no doubt against all my better judgement, I appear to have decided to play along with you clowns, and, from the look of you, I'm guessing hijinks ensued."

Soldier Spider smiled, thinking back. "Yeah, hijinks have indeed ensued."

Spider was shaking his head, pissed off at himself. "So," he said, "was it at least something, you know, good and worthwhile that got me to sell myself out?"

The old man in black took a long moment to think about this. At length, he said, "At the time, and this is going back a long while now, when I was where you are now, I didn't think anything could get me to help these bastards. I was furious, just furious, not just at being kidnapped, not just at being so thoroughly fucked around with — I mean that weird business with that other Future Spider was still fresh in my memory, plus," he paused, shaking his head, "the murdered future me, and, of course, sleeping with Iris... I was just fed up to the back bloody teeth with all this time travel bullshit! I'd had a bellyful! All I wanted to do was go back and fix stupid time machines for stupid owners so they could go off and do stupid things with them. I'd always hated the whole time travel thing, but compared to all this other stuff, the plotting and scheming, the whole 'Secret Squirrel' thing" — He sighed, remembering every-thing— "Well, it made being a time machine repairman look pretty damn sweet, to be honest."

It was eerie, Spider thought, watching and listening to this. The old man really knew him, to a degree that was downright spooky, like a violation, only of course it wasn't, not at all. For the old guy, Spider's current life, such as it was, was a distant memory, something he'd given up for some greater good, but which he still remembered, from time to time, and hated that he'd been living such a shitty life. Spider thought about it, allowing himself, just for the sake of argument, to consider the possibility that there might be something worthwhile in his future, if he would only accept this dubious fate.

If he were to go along with all this nonsense, would he miss anything? Sleeping in a smelly, stale plastic capsule at Mrs. Ng's, eating not much more than instant noodles and similar shitty stuff because it was all he could afford? No, he wouldn't miss that. He would miss Molly, he knew, and his mum and dad. And Charlie, who made getting through each day at the shop that much easier, a good and unexpected friend to him at a time when he'd had no friends. For that matter, he even quite liked young Malaria, though he hardly knew her.

He found himself picturing Iris Street in his mind's eye. Not the cold female inspector she was now, but the Iris he'd known when they were both young. Their affair, if you could call it that, had lasted no more than ten breathtaking days, but what days those had been! Even at the time he'd known the relationship was a hopeless cause. Iris, always ambitious, was already planning her ascent through the Police Service, putting in long, hard hours studying, reading old case files, training, always training, doing her damndest to be the best, most go-getter copper she could possibly be. After they'd made love, and they were lying there tangled together, and he marvelled at her spectacular passion and sublime body, she'd be talking about how she wanted to make inspector before she turned thirty-five. It wasn't what he'd had in mind by way of pillow talk. More recently, when he had been around Iris, remembering those extraordinary ten days, it was hard to believe this was the same woman — and yet he sometimes caught himself wondering, particularly late at night trying to get comfortable on her couch, aware of her natural scent everywhere, if she still harbored those same amazing passions. And realizing, well, yes, she evidently did still have at least some access to that part of herself, if what she blushingly admitted about her night with the other Future Spider was to be believed.

Spider, sitting there, overwhelmed with strangeness, found himself reaching for the familiar, for things he already knew, for the world he might well have lost. Thinking about Iris, and what he knew about her — that she might be part of the whole Zeropoint apparatus. Could she have deliberately lied to him about that night with his Future Self? It was a maddening thought, the kind of thought that led nowhere good — but at least it was a familiar kind of madness, a madness he could understand. The alternative, to embrace this Future Spider's world and perspective, was a pathway to an entirely unfamiliar, terrifying madness, and Spider was determined to resist.

With that decided, he said to his future self, "I'm not prepared to give up my former life."

Soldier Spider smiled and nodded, in a way that Spider was learning to hate. The old man said, "Nobody wants you to give that up."

This was the last thing he expected. Uncertain, he said, "So I'm going back to my life?"

"Of course," Soldier Spider said. "What did you think was going to happen?"

Spider shook his head and rubbed his face. "If you're really me, you know damn well what I was thinking."

He smiled again. "Yes, we want you to help us. That's correct. We're in trouble. Things are bleak."

"How bleak?" Spider said.

"Well, since you ask..." the old man said, "This gets kind of involved, and there's quite a lot to take in, but I'll try to be brief."

"Oh good," Spider said, not looking forward to the presentation at all. "An info-dump!"

The future Spider smiled wryly. "Now, now. No need to be rude."

Spider grinned for a moment, despite himself. "Sorry."

"Okay. Where to start?"

"You said this is the 'End of Time.' My first thought, I have to say, is, 'Bullshit!'"

The old man laughed. "Yeah, that's right." He nodded a moment, remembering, then turned more serious. "Thing is, though, it's true."

"Yeah, but what does it mean? I mean, how can something like time have an ending?"

"You'd be surprised," he said. "Maybe even a little alarmed."

"Ooooh," Spider said. "I'm all scared."

Ignoring Spider's sarcasm, Soldier Spider explained that the "End of Time" was a term of convenience.

"Well, to give you some idea," he said, "matter is long dead. There are no galaxies, no planets, no rocks or stray moons. No stars, either. All there is, is space itself. Wait, that's not precisely true. There are 'things' still eking out a sort of existence, things adapted to this environment, if you can call it that, and if you can call their agonizingly slow metabolic activity 'life.' Anyway. The thing is, the entire fabric of space-time is flinging itself apart, faster than the speed of light. It's kind of hard to visualize." Spider told him he was right about that, and asked about the Einsteinian idea of things not being able to reach the speed of light.

Soldier Spider looked bleak. "He was right. But I'm not talking about things moving *through* space-time; I'm talking about space-time itself. It's not covered by that rule."

Spider had thought about this, as much as he could, and said, "So if there's not much here, what's the big war about?"

And his future self sighed. "What's it all about? It's about many things. It's complicated."

"Try me," Spider said, not in the mood for evasive bullshit.

"I don't remember being that dubious when I was you."

"Things change."

Uncomfortable, Soldier Spider launched into an explanation. "There are two main problems. One is more tractable than the other. The more tractable problem concerns the other Zeropoint operation, which is, possibly, putting it too simplistically. Um," he grasped for words. "In a near-infinite set of parallel realities, most are dominated by a Zeropoint organization bent on gaining full control of all of history, with the aim of making it easier for the Vores to—"

He'd heard of the Vores. "And they are?"

"Nobody is quite sure exactly what or who they are. We know that they are, at minimum, organic machines, parasites of a type, stuck on the *outside* of the universe — you have to imagine the entire universe — really, the entire manifold, I suppose — as a very complex hypersphere, as seen from a higher-dimensional viewpoint."

Spider began to regret asking for an explanation. "'Higher-dimensional viewpoint.' Right."

"So you've got these things feeding on the substance of the universe itself, eating it, and shitting out entropic waste... Uh, Spider?"

He was doing his best, but it was not easy. "You're saying there are things literally eating the universe?"

"Yes, that's right."

"Why would they do that?"

"We don't know if they're conscious, or intelligent creatures. For all we know they could be mindless, self-replicating Von Neumann machines. What's important is that they're consuming the order of structured matter and energy in the universe, and spewing out chaotic energy and gas and whatnot into that higher-dimensional space. Other creatures in that realm, which is otherwise cold to the point of absolute zero and pretty bleak, they are drawn to this source of energy, which shows up like a huge burning star to them, and they come and feed on that, and next thing you've got a whole bloody ecosystem going, all dependent on these Vores for sustenance. And the more the Vores multiply, the more this bizarre ecosystem grows and expands."

Spider was thinking about the vents on the deep ocean floor, spewing hot, chemical-rich materials, and drawing in all manner of strange, otherworldly deep-sea lifeforms, none of which ever saw the light of day, evolving and growing and developing deep in the hot darkness at the bottom of the sea. "All right," he said, nodding a little. "So far so good."

"You did ask, Spider. It knocked me for a loop, too, when I heard about it."

Spider wished he wouldn't keep referring to "his" past that way. It was easier for Spider to deal with Soldier Spider if he could keep from seeing the old bastard as a future version of himself, with all that that implied about his own future choices and beliefs. He said, "How long have these things been at it?"

"Eating the universe?"

"Yeah."

"Dunno, to be honest with you. Long enough. Long enough to make certain the universe is flat, that it will keep expanding indefinitely."

He had heard something about the "flatness" of the universe, that it had to do with whether the expansion would ever stop, and start to reverse itself, ultimately squeezing down into a so-called Big Crunch. The key question involved the quantity of mass and energy available in the universe: if the total was greater than a certain value, the universe would slow and reverse its expansion and go crunch; if lower than that value, the expansion would spread out forever. Were the Vores aware they were changing the ultimate fate of the universe? Or were they just eating because they could, and there was plenty of available food? Did it matter? Spider thought, no, not really. He couldn't imagine being able to do anything about them.

What did concern him, now that he could, sort-of, picture the whole thing, was that, given enough time, the Vores could work their way from the distant future down to his own time. The very idea of "the future" was disappearing. Even as the fabric of space-time flung itself apart at unthinkable speeds, it was disappearing; the sheer size of the universe was contracting: that "complex hypersphere" containing the entire manifold would be dwindling slowly away. The future was not what it used to be.

"All right," Spider said. "I can kinda see it. Kinda."

"Good."

"And then there's you guys, countless versions of Zeropoint, all spread across all the different timelines, only most of you are bad guys?"

"Not so much bad guys as guys with very different aims."

Spider swore. "Good grief."

"You need to understand this," Soldier Spider said, making a big point of it.

"Why?"

"Because, like it or not, this is your future. I am you."

Spider held his head, resting his elbows on the desk. "It's kind of a lot to take in, all at once, you know."

"Can't be helped."

Spider sighed, well aware that he had not merely been shanghaied here, but that he was also being set up for an exciting career in some unimaginable military service. Though exactly how you might go about fighting "things" stuck on the outside of the universe — his mind boggled more than a little at the idea — while you were stuck inside said universe, he could not say. Of course, he also realized that if he were to ask such a question, this future version of himself would only be too pleased to tell him. "Well, Spider," he imagined his future self telling him in his best sarcastic tone, "first you need to take this fantastic super-scientific, mega-powerful Blat-O-Matic, see, and you basically use it like an oxy torch to cut a hole in the wall of the universe, and then you climb outside, and well, then you just need, say, a giant atomic-powered chisel thing, and you just pry the Vores off the outside of the universe like they were so many barnacles..." The idea was amusing, and distracted him for a moment.

"You were thinking about the Blat-O-Matic just now?"

Spider, fed up, said, "Oh, fuck off."

"Sorry. Just, you know..."

"Yeah. Remembering. I get it. Just stop it, all right. It's annoying."

"Sorry, Spider."

Slightly mollified, Spider thought he should cooperate, even if only a bit. "So, big scary Vores are, um, eating the universe. Horrors! But then you've also got these other guys, these Zeropoint fellows, who are opposed to what you're trying to achieve, and they've got their own plans. You're down to just this one ship. I'm guessing they have more than that?"

"They have millions of ships, spread across countless timelines."

Spider coughed. "Millions, did you say?"

"We don't have an exact figure. It's a bloody shitload, basically."

He nodded. "Ships like this one?"

Soldier Spider turned glum. "Nah. Their ships are really cool."

This was not what Spider was expecting to hear. "'Really cool,' huh?"

"Hence the, er, one of us, and the millions of them. They've been wiping us out pretty methodically. If we hadn't managed to implement the flux-proofing when we did, we'd have been stuffed."

"Shit."

"It gets better. The opposition, they seem to know every move we make, usually before we make it."

"So you've got a mole?"

"Or something."

"Is anybody missing? I mean, on a ship like this, wouldn't you miss someone if they just vanished?"

"Not everyone in our branch of Zeropoint is on this ship."

"Ah," Spider said, not much wiser.

"Cross-time intrigue. Big fun," the older Spider said.

"So," Spider said, getting impatient. "You tell me all this stuff about the End of Time, bizarre critters literally from beyond time and space, and a war between different parts of the same organization for, I suppose, all the marbles that have ever existed, in every possible universe.

"I wouldn't be quite that flippant about it," Soldier Spider said.

"No, I suppose not. But I'm not you. Not yet. I'm still me, and liking it that way. I don't want to be you. I don't want to sell myself out. Obviously, at some point, yeah, fine, I can see that I do somehow reach that point, but right now, no. Not sold. And, to be really honest with you, starting to wonder where I fit in with all this craziness."

"You're here, Spider, because we need you. Yes, you. Nobody else but you. Not me; you."

"Uh-huh. Yeah. I got that, thanks. Still not seeing anything—"

Soldier Spider interrupted. "You want to see something that might justify your being here?"

"Yes, please! Absolutely!"

"You're sure?"

"I'm real sure, yeah."

"It doesn't occur to you that this is the sort of conversation where the oh-so-cynical one winds up wishing he hadn't been such a wiseguy?"

"It doesn't occur to you that I just don't care, and would really like to just go home and fix stupid busted time machines?"

Soldier Spider got up. In that spec-ops gear, he looked a lot bigger than Spider realized. And he had a look on his face, a very definite "fuck you!" look, that Spider matched with one of his own. "You. Come with me. I'll show you something that might just get your attention."

At this, hearing the tone in Soldier Spider's voice — the softness, even what had to be vulnerability, Spider started paying attention to what was happening here. Something, he saw, was wrong, more wrong than he thought. He felt a trickle of cold fear in the depths of his belly, a dread that he was going to get his wish.

Soldier Spider led the way out of the cramped cell and into the rest of the ship.

CHAPTER 14

His future self led Spider out of the interrogation room, and showed him through what he gathered was a very limited section of the *Masada*. Spider was surprised at the tight confines of the passageways, through many of which they could move only sideways, and crouching. Here and there they found what Spider guessed were lower-ranked crew intensely cleaning surfaces, walls, fixtures and fittings that looked already clean. The older Spider explained that "humans constantly shed skin cells, hair, eyelashes, and you don't want to know what else, and it all builds up, to say nothing of bacteria. Leave it long enough and everything stinks and you wind up with infectious diseases laying people out. So, we clean, and we clean again, from stem to stern."

Temperatures varied greatly in different parts of the ship, too, Spider noticed. Where the interrogation room had felt more-or-less room temperature, at least as he understood it, other areas were surprisingly cold — he could see his breath in some places — and others unbearably warm. He tried asking why, but was told to just keep moving, they were short on time.

At length, they squeezed into a larger room that was more familiar; it looked to Spider like the procedure rooms he remembered from the Perth City Mortuary, all very clean, cool, and with an array of steel dissection tables, each with grooves and drains. Along one wall was a row of four square doors. In one corner was a collection of sophisticated machinery Spider did not recognize, but whose purpose he could guess. And on one dissection table, covered in a white sheet with only her badly damaged head showing, was the body of Spider's sort-of ex-wife, Molly Webb. Spider gasped. He couldn't help it. At first, standing there, staring at her, he thought he must have been mistaken. That wasn't Molly. Molly was in Bangkok. She was fine. He spoke to her just the other day.

He took a step closer, and then another step. His legs felt weak. He felt cold all over. Glancing at Soldier Spider, he saw that his future self looked much the way he felt, or maybe worse. Soldier Spider had a hand over his mouth, and his eyes closed.

Then Spider was there, standing close enough to Molly's body to touch it. He could see that it was Molly. He said her name, as if trying to wake her up, but she did not respond. "Molly, come on," he said. "What's going on?"

Trembling, he touched her face. It was cold and hard. "Oh God," he said, starting to get it. "Molly..." He covered his mouth; his eyes began to tear up; his throat tightened.

Spider looked up at Soldier Spider, who nodded, and moved around to join Spider. One arm around Spider's shoulders, he led Spider out of the room. A technician in surgical scrubs drew the sheet over Molly's face.

In the chilly corridor, Soldier Spider explained. "Molly was coming back from her trip to Bangkok. You were supposed to have met her at the airport, to pick her up, but you didn't get there in time. She took a taxi home." At this point Soldier Spider paused, closed his eyes for a moment, and took a breath. "On the way home, there was an accident, and the taxi crashed. Molly and the driver both died."

Spider was speechless. He wanted to say so many things, but couldn't. At first he suspected that Soldier Spider and his Zeropoint buddies had for no doubt bizarre reasons arranged for that taxi to crash. Another voice in his head wanted to question whether that really was Molly, or some kind of android replica. Maybe, he thought, the real Molly was just fine somewhere, and wondering why Spider couldn't pop round to fix her toilet.

"She never..." It was hard to speak without breaking down. "Told me I had to pick her up." He wiped his nose and his eyes on his sleeve.

"That's true," Soldier Spider said, "from your viewpoint."

"Oh, shit," Spider said, seeing where this was going.

"The thing is, and this is hard to fully accept. I know I found it just about impossible—"

"Just stop with that right now, all right?"

"Sorry."

"Can you bring her back? You said yourself this is the End of Time, right? Surely—"

"Not the way you think—"

"But there's a chance?"

"It's complicated."

"Well, start uncomplicating it right now you treacherous bastard."

"The problem," Soldier Spider said, "is that we are in the shit. One ship against millions. We're low on power, life-support, able-bodied crew, you name it. The ship's flux-proofed, but only the outer hull, it's all we can manage like this. We're hanging on by our fingernails. The other team, though, Dickhead's team, they—"

"Dickhead? Dickhead McMahon? *My* Dickhead?"

"The same. Mr. Zone-of-Control himself."

"What?"

"Long story. But listen to me—"

"What the fuck could Dickhead McMahon have been up to?"

"Trying to win the universe, same as everyone else. Trying to commune with the Vores. Trying, in fact, to kill us."

"But that's... That's nuts!"

"And yet, here we are. Now, listen to me. I need your help."

Spider thought his head might explode. It was too much. He paced up and down the corridor, trying to think, to make sense of everything, talking to himself, going over and over everything he knew, or thought he knew, trying to make everything fit together. Again and again, he came back to the one thing he cared about above all else. He said to Soldier Spider, "Is she really dead?"

"She is. I can't tell you how sorry I am."

"And she's dead because of me, because I let her down?"

"Indirectly, yes."

"Okay. Send me back."

"Not just yet."

"What now?"

"I need you to do a job for us."

"Fine. I'm in. Just send me the hell back there."

"It's not that easy."

Spider wanted to pull his hair out. "I'm ready to go right now."

Soldier Spider grabbed Spider's overalls, picked him up, and pressed him up against the wall. "Shut the fuck up, settle down, and listen to me. I have to tell you a bunch of stuff you won't like. We've got a plan. You're the star of the plan. But there's a catch you'll absolutely hate, okay?"

"Fine."

Soldier Spider put Spider down and straightened his overalls. "Right," he said. "The good news, the one thing you need to hear up front, is this: if you carry out the plan to the letter, Molly will live. The taxi accident will never happen."

This got his attention. "I'm listening."

Soldier Spider sighed, exhausted, and managed a weak smile. "I don't remember being quite this difficult when it was my turn."

"Still listening!"

So Soldier Spider told Spider the plan. As Spider stood there, taking it in, and realized just what was being asked of him, he wanted to refuse. "There is no way, right? No. Way. In. Hell. that I'm doing that."

"No one else can do it, Spider."

"Molly would never speak to me again."

"That's true, yes. You're right. She doesn't."

That was a blow, right there. "She lives, but she hates my guts forever?"

"She lives, hates your guts forever, but the universe is saved, at least for now."

"I don't care about the universe," Spider said and slumped down and sat on the floor, his legs stretched out.

Soldier Spider squatted next to him. He said nothing for a minute or two, then nodded, clapped Spider on one of his knees, and said, "Okay, fair enough. Good point. You're right."

"What?"

"You're right. It's too much to ask of you."

"So you're sending me home."

"Sure."

"Just like that."

"Just like that. Come on, get up."

"What's the catch?"

Soldier Spider offered him a hand to help him get up. As Spider got to his feet again, he felt more than a little suspicious.

"There's no catch. Look, here's what happens."

"Here comes the catch," Spider said.

Ignoring that remark, Soldier Spider led Spider along the corridor. He said, "We'll send you home. You'll arrive a moment after you left with me. You'll remember what I told you about picking up Molly from the airport, but you've got a meeting with Dickhead. You could blow that off, I suppose, but either way, you go out to the airport to get her. You get there just in time. Like always, Molly treats you like shit, but you love her anyway. You pack her stuff into the van, you get in, get moving, and head back to her place. Molly's in a pretty bad mood. The show in Bangkok didn't go that well. You try to cheer her up."

"Oh, God," Spider said, seeing where this might be going.

"That's right. You wind up in an accident. Van's to-talled, and so are you and Molly. Here, check it out..." Soldier Spider led him into another room, much like the previous one, only this one had several dissection tables. Two of them were occupied. Soldier Spider indicated to a technician to expose the bodies' faces.

It was bad enough, Spider thought, seeing Molly again like that. What tilted the entire business into a new dimension of weirdness and horror was seeing the other body — himself, clearly himself, lying there.

"You sick fuck," Spider said.

Soldier Spider nodded toward Molly's body. "This is not the same body from the other room."

Spider advanced on his future self. "How dare you?"

"The thing is," Soldier Spider said, not moving, "this happens in every timeline we've examined. Every single—"

Spider lunged forward and hit Soldier Spider, as hard as he could, in the man's jaw; he felt some teeth crunch, but he also felt one of his own knuckles crack. Soldier Spider staggered back, but remained standing. He winced, touching his face. "Damn," he said, and went to a stainless steel trolley nearby, opened a drawer, and pulled out a small, paper-wrapped item that looked, Spider thought, like a boiled sweet. Soldier Spider put it in his mouth, and started sucking on it.

Spider's hand hurt like crazy. He'd broken the skin over two knuckles, and they were starting to bleed. The pain was much worse than he had expected. "Shit," he said, shaking his hand, and, the adrenaline rush subsiding, starting to feel a little ridiculous. He apologized to Soldier Spider. "Look, I'm really sorry. It's just, it's too much, I can't stand it."

Soldier Spider tossed him one of the boiled sweet things. When Spider unwrapped it, he saw it looked very similar to the thing he was given by his other Future Self that long, strange night in the car, the thing that rebuilt his mouth. He stuck it in his mouth. "Do I thuck on thith fing or what?"

"In your case," Soldier Spider said, his reconstructor pellet stuck in the side of his mouth, "swallow it. You'll be good as new."

Neither said anything for a while. After a few minutes, the stinging sensation in Spider's hand subsided and was replaced by a hot tingling. As he watched, the skin on those two knuckles knit back together, and he swore, amazed to see it happen. It took longer to rebuild the cracked knuckle.

While he waited for the agents to complete their work, Spider found himself staring at his own dead body. It was one thing to see massive head trauma on someone else, the way he did back when he was a constable, attending the scenes of traffic accidents. This, this was different. His dead self's head had been caved in from one side; he guessed the shop van must have been hit from the driver's side. There was a lot of bruising, and the neck looked wrong. He touched the corpse's face: it was cold and hard. It gave him the horrors, seeing himself like this, imagining what it must have felt like. This, he understood, was his immediate future. If, that is, he didn't cooperate with Soldier Spider's desperate plan.

He said to Soldier Spider, who'd been quietly watching him, "How do I know any of this is true?"

"Why would I lie to you?"

"You could lie to me if it was in your interest."

"Spider, I'm you, more or less."

"You're what? Thirty, forty years older than me?"

"Ah, actually, quite a bit more than that."

"My point. You're not me, not anymore. You've followed a different path. It's changed you. So why should I believe anything you tell me?"

Soldier Spider took this in, nodded. "Yeah, fair enough. So. You want me to send you back so you can take your chances avoiding all this?"

"The alternatives," Spider said, "are not great."

"They're never great, Spider. It's always Hobson's Choice."

He found himself looking again at Molly's body, glad the sheet was there, concealing the full extent of her injuries. The fact that her body did not lie straight on the table was bad enough. "You say she'll live?"

"She'll live, yes."

"But she'll hate me."

"Oh yes." Soldier Spider, for all his years, looked like he remembered Molly's hatred only too well, and it still hurt.

"Good God," he said, dismayed at the choice.

"I wish there were some other way."

"Dickhead's ships are all flux-proofed, too, right?"

"Their entire existence, from plan to finished ship to ultimate decommissioning, yes. We can't touch them, and they can't touch us."

"Why do I feel like Winston Smith, confronted with the rats in Room 101, telling Mr. O'Brien to do it to Julia instead?"

"Dickhead needs someone close to you, Spider. It's basically Molly or your parents."

He was starting to find it hard to remain standing. He thought he was going to be sick. "I feel ill."

Spider knew, in his roiling gut, that he'd made his decision, and he despised himself for it. "Shit," he said, mainly to himself.

Soldier Spider nodded. "Thank you," he said.

"Fuck off."

"I need you to come with me now. There's still a bunch of stuff I need to tell you..."

At the end of the new briefing, Spider felt overwhelmed. He said, "I think we'd all be a lot safer if it was you taking care of Dickhead, actually."

"But I already did. Now it's your turn."

"Wait a second. Wait just a second. You remember taking care of the Dickhead problem when you were me."

"That's right."

"But now, you're older, and yet somehow Dickhead's back?"

"Think of a hydra with billions of heads, each one from a different timeline, and each one pure Dickhead McMahon. Think about it."

Spider thought about it. He swore for a couple of minutes. Soldier Spider nodded and told him he was now starting to get it.

"Now remember," he told Spider, giving his shoulder a reassuring squeeze, "take no prisoners, okay? Believe in yourself. You can do this. If in doubt, improvise. And, whatever happens, kick butt!"

And with that, they sent Spider back home.

§　§　§

Spider arrived back in his office only a second or two after Soldier Spider had whisked him away to the *Masada*. It was 4:42 p.m. He could hear Malaria on the phone, listening to people explain the weird stuff their time machines were getting up to and doing her best to diagnose the truly simple stuff, working from the office copy of *Time Machines for Dummies*, so that Spider and Charlie wouldn't have too much of their time wasted. From the way the phones kept ringing, Spider could see that business was good. If bloody Dickhead would put on an extra technician they could really get some throughput going, he thought — and then he stopped hard, his brain screeching to a halt like something in an old cartoon.

Dickhead. Yes. Dickhead is a bad guy. Zeropoint. The mission. Right.

Strange the way he'd nearly forgotten about all that. It was, after all, only a minute or two ago that he'd been sitting on a *timeship*, the last such ship at the End of Time, engaged in an existential conflict with otherworldly things called Vores that were destroying the universe one bite at a time. He remembered wondering how a vessel like that, way off in the unthinkable future, could be so, well, primitive — albeit capable of sliding like a bead along the long thread of time, sure, but still primitive in conditions and such. Soldier Spider had tried to sketch in for him the idea that on the *Masada* something like ninety percent of the available energy went into running the vessel's mighty translation engines; only ten percent was left for crew life support, and that meant living squeezed into cramped spaces.

On the way back to his desk, his phone patch went off. "Webb, hello."

"Hello? Spider?" It was Rutherford, and he sounded rushed, breathing fast. There was the sound of running footsteps on wet pavement, and in the background deafening traffic: dozens of bikes, jangling bells, people shouting; and motorized traffic inching its way along, drivers shouting abuse, honking horns.

"James? Uh, hi. What's up?"

"Just... running for the bus. Hang on, let me just get under some cover." More running, edging his way through crowds, and then, "Right, that's better." Spider could hear rain hitting the roof of the shelter, and people around him talking on their own phones. "Okay, good," James said. "Listen. Are you busy tonight?"

Tonight? Spider found himself wondering, *What is significant about tonight? Soldier Spider didn't tell me anything. Damn!*

"Yeah. If it's not convenient..." James trailed off. He sounded distracted, even distant.

"No, that's okay. What's up? You okay?"

There was a painful pause, then James said, his voice straining, "I need to talk to someone, Spider. I'm in trouble."

Intrigued, Spider asked, "Is this to do with the business you told me about?"

"Um, I can't talk about it over the phone. Could we meet somewhere?" James said. In the background Spider could hear a bus pull in to the stop, its tires hissing on the pavement, brakes squealing. "You know Café Fuego, at Crawley?"

Spider knew of it, an upmarket café with a spectacular view over the Swan River and the city skyline. "Yup. How's eight o'clock?"

"See you then." James killed the link.

Spider sat, thinking about what he'd just heard. James sounded preoccupied, his voice flat. *What the hell?* Spider thought to himself.

Then, right on schedule, according to the instructions Soldier Spider had given him, Malaria appeared in his doorway, and said, "Dickhead just arrived, Spider." She was full of dread, anticipating Dickhead's unique charm. "I swear, if you don't get him to leave me alone, I'll bloody kill him."

"And so it begins," he said. He told Malaria that he would sort Dickhead out. No problem.

Her arms crossed, turning so she could see out the front window and watch Dickhead parking his immense Hummer, she told Spider, "If I don't get a personal apology from him, today, I'm out of here."

"I said I'd handle it," and he flashed his best attempt at a reassuring smile. Hardly mollified, Malaria went back to her desk and braced for impact.

Right on schedule, Dickhead squeezed through the office door, damp from the drizzling rain outside, and shook his boxy head. "Since when did bloody May get so miserable and wet? I tell you, it never used to be like this, not when I was a kid. God, May used to be maybe a bit cool, maybe the odd handful of rainy days, but nothing like this! Have you seen it out there? Parts of Perth are actually underwater, the river's burst its banks in places — don't you listen to the news here? My God, it's a bloody scandal, you mark my words! Good thing I've got the Beast out there" — the Beast was his Hummer — "or I'd be underwater, too, for God's sake! And it's not even properly winter yet! It's just insane out there." He paused for breath and smiled at Malaria. "Ah, the lovely Malaria! And how are you this afternoon? Not working too hard, I hope?" He chuckled, looming over the front counter so he had a good view of Malaria at her desk.

"Bugger off, Dickhead," Malaria said, this time with no undertone of good humor.

Dickhead, quite unfazed at Malaria's suggestion, saw Spider lurking in the doorway behind her, and winked at him. "Spider, the fair Malaria here sounds a bit overworked. Things must be looking up!"

Malaria glanced meaningfully at Spider, and went back to her work.

Spider said, "Dickhead, we need to have a little talk."

"Any chance of a double macchiato?" Dickhead asked Malaria, who flinched but said nothing.

"Droid's not working," Spider said as Dickhead pushed past him like an iceberg in a wool suit.

Dickhead complained bitterly about the coffee situation, and when Spider offered him a cup of instant he protested noisily and went on about what a hard day he'd had, going around all the other Time Machines Repaired shops in the metro area, and how for some reason all their coffee droids were broken, too. "But I got all those coffee droids in a deal!" he said, settling into the guest chair in Spider's office. "I tell you, Spider, you can't trust African workmanship anymore, it's a bloody disgrace, a bloody disgrace! After all we've done for them, too! God!"

Spider settled behind his desk. "Dickhead, before we begin, I've got a bit of a problem."

Dickhead looked like he was considering the idea of treating Spider's comment as a hook for a joke, but changed his mind, going instead with an expression of serious concern, tempered with delight at being the one to whom Spider turned for help. "Anything I can do?"

"In a word, yes. Look, it's about Malaria."

"Delightful creature," he said, smiling. "I'm trying to get her to go out for dinner with me, but so far she's playing it cool."

Spider sighed and shook his head. "Well, about that, just stop it, okay? Leave her be."

"Um, what?"

"I said, and I quote, Leave Malaria alone. She's a great worker, and she's doing a good job for the shop, so show a bit of bloody professionalism and leave her alone. She's not interested."

"What are you trying to say, Spider?" He looked baffled.

"You're always trying to chat her up. I'm telling you to stop it."

Dickhead stared at him, astonished, then got up and went to the door, opened it, called out to Malaria, "You know, Malaria, if you had a problem with me, you could have spoken to me directly. There's no need—"

Malaria yelled out, "Spider!"

Spider was out of his chair and at the door, behind Dickhead's bulk. "What, are you drunk?" He shut the door. "She just wants to do her job and go home. She's not interested! You're giving her the shits!"

"You know, Spider," Dickhead said, turning to stare at him, "I decided today was a good day to launch the next phase of my little project, and I thought, I know, I'll get Spider to come on board, he's a good bloke, reliable, hard-working, imaginative — plus of course you owe me — so

I came out here, all set to give you the big spiel, lay it all out for you, the whole thing, the vision, if you will — and here you're telling me off for sweet-talking your reception-ist. And I'm all confused, frankly, I really am confused, because all this time, I thought I was your boss. I thought I *owned* you. Now I find out I was mistaken. All this time I was proceeding from a false premise, as they say. All this time, somehow, despite the lack of money in your bank account, and the rather large amount of money in my bank account, and all of that, it turns out that you're *my* boss instead!

"You can see how this would come as something of a shock to me, Spider, particularly after everything I've done for you over the years, and without ever seeking a word of thanks, or gratitude, or even recognition! And now here you are, talking to me like you're some kind of, God, I don't know, like an *equal*! Help me out here, Spider. Help me out."

Spider wanted to hit him. He could feel the urge build-ing in his arm, in his solar plexus, his whole body wanted to hit the bastard hard, put him down — not that he'd done such a stellar job of that with Soldier Spider, he thought, but he was different: he was a trained military guy. Dickhead was just a big lump of nastiness, more nastiness than Spider would ever have believed possible, he now understood — but he knew that would be the end of him. No more job. Certainly no reference. He'd be in deep shit. Spider was forty-four years old — not ancient, by any objective standard, but forty-four was sufficiently old that finding another job would be difficult. For one thing, he'd have to go back to school, and that meant back to TAFE, the technical college where he'd studied for his only non-police qualification, his Certificate in Chronosystems Maintenance and Repair, Level III, and that had taken three years' full-time study, plus three days a week work expe-rience on top of that. It had been insanely hard juggling all of it, but it would be much harder now, years later, with him that much older, and with that much less stamina.

He knew he could always get some kind of unskilled, entry-level laboring work, but to make more than poverty-line wages you really needed at least two or three such jobs, and that meant no sleep. Spider was up against it, and he knew that Dickhead knew that, too. Dickhead had him by the short and curlies, as Dickhead himself might say. It wasn't like Spider could get another job in the time machine maintenance industry, either, not if Dickhead put the word out that Spider was no good.

He supposed he could freelance, work in people's garages, that kind of thing, but he'd never make the same kind of steady money, such as it was. He had no idea where he would even live, if it came to that. Buying his own tools, that would cost money he didn't have. When he was studying, he'd had to buy some basic tools, but the school provided all the heavy-duty diagnostic gear, stuff that cost tens of thousands of dollars. Without access to such equipment, Spider would have a very hard time working the freelance angle.

All of which left the blunt reality: he would have to go back to school and learn something else, and somehow defer the considerable expense involved in such training until after he graduated, so for the first ten years of his new career he'd only get a fraction of his real wages. What would he live on in the meantime? Where would he sleep at night? He imagined going up to Iris and telling her that he would need to crash on her couch for another three years or more. "Yeah, that's going to work," he muttered.

Still, Soldier Spider had told him a situation like this would come up. "You'll have to make a stand against Dickhead over something. No, it's all right. He respects that kind of blunt-force approach. You have to make him see that you're not a spineless wimp."

"But I am a spineless wimp," Spider had told his future self, full of self-pity.

At this, Soldier Spider punched him in the gut, and Spider crumpled to the ground, all fetal and struggling for breath. "Hey, if you say so, Spider," he said. "You're not spineless. You did the right thing about Superintendent Sharp, remember? You took them all on. You stood up to all his minions, even when they were threatening your life

— and not just *your* life. Remember those letters, threatening Molly and even your mum and dad? Remember that?"

He remembered. Only in his memory, that entire business was the worst thing that had ever happened to him, and it felt like a comprehensive defeat. It had cost him his health, even his mental health. If it had been any kind of great victory for the forces of clean policing, he had often thought, he'd be the commissioner now, right? He wouldn't now be a pawn in some mad game of cross-time chess.

So, praying that his future self's analysis of Dickhead's character was correct, and that the boss would respect him if he pressed his point, Spider fought back the impulse to hit the bastard. He stepped back, and did his best to control his breathing. "Malaria," he said, "is a good kid. Apologize to her."

"You were gonna give me one just now, weren't you, Spider?" He was grinning.

"I said, apologize to her. Now."

"Hmm," he said, "that whole speech I just gave you, concerning the matter of who owns whom, that didn't really penetrate, did it?"

"Apologize, or I'm gone."

Dickhead was amazed. "Threats, now? Spider, I'm almost impressed."

This wasn't going the way it was supposed to go. It was going to shit, and Spider could see it. Dickhead did not look at all like a man who could see that Spider was a credible equal; he looked like Sharp had looked on that long-ago morning when he'd told Spider what he thought of Spider's "underhanded, backstabbing, cowardly" attack, following him around in ghost mode with a camera, instead of coming right out with his accusations, to his face, like a real man. Spider felt like a bug only too aware that it was about to be crushed. What should he do? He could persist with this issue, stick up for Malaria, do the right thing, fight the good fight, or he could fold. He knew Dickhead wanted to make him some kind of big offer. That would be the Zeropoint thing, Soldier Spider had told him.

Dickhead wanted to recruit him into that other mirror-image version of the outfit, supposedly. It was important, he'd been told, that that recruiting effort succeed. They needed Spider to gain access to the other side.

It was just that Malaria needed him to stick up for her. If his situation was precarious, hers was just as difficult, and forcing the issue with Dickhead directly, face to face, would only get her fired with no legal recourse. Yes, she was young, and with her skills she could probably get another job relatively easily — Spider knew qualified baristas these days could sometimes write their own ticket. He remembered Malaria telling him, at her job interview, when he asked her why on Earth she wanted to work at a lousy time machine repair shop, "I just, you know, think time machines are really cool? Thought it'd be fun?" And that had been that. She got the job. Everyone else he'd interviewed — well, the three other candidates — told him, "I believe I can excel in this business environment, sir!" He still had nightmares about those candidates. All of which left him thinking he should have stayed in bed this morning.

Dickhead, meanwhile, was advancing on Spider, backing him up against his desk, "You really care about her?"

All right, then. Moment of truth time. Trust the future. He said, his legs weak, "I do, yes. She deserves to be treated properly in her place of work."

"And you're prepared to go to the mat for her?"

"Yes."

"Even given the way we met, the state you were in?"

"Are you a man, Dickhead, or just a cheap bully?" His pulse boomed in his ears, deafening. He had no idea he'd been about to say such a thing, but out it came.

Dickhead stared at him, stared hard, standing so close to Spider that Spider knew what he'd had for lunch.

Then, Dickhead backed off, glaring, and adjusted his tie and his jacket. He was breathing hard through his nose. After one more hard look at Spider, he yanked the door open, yelled out, "Malaria! A word!"

Spider shriveled inside, feeling cold and shaky.

Malaria said, "Sir?" She didn't call him Dickhead this time. Listening to her voice, Spider knew she was feeling the way he felt, just waiting for the blow.

"Malaria," Dickhead said, his tone gruff, "I'm sorry. I have been entirely unprofessional in my behavior towards you. Please accept my apology. I will do better."

She was silent for a long moment. "Yes, sir," she said. "Thank you, sir."

Dickhead strode back into Spider's office, performed an elaborate bow and said, "There. Feel better?"

Spider was speechless. He sat on the edge of his desk, breathing deeply.

Dickhead stood there, hands on his hips, and said, "Anything else on your mind, Spider?"

CHAPTER 15

While Spider was grateful that Dickhead had at last done the right thing, he hated having had to ask Dickhead to do it. McMahon should have treated Malaria properly all along — or, if he really did fancy her, should have set about wooing her in a very different manner. There were times Spider hated Dickhead, but then there were other times when Dickhead would inexplicably turn genuinely decent and sympathetic. It was maddening.

Now, he thought, watching Dickhead, he could see that the bastard's unexpected turn of decency was largely for show. Dickhead had gone along with apologizing to Malaria not out of an awareness that he had behaved inappropriately in the workplace, but on a whim, because he could. Spider's situation had not improved, and neither had hers, while Dickhead got to look all magnanimous. Feeling cold and a bit nauseated, Spider went and collapsed in his chair.

Dickhead grinned at him and said, "Who's for a coffee?" Before Spider could offer an opinion, he had disappeared into the break room. Spider could hear him rinsing out coffee mugs and mumbling under his breath about the evils of instant coffee, "in this day and age."

Without Dickhead using his zone-of-control powers in Spider's tiny office, the room suddenly felt huge and spacious; he felt he could breathe again. Soldier Spider was right. Dickhead had done the right thing, and Spider had, in a roundabout sort of way, kind of won. Or at least Dickhead had let him win, which wasn't quite the same thing. Better, his heart was starting to settle back to something resembling a normal rhythm. Now he just had the post-confrontation shakes, as all that adrenaline worked its way through his system.

While he sat there, staring at nothing, going back over and over that business with Dickhead, Malaria popped in, smiled, and whispered, "Thanks!" He nodded, too exhausted to do much else. This had been one of those days, what with the unexpected jaunt off to visit the timeship *Masada* and all. He could hear Dickhead in the break room, loudly stirring coffee, working the teaspoon like a percussion instrument. The high-pitched ding-a-ding-a-ding-a-ding as he stirred jarred Spider's weary nerves, and he was grateful when Dickhead was finished. He braced for the big man's return to his office.

"I see you're out of bloody biscuits and all!" Dickhead said as he brought in a tray bearing two large mugs of coffee.

"Bitch, bitch, bitch," Spider said, and took the mug Dickhead offered him.

Dickhead said, his face straight, "Nine sugars for you, wasn't it, Spider?"

Spider very nearly fell for it, but realized in time. He performed an impression of a "ha-ha, very funny" smile for his boss's benefit, but all the same decided to leave the coffee to cool for a bit before trying it. One never knew, with Dickhead.

"So," his boss said, between sips.

Spider, slumped back in his chair, hungry and tired, said, "So what?" He knew very well what Dickhead had on his mind, thanks to Soldier Spider's briefing. The question at hand, from Spider's point of view, was whether he had the nerve to go through with it. It helped him to think that all he could do at any given time was just work on the problem in front of him, and worry about later problems when he got to them. Right now, all he had to do was convince Dickhead he had no clue what Dickhead was really all about. *Well*, he thought, trying not to look tense, *here goes nothing...*

"I'm trying to decide," Dickhead said, staring into his coffee, "whether to go ahead with my original plan for today."

"Let me know when you decide, then," Spider said, reaching for his own coffee.

Dickhead worked his mouth into a humorless smile for a moment. "When I took you on, lo these many years ago now, I thought you might grow into a useful asset."

Spider's coffee was too sweet, but not insanely so. He sipped and waited. Here it came. The big pitch, the invitation. All the previous business, he'd been told, was just sparring: "Basically bullshit," in his future self's words. "It's a big thing he's got in mind for you, and he can't just bluntly come out and say, 'Well, Spider, how'd you like to join us in the Great War at the End of Time' or anything like that, because you'd laugh, you'd think he was nuts. He has to introduce the topic a bit at a time, ease you into it. Otherwise, well..." He'd trailed off, and Spider could see why. But now, seeing Dickhead there on the other side of his desk, knowing what was on the big bastard's mind, it still felt like a weird situation.

He'd asked Soldier Spider, "Why? Why's all this happening to me?"

"Why you?" his future self had said sourly. "Well, why not you? Wasn't it pure chance that you happened to go to that particular pub the night you met Dickhead? You could have gone to some other place and avoided him, maybe, though our simulations suggest he was actively looking for you."

"What?"

"Yeah. And then of course, you're the one who wound up finding Clea Fassbinder's body." Here Soldier Spider sighed, tired and sad. "She was one of our best people. Damn shame."

This revelation jolted Spider out of his "why me?" funk. "Oh," he had said, sitting up, staring at his future self, and remembering Fassbinder's body wrapped in that blue plastic sheet.

"Very sad case," Soldier Spider went on, distracted, clearly wanting to talk more about Dickhead and the mission.

Spider didn't want to let it go. "Who was she, anyway?"

"She was one of us. A soldier."

"That's it?"

"She made her choice, Spider."

"Choice? What choice? 'Why, yes, I'd love to wind up slaughtered like a pig inside not one but two bloody time machines in the 21st century?'"

"Clea knew she died in your time. It freaked her out, knowing that, wondering why, how it happened, the whole thing. Then, when she found out she'd been murdered, well, it was like she had to find out all about it."

"She went to investigate her own murder?"

"She knew we weren't about to authorize something like that, so she spent a lot of her free time trying to investigate what happened to her from here, using our resources."

"I'm guessing you weren't crazy about that, either."

"Let me just say," Soldier Spider said, "Clea was getting a bit obsessed about it. Felt like her whole life was on rails. Occupational hazard in this line of work. And always, always asking, 'why the fuck am I even in 21st century Perth, Western Australia in the first place? I mean, of all places to meet a sticky end, why there? Why not someplace *interesting*?'"

Spider felt a sharp pang of defensive pride about his home town, but wasn't prepared to argue the point with someone from the End of Time, for God's sake. "So what happened?"

"A job came up."

"Ah," he said.

"260th century AD. We're conducting a covert op, don't even think of asking the details. Out of nowhere this bloody space probe thing from the 21st century appears, and starts snapping photos."

All at once, Spider felt large pieces of the puzzle grinding like heavy stones into place. "*Kronos*."

"You've heard of it, then?"

"Time probe. Doing for the future what *Voyager* and *Galileo* did for the solar system. Hop-scotching across the future, sending back reports."

"Exactly."

"Surely, though," Spider said, thinking about it, and thinking about James Rutherford's strange story, "you could have easily avoided it?"

"By the time we spotted the thing, it had already snapped several terabytes of pix, run all manner of scans, and squirted it all back home, to your time."

"Yeah, but if you just moved your covert op a light-year to the left, then the probe thing—"

Soldier Spider gave Spider a tired, sour look. "Been there, tried that. Over and bloody over. The fucking probe keeps turning up, like it's hunting us, for God's sake!"

"Ah," Spider said."

"You see the problem."

"Even so, though. What would observers back in the creaky old 21st century even understand of stuff the probe showed them? Surely it'd be all very, 'Uh, what the hell is that?' and 'It kinda looks like an espresso pot mating with a waffle iron.' That kind of thing. So what's the problem?"

"The problem, numbnuts, is follow-up probes. The morons not just back in your time but for thousands of years after that see they've found a manifold hot-spot, with interesting and colorful locals doing fascinating things. Let's have a closer look, shall we? And next thing, more cameras are turning up to investigate our covert op than visit the Kennedy Assassination and the Crucifixion combined!"

"I suppose Dickhead somehow gets involved, too?"

"Of course. We think Dickhead's people are the main reason the probe keeps finding our op in the first place, the bastards."

"So. Problem."

"Someone has to go back to your time and take care of it. Guess who volunteers?"

"You couldn't stop her?"

Soldier Spider sighed. "I tried. I talked to her. Picked someone else for the job, even. But in the end, against orders, Clea went." He shook his head, the memory painful even now.

Spider nodded, thinking about how it must have been. Then, a thought. He said, "By the way, does the name James Rutherford mean anything to you?"

"Rutherford was one of several people with access to the probe's nav system software. High-level access, lots of influence, a heavy-hitter in all respects. Impeccable credentials, of course."

"Of course. So Clea volunteers?"

"We try to talk her out of it, but by now she's got something like a death wish."

Spider tried to imagine what that might be like. He remembered a couple of guys in WAPOL who'd gotten a bit that way, seen too much, nothing but trouble on the home front, self-medicating with booze and dope to get through the days, taking stupid risks, convinced there was no hope of helping anyone, everything was going to hell, society was in the toilet. You couldn't help guys like that.

"So she goes back, meets up with James—"

"No, she goes to meet all of our target candidates. Only Rutherford goes along with it."

"They have an affair?" Spider was thinking about James's wife's suicide, and his subsequent stay in hospital. *Oh, James, what have you done, mate?*

"The affair was not part of the brief. That just happened. We strongly suspect she wanted it to happen, strangely."

"And that's what got her killed?"

"We think so."

Spider nodded. "Okay, then. So when are you bringing James in?"

"I never said Rutherford was the murderer."

"But—"

"Spider, yes, we do know who killed Clea. We know the whole story of what happened that night, how she got hidden away in the two time machines, everything."

"Why have I got a bad feeling about where this is going?"

"We do not have the resources to chase murderers. We're not a police agency."

"You could tell me, and I could go—"

"You are not yet one of us, Spider. Think about it. Operational security. If I told you how we know what happened, I'd be in the shit, and you could infer things about our intel-gathering capabilities, or Dickhead could, if he questioned you about it. At the moment our ability to snoop about is one of the only things keeping us going."

"So Clea's killer gets away with it?"

"I didn't say that, either, Spider."

"What?"

"The universe takes care of all things in time. Believe me."

"Um..."

"Trust me, Spider. The killer does not get away with it."

He didn't know what to make of that remark. "It's just, Good God, I can't believe I'm saying this out loud, I need to know what happened to her. Her body fell right at my feet, and there she was, dead, murdered. She was a case, an actual case! Have you been doing this so long you've forgotten what it was like to be a cop? Is that it?"

"I haven't forgotten. I remember that day in the Bat Cave very well. Thinking back, I remember, too, the way James Rutherford looked so sick when he saw Clea's body."

Spider seized on this. "Yes! Because he knew her."

"Maybe he even knew what had happened, who killed her, everything."

"Are you suggesting I go back and grill James?" Spider remembered that James wanted to talk to him "tonight", about something urgent. The way he'd said he was in some kind of trouble. Did he want to confess everything? Was that it? Or was the real murderer putting some kind of pressure on him? Spider remembered that night in the shop's break room, the way James had looked like he was starting to break down, and the way he stormed off without explaining, and then couldn't be reached. Spider could feel that he was very close to sorting it all out — if he could just get through all this bullshit with Dickhead first.

"So, you can't tell me anything. Is that right?"

"Right. If you eventually become me, of course—"

"If? What do you mean, 'if'?"

Soldier Spider was getting fed up. "You are not guaranteed to end up as me."

Spider remembered something his other future self tried to tell him, about timelines growing like weeds from every possible choice you make. "So there's only a chance I end up like you?"

"Only a chance. In fact, there's every chance that you die."

"I could die?"

"Yup."

"Shit!"

"Sorry."

"Shit!"

"You did ask."

"Yeah, but..."

"It's just an eighty-four percent chance. It's not inevitable."

"Eighty-four percent! Fuck!"

It took Soldier Spider a long time to get Spider to settle down and see things differently, and it wasn't easy. Spider had long nursed a sense of impending doom about this whole affair, and now, to make it worse, he had an actual number to put to it. "You're saying I've got just sixteen chances out of a hundred to make it through to, I guess, being you."

"I didn't want to know the exact figure, either, believe me."

He shook his head, feeling dismal. Then he thought about it a bit more, trying to look at it from different angles. "But in some timelines this plan of yours actually works out, we get Dickhead, I get Clea's killer, and everything works out okay?"

"Except for Molly never speaking to you again, yes."

Spider was still having a tough time dealing with that prospect. Try as he might to keep thinking of the greater good and all that, it was still a hard one to accept. "So how do I improve my chances? Can't you guys shunt me onto a more favorable timeline. I mean, you've done it before, right?"

"That wasn't us, Spider."

"What? Are you saying it was—"

"Dickhead, yes. He's pulling out all sorts of bullshit. Sometimes he wants to help you, and prevent you becoming me, other times he wants to kill you and stop you becoming me, too. And sometimes he just likes to mess with people, make 'em crazy."

"Well," Spider said, astonished, "mission bloody well accomplished!"

Soldier Spider managed a weary smile at this. "Sorry I can't be more helpful."

"So you can't make sure I turn into you?"

"Not really. That's up to you."

"So what did you choose at this point?" Spider asked. "I mean, here you are. You clearly survived."

"Yes, I survived. Yes, I made it to now, and I'm old and pretty much had it, yeah, sure. The thing is, *I never figured it out*. I never had a bloody clue. Never saw it coming. I thought for sure James Rutherford was the guy, just like you, but somebody attacked me late one night, I never saw who it was, he came from behind, and I went down like a sack of spuds, and I woke up in hospital days later, and the doctors were all, "Oh, Mr. Webb, we very nearly lost you, blah de blah de blah. And that's my inglorious tale, all right? I don't know what happened. Just remember this: James Rutherford is trouble. Leave him the hell alone. The man's lost his bloody mind, he's self-destructive, and he'd be quite happy to take you down with him, just like he tried to do to me. You, my boy, get another chance. Rutherford will call you, wanting to see you. I went, and nearly died. If you go, you just might wind up in that 84% I told you about. You'll never find out who killed Clea, you won't stop bloody Dickhead, you'll never get to sleep with Iris again, you'll just be one dead stupid fucknuckle. So don't go and see him, okay?"

"I get to sleep with Iris?" He knew this thought made him officially a giant scumbag, but there was a part of his mind that calculated, if Molly is going to hate me anyway, well, why not? He sighed, shaking his head.

"She kinda likes you, kid," Soldier Spider said, waggling his silvery eyebrows.

"Cool."

After that there wasn't a lot to say. Spider moped about a bit, trying to take it all in. The thing that kept giving him trouble was this whole issue of multiple, even infinite, alternate timelines. That was hard to think about, whole armies of guys named Spider, each trying to crack the same case, each making different choices, reaching different conclusions, some succeeding, most failing, and some even dying. Soldier Spider took him aside after dinner, and tried to explain the Zeropoint problem in more detail. Spider wanted to know how people in other timelines, following their own decisions and so forth, could pose a threat to people in this timeline. Soldier Spider said, "Spider, at this point, we're no longer confined to our own timeline, or even our own sheaf of timelines. We can go across to them, and they can come across to us. Every physically possible universe — well, at least all the inhabitable ones, anyway — is up for grabs. Whoever controls most of those universes wins, but if the other guys win — if Dickhead's guys win — then the Vores will turn up a lot sooner and destroy everything before we even get started."

"Uh-huh," Spider said, still feeling way out of his depth. "Why would they do that? What's in it for them?"

"We're not exactly sure, to be honest. It seems like a crazy plan. Why would you want to bring forth your own destruction?"

CHAPTER 16

Spider sat back in his office chair, watching Dickhead trying to make up his mind. Spider hoped he'd done enough with the epic standoff over Malaria's future to convince Dickhead he was the right man for the job. Then again, he thought, if Dickhead's people had so many troops, and so many ships, and so much of everything, what possible difference could a schlub like himself make to anything? Surely it was already a lost cause. He didn't get it. He was also watching Dickhead, who seemed like a perfectly ordinary twenty-first century businessman in his off-the-rack suit, cheap aftershave and ten-dollar haircut. Could this man be the crazy bastard Soldier Spider had told him about? Even now, as he sat there sipping bad instant coffee, lost in thought, was he thinking crazy thoughts about how the Vores would grant him and his followers some fabulous boon in return for helping them destroy the universe?

Dickhead, after a lot of thought, leaned forward, set his coffee on the edge of Spider's desk, and looked him in the eye. "I'm, hmm, how to put this, sorry, um, for that business earlier, over Malaria. Not exactly my finest hour, huh?" He looked genuinely embarrassed about it. Spider let him talk. "It's just, well, not that there's any excuse, of course. I realize that. It's just, I've got a lot going on right now. Lots of stress. Big plans in the works, very big plans."

"Sure," Spider said, tense but trying not to show it, "sounds exciting."

"Yes, very exciting. Absolutely. Now, you and me, we go back a fair way, don't we?"

"We do, yes indeed." Spider thought it would be bad form to remind Dickhead of that whole "I own you" thing he'd used on him earlier.

"Yes. I was right about you, too. Didn't I say to you, all those years ago, that if you just stuck with me, you'd do all right? I was going places, and I was taking you with me. Isn't that right?"

"What's on your mind, Dickhead?"

The big man shifted in his seat. He said, "An opportunity's come up in one of my other business units, Spider. A big opportunity. Something I think you'd be well suited for."

"Is that right?" Spider asked, trying not to be too eager.

"Now, this is exclusive stuff, Spider. Strictly need-to-know, all right? Not a word to Malaria, and not a word to Charlie, okay? Good. It's just, well, I cannot tell you just how exciting this whole thing is going to be, Spider. It's massive, it'll be huge, and we'll be right there in the heart of things."

He was beaming, staring off into space, his eyes shining. Spider could see the man was quite insane, just as his future self had told him. Dickhead went on, now looking at Spider. "It's called Zeropoint, Spider." Smiling, he gestured in the air over in front of him, as if showing a theater marquee sign. "That's 'ZEROPOINT,' all in caps!"

"Gosh," Spider said, doing his best to mean it.

Dickhead said, "Zeropoint is a new kind of business, Spider. Something we've never seen before in the history of the world! New ideas! New thinking! And you're the best man for the job, Spider, the very best man!"

"You going to tell me about this job, or do I have to guess?"

His phone went off again. Dickhead offered to step into the break room to give Spider some privacy, which made Spider peer at him, trying to discern hidden layers of meaning. He said it was fine. Dickhead said he needed to freshen his coffee anyway. "Talking too much," he said. "Getting coffee mouth, blagh." Spider waved him off as he left the room, then he answered the phone.

"Webb, hello," he said quietly, and felt his gut clench afresh.

And sure enough, it was Molly, just back from Bangkok. Molly, who had a special role to play in the forthcoming events, but Spider could not tell her about it, warn her about it — or save her from it. This, he thought, was one of the last times he would ever speak to her.

"So", Molly said, all tired and stressed, "Al! Where the hell are you?" He could hear a lot of people talking in the background, PA announcements, even a dog barking way in the distance. She was at the airport, and she believed he should be there to bring her home.

He said, his mouth suddenly all dry, "Hi Molly. You've just arrived?"

She told him, at great length, that yes, she had just arrived. Quarantine people had given her enormous grief about some "perfectly harmless bananas" and threatened to hit her with "this huge fine".

He cut her off before she could get too much of a head of steam going. "It's okay. Don't panic. I'll be right there."

"You were supposed to be here now, Al!" she said, her voice taking on a certain tone he recognized only too well. This was her calm-before-the-storm tone, that very measured way she bit off the words in a quiet, precise voice. She only used it when she was bone-tired, on the verge of a sinus headache, or in situations where things were going absurdly bad and she was trying to retain a semblance of control. This was Defcon Two, Spider knew. You did not say you couldn't help Molly out when she reached this point. You would live to regret it, and he had the scars to prove it.

He called out to Dickhead, who was still in the break room, "Look, can we pick this up tomorrow, maybe?"

Dickhead leaned into Spider's doorway, surprised. "What?"

"It's just, something's just come up. I gotta go right now."

A little confused, a little disappointed, Dickhead knotted his mighty brow, glanced out the window, then said to Spider, "I don't know, Spider."

"We can pick it up tomorrow. It'll be fine. You can tell me all about Zeropoint. I'll be all ears. It's just, I've really got to go."

"Hmm," Dickhead said, thinking big thoughts. "I see. I do. It's just..." He took a breath, stared into a realm of fantasy only he could see. "Zeropoint is special, Spider. It's real special, and you're just the fellow to carry out my vision, you see. It's very important, Spider."

Spider thought he was going to explode. "Yes, fine, good, but surely, tomorrow morning..?"

His boss lowered his gaze and met Spider's eyes, cool and remote. "Tomorrow, Spider, this offer might not be there," he said.

"What offer?" He knew very well what Dickhead was going to offer, but he had to play his part. "You haven't told me a damn thing yet!"

Dickhead went back to the break room, and Spider could hear Dickhead *ding-ding-ding-dinging* his coffee cup again as he stirred.

His future self had not warned him Dickhead might be quite this unpredictable. "I thought you wanted me in on the ground floor, and I was just the person you needed, and all that?"

Dickhead called out, "Yes, that's right. But if you're too busy..."

Exasperated, he told Molly to hang on, he'd be right there. To Dickhead he said, "My ex-wife needs me to come pick her up. She's at the airport."

Dickhead came back into the room, bearing coffee. He said, "Opportunity knocks but once, Spider."

"Look, we can pick it up later tonight."

"The opportunity train is leaving the station, Spider. Are you on it or not?" Dickhead stood there doing a strange steam train impression, pumping his arms, making "choof-choof" noises, as he went back to the break room.

Even though he'd been told that this would happen, and even though he was doing his best to play his part, he found he did not have to fake anything. The exasperation, the infuriation, he felt about Dickhead's manipulations were genuine. The bastard was driving him nuts. Then he had a terrible thought, one he wished he could unthink, but couldn't. He found himself wondering if Dickhead was really working with Soldier Spider, not against him? What if Dickhead was, and always had been, part of the *Masada* crew, and he and Soldier Spider were working some con game on Spider to get him to do some terrible thing for them, or maybe it was some arcane initiation stunt. *Surely not*, he thought. *That would be too evil.*

Molly, meanwhile, was yelling on the phone, filling his head with loud and piercing abuse. The phrase "useless, spineless sack of shit!" came through very clearly. It was like old times. "Look," he said to her, "I just need a minute—"

"Okay, fine. Thanks!" she said, hanging up, and sounding anything but grateful. Spider felt as though he'd let her down somehow. He shook his head, wiped his face, the tension unbearable. All he could think was that right now Molly was very likely starting to look for a taxi to take herself home. The sight of her mangled body on that morgue dissection table filled his mind.

Spider went to the break room. Dickhead was scribbling something on his watchtop, a cryptic smile on his huge face.

"Dickhead, I really gotta go. Molly, she's—"

"At the airport?" he asked, faintly amused. "You said."

"Yeah. Have to go get her. Said I would, apparently."

Dickhead was now humming a little tune, and reading back what he'd written, looking pleased with himself. "So you're saying no to my offer?"

"Look," Spider said, genuinely frustrated and angry, feeling like an injured mouse caught in a game between two hungry cats, "I have to go. You don't know what Molly's like. And, shit, it's only a day. Come back tomorrow morning, first thing, you can talk to me all you want about this zero-thingy, okay? It's the best I can do."

Dickhead looked at him, studying his face, turning his head this way and that, trying to make up his mind. "Hmm, I don't know, Spider. I've got two or three other people in mind for this little opportunity."

"Oh for fuck's sake, Dickhead!"

Dickhead straightened his jacket, leaned forward, extended his big right hand. Spider shook it, feeling cold and wretched and used, hating every moment, hating himself. He was a shit. All those years ago, he'd stood up to Superintendent Sharp and all of his vile pedophile buddies, he'd gone and testified at Sharp's trial, and he'd told the bloody truth, and it had cost him everything he had. He had thought he would never feel worse than he felt then. He had been wrong. Dickhead looked him in the eye, grinned mischievously, and said, "Good night, Spider." Not "See you tomorrow," or "Later, mate," or anything suggesting Dickhead would come back and repeat his big offer. In fact, Spider thought, watching Dickhead leave — without saying a word to Malaria — he might just have blown the entire operation. Suppose Dickhead did have other people in mind for the Zeropoint project, and he was off to see one of them right now? His future self was going to kill him.

§   §   §

It took more than two infuriating hours to drive to the airport — normally a twenty-minute jaunt — in one of the shop's beat-up, fuel cell-powered vans, stop-start, stop-start, rush hour traffic, inching forward occasionally, spending long periods enduring constant horn-honking, bicycle bell-ringing, driver-screaming, traffic gridlock. He spent a lot of the time just sitting there, the van's wheel engines switched off, brooding about how he'd screwed up the interview with Dickhead, ruined everything, the entire future of the universe down the toilet, all because of bloody Molly. He'd known she would call, and he'd known Dickhead would make his big pitch. His instructions, though, had been to let Molly know he'd be there to get her — but also to accept Dickhead's offer, or at least indicate to Dickhead that he was very interested. There'd been no suggestion that Dickhead had other guys in mind for the job. His future self had assured Spider that the entire thing would go like clockwork, and all he had to do was hit his marks and say the right things. The future would take care of itself, he'd been told. Spider wondered at just what future point he had turned into such a manipulative, mendacious swine.

Traffic moved a little, as if it were on its last iota of life, and could only move a smidgeon at a time. Spider swore at Dickhead, at his future self, at Molly, at the whole bloody universe itself. He thumped and bashed the van's steering wheel so much his hands and wrists hurt, and he got so caught up in this aggravation that several times he very nearly ran over cyclists, and only managed to avoid them by jamming on the brakes and risking rear-end collisions from all the other cars and bikes behind him. It felt as if his nerves were burning up.

Then, once he reached the airport, and cleared Traffic Security Pre-Screening, it turned out there were no available parking spots. This meant spending ages driving slowly up and down, and up and down, and around all the different carpark areas, reading off the *Available Spaces* displays everywhere for a reading other than *Area Full*. It was maddening. Spider shouted at other drivers, all of whom were doing the same delicate dance, following each other around and around, whole convoys of vehicles looking for vanishingly few spots. Spider remembered wonderful games from his teenage years, like *Car Wars*, where you could mount heavy weapons on your vehicle and deal with bastards like these most efficiently. Those had been the days.

In the drop-off and pick-up lane directly in front of the Terminal entrance, taxis, their horns blasting each other, jostled for space, risking fender-bending collisions, and traffic cops employed by the airport corporation did their best to keep the taxi drivers from killing each other. Spider was painfully aware that he had to make this whole charade look good. The idea, bizarre as it still seemed to Spider, was that any scenario in which Molly either took a taxi or allowed Spider to collect her, would end in at least Molly's death, and possibly his own, too. Not that he cared too much about his own useless life just at the moment. The optimal scenario, Soldier Spider had explained, was the one where Dickhead's trained monkeys — perhaps too kind a term — collected Molly instead. Only if Spider helped arrange Molly's capture was she assured of surviving. It was killing him inside, thinking about it, and now, having to organize it in such a way that Dickhead's goons didn't realize that he, Spider, was in on it.

Dickhead's agents had to believe that he was doing his very best to pick up Molly. He knew Molly was likely already long gone, in Dickhead's custody. He had knots in his guts, so painful he could hardly sit up straight, and he felt hot and feverish, almost vibrating with anger — and could he just find *one lousy parking spot*?

It took almost thirty minutes, but he did find a spot, way out on the perimeter of the parking area, so far away from the Terminal building he could hardly see it. It was getting on towards late evening, cold and wet, with a nasty wind slicing through his clothes. Widebody jets heading for Southeast Asia roared into the sky every five minutes, even as others were visibly stacked up, ready to land, way out in the distance, their lights glimmering in the twilight sky. The rotating beam of light from the control tower swept overhead like a luminous knife.

Spider managed to get a lift on one of the crowded carpark shuttle buses, and at last made it to the Terminal, breathing hard, a nasty pain in his chest, and dripping sweat. The armed troops positioned at the Terminal entrances waved their millimeter-band scanners at him once it was his turn, but didn't like how sweaty and aggravated he looked, so they took him aside to ask him a few questions. Spider knew better than to take out his frustrations on these guys, and they let him go with a caution, suggesting he just settle the hell down. Inside, pushing and shoving his way through the hot and pressing crowds of people waiting to check in and people waiting to leave, he thought about his situation. Since he was obviously far too late, he had only one option.

Glancing about, he took in the countless brightly-colored kiosks around the Terminal. The weary traveler could rent a car or a bike, book a package holiday, buy some shiny souvenirs of Western Australia, get their clothes cleaned in an instant, buy something to read or watch or play, rent a phone or even a watch, and much else. And, at last, its little kiosk all lit up bright blue and brighter yellow, there it was: Jiffy Instant Time Travel, with its tag-line, Never Miss A Flight Again!

Spider joined the line and tried to calm down, to control his rapid breathing, worried about the pain in his chest. He wished he had some water, and looked around for one of the wandering vending droids, and in the process saw that there were already lots of people in line behind him, so he was stuck. Sweat rolling off him, he stood there, eyes closed, wondering about the symptoms of heart attacks, wishing Molly was indeed still there, wishing he and Molly were still together, wishing — he could not believe he'd been reduced to bloody wishing! *Forty-four years old, fat and going gray, and I'm standing here wishing for things.* He was disgusted with himself. *You might as well wish for a bloody pony!*

He'd asked Soldier Spider, when the bastard first presented this little detail, just what they would do to her, and the older Spider had shrugged. He didn't know, he said, and Spider didn't know if he was telling the truth or lying. Spider asked why she even had to be mixed up in the whole stupid caper in the first place. The old bastard had told him, matter-of-factly, that Dickhead wanted to get an "edge" over Spider, to get him to cooperate. Dickhead's people had plans for Spider, plans he suspected Spider would not be willing to carry out.

"What kind of plans?"

"I can't say. I mean the timeline will be shifting and your future will no longer be my past. All I can say for certain is his plans are aimed at us."

"But you know an attack's coming?"

"That's right."

"And somehow I'm involved."

"You make it possible for Dickhead to attack us. Otherwise, the—"

"Flux-proofing thing."

"Exactly. He can attack our people, but he has to get inside the ship first. You make it possible for him to do that."

"Because I'm you."

"Got it in one, Spider," his future self said. "Our ship's flux-proofing is like a firewall, with open ports corresponding to her crew. I'm part of the crew, so the firewall lets me though. And because it lets me through, it'll let you through."

"Uh-huh," Spider said.

"So, since you're reasonably likely to object to leading an attack against us, Dickhead needs a way to persuade you to see things his way."

"Shit."

"Yeah."

"Are they gonna hurt Molly?"

"Probably."

"God," Spider said, anguished.

"Sorry," Soldier Spider said, and he looked genuinely upset at the idea. "Imagine how it feels for me to tell you all this."

"Mmm."

Now, back in the Terminal building, remembering that exchange helped, a little. The older Spider recognized, indeed understood only too well, how hard this was for Spider and his hopes for a reconciliation with Molly. He could imagine what she was likely to say, if he got a chance to talk to her again: "And you let them?" No amount of handwaving about the End of Time and parasites stuck on the outside of the universe, eating reality, was going to cut any ice, not with Molly. She would only see that he had let her down. Had exposed her to who-knew-what kinds of suffering. Standing there, withered and alone in this deafening, bustling, smelly crowd, hearing nothing but Molly's voice ringing in his head, telling him she wanted nothing more to do with him, Spider found himself remembering the night — it felt like ages ago now — that the first Future Spider had shown him those crime scene photos of Molly, murdered, dead, sprawled on the floor of her house — the house that had once also been his. It had all happened in a different timeline, the result of a whole bunch of different choices. The memory ached, seeing Molly like that, on the receiving end of a brutal death. To say nothing of the sight of her body aboard the

Masada, being able to touch her, knowing it really was her, and she really was dead, not just an image on a handheld. Would it now come true? Was this one of those events in the torrent of history that "wanted" to happen, no matter what changes time travelers tried to make?

Spider seethed, standing there, thinking of Molly, loving Molly. It had been Molly who wanted the separation, not Spider. He'd gone along with it because, above all, he wanted her to be happy, and if that meant not being involved in her life, well, that was okay. He'd do it, not make a stink about it, and hope for the best.

Thinking about Molly, remembering their wedding day, on Cottesloe Beach at dawn, surrounded by family and friends and well-wishers. Molly, luminous in dawn twilight; him, with a tux a size too small.

He wiped his eyes, and started to think about things in a way he had not thought about them before. All that mattered, as far as he was concerned, right now, was Molly. Right? He didn't care about anything else, not Clea Fassbinder, not James Rutherford, not even the future itself. His whole universe was and always had been Molly. She was everything, and, he knew, would always be everything.

It was the kind of thought he used to have all the time, back when they were young and the future beckoned across the years. He realized he had not thought of Molly this way recently, not at all. The image of Molly he carried in his mind lately was the annoyed, peeved Molly, the Molly rolling her eyes at him, but still wanting him to fix her broken toilet, or put up a fence in the yard, or mow the lawn — once he'd fixed the mower first, of course. He hadn't thought of their wedding day in years.

How could he have been so stupid?

Standing there in the Jiffy Time Travel queue, still several customers away from getting help, an idea formed in Spider's overheated mind. Maybe, he thought, it was time to go off-script. Screw the future. Soldier Spider had said himself that all things are possible; not every timeline led to that future. Some timelines, surely, Spider thought, led somewhere better.

CHAPTER 17

Spider, already feeling lighter and more relaxed now that he had a plan of his own, went up to the Jiffy counter and, once he got to the front of the line, told the pretty young woman staffing the shop he wanted to rent a "Jiffy," as their units were known.

She had been smiling — the shop was doing great business — but on hearing Spider's request, she turned apologetic. "Actually, I'm really sorry, sir. All our units are busy just now."

For a moment he thought he'd scream. Then he thought things through. "Busy?"

The young woman checked her screen. "One will be available in twenty minutes, as soon as I have it cleaned and prepared. Can you wait?"

"Oh," Spider said, smiling now, too, "I can wait with the best of them."

§ § §

Exactly twenty minutes later Spider returned to find the very same young shop assistant standing next to a recently returned and spotlessly cleaned Jiffy Time Machine. It was a one-man, booth-type device with clear plastic walls and simplified controls. Spider briefly chatted with her about the technical specs of the unit. He knew they were limited to hops of no more than twenty-four hours in either direction, and designed to auto-return. Built in Shanghai, they were very popular and, it turned out, easy to maintain.

"There you go, Mr. Webb," she said, smiling. He thanked her and she gave him a screen containing the end-user release, in which he promised not to use Jiffy products and/or services in order to gain unfair commercial or pecuniary advantage over other people with regard to games of chance, sporting events, or financial transactions on pain of severe penalties under the Act — all standard chrono-industry boilerplate. He signed, and she handed him the unit's key. He stepped into the unit. There was a simple numerical keypad, a small display, "+" and "-" buttons, and the big green GO button. Next to the button was a coin slot: each hour of travel in either direction would set you back one dollar. He fished out a two-dollar coin, fed it into the coin slot, punched in "-2", and hit the GO button. He heard the familiar three-chord jingle, and a voice said, "Thank you for taking a Jiffy!"

The only real indicator that anything had happened was that the sky outside the Terminal was noticeably brighter. Certainly the crowds inside the Terminal were no less bustling. Once out of the machine, it vanished, heading back to its "present". Thinking about what to do, Spider popped his watch, which was receiving updated information about flight arrivals and departures, and checked that Molly's Thai Airlines flight was, in this timeline, still on time. It was, and scheduled to arrive shortly. *Right*, he thought, furling his watch-screen. On landing, Molly would have to wait around while the aircraft was taken to its parking slot — which, given how congested the airport was right now, could take a while. Deplaning, working through the endless duty-free areas, baggage claim — though that could take time as well, he realized — and then the line-up for Immigration and Customs. He realized it might take nearly an hour for Molly to get out to the arrivals hall. She had complained in her phone call that she'd encountered trouble with Quarantine over a bunch of bananas, and who knew how long that might take? The problem was that Dickhead's goons could snatch Molly before she made it out here to the arrivals hall, and there was no way he could get through the near-military-grade security apparatus to reach her in time. He'd have to wait. Muttering to himself, Spider bought himself a vending machine coffee and a chocolate bar and sat himself down where he could keep an eye on the doors leading out to the arrivals hall.

This was fine for a few minutes, but soon he started feeling nervous. It was hard to just sit and relax. Everyone he saw somehow looked suspicious, especially all those people who appeared perfectly innocuous: nobody who looked that innocuous could be anything but guilty, Spider thought. Fortunately, he realized that was madness talking, started thinking about a different approach, and soon formed an idea. He got on the phone and called Molly.

She answered almost immediately. "Molly Webb, hello?"

It was wonderful hearing her voice. "Hi, Moll, it's me. You okay?"

There was a brief pause, then she said, "Al? That is you, right?"

"Yeah, hi. How are you going?"

"What are you calling me now for?"

"Just letting you know I'm here at the airport, like we arranged." Never mind that if he was here, waiting for Molly, then she had no reason to phone him later to protest that he wasn't here. He figured in the overall scheme of things, where every possible reality occupies a separate timeline or world, both realities had plenty of room.

"Well, that's great. Thanks," she said, still surprised, but also sounding a little peeved that he'd bothered her during the flight.

Should he tell her there was a possibility — indeed, a likelihood — that bad guys were going to kidnap her? Sure, why not? Except, she'd never believe it, and why should she?

"How'd the exhibition go?" Spider asked, trying to find something to talk about, to keep her voice in his head as long as possible. Soldier Spider, he recalled, had suggested the exhibition had not gone well.

"Okay, you know. Made some good contacts."

"Great!" he said, smiling too hard.

"Look, it's lovely to hear from you, it's just, I'm really worn out. I was just getting a bit of sleep when you..."

"Oh," he said. "Oh, I didn't know. Sorry."

She managed a small laugh. "No worries. Look, I'll talk to you soon."

Panicking a little, knowing this might be the last conversation he would ever have with her, he flailed about trying to think of something to say, anything would do, just to keep her on the line. "See you," he said at last, unexpectedly upset, and killed the link. "Shit!" he said under his breath and wiped his eyes.

Molly's flight was twenty minutes late. Spider, who'd felt so clever and resourceful when he was executing his brilliant plan, now found himself sweating and tense and frustrated. After a while, with people crowded in around him, Spider found he could no longer remain seated; he got up and tried to press through the crowd so that he could be as close to the doors as possible; with a bit of luck he might minimize Molly's exposure to any lurking bad guys. But once he reached the front of the pressing crowd, breathing hard, he started looking at these other people with him, and it was amazing, he thought, just how wickedly guilty they all looked! *The bastards! Each and every single one of them, all doing their best to look like regular civilians, mostly dressed casually, some of them wrangling small and disagreeable children — they're all clearly evil and bent on subduing me and making off with Molly, and the fate of the entire universe hangs in the balance!*

And, once he caught himself thinking like that again he stopped, glanced around, and now saw only a bunch of tired, anxious and unhappy people — particularly the ones with fractious children — all of whom wanted nothing more than to pick up their friends, their partners, their family members, and get them the hell out of this wretched airport as soon as humanly possible. All of those people who looked so innocently full of evil intent, he noticed, couldn't really give a bugger about him. All of which, he thought, made much more sense.

In fact, and this thought rocked him back on his heels, he had no real proof that Molly had not, the first time round, after calling Spider to complain about his lack of presence, simply gotten herself a taxi and gone home. Who knows? he thought, she could be there right now, in the other timeline, having a shower, getting something to eat, maybe even having a nice, safe nap in her own bed.

Wait a minute, he told himself. If Molly had left without him, taking a taxi, then she would have died — at least according to Soldier Spider. Any scenario in which Molly decided against waiting for him led to her death. "That's right", he said aloud, remembering the sight of Molly's cold body in that procedure room on the *Masada*, "You're trying to save her life. Focus, Spider."

It was, for Spider, a moment of clarity, something he'd sorely missed since his life had skidded way off-course with the discovery of Clea Fassbinder's body so long ago. *You're just one man, Spider*, he told himself. *Take it easy, you'll get through this.*

When, at last, the doors opened and torrents of weary travelers, each pushing trolleys stacked with bulging bags, began flowing into the arrivals hall, Spider found himself first smiling, then starting to panic again, trying to peer through the turbulent crowds, hoping to spot Molly, only Molly did not appear. Hundreds of other non-Molly people appeared, some of them even looking vaguely like her — that same cranky set to the mouth, the same "I can't do anything with this hair!" — but his former wife was a no-show. Spider's hopes were sinking fast. *She can't be gone already!* He imagined Dickhead had paid off air-side employees to do a little job for him, to take one particular passenger aside for a little chat, to clear something up, just an administrative thing, nothing to worry about, you're not in any trouble, now just step in here, that's it, and *wham!* Next stop, End of Time!

"God, what's the matter with you?"

He jumped, startled, and found himself looking at her, at Molly, the one and only. Thinner and older than he remembered, more careworn, showing a little sunburn on her cheeks, nose and shoulders, her freckles blazing, but the same intelligent gaze, the same disappointment in him. It didn't matter. "I didn't see you," he said, knowing it was stupid as he was saying it, but beyond caring.

"Well, then," Molly said, "where are you parked?"

Now she was here, Spider realized, things were about to get lively. Once more he turned his gaze to the throngs of people all around them, looking for anyone who might be working for Dickhead. For a moment he watched eager Customs beagles and their handlers.

"Well, are we going or not?"

Spider flashed an awkward smile, trying to convey the idea that everything was fine, nothing to worry about. Molly's trolley, burdened down with several huge suitcases, was very nearly immovable. He wondered how on Earth she'd managed to propel this load all the way from baggage claim. It was so heavy he thought he'd need a tractor.

"You sure you're all right, Spider? You look like shit, you know that?"

"People keep telling me," he said, glancing about. He knew she was right. How long had he been wearing these same white overalls? Spider went on to tell her they had quite a journey across the endless parking lots to where he had parked his van. Molly suggested he go ahead of her, grab the van, and bring it round to the pick-up/drop-off area in front of the Terminal. The very idea terrified Spider, so he made a show of not minding the enormous effort involved in keeping the trolley moving, and the heap of her bags reasonably steady. Molly offered to personally carry one of the smaller bags.

They made it almost a hundred meters through the parking lot, with Molly constantly bitching at him to go and get the bloody van, when Spider noticed a blue VW van slowly approaching. He didn't recognize the guy driving, but something about it looked like exactly like the kind of thing he had been watching out for ever since he got here.

He had a choice, he realized, watching the van. He could let the bad guys take Molly, as he'd been told to do, because, after all, everything was at stake. All he had to do was willingly send Molly into a situation where she would suffer, but survive, and hate him forever.

Or — the side door of the van was opening, and Spider could see a couple of guys in black hunched inside, ready to leap out — he could try something else. "Get behind me, Molly," he said to her in a voice something like his old "Stop, Police!" voice. It worked, too: Molly blinked and immediately ducked behind him, but then started in with the questions and the indignation.

Spider said, in a loud voice, speaking to the air around him, "Spider, if you're following this, you know that more than anything I want Molly to be safe. You know how I feel about her. You—"

"Al, what the hell are you...?"

He went on. "I will not let Molly be taken by these goons. I'll fight the bastards, and I am prepared to risk my own death if necessary. You know that. So here's the deal. You take her. Take her to the *Masada*. Look after her. You told me Dickhead can't touch anybody aboard your ship. So you take her, and protect her. In return—" The van stopped. Spider could smell its deep-fryer exhaust. Two guys leapt out, dressed the way Soldier Spider dressed, all in black spec-ops gear, faces obscured, hands in gloves. One was telling Spider, "Now, let's not be stupid about this, okay?"

Spider said to the air, "Take her now, and I'll do whatever the hell you want. Anything you want. Just protect Molly. I don't care about anything else, okay? Okay?"

The other of the two goons produced a stun-gun, and leveled it, aiming it at Spider.

Molly, hiding behind her stack of bags, was shouting, "What the fuck is this? Al? What's going on?"

"Hand her over, Mr. Webb," the first one said, sounding reasonable.

"Anytime now, Spider!" Spider yelled at the sky.

Molly vanished.

The goon with the stun-gun swore and shot Spider. He went down, twitching, gritting his teeth, the great tottering tower of Molly's luggage the last thing he saw before blackness swept over him.

CHAPTER 18

Spider was sitting in what looked and felt like a regular office chair, in front of a spartan desk, in a small clearing in — as far as he could see — a vast field of towering sunflowers. The sunflowers made him think of triffids. Then again, he realized, the whole scene looked like parts of rural France he'd seen in coverage of the Tour de France. It was a baking hot day; the sun, looming overhead, was huge and reddish, casting menacing purple shadows. Millions of bugs hissed and whirred about. Way in the distance, Spider spotted a big bird of prey, possibly a hawk, hovering over a particular spot in the field, peering down, watching something which didn't know it had only moments to live.

The last thing Spider remembered was — now, wait a minute, it would come to him if he concentrated — the airport? Molly? Some kind of trouble, hmm, that sounded familiar, and now that he thought of it, his joints felt sore, and his breathing wasn't quite right, and he coughed a bit, though that might have to do with all the dust in the air from the sunflowers.

Then he remembered. "Oh, shit," he said, horrified, and got up from the chair. Standing there in the clearing, staring around, trying not to hyperventilate, trying not to panic, he thought, *It's gotta be a sim. And if it's a sim, there'll be some way to tell, right*? Actually, thinking about it, that might not be the case. Even so, he did not believe he really was sitting in the middle of a field of sunflowers in rural France on a hot summer's day. One look at that sun up there, that wasn't right. Then he thought, *God, what if that is the sun? What if this is way in the future? Soldier Spider took me off into the future, and he said Dickhead would probably do much the same, so this could be...* He had to look away.

Then he heard a rhythmic thrashing noise approaching from the distance; someone was coming to see him, he figured, and it was likely going to be bloody Dickhead McMahon, keen to take Spider aside and show off. Soldier Spider had told him that if Dickhead wanted to show off, then by all means let him. It was possible the bastard might let something crucial slip in an unguarded moment, something that would be useful later. *Right,* Spider thought. *Fine. I'll just stand here, not panicking, not furious, not worried about Molly even a bit, and let Dickhead schmooze me all he wants.* He figured he'd want dinner and a show afterwards, though.

Then a bunch of sunflowers at the edge of the clearing were pulled aside, and there he was in all his glory: Dickhead McMahon, still dressed in that same business suit that he got off the rack at K-Mart. He nodded hello, and took a moment trying to brush dust off his suit with his hands. The bugs were bothering him, too, Spider noticed, so that was something: whatever the hell this was, it wasn't just his own hallucination, and that, oddly, was a comfort.

Dickhead finished dusting himself down and started to stride across the clearing, coming around the desk, keen to give Spider a big buddy-hug. Spider saw him coming and the first impulse that came to him was to hit the bastard. He'd held himself back the last time he felt like hitting Dickhead, and regretted it. This time Dickhead had it coming. Spider remembered getting stun-gunned, the way it felt, his whole body on fire, convulsing on the filthy floor of some rented van.

Then Dickhead was right in front of him, beaming, saying, "Spider! So good to see you!" and his arms were out, ready to smother him, absorb him — and Spider snapped. He'd had enough. Glaring at Dickhead, he took a step back, out of the man's grasp, then hauled off and hit him hard across the cheek. Dickhead staggered and groaned, reaching a hand up to touch his face, and he looked at his fingers — there was no blood, and then he looked at Spider, dismayed and confused, then angry, and Spider knew Dickhead was thinking about hitting him.

Spider was boiling with adrenaline, up on the balls of his feet, ready for anything, watching Dickhead, trying to read his face. Spider's hand was starting to hurt, though. Was it broken? His fingers weren't responding properly, and there was a blinding, piercing pain in his knuckles, and he thought, *Shit! Not again!* He held that hand lightly in his left hand, probing it for damage. Dickhead, still holding his face, nodded at him, and smiled. "Out of practice, mate," he said, goodnaturedly.

"Yeah, a bit," Spider said, and felt stupid.

Dickhead went to the desk, touched it, and a control panel appeared. He called for medical assistance, and presently a smartly-dressed female robot assistant came whirring through the sunflowers. Dickhead told the machine to see to Spider first, which she did, quickly examining his hand, determining that nothing was broken, but that Spider should probably rest the hand as much as possible. She applied a cold, antiseptic-smelling gel that tingled and then burned down into his knuckles and finger joints, and after a moment his hand felt almost as good as new. He said thanks.

The bot smiled and went to deal with Dickhead. Dickhead's face was red where Spider had hit him, and he was trying to tell if any of his top teeth had come loose; it looked as if a few of them had been damaged. She took her time, working over his cheek and inside his mouth, applying various treatments. Dickhead winced and grimaced, and told the machine, "Hey, he started it," which Spider heard and which made him want to protest that if Dickhead's goons hadn't abducted him—

Dickhead said, "Look, fair's fair, you've got a legitimate grievance, Spider, and I do apologize for that. The pickup did not go as planned, and the boys truly fucked it up. I told them not to rough you up in any way, that you were to be treated as a guest, but they didn't listen, and now they're, well, let's say they're exploring other employment options. If you can't follow simple instructions, you've got no place in Zeropoint, that's what I say."

All of which left Spider, flexing his fingers, astonished. "That's it?"

Dickhead was leaning against the edge of the table. "What more do you want? I said I'm sorry. It's not at all how I wanted you brought into the operation. I don't blame you a bit for taking a whack at me. I'd have done the same."

"Right, I see," Spider said, still surprised at Dickhead's graciousness.

Dickhead got up, clapped his hands, beamed, his face looking fine, and said to Spider, "God, I'll bet you're hungry. What do you feel like?"

Hungry? The word "hungry" didn't begin to cover it. Spider was starving. It felt as if he hadn't eaten anything substantial in ages. He decided to chance Dickhead's hospitality. "What have you got?"

Turning to the robot assistant again, Dickhead said, "Two steaks, eggs, chips, onions, medium-done." Then to Spider, "Don't know about you, but I could murder a coffee. What do you reckon?" Before Spider could answer in the affirmative, Dickhead told the assistant to also bring them both long macchiatos. The assistant nodded, repeated back the order, and left, disappearing back into the sunflowers from whence she came.

"Take a seat," Dickhead said to Spider, pulling out the chair for him. He went around to his side of the desk, still touching his cheek gingerly, and pulled out his own chair. Spider noticed that Dickhead's chair was noticeably bigger than his, and thought, *Typical*. Spider's chair was comfortable, and seemed, surrounded by all this rolling French countryside, quite out of place. He took a moment, now that things were as normal as they were likely to get, to admire the realism of the illusion.

"Got your own holodeck, huh, Dickhead?"

"It's a 'Display Room,' actually, Spider. We do much of the running of the ship from here."

Spider glanced sideways at his host. "So we are on a ship? I wondered."

"Oh, pardon my manners. Yes. Welcome to the Timeship *Destiny*, Spider. You are an honored guest. Once we've eaten and had a bit of a chat about things, I'll show you your quarters."

"So I'm staying a while, then?"

"Well, actually, no, but I'm hoping you'll be back, and when you do return, there will be a place for you here aboard this flagship."

Doing his best to keep up, Spider nodded. "So all this, this is just you showing off for my benefit?"

"I wouldn't call it showing off, exactly," Dickhead said, clearly stung by the accusation.

The assistant returned, this time bearing dinner. The steaks were enormous; the eggs perfectly done; the chips were hot and fresh. Hungry as Spider was, there was no way he could possibly eat all of this. The coffee, when he tried it, was strong almost to the point of being unbearable, but not quite. In short, it was divine. Spider sat looking at everything, taking in the marvelous aromas and the steam, and tried a chip — perhaps too hot just yet — and found himself thinking that if this is how the bad guys eat, maybe being a bad guy was okay.

Then he stopped, realized what he was thinking, and felt, for a moment, like pushing everything away. Except he really was desperate for something to eat.

Dickhead dismissed the bot and told Spider to get down to business. Spider didn't need further encouragement.

Later, once the dishes had been cleared away, and Spider was on his third coffee, Dickhead asked him, "So, Spider, any questions?"

Spider had quite a few. "Well, since you ask. You said we're on a timeship, not a starship, or whatever."

"That's right. Basically, an extreme development of existing chronotechnology. With one small twist: we can hop across from one universe to the next, playing with timelines, preferencing some over others. It's made us strong, Spider. Very strong."

This was much like what Soldier Spider had told him, but he couldn't let on to Dickhead that he already knew what was going on. He'd been a little anxious about that during dinner; he hadn't said anything about the whole "timeship" thing, mainly because the food was so good, and there was so much of it, all he wanted to do was dig in and eat up. Now, stuffed to the point where he had to adjust his belt, and planning to stay seated for a good long time, he could start playing the innocent time machine repairman, just as Soldier Spider had told him. "Really?" he said, doing his best to look all saucer-eyed with surprise. "Does that mean you can choose...?"

"Yes, we can manipulate events, even history, up to a point."

Spider nodded. "I hope you're using your powers for good, Dickhead."

Dickhead smiled. "Of course!" he said, and laughed.

"That's good to hear." Spider didn't believe a word of it, but remembered what Soldier Spider had told him, that it had been Dickhead's people manipulating Spider's timelines. "So, what? You've been living here, on this 'timeship'" — He used giant air-quotes to emphasize the weirdness of "timeship" as an idea, and hoped he wasn't overdoing it— "all this time? What about your wife?"

Dickhead hardly blinked. "Sarah's fine, thanks. I've got a condo in Perth. She lives there, and I can use time-travel in such a way that from her perspective I'm a regular businessman, taking care of things. Anyway, I pop back here from time to time to touch base, update everyone on what's going on, upcoming projects, that kind of thing."

"Okay, right. Hmm. So where — um, when? — are we, exactly?"

Dickhead consulted a panel on his control display, then looked at Spider. "I don't want to alarm you, Spider, okay?"

"Okay. Not alarmed. Not too much, anyway."

"This is the, um, 'far future.' The way, far future."

Spider did his best to look suitably shocked and impressed. "Oh. Okay. So, um, how far is 'way far?'"

Dickhead folded his hands together, thought about it for a moment, scratched his chin, then looked Spider in the eye. "It's hard to say, exactly, in terms of years."

"Um, what?"

"It's difficult, all right? There comes a point when you're so far uptime that numbers no longer cut it, that's all."

"I see," Spider said. He was having no trouble faking how impressed and even scared he was. The first time round, when Soldier Spider had introduced him to all this, it had been bad enough, but even on this, his second exposure, it was still a freakish thing to try to handle. "Okay."

"Spider," Dickhead said, "I could probably get someone to give me a figure, okay? If that would help. It's just that any such figure would have to be expressed with scientific notation, it's so far from your own time."

"Oh. I see. That's..."

"Alarming?"

"Yes," he said, nodding, "yes, very alarming. It's also making me wonder just how in the hell you're able to get a time machine to reach so far. Translation engines, um, back home, the best recorded time displacement is, uh, almost three thousand years? Something like that?"

"We've got time engines that would make God envious, if you'll pardon me saying so, Spider."

"Right. Of course you have. Typical, even." Good old Dickhead, always having to have the biggest, the most powerful, the most obnoxious, even when it came to timeships! Spider was impressed, sort of.

Dickhead added, "It's very peaceful, though. Very quiet. Spacious, you might say. More coffee, Spider? Something stronger, perhaps?" He had his finger poised over a tab on his control display, ready to summon his assistant again.

"You could tell me what the hell's going on. This is all very impressive and, frankly, shiny, Dickhead, but so what? What's the point?"

"The point, Spider, is simple. There's a war on. It's a bad one, stretching across the end of the universe, the end of time itself. Every timeline, every alternate or parallel world, it all winds up here, at the end of all things. It's been a long war, but then again, it's barely started, depending on your perspective. Everybody who's ever thought about it has tried to get here, the Everest of the Cosmos, if you like, the ultimate summit, the deepest abyss of the ocean. Everyone wants to be here, because from here you get the best bloody view, Spider. You can see all of history, gazillions of years, whole epochs like blinks of an eye. And from here you can fiddle with all that's gone before, pulling the strings of the past, making things the way you want them. It's strong stuff, my friend. The strongest. The urge to fiddle, well, it's unbearable..."

This was not exactly what Soldier Spider had told Spider. "The end of time? How can there be an *end* of time? Surely it just goes on and on, endlessly. Are you saying there's a Big Crunch, and we're circling the ultimate drain, or something like that? Is that it?"

"Oh, no, nothing like that. Space-time turns out to be flat. Just flat. No 'Big Crunch,' no 'Big' anything, in fact. The universe, all the universes, just spread out forever and ever, amen."

"Then I don't see how the universe can just end, you say yourself it goes on forever."

"Yes, Spider. That's right. And I'm trying to tell you — and forgive me for trying to dress it up a bit to make it interesting — the thing is, hmm, okay, think about protons, okay? Protons last practically forever, right?"

Spider nodded, thinking hard. "Ten to the power of 35 years, plus or minus?"

"Exactly. And what I'm saying is, we're well beyond the Proton Age here. It's just an infinite void, only the void itself is flinging itself apart: every bit of space-time hurling itself the hell away from every other bit, stretching it all out in every direction, all at once. You'd think sooner or later the rate of expansion would make it rip itself, and you'd get a whacking big hole, and the whole universe would flutter and whiz about in higher-dimensional space like a deflating balloon — but it never does. It never tears, it never rips, it just constantly expands."

Spider had heard about this accelerating expansion, and heard that it was likely to do with a mysterious force known colloquially as "dark energy" that was bound up with Einstein's "cosmological constant." It was one thing to read about such things in the pages of *New Scientist*, or on the tubes, but quite another to find yourself in a timeship in — he was told — the midst of that void. He found himself looking down at his own body, checking his feet, legs, arms and hands. Everything seemed okay. He didn't appear to be stretching apart at impossible speeds. "Uh, Dickhead, small problem."

Dickhead nodded. "The stretching apart thing?"

"Yeah."

"It's happening to us as we speak."

"It is?"

"Oh yeah. Nothing to worry about. Your subconscious mind handles the whole thing behind the scenes."

"But I look... I look exactly the same. You look the same."

"It's all in the mind, Spider. Relax."

"But—"

Dickhead cut him off. "Mind over matter, Spider. It's not that you're exploding, Spider, or anything like that. It's that the space-time in which you're embedded is itself stretching. This means that everything embedded in it stretches with it. In reality, the atoms and molecules of your body are being pulled every way from Sunday, and mine, too — but our minds, Spider, our minds present us with the illusion that everything is perfectly fine."

"Holy shit!" Spider said.

Dickhead went on, telling Spider most of the same things Soldier Spider had told him on the *Masada*, which was fine, and Spider did his best to look all amazed and troubled and dizzy at the thought of it all. But Dickhead told him things Soldier Spider had not said. "The End of Time, Spider, is like the bottom of the deepest ocean trenches. There are things alive here, uniquely adapted to this most extreme of environments—"

"Uh-huh..." Spider said, thinking about what his future self had told him. For one thing, Soldier Spider had told him there were odd things living on the outside of the universe, feeding on the exhaust of the Vores. "Go on."

Dickhead said, "So this is the Great Abyss. Things adapted to live here are not actually from here; they started as things brought here by other time travelers, and left behind, like waste ballast water dumped by container ships that turns out to contain all manner of nasty parasites that take over and destroy local ecosystems."

"You said there's no matter, though."

"That's right. No *native* matter. These other things, they were, as I said, brought here. They're fine. They're cold, of course, and they grow slowly, do everything slowly. But they've been out here, growing, adapting, changing, for, well, pardon the unscientific turn of phrase here, but they've been out here for zillions of years."

"Oh, zillions. That impresses me," Spider said, folding his arms and leaning back, and trying not to panic.

"Look, the point is, Spider, that 'the End of Time,' like the bottom of the deepest parts of the ocean, is far from an arid wasteland. The place is alive, Spider! Things are going on, civilizations are rising! It's a land of opportunity, sort of!" Dickhead was staring off over Spider's head, his face full of rapture, a convert, a true believer.

Spider knew he was in big trouble. "This is all great and all, Dickhead, but, um, like I said, so what?"

Dickhead blinked a few times, came back to himself, and looked down at Spider, a little disappointed. "You can't see it?"

"See what? All I see is bloody sunflowers!"

"Spider, I'm trying to do you a favor."

"Well, do me a favor by telling me what the hell is going on!"

"All right. Fair enough. You're right, you're right. It's just, well..."

"Complicated?"

"Yeah. Complicated."

"Okay," Spider said. "Here we are. End of Time. Creepy-crawlies. Woo."

Dickhead sat down again. He touched a control on the desk. The scene around them changed: from the middle of a sunflower farm in rural France, to the deepest of deep space, deep time. Blackness that had to be seen to be believed. A lack of color, lack of anything at all, that defied description. An emptiness that hurt the mind, that seemed to cry out for something, anything, to fill it. Spider, confronted with it, seeing it all around him, felt his mind revolt. It was the sort of overwhelming emptiness that makes the worst kind of darkness: the emptiness that your mind cannot help but populate. Before you know it, it's not empty at all, but teeming with all of the things you've found terrifying throughout your entire life, dating all the way back to things that scared you in your mother's womb. Just looking out at that darkness panicked Spider. He could hardly breathe. His heart boomed and pounded in his throat. He wanted to run and run and never stop, and it was only the obvious fact that there was nowhere to run that kept him sitting there — and the fact that he could still feel the solidity of the desk and his chair that kept him anchored to reason.

"Okay," Spider whispered, terrified, "this is freaking me out. Can we go back to the sunflowers now?"

"This, Spider, is a representation of the view outside. It's more complicated than it looks, because of the expansion and so forth, but, just for the sake of argument, this is it, the End of Time. We call it that because there's nothing really to measure time against. There's no heat, for example; out there it's absolute zero. The cosmic microwave background radiation, the fabled evidence of the Bang, well, it's gone, it's over. Think about that, Spider. Absolute fucking zero. It's a breathtaking thing to contemplate. It's like, even though it's a vacuum out there, it's also like solid ice, ice you could never break."

Spider was gripping his chair so tight he had punctured the seat cushion with his thumb, and he hadn't noticed.

Dickhead was still talking, as if narrating a nature documentary, as if everything was perfectly fine. "Now, this is the interesting bit, Spider. You see, looking out at that, thinking about the temperature, you'd say to yourself, well, nothing can live in an environment like that, and you'd be pretty well right — except, you'd actually be dead wrong. If we adjust the colors, just so..." He touched a control. "You can start to see..." Gradations in the blackness became apparent. With those came what Spider first took to be dark points of some kind in what he guessed was the distance, but there was a large sphere in the foreground that had the same lack of color. After some more adjustments, the distant points and the nearby sphere turned a dull, brownish red, and he could see — what was it, texture? — on the surface of the sphere, some kind of stubbly, knobbly texture.

"Is that some kind of dead star or something?" he asked, his voice barely audible. There was no earthly reason why something as ordinary as a dead star should even still exist in such extreme conditions, and he knew that, but he felt lost and petrified, and his mind reached for the familiar.

"Actually, no. These are much smaller than stars. These are not much bigger than a clenched fist, or maybe a softball. These are colonies, like the colonies of bacteria you'd see in a petri dish, but on a much, much bigger scale. Each of the knobbly bits you can see is a lifeform, a tiny lifeform, and they huddle together like this to share what little heat they have. Over time, they circulate into the center while others rise to the outside. Not unlike penguins huddling against antarctic storms, actually. Now then..." He made more adjustments. The foreground colony turned bright red, with even brighter patches that shifted hues; in the background the other colonies grew brighter as well, but were joined by many more points, showing as a dull gray. There were far more of these gray colonies than red ones.

Spider said, "Dead ones?"

Dickhead nodded. "Natural selection at work."

It was a lot to think about. The gears of evolution still grinding blindly away, even here, Spider thought, at the end of everything. "It must take ages for anything to happen, though," he said, watching, starting to feel less freaked out now that he saw something familiar going on.

One of the "living" points in the background grew much bigger as Dickhead zoomed the image. Here was a colony visibly under attack: only portions of the surface showed up as alive; other areas showed the red much brighter, but blighted with something black, like a plaque. Dotted across the black plaque were dazzlingly bright points that looked like they were white-hot luminous vapors suspended in space. "Marauders," Dickhead said, his eyes shining, again full of that worrying rapture Spider had seen earlier.

"They're something like the Crown-of-Thorns starfish destroying the Great Barrier Reef," Dickhead said. "Only they're conscious, intelligent, and very, very determined. They're the dominant form of life in this environment. They spread by spores that take millions of 'years' to travel from one colony to the next, they land, and they take what they need, kill the weak, and move on. We think they're kinda cool, frankly, Spider."

Spider was less impressed. "So you're saying they're sorta like ancient Vikings or something?"

"They're survivors. Faced with impossible conditions, they're making a go of it, and they're learning. Their tactics change over time. They're starting to build things. It's breathtaking!"

"Okay, fine, no worries," Spider said, sensing something wasn't quite right with this picture. "So where's the catch? What's wrong?"

"What's wrong, Spider, is that all this is under threat."

"Something worse than these Marauders?"

"These little guys are, in the scheme of things, pretty small beer. They're starting to put together a uniquely adapted civilization. It's taken them billions of years of hard work. Think of that. But something new is coming. Something bigger, and much more threatening."

"And these new guys, they're not so cool as your pet Marauders here?"

"They're called 'Vores', Spider, because they eat everything. Space, time, energy, matter — the substance of the manifold itself."

"Fuck," Spider said. He'd been wondering when the Vores would enter Dickhead's strange universe.

"We believe they are Angels sent by God Above to cleanse the universe."

Spider coughed. "I beg your pardon, Dickhead?"

"Angels, Spider. They are burning the universe."

Spider's mind reeled. He remembered, the other day, Dickhead asking him if he believed in angels. Remembered the way all those bloody motivational posters everywhere featured angels going about their ineffable work. Dickhead," he said, hardly able to speak.

Dickhead went on. "God has decided it is hopelessly corrupted and foul and it must be destroyed to make way for a new Creation."

"Cosmos 2.0? Is that it?"

"Spider, listen to me. This is the important part." Dickhead was getting a little sweaty, Spider noticed. He imagined Dickhead drumming this into his followers' heads again and again until they Understood the True Importance of Their Mission.

"I'm all ears, Dickhead."

Dickhead clearly didn't care for Spider's tone, but he went on. "We can't attack the Vores directly." He went on, describing the Vores in similar terms to the way Soldier Spider had described them to him not long ago. Higher-dimensional space. Hyperspheres. End of Reality as we know it. Where Dickhead differed from Soldier Spider was in his vision of the Vores as Angels of Destruction. "We believe, and I need you to take this on board, and make it part of your own beliefs, Spider, you mark my words, this knowledge will save your life, we believe that the Vores must be allowed to do their sacred work."

"Uh-huh," Spider said, trying not to panic. "Do go on."

"Those who assist the Vores will be rewarded, Spider. I see you don't believe me. That's understandable. It's a lot to take on board, but you mark my words, son—"

"Dickhead, I gotta tell you, I don't know about this."

The huge old bastard sat there, looking at Spider, dripping the sweat of great passion, his eyes red and weary. He loosened his collar, sat back in his chair, taking a breather, thinking how to convince Spider. At last, he said, "Have you heard of the 'Final Secret of the Cosmos'?"

He thought, *I'm about to hear all about it.* "I have to say, no, I have not heard of the Final Secret of the Cosmos. Why don't you enlighten me, Dickhead?" He was wishing Soldier Spider had warned him in more detail about the extent of Dickhead's craziness.

"At the end of the universe, in the final moments before the last iota of space and time is destroyed in the last great fire, the Vores will communicate a message to the True Believers. Those who have helped the Vores, who have worked against the Doubters and the Skeptics, will be rewarded with the Final Secret. The last truth, the ultimate revelation." Dickhead was nearly weeping with joy at the prospect of it all.

"So what is this Final Secret? Any ideas?" Spider asked, trying to sound reasonable.

"We don't know. We just don't know. All we know is what the Vores have communicated to us so far."

"Right," Spider said, nodding, hating every moment of this nonsense. "And when you say 'we' and 'us', what you really mean is 'you', yes?"

"They communicate through a living channel, yes, and that is, of course, me."

Spider stared at him. Despite the terrors of the End of Time, and the sense that there was no floor under his feet, Spider heard that tone in Dickhead's voice, and wanted to run. He tried to kid McMahon along a little, and said, "You do know that sounds like so much bullshit, don't you?" He said it with a smile.

Dickhead glanced at him, and all the weird messianic glow was gone from his face. He looked like the Dickhead he remembered from the shop. He grinned, nodded, and said, "Oh yeah, sure. I agree, absolutely. And I would have thought so, too, but one day — okay, this is going to sound awfully clichéd — well, I had this dream, Spider."

"Oh, kill me now," Spider said, shaking his head. "Not bloody dreams."

"You don't understand—"

"You had a dream in which, let's say, some kind of angel appeared to you, and told you your destiny" — Spider made a show of saying the word, to emphasize its full ridiculousness. "And you thought, unlike anybody else, who would have said, 'Hmm, too much cheese before bedtime,' you thought, 'Cool! Where do I sign up to be part of this awesome destiny?' Right?"

Dickhead was peeved. He glared at Spider, working his jaw, clearly straining to avoid saying all the things that were right there on the tip of his tongue, right now. For some reason Dickhead appeared to need Spider's ... approval? Understanding? Help? It was puzzling, and more than a little worrying. Dickhead said to him at last, "It wasn't quite like that. But I did receive a 'call,' if you like. I knew I had to do this, that it was what I was put into the universe to do. Everything else, my whole life up to this moment, has been about getting here. Spider, I want to know the Final Secret of the Cosmos."

"What about your gung-ho little mates out there, the Marauders, and all the rest of 'em? What are they supposed to do when they get all wiped out? I mean, all those billions of years of development, for nothing? That's not fair, is it, Dickhead?"

Dickhead smiled. "We're attempting to contact the Marauders."

Spider tried to imagine how long it might take to communicate with a lifeform evolved for the absolute zero environment. "Let me guess. You think you can talk them round to joining forces with your lot?"

"We think they have a lot to offer, the Marauders."

"I see," Spider said.

He sat there, arms still crossed, starting to feel more terrified of Dickhead than of anything else he'd seen or heard. Clearly, the man was crazy. Something was definitely going on "here" at the "End of the Universe." He was quite happy to accept that part. That it had anything to do with "God," or with a higher consciousness or divine entity of any kind, Spider was not so sure. "Okay," he said at last, knowing Dickhead had some very bad news for him, "where do I fit into your insane little plans?"

"I'm glad you asked," Dickhead said, smiling, looking like a salesman again. "It's very simple, I assure you."

"Do tell."

"It's like this, Spider. My organization here is called Zeropoint. I mentioned it to you back at the shop, right?"

"Uh-huh."

"The thing is, like I said, we're at war."

"Of course you are."

"It's true. We're in a war with another version of our own organization."

"What?"

"It's a bloody civil war, Spider! The other side is led by a man called Webb."

Oh, no, Spider thought. He suddenly saw everything very clearly. "Aloysius Webb, Dickhead? Spider Webb? Me? Is that why you brought me here, because I was already here, but working for the wrong side?" He was flashing back to that night, years ago, the night he met Dickhead in a pub. Now he could see that Dickhead had been looking for him, hoping to solve a difficult problem in the remote future with a simple fix back in the past. All he had to do was go back and recruit Spider to his own side ahead of time, and maybe prevent the civil war...

"The war has reached a very difficult point, Spider," he said, ignoring Spider's protest. "Their side is down to one last ship. They call her the *Masada*." He shook his head, no doubt hating them for using such a pretentious name. "Do you know the story of the siege of Masada?"

"I've read the Wikipedia entry."

"Ah. Well, never mind. Anyway, the people on that ship, Spider, think they're the last honorable, noble, decent people left at the End of Time. They think they're the good guys. They think their shit doesn't stink. What's worse, though, is that they're trying to undermine our campaign with endless lies and propaganda, and it's starting to work. What they can't do through sheer force, they can do with bloody propaganda! They will tell you that the Vores must be stopped, even killed, if possible. They will tell you God is not involved, that there is no God. They will tell you the Vores are just a bunch of aliens, and maybe not even real lifeforms. They don't care about the Final Secret, Spider. They just don't care. They say there is no Final Secret, that it's all a delusion, a myth!" Dickhead was getting worked up again. Spider edged his chair back from the table.

Spider said, "How do you know they're wrong?"

Dickhead looked at him as if he thought Spider hadn't been paying attention, and maybe even that he was a little stupid. Then he smiled indulgently, and said, "Spider, I know what I'm talking about, okay? I know. The Vores are agents of God. We are fighting the good fight."

"Okay, fine," Spider said, and managed a cheery smile. "Sure, why not?"

Dickhead was enormously relieved. "Thank the Lord!"

"There's just one thing I'm a bit hazy about."

"Let me guess," Dickhead said, leaning forward, hands clasped together, looking all earnest, "you're wondering where you fit into the project."

"I was wondering."

"It's like this, my friend." McMahon touched a control. A large portrait-format image appeared floating in the air above the table. "The problem is this man, Aloysius 'Spider' Webb." Next to Dickhead's messianic bullshit, Soldier Spider looked like a hero.

Spider looked, sighed, then did his best to feign puzzlement. "Who is that?"

"Hmm," Dickhead said, "this is a bit difficult. You see, this is you."

"I beg to differ, mate!"

"No," he said, "it is. This is you, decades from now. He's an old man, fixed in his ideas, a bit funny in the head, frankly, and he's the man we have to eliminate." He left that word, "eliminate," hanging in the air between them.

At last, after all the previous blather, Spider thought, *we finally reach the crux of the matter, the bitter fact, the hard ask.* "You want me to eliminate my own future self?"

CHAPTER 19

"He's a dangerous old man, Spider."

"You could just blow up his ship, couldn't you?" he said, feigning ignorance.

At this, Dickhead pursed his lips, looked at the image of Soldier Spider, sighed and sat back in his seat. "Actually, no."

"No?"

"No. Not as such."

"You said you've got millions of ships, and they've only got one."

"Yes," Dickhead said, sounding tired, "that's all true."

"So what's the problem? Pound the shit out of 'em!"

"The problem, Spider, is that their ship is flux-proofed."

"Which is?"

"Which makes the ship itself pretty much untouchable. Its complete timeline, from the first day at the shipyard when the keel was laid—"

"Timeships have keels?"

Dickhead carried on. "Its entire existence has been sealed away from attack. You can't attack it today because it continues to exist a year from now. It exists for the entirety of its natural lifespan as an object, until such time as they switch off the flux-shield, and decommission it. Likewise, you can't go back in time, say, a year, and try to damage it then, because it still exists today. It's a real problem for us."

Spider took this in, noted that it agreed with what he'd been told before, and asked, "What about your ships?"

"Same. We're all flux-proofed."

"So what you're saying is, you're all screwed, attack-wise."

"We can't hit them; they can't hit us, yes. That's why we need you."

"What can I do?"

"You can get onto the *Masada*."

"I beg to differ," Spider said again, trying to laugh dismissively, but not sounding all that convincing, even to himself. Only too aware of this, he tried to cover the lapse. "What makes you think I can—"

"Because," Dickhead said, interrupting, "you've been there before."

Oh, shit, he thought. "I've what?" He felt his cheeks burning, and his stomach was in knots. All this time, Dickhead had been playing him along, the bastard!

A silence fell between them. Dickhead sat back, watching him, all trace of apocalyptic messianic craziness gone, and replaced by the stone-hard face Dickhead normally reserved for discussing Spider's shop's sagging bottom line. Spider did his best to look innocent, but he knew it wasn't working. The silence was brutal. It begged to be filled. He recognized the technique, of course. It was an old cop trick, something to pull out when questioning a tricky suspect. You just shut up, sit back, cross your arms, or maybe just sit there, tapping a finger on the table, and let the silence, and the tension, accumulate, like an electric charge. In time, with most suspects, the tension becomes unbearable, and they start talking. In fact, with some suspects, the hard part is trying to get them to shut the hell up. He didn't appreciate finding himself on the receiving end of this tactic. The thing to do in this situation was to play it ice-cool. To sit there, quite unbothered, all the time in the world, so to speak, minding your own business, and just wait out the copper. The whole tactic rested on the idea that silence was oppressive, that you had to fill it, like a vacuum. But for some suspects silence was just fine. They could sit there and say nothing at all, maybe for years on end, and they'd never feel even a moment of anxiety or stress about it. Spider had dealt with a couple of guys like that in his time, and he had found them to be spooky bastards. Men quite happy with their own company, who probably never said more than two words every few days even in their normal lives, when they weren't up to no good, of course. Spider tried to think the way those guys thought, to get into that same frame of mind, where silence was easy, and talk was a rude interruption, and couldn't do it. He muttered, "Damn it," and looked across at Dickhead, who smiled.

Spider said, "I'm not a killer, Dickhead. Forget it."

"You're not?" He sounded all surprised, and even a little disappointed.

"No."

"You're sure about that?"

"Yes, I'm sure."

"It would be very much worth your while, Spider."

"No. Not for anything."

"Nothing?"

"Nothing."

"Well," Dickhead said, scratching his chin, "this is kind of a problem."

"You could send me home."

"Why would I do that?"

"I could go back to fixing time machines."

"No," he said, "I don't think so, Spider."

Spider felt great forces moving around him, forcing him in one direction and one direction only. "So if I don't do the job, you'll fire me? Is that it?"

"No, not at all. If you don't, or won't help me out, I've got no use for you. That was the deal all along. I took you on when nobody else would touch you, Spider. I picked you up out of a puddle of your own squalor, you were broken, useless, full of self-pity and self-destruction. You were pretty much homeless, remember? Do you? And I came along, and I saw you, and I saw potential in you. I saw that I could do great things for you, and you could do great things for me. That's the secret of a successful business, that is, you mark my words. It's not about dollars and cents and accounts receivable and all that bullshit, it's about knowing people, Spider. Knowing what a person can truly achieve, if he's motivated enough. Your problem, as I saw it, was that you never had the right motivation. You never had the right guiding hand showing you the way."

Dickhead was killing him with this speech. Spider did remember those days, remembered them only too clearly. "I can't do it, Dickhead," he managed to say. "I just can't. I'm not a murderer."

"That's all right, mate," Dickhead said, his voice full of kindness. "It's okay. I understand. There are no born murderers. You used to say that yourself, remember? There are people who are very likely to go down the wrong path, you used to say. People who are almost forced by the circumstances of their lives to make the wrong choices. I understand. I get it. But you used to say something else, Spider: you said anyone could become a killer. Anybody at all, from a little kid to a saintly, old, white-haired grandmother who always rescued daddy longlegs spiders from the shower cubicle. They just need the right motivation, the right combination of circumstances. Can happen to anybody, right? Didn't you used to say that, Spider?"

Spider didn't remember having this conversation with McMahon, but that was typical of his life lately, wasn't it? Forces beyond his control plucking the strings of his life like a harp, shifting him from one timeline to another. So who knows? Maybe some version of him had told Dickhead all this about the people who kill people. It was certainly true, though, that was for sure. Again, he felt those huge forces squeezing him down one particular channel, putting him in a situation where he would have only bad options. *Dickhead looks too cocky*, he thought. *He's got something up his sleeve. Something very bad.* Spider was so tense, his whole body knotted up with dread, he hurt all over, waiting for Dickhead to reveal all.

For now, Dickhead was content simply to stare at him, a tiny smile curling his lips. Spider could see, even if he had never seen this before, that Dickhead had never been any kind of real friend to him. He had always been an opportunist, had always only been out for his own goals.

When Spider could take it no longer, when the pain of waiting was almost too much to bear, he said, "You can't force me to do it. You'll have to kill me."

Dickhead looked all shocked. "Kill you? Why would I kill you? You're my friend, Spider. You're my responsibility. No, don't be silly."

"Well, you'll have to do something about me, 'cause I'm not killing that guy."

"I think you will. I think you'll do it cheerfully. I think you'll be grateful to do it, in fact, and you'll come to me afterwards, and you'll beg me to let you kill other people. I think, contrary to what you told me, Spider, that you're a born killer. You just haven't opened yourself to the possibility before. What do you think?"

Spider felt tears welling in his eyes. "Fuck you, Dickhead."

It was as if McMahon never heard him. He carried on. "It's like I said. You just need the right motivation." He glanced at his control display, and touched two buttons. "That should do it. Ah yes," he said, smiling, looking at the video window that had opened up in the air above the table. "Can you see that all right, Spider? I can adjust the brightness if you like?"

And there she was, not safe and sound in the care of Soldier Spider and his merry men as he'd planned. No, Molly was right here. He felt his heart stop. He didn't want to look. Just listening to the audio feed was bad enough, but he knew he would have to look at her. He would have to take in the full measure of his failure. Tears spilling down his cheeks now, he looked at the window. The scene was dark, but clear enough. She was suspended by her own arms, which had been wrenched back and upward, the wrists cuffed together. Her feet hovered mere centimeters above the floor. It was hard to see Molly's face, but he could see enough to know she was sick with agony. With each of her rapid, shallow exhalations, her breath misted the chill air. Nearby, a humanoid robot similar to the one Spider had seen earlier delivering dinner stood, bearing what was unmistakably some kind of gun. Spider could not speak. His mind fled in horror. His genitals retracted. He felt sick, but could not look away. He tried to say, "Molly..." but his voice wasn't working.

Dickhead looked at him, took his time about it, scowling, weighing up the effect the image was having on Spider, then touched the controls again, and the image disappeared.

Spider said, "What do I have to do?"

Dickhead said, "Here's the plan..."

§ § §

Spider's office, late afternoon, raining outside, gray and overcast. Sounds of traffic nearby. Malaria in the outer office, talking to someone on the phone, trying to help diagnose a problem with a wonky time machine. Out the back, in the workshop, Spider hears a heavy metallic tool hit the concrete floor, and then hears Charlie Stuart swearing a blue streak.

He shuts his office door, collapses into a chair, closes his eyes, holds his head, trying to block it all out. It's too bright, too loud, too smelly, too everything! One moment he'd been adrift in the mind-sucking void of the End of Time with Dickhead, aware of his senses almost turning his brain inside-out in their desperate hunger for stimulation, and the next he's here in the overwhelming past. Even his chair feels too vivid.

He gets up, paces back and forth, tries not to think of Molly. Molly standing there — no, Molly dangling there, in unthinkable pain, hoarsely screaming — and he feels himself crumbling again, cracking apart, the tears flowing, gasping great sobs.

Malaria appears, asking if he's all right, but there's nothing he can say, nothing at all. She tells him that James Rutherford called again, and he sounded all weird on the phone, but he wouldn't say what was wrong, he just wanted to talk to Spider, and there was this, she didn't know, this "edge" in his voice. It was strange, she says. Spider wasn't there, so she talked to Charlie about it, but Charlie didn't know what to make of it either. What should she do? Spider remembers he has to visit Rutherford—

Malaria tells him if he doesn't feel well he should go home and get some rest, he does look pretty bad, if he'll excuse her saying so. He tells her to mind her own fucking

business, everything's fine, just get back to work. She stares
at him for a moment, then goes back to her desk, and the
phone's already going nuts. With the door shut, he rubs
his eyes with the heels of his hands, and feels like shit for
talking to Malaria that way when she was just trying to
be kind.

He goes back to his desk. On the floor, next to his chair,
there's his new backpack, the one Dickhead gave him. The
one containing the device. He picks up the pack, puts it
on the desk, lifts the flaps, and there it is, surprisingly small,
no bigger than a golfball. He dares not touch it. There is
no digital countdown, no complicated red and blue wires,
nothing at all other than fine-print warnings that tell him
it is a *Class III Causality Weapon: Handle With Care, Caution
May Delete Timelines, Beware Temporal Flux Field Effects,
Conforms With ISO-54060 Standards Governing Temporal
Weapons, Manufacturer Not Liable For Damage Deliberate or
Accidental.*

Spider thinks it very thoughtful of them to print all these
warnings. *Having read all that, you'd be a moron if you actually
let yourself get hurt by it, wouldn't you?* he thinks, in a mental
tone of voice so reasonable, so mild and half-amused, you
wouldn't know he's exploding inside his own head, that
his conscious mind is running on automatic while the rest
of his consciousness, everything that makes him Spider,
is a firestorm of panic and hatred and fear — and the
sharpest, most penetrating, lacerating guilt.

Standing there, looking down at the device in the bag,
remembering Dickhead's briefing, he feels, for the nth time,
like a fool for ever listening to the man, for ever accepting his kindness and help. Maybe, if he survives, he thinks,
he'll go back in time and make damn sure Broken Spider
never meets Dickhead McMahon. Better to be a wreck of
a man than to wind up like this. Or better yet, to go back
in time and use the Weapon on Dickhead. It seems like a
brilliant idea, and maybe a way out of his bind. If Dickhead
never existed, he could never recruit Spider, never go on
to lead a fleet of a million ships in a titanic war at the End
of Time. Best of all, Molly would be fine. Prickly as always,
passive-aggressive, but fine. *Hmm*, he thinks, *that all sounds*

pretty good. It does mean that Broken Spider would be left to rot, to take his chances with destitution and bitterness. *Compared to what I'm going through — and more important, what Molly's going through — right now,* he thinks, *destitution and bitterness sound pretty damn fine.*

But what if it doesn't matter? What if the universe finds some other idiot like Dickhead and shows him the dream with the angel and fills his head full of glory and power and destiny? Did it matter that it was Dickhead McMahon who came upon him that night, or would any similar guy do just as well? *In other words,* he thinks, seeing how this line of thought would end, *would the show still go on, just with different actors in the key roles?* He has a horrible feeling it might. So erasing Dickhead is no good. The problem is that, from Soldier Spider's point of view, all of this has already happened, long ago. Past Spider has already carried out the mission. It would be very hard to keep it from happening now.

"Fuck!" he mutters, with considerable feeling, thinking not only about his particular problem, but about the larger issue: was there, in the end, any such thing as free will? It was looking like maybe not, and that was a hard thing to accept. No matter what he chooses to do now, whether he carries out the plan as instructed or tries something different, it's already been decided. All possible outcomes have played out — and they've all ended up at the End of Time with Dickhead, Master of Destiny. Who knows, though, maybe Soldier Spider faked him out, gave him all these instructions and guidance with the specific intention of overwhelming him and forcing him to try something different to escape from it all. Either way, looking back from the End of Time, it's all already happened, every possible variation, and all for nothing. Spider noodles with the idea of going back to the *Masada*, pinning Soldier Spider to the deck, and forcing him to tell Spider just what he did when it was his turn, so he'd know what to do now — but he suspected the old bastard would not help him. Why should Soldier Spider help? When it had been his turn, he'd got no help.

What if the future isn't so predetermined, though? He knows that history possesses surprising momentum, that it resists change but it can be changed, if you try hard enough. Suppose the whole business with the End of Time could be averted? Where would you have to be to make the critical change? He doesn't know, but he suspects the critical point would be somewhere deep in the past, and right now he does not have the time or the resources to mount such a search. He is broke. He'd have to borrow one of the time machines that are in the shop for repair, and hope for the best. And, all the while, he'd still know that way off in the remote future, Molly was suffering while he muddled about.

He pulls out the coin-sized, black key-ring device, the one Soldier Spider gave him at the end of his visit to the *Masada*. Dickhead had given him one just like it, that would take him back to the *Destiny*, once the job was done. Both are keyed to his unique biochemical signature. Both are one-shot devices.

There is no stopping it, Spider can see that, but he can't accept it. It isn't right. It isn't just. He remembers Soldier Spider telling him that the only chance they had on the *Masada* was for Spider to do what he was told exactly the way he told him to do it. There could be no variation. Spider had to follow the script, whether he liked it or not. The *Masada* was low on supplies and power. They had one chance to take out the top leadership of the other Zeropoint organization, and Spider had better not screw it up, because if he screwed up, not only would they all die of starvation and thirst, but, worse, Molly would also die.

Yes, he thinks. He gets all that. He really does. It's just that he has now learned that Dickhead is at least two moves ahead. The fact that Dickhead knew that Spider had been to the *Masada* proves that. The fact that he could arrange to intercept Molly's transfer to the *Masada*, too, only rubs it in Spider's face. Dickhead must know what is going to happen. Maybe he's received a visit from a future version of himself, who's told him all about Soldier Spider's little plan. It is impossible to know.

One thing Dickhead told him, before sending him back here, was that if he carries out his mission faithfully and carefully, and survives, he can come back to the *Destiny*, and be reunited with Molly. Not, of course, that she would have him, he knows that, but still. Either way, Spider and Molly would be right there, in pride of place, ready to partake in the Final Secret of the Cosmos. It would be, Dickhead said, so cool!

The key-ring remote in Spider's hand is cold to the touch. He wonders what would happen if he destroyed it, crushed it under his Doc Marten heel. Without the remote he couldn't go to the *Masada*. But his future self, he realizes, already knows just what Spider chooses to do in this situation, and has given him that remote anyway. If he tries to go off-script at this point — and didn't doing that work out so well the last time he tried it? — the most likely outcome is just that either the remote proves indestructible, or another one turns up in his pocket.

Okay, he thinks, What if he detonates the Class III causality weapon right here, now? From what he understands, it features a powerful conventional explosive, and a timeline-erasing effect. Which only leaves a mysterious body nobody recognizes or can identify. Spider had asked Dickhead, when the bastard was explaining the weapon to him, that surely in erasing Soldier Spider's timeline it would also erase his own. Dickhead reassured him that he would be fine, because there was no guarantee that Spider and Soldier Spider were part of the same timeline. Spider remembered his future self telling him much the same thing, that Spider might not become Soldier Spider. He wasn't so sure. It sounded like bullshit to him, but what choice did he have?

What would happen, he wonders, if he were to use it on himself? For a start, nothing he's done or experienced would ever have happened. Nobody he's ever met would remember or recognize him. If the cops brought in his own parents to identify the body, even they would not recognize him, because he was never their child. They would have had some other child. Molly would have got involved with some other guy or guys; she'd probably still have become a mad sculptress, and would probably still be difficult, and brittle, and demanding. Dickhead McMahon would have found some other poor bastard to recruit, and that poor bastard's sort-of ex-wife would probably have got shanghaied off to the End of bloody Time to be tortured.

So, after all that, using the device on himself would achieve no real benefit to anyone. He'd be handing his special bundle of misery to some other poor bastard. *Who knows?* he thinks, *maybe in a previous iteration of time, some other guy was in exactly this situation, and he did detonate the Class III causality weapon, wiped himself out, thus handing the whole mess to Spider*. The lesson, he now sees, is that at this point in space and time someone has to do this job. It doesn't even matter who, exactly. *Some events*, he thinks, *want to happen*.

And that gives him an idea. Probably it's a crazy idea, and he can think of a dozen reasons why it wouldn't work, but it's all he's got. It's been bubbling away in the back of his mind since Dickhead told him about the Class III causality weapon's properties. The bastard told Spider, "Now treat the thing like the finest crystal, all right? The circuitry in there, well, let's just say, it's delicate. Very bloody delicate. No throwing it around. No dropping it. No juggling!"

Spider had objected at that point, but only to see the sour look on Dickhead's face, which was priceless. Spider could see that Dickhead had been waiting a very long time for Spider to be right here, in this situation, poised to take out his greatest enemy. The irony was delicious. He was practically salivating at the prospect, Spider noticed, even more revolted. He asked Dickhead, "What if I get caught in the blast radius, though? If my timeline ceases to exist, to have ever existed, I can't wind up here, under your thumb, can I?"

Dickhead had smiled. "There are any number of Spider Webbs, moron. Any of them will do. If not you, it'll be another you. Worry not."

That was when Spider decided that Dickhead had to die. He didn't know just how he could achieve this goal, but right then it didn't matter. The man had to be stopped, and not just this iteration of him, either. Just as he, Spider, had countless other selves stretched across the timelines of the manifold, so too did Dickhead. Ideally, Spider thought, all of them would have to die. Dickhead had not only to be killed, he had to be erased.

Back in the here and now, Spider takes one last look at the device in his backpack, makes sure it's sitting nice and secure, and double-checks that it's not currently armed. The last thing he needs is for the thing to go off because of his trip through time to the *Masada*. Just to be sure, though, he pulls over a screen from his desk and runs a search on "electromagnetic pulse — EMP" weapons. "Hmm," he says, working through the many results, skimming here and there, reading up. "Shuts down electronic circuitry." This is what he thought EMP weapons did, but it is worth checking, considering what is at stake.

Okay, then. Just a few loose ends to tie up. He doesn't expect to survive this mission, one way or another, and isn't sure he even wants to survive, knowing what he knows about the future. Dickhead must be stopped. That's all that matters. It occurs to him that with that thought he might have just taken the first step on the path to becoming Soldier Spider. *If so, cool. No worries.*

He gets on the phone, and tries to call Iris. Her phone's switched off. He leaves a message, sketching in what's going on, what he's trying to achieve, and asks for any help she can provide at this end. Finally, he calls his mum and dad, and they, too, are out. It just about kills him that they're out of reach. For a long moment he doesn't know if he can go on without saying what he needs to say to his parents. At length, he gets his breathing under control, wipes his eyes, and tells them he loves them, and that makes him blubber afresh, so he rings off, feeling wretched and alone, hardly able to stand under the vast weight of responsibility he feels crushing him down.

He slings the backpack over his shoulder, and goes out to the workshop, says g'day to Charlie, shakes his hand, tells him, as he should have told him long ago, that he is a great guy, and it has been a rare privilege to work with him. Charlie is all surprised, then disturbed, and finally starts freaking out, and wants to know if Spider's dying or something, because, God, why would he talk like that? Charlie even starts getting upset, and Spider feels awkward; he doesn't want a scene like this. Charlie comes and hugs him, and tells him they'll all help Spider work through whatever the hell it is, because they're mates, and mates stick together. Soon Spider's blubbering, too, but he can't tell Charlie what's really going on. He pats Charlie on the back, thanks him, and says he has to go.

He stops to see Malaria and apologizes for speaking to her that way earlier. He had a lot on his mind, but he shouldn't have taken it out on her. Also, he tells her that she's doing a great job. She's all confused, and worried about him, but she can see he's not about to explain what's going on. She does ask if she's going to need to find a new job. He says he hopes not and leaves the shop through the front door.

There's now nothing else for it. He takes the remote, and, closing his eyes, holding his breath, nervous as hell, he hits the go button.

CHAPTER 20

"Hey, Spider," said Soldier Spider.

He was there. He recognized that smell, only now it was worse. Things were failing and breaking down. It was cold; he could see his breath; it reminded him of Molly, and that shook his resolve.

"It's okay. Believe me. It's okay. You'll get through this," his older self said, and reached an arm around his shoulder and led him through the cramped and noisy passageways of the ship.

"How are things going?" Spider asked as they made their way forward.

"Not good, not good. Everyone's on emergency rations. There's a problem with the water recycling system, too."

Spider understood what Soldier Spider was telling him. "Infections?"

"We've got nine people out of action right now, and we're doing our best to make sure everyone only drinks and uses boiled water, and practices medical-standard hand-washing. It's been ten hours without anyone else going down sick, so we might be okay. Of course, then you've got the issue of electrolyte maintenance, and of course the sick folks are using the same water supply. It's tough."

"Can I help?" he asked.

"I don't know, Spider," the old man said. They had to stop and press themselves against a bulkhead as two other crewmembers squeezed past going the other way. "Can you?"

He was standing right next to Soldier Spider; and could feel the man's body heat, even through his spec-ops outfit.

When he looked at him, he could see him sweating. Spider said, "Are you sick, too?"

"I'm doing okay, keeping out of trouble."

"You didn't get my message."

"Message?"

"About Molly? At the airport?"

"You..." He frowned a moment, then remembered. "Oh, yeah. Right. Yeah."

"I thought you guys were watching me."

"Limited resources, Spider. Limited resources. Just keeping up with Dickhead's various activities across the manifold keeps us surprisingly busy and stretched pretty thin."

The image of Molly suspended like that would not leave Spider's mind. It was worse than seeing her dead and mangled body. Much worse. When you're dead you're past all of life's suffering. You're at rest, such as it is. What was happening to Molly... It was too much. There were no words for it, just cyclonic anger.

"Easy, mate," Soldier Spider said, gently, giving Spider's shoulder a squeeze. "Try not to blame yourself."

"I had it all worked out."

"You did what you thought was right."

"You were supposed to take her and keep her safe."

Soldier Spider nodded, and looked achingly sad. "Come on. Let's get on with it, shall we?"

They moved up through the ship. That smell was everywhere. Spider hardly saw any of the ship's crew; only a handful of different sorts of robots worked cleaning duty, but did so with unflagging diligence. Some of those robots, Spider noticed, looked like they'd been built out of spare parts from other robots.

Soldier Spider led him to a cramped ward room, sat him down at a table. "Wish I could offer you something to drink, but we're rationing the water at the moment."

Spider was looking around at the décor. There was a wide photo showing all the ship's crew, beaming, in crisp uniform, on a sunny afternoon, with the great black bulk of the ship behind them. Sitting in the front row, with a plaque containing the ship's name and registry code, was a younger version of Soldier Spider. He looked happy and proud. Surrounding this photo were images, postcards and small novelty souvenirs, from different times and places, all of them spacious, warm and beautiful, sent by crewmembers away on holiday. On the opposite wall was a gallery of images of crew members, solemn, in impressive uniform, against a background of dark velvet, each captioned with the officer's name, rank, and the relative space-time coordinates of their death. There were, Spider counted, well over one hundred such images. Under the display, the simple message, in stark lettering, "LEST WE FORGET". Spider felt a lump in his throat, and looked away, wiping his eyes.

Soldier Spider, sitting opposite Spider, had his eye on Spider's backpack. "Is that it?" he said.

Spider lifted it up onto the narrow table. "Yup. Got a present for you."

"Oh, I like presents," the old man said, not smiling.

Spider reached in and, taking great care, took out the Class III causality weapon, and set it on the table between them. "You won't like this one."

"Is it armed?"

"No, I checked."

Soldier Spider peered at it, thinking hard. "Just trying to remember when it was my turn," he said.

"Dickhead did tell me how to arm it."

"Very thorough, that Dickhead," Soldier Spider said. Even at rest like this, it was obvious the weapon was a delicate instrument, built from, it appeared, millions of components, a triumph of anti-personnel chronotechnology. "So," Soldier Spider said, "multi-modal?"

"Causality effect plus conventional warhead, yeah."

"Nice. I'd forgotten just how cute the little thing was." He was smiling, a little sadly.

Spider, for his part, was terrified of the thing, and could not understand his older self's *nostalgic* reaction on seeing it again. "It doesn't concern you, having this thing on your ship?"

"Spider," he said, meeting his younger self's worried gaze, "it does, and it doesn't. It's complicated. Yes, it's trouble. It's bad news. It's, well, it's many things, all wrapped in a surprisingly small bundle. It could cripple our power supply, no question. We'd be dead in the water, so to speak. Probably shut down our flux-shield. And, of course, being a causality thing, it would delete me, and maybe you, too."

"I've had a thought about that," Spider said.

"EMP?"

"Great minds think alike."

Soldier Spider snorted. "Yeah, right. Interesting idea."

"Think it'll work?"

"Depends."

"Depends on what?"

"Depends if it's hardened against EMP."

"Was yours?" Spider asked.

Soldier Spider thought back. "I don't think so, but I think there was something else about it... Damn, what was it?"

"What? Like a booby trap?"

He was trying to remember. "Let me just check some archives a moment." Soldier Spider pulled out a small screen, flipped it open, pulled out a pair of battered reading glasses, put them on, and started searching. After a moment, he said, "Yes. There. Look." He showed Spider the screen. It was displaying an archived record of this meeting.

Spider read the notes regarding the weapon. "Hmm, armed, no, that's good, tried an EMP shot..."

Soldier Spider said, "Shut down the causality effect, but not the explosive." He nodded, satisfied. "Sounds about right."

"You're very casual about it, don't you think?"

"Off-brain storage, Spider. Gotta love it."

Spider stared and stared at him, horrified.

"Listen to me, Spider," his older self said, leaning forward, speaking softly, "I'm well aware of what this thing can do. I've seen them before, this and variations of it. Very popular weapon type. Very effective. Lost a lot of good people to them — and very likely a great deal more who none us even remember."

Spider was chilled, thinking about it, wanting to get on with neutralizing the thing before one or both of them vanished from all existence and memory. He didn't understand how Soldier Spider could be so, well, flippant about it all.

And there was more where that came from. "The thing is, you get to a certain age, you see things differently from how you see them when you're a young 'tacker' like yourself. You get a broader perspective. You get sick of war, sick of conflict for its own stupid sake. I mean, take this whole bullshit war we're in here, us and Dickhead's bunch. How much time are we wasting trying to kill each other when we could be tackling the Vores themselves? Bloody Dickhead's a stupid delusional fuckwit, pure and simple, Spider, and you can tell him I said so."

Spider remembered how he felt, not that long ago, telling his employer he was a cheap bully, and how, while it felt good to say that at that moment, he knew he was pushing it, and Dickhead's good will, right to the edge. Telling him he was a stupid delusional fuckwit, with that same tone of not giving a shit what Dickhead thought about such a comment, was breathtaking. Spider hoped he lived long enough to try it out for himself.

Soldier Spider, sitting there, weary and demonstrably not too well, was looking at the causality weapon, sighing. He went back to his screen, touched a control, and said aloud, "All hands. Prepare for EMP shot. Shut down all non-essential systems now. Any problems, see your designated damage control officer. EMP shot on my mark." He glanced at Spider. "All set, Spider?"

"You're sure this won't just set it off? Surely Dickhead would—"

"Dickhead is many things, but he's no evil genius."

"But—"

Soldier Spider said to his screen, "Mark."

There was a heavy, sub-audible THUNK that Spider felt more than heard, a waft of warm bad air came through the vents, and the lights went out, quickly replaced by red emergency lights. Soldier Spider was peering at his glowing screen, watching developments unfold. "Damage report?" he said.

Spider heard several voices report in. Things appeared to have gone well, but main power was out for the moment, life support was still running at minimum, and ninety percent of hardened systems survived the shot. There were no casualties. All personnel in sickbay were okay, for now.

Then Spider noticed he was not alone on this side of the table, and he jumped. Soldier Spider laughed and clapped his hands. Spider peered at the thing on the seat next to him. At first he thought it was a dead body, but it wasn't. "Oh God," he said, "it's a robot!"

Soldier Spider laughed again. "I just about shat myself when that happened to me," he said. "Just priceless!"

"This is your idea of a prank?"

"No, mate. This is Dickhead's idea of a prank. Take a closer look."

He hefted the thing's body until he could see the machine's face. "Oh," he said, recognizing it. "It's Dickhead's personal assistant. Or something very like it."

"Ghost mode. Gets you every time," Soldier Spider said.

"Shit! How long have I been trailing that around with me?"

"Since you were on Dickhead's ship, I'd say."

"So it's been transmitting back to Dickhead this whole time?"

"Yeah, but so what? We haven't said anything yet."

"Um..."

"We haven't said anything operational."

"Ah."

Soldier Spider looked pleased with himself. "So, got that remote?"

He handed it over. Dickhead's idea was that once Spider planted the causality weapon, he'd use the remote to return to the *Destiny*. At the time Spider did not believe the thing would actually work; he figured Dickhead would be just as happy if Spider died here.

Soldier Spider looked at it up close: it, like the one that got Spider here, wasn't much to look at, a simple disposable one-shot device. Using his screen, he called someone named Wendy to come and pick it up.

Wendy turned up, looking pale and sweaty with illness, nodded hello to Spider, and Soldier Spider handed her the remote. "Can you do it?"

She studied it for a moment, then said, "Yeah, no worries. Should take about twenty minutes."

"You've got ten."

"Aye, aye, Skipper," she said, leaning on the sarcastic, and left. Soldier Spider watched her go, amused, at least for now.

"What about the bomb?" Spider said.

"Yes, what about the bomb?" Soldier Spider said, still strangely amused. He got up from the table, and grabbed the weapon. "Come on."

Spider joined him. "Where to?"

"Workshop." They set off through the confining red-lit corridors of the ship. Where before there had been cool and warm areas, depending on the ventilation and the presence of heavy machinery nearby, now it was frigid almost everywhere. Spider was shivering, and he was sure his breath would be misting if he could see it. His older self, striding along, appeared fine. Carrying a live bomb, but fine.

Spider also noticed there was no one around, not even cleaning bots. When they reached the workshop, Soldier Spider asked Spider to seal the door behind them, locking them in. "Just in case," he said. The workshop, like all the other living spaces on the ship, was cramped but spotlessly clean and tidy, like an operating theater that dealt mostly in heavy machinery and robots, Spider noticed, looking at things tidily stacked here and there. It was strange to see robots in pieces; it gave him a very distinct science fictional frisson, that feeling he was inside a movie from his youth. "Gather round, Spider," Soldier Spider told him, indicating a bench. "All right, then," he said to his younger, petrified self, "what do you know about bomb disposal? As I recall, not bloody much, yes?" He was looking at him over the rims of his glasses.

"That would be correct, yes. Still, I can pass tools with the best of 'em. You name it." When Spider was a kid, he often helped his dad fix up old bits of dead machinery, which Dad would then sell to make a little extra cash. It was weird seeing his future self like this; taking out the bizarre sf buzz from the scene, it was only too easy to see himself as his much younger self, and Soldier Spider as his father. It was sort of comforting, familiar. Almost enough to make him forget that he could die at any moment.

A small window in Soldier Spider's screen lit up. It was Wendy. "Got it in seven minutes, Skipper. Do I get a biscuit?"

Soldier Spider was hunched over, studying the bomb in detail under a large illuminated magnifier not that different from similar tools Spider had in his own workshop. "I'll have to owe you the biscuit, Wendy, but good work. How many'd you get?"

"Enough," she said, sounding pleased with herself, despite being sick.

"Tell the lads to start suiting up. We'll be along shortly."

"Okay," she said, and was gone.

"Her name, Spider, is Wendy Pheromone Clavier-3. That's a numeral '3', by the way, not the word 'three'. Very important. You'll meet her, if you get to be me, at a yachting regatta off Jupiter. Very handy woman. Capable. Sense of humor. Useful. Now, hand me that phase-cutter. No, that one. Thanks." Soldier Spider had the bomb seated in a three-pronged mechanism which itself was inside a large tank made of what appeared to be very thick, multi-layered anti-ballistic plastic. Spider was reminded strongly of the Bat Cave. Soldier Spider took the phase-cutter in his right hand, made some fine adjustments with the controls on its handle, and gently touched the working tip of the device to the skin of the bomb. "All right, then, time to light the blue touch-paper," he said.

Spider said, "Permission to shit my trousers, Skipper?"

"Permission granted," Soldier Spider said, amused, and hit the trigger. There was a faint hum. The tool started making impossibly precise, steady, delicate incisions in the shell of the bomb. Spider was holding his breath; his heart was in his mouth, taking up a lot of space. In his mind, the only sound he could hear was, "Shit, shit, shit, shit, shit," and so on. He did not want to die. Not now, not here. Not without Molly. And not without taking care of Dickhead Bloody McMahon.

Soldier Spider shut down the phase-cutter and set it aside on the bench. With a tool that reminded Spider of surgical instruments, he removed a small rectangular piece of the bomb's shell, revealing a small, glowing red light. "There you go, Spider, have a look at that."

Leaning in with great reluctance, Spider spotted the light. "What am I looking at?"

"That is the system readiness indicator for the causality weapon. The EMP shot worked!"

"Imagine my boundless joy," Spider said, still terrified. Then, thinking about the situation, he said, "You know, wouldn't it have been much easier all round to have some robot do all this?"

"None of the working bots have sufficient fine hand control. And, before you say it, we also couldn't just shove the thing out an airlock."

Spider had been thinking about suggesting this very thing. "Problems?"

"Big problems. Little bastard's pressure-sensitive. We learned that the hard way." He stared off into the distance for a moment, then reached for another tool, and went back to work on the bomb, removing screws Spider could not see with his naked eyes.

Spider could imagine just what the "learned that the hard way" might mean, and tried to imagine Soldier Spider, in his own place, faced with this same situation, and losing the old man due to a stupid mistake. "That must have been tough," he said.

"You have no idea. Trashed a lot of the ship."

"Even with the flux—"

"Ordinarily, the flux-proofing would protect the ship's entire structure, but that costs energy we don't have. So we just protect the hull, and take our chances with the inside. The game is about getting a weapon past the shield's firewall. Listen, hand me a staser, would you?"

"What the hell is a staser?"

Soldier Spider glanced across at him, surprised, then not surprised. "Ah, right. Yeah. Sorry. Listen, I need this thing called a staser. It's a stasis device. Also works well as a weapon, actually. Anyway, need one. Looks like Mike's made off with the one I keep here, so I need you to scuttle off to Engineering to grab it for me."

"And Engineering would be, er, where, exactly?"

Soldier Spider handed him his screen. "There you go, punch up the ship interior layout diagram, and follow your nose."

Spider found the interface surprisingly usable, and soon brought up the diagram. His eyes widened. "Ship's bigger than I thought."

"Used to be a bloody brilliant ship, back when. You'll like her a lot."

"So," he said, looking at Soldier Spider, thinking something was more than a bit odd about all this, "find this Mike guy and get your staser back."

"Mike's sick. You'll need to talk to a bot. You'll be fine."

He nodded, frowning. "Okay. Right." He knew he had to go, but he didn't want to leave.

"Sometime this year, Spider?"

"What's going on?"

"Nothing's going on. I need a tool. I need you to go and get it and bring it back."

"Couldn't someone bring it here?"

"You need to get familiar with the ship, Spider. If you end up—"

"So you're letting me in on all the secrets?"

"No, I just want you—"

"You said before there were things you couldn't show me on this ship."

"Tool, Spider. Go and get the fucking tool."

Spider had the worst feeling in the world about this little errand, but he could see that Soldier Spider was prepared to practically throw him out by his ear if he had to, and, even though an old man, he still looked a lot stronger, and a lot fitter, than Spider. "Bugger," he said, feeling sick in his guts, and turned to leave.

Soldier Spider said, "Oh, um, by the way."

"What?"

"I'm very sorry about Molly. Just... dreadfully sorry about everything."

"You said, I know. I understand."

"No, actually, um, you don't."

Spider stood there, staring at the old man, and felt everything fall out from under him. Every assumption, every belief, everything he ever held dear and true. "I beg your pardon?" He could hardly speak.

Soldier Spider was staring back at him, ashen, lips pressed tight together. Unable to speak, he just shook his head, his eyes shining slightly in the weak light.

"Oh my God. Did you...?"

"I need that tool, Spider."

"You lied to me?"

"You don't know how hard—"

He could hardly think. It felt like his heart would burst. "You lied to me about Molly? You said she'd survive."

"I—"

Spider, aghast, stared at his future self, saw his future, in which he would, without batting an eyelid, without looking away from him, with a perfectly straight, convincing face, quietly betray his own younger self. He managed to say, "Greater good, was it?"

"We needed a way to get inside Dickhead's flagship."

Speechless, shaking with horror, Spider stared at his older self one last time, turned, and went for the door.

"You'll do it, too, Spider."

He closed the door behind him, blinked several times to clear his eyes, and glanced at the ship's map laid out on the screen he held in his shaking hands. He thought of Molly. Thought about that time Soldier Spider showed him her dead body in the ship's morgue. Killed in a dreadful car crash? Or dead after succumbing to torture on Dickhead's ship and politely sent back, to be a torment to two versions of the deceased's husband? He shut his eyes, trying to get past the roaring sound in his head, to reach a point where he could think without wanting to kill everyone on this whole fucking ship.

It took a long time. At length, he checked the map again, nodded, and took a deliberate step in the direction of the Engineering Department. That bomb had to be neutralized, he told himself, so that he could then kill Soldier Spider himself, with his own hands. That thought kept him moving. The air, not that there was much of it, thin and metallic, was so cold it burned in his nose and lungs.

Spider was in sight of the main entrance to the Engineering Department, easily more than two hundred meters from Soldier Spider's workshop when—

The sound of the blast, a flat, heavy eruption of low-frequency noise, followed by the howling of emergency sirens and klaxons, reached him moments before the blast's shockwave. Channeled through more than two hundred meters of tight, confining passageways, when it reached Spider it knocked him against a bulkhead, and he fell in a heap onto the deck, stunned, shocked, and wondering what the hell had just happened. After a minute or two he was able to get to his feet, dizzy, his head hurting, and he started to make his way back to the workshop, full of confused dread and rising panic. His first thought was that Soldier Spider, the treacherous bastard, had just "thrown himself on the grenade", just like a heroic soldier in one of those ancient World War Two movies Spider remembered from his childhood. "You mad bastard!" he muttered, making his way through the baffling, twisting corridors, everything in smoky darkness. He knew he was getting close when he could smell fire, smoke, bitter explosive residue, and some other strange noxious chemical odor he guessed was some kind of fire suppression system doing its job. And, once he was aware that something really had happened up here, something bad, Spider felt something in his heart flip over. Where before he'd been a guy completely out of his depth, doing what he was told, not really believing in any of this crazy nonsense about the End of Time and the Vores and all of that — now, viscerally aware that a man had sacrificed himself for the greater good, Spider felt as if he was only now finally arriving in this present moment, in this situation. And, worse than that, the man who had been his only reliable source of information and guidance about this world was gone. As much as Spider had hated his future self always droning on about everything, now he felt a piercing anxiety. He was on his own now. "Oh, shit," he said to himself, breathing fumes, feeling woozy, like he was starting to drown in future shock.

A figure in black spec-ops gear like Soldier Spider's, but wearing a face-mask against the smoke, appeared out of the darkness and intercepted him. "Mr. Webb? Are you okay? Can you hear me?"

It took him a moment to register that someone was speaking to him. "Oh. Right." He coughed, a horrible wet sound. His eyes were sore and he was constantly rubbing at them. "I hit my head."

"You need to come with me, okay? It's not safe here."

"How bad is it?"

"Pretty bad. The whole sector's trashed. Huge damage, we're still working out how bad it is. Here," he said, handing Spider a mask and showing him how to put it on and make it work. The air it produced had an unpleasant but familiar bitter, rubbery taste Spider could have done without, but at least he could breathe properly.

"I'm guessing your illustrious leader..." he said, and immediately regretted his tone, and felt like a shit.

The soldier couldn't speak for a long, agonizing moment. "I need you to come with me. Oh, and by the way, I'm Cavers. Call me Steve."

"Spider." They briefly shook hands. Cavers' gloved hands were enormous. "Lead on," Spider said, and Cavers set off, with Spider in tow, through a different set of passageways, in the frosty darkness. Spider felt utterly lost, confused, aware that enormous, complex emotions were swirling around over his head, and would at some point swoop down and envelop him like a giant hot wave of wretchedness. So far, he only felt numb, shocked, a little strange. It had occurred to him that everyone on the ship would look to him to take over where his future self left off. That, he resolved, was not happening, no matter what. He was just some idiot who fixed time machines, and that was all, he told himself. No way was he some kind of military leader, no way in hell. He wanted no part of any military service. Yes, he'd been a policeman, but that was entirely different, he told himself, very convincingly, he thought. He was not necessarily doomed to become Soldier Spider. He clung to that notion, a life-belt in rough seas.

It also struck him, as they made their way forward, that Soldier Spider had deliberately waited until he was well clear of any possible blast effects before letting the bomb detonate. The old bastard trying for some kind of redemption? Possibly, he thought, trying to think his way into the other Spider's devious mind. It did make him think twice about what he'd been told about Molly. Could the old man have lied about Molly's death as a way of getting Spider out of the room? He remembered that strange feeling he had, just before Soldier Spider revealed that little nugget, like something was wrong. He wanted Spider to go and fetch some stupid tool that anybody on the ship could have located for him, and much faster than he could. "You mad, crazy bastard," Spider said, thinking about him, and thinking that Soldier Spider must have remembered standing there with his own future self, and having that same intuition, that something was up, something bad.

Could Molly still be alive? Would Soldier Spider lie about her specifically to get Spider so furious that he'd leave the workshop? The answer, it seemed to him, was hell, yes! He would know that Molly was Spider's most fundamental vulnerability — was, in fact, his own vulnerability, too, for that matter. Why wouldn't he use it against Spider to get him moving, out of harm's way?

Chewing this over, Spider found himself not sure what to think about his future self; it felt like a million different feelings and thoughts all jammed together, trying to figure out what was true, what was lies, and what it all meant.

Cavers' voice came to him through a radio connection in the mask. "You still with me, Spider? You okay back there?"

Startled out of his reverie, he said, "What?"

Cavers was right in front of him, and Spider hadn't noticed. "Are you okay? You've been very quiet."

"No, I'm, well, lots to think about."

He nodded. "Yeah, I reckon."

"Where are we?" The sirens had subsided; the stink of smoke and burning had dissipated. Now it was cold and dark, full of memories and torments and things he didn't want to think about.

"You still got the screen he gave you?"

"You know about the screen?"

"Standard issue. Everyone gets one."

Spider checked his pockets. No, he did not still have it. "Shit," he said, with feeling, and was surprised at how upset he felt at having lost something Soldier Spider had given him. It was only something simple, he told himself, yet now it seemed as if it was heavy with significance. He had to get it back, he thought, and felt ridiculous for feeling like this. His eyes stung, but he couldn't wipe them with the mask on.

Cavers gave his shoulder a reassuring squeeze. "It's okay. I'll get you settled and head back for it."

"You really don't have to," he said, now channeling his mother, never wanting anybody to go to any fuss over her. "It was just a map. I'll get another."

Cavers said, "Ah, no, mate. Not just a map. Trust me."

Spider nodded, baffled, and let the guy lead the way. Soon they arrived in a makeshift sickbay, no bigger than Spider's office back at the shop, lit with handheld lanterns hanging from bits of wire. There were three beds, two of which were occupied with unconscious patients, members of the crew. Cavers indicated that the ship's medic wanted to give Spider a quick once-over before certifying him okay to join the assault on Dickhead's flagship. "He'll be along in a jiff. Meanwhile, I'll just duck off and get that screen for you. Take it easy." And, before Spider could say anything, he'd left, leaving Spider on his own, listening to strange new sounds creaking, groaning and sighing through the ventilation system. He wondered how bad the damage might be. Wondered what it must have felt like, for Soldier Spider, when the bomb detonated. Wondered, in fact, about death itself. So far he'd been confronted with the prospect of his own death in various ways, an utterly unnerving thing. Was there an afterlife at the End of Time? Had Heaven dissipated along with all the universe's protons? Not that Spider had ever been religious, but he had often speculated and pondered what might await those who passed from this life. He had a horrible feeling that out here, beyond all that was rational, beyond any trace of light or heat, there was only the abyss — and the constant chewing of the Vores, coming to get you.

The ship's medic turned up, an exhausted, pale, young man whose lab coat did not fit well, with a stethoscope slung around his neck, and who gave off a sense that he'd been awake for four straight days now, and was hanging on out of sheer bloody-minded persistence, and probably a lot of caffeine and God knew what else. Spider had a feeling this was not a guy with whom to engage in light chat. He answered the medic's questions as honestly as he could, told him about hitting his head, but was told he did not have a concussion. The medic listened to Spider's booming heart, took his racing pulse and checked his respiration. "You're clearly in shock. That much I can tell you for sure, Mr. Webb. I'd like you to stay put in here for the night, get some rest, okay?"

"I don't feel too bad, really," Spider said.

The medic had no time for this. "My order is final, Mr. Webb. I'll try and get the galley to send you something to eat later. For now, you need to keep warm, I'll fetch you a nice hot cuppa—"

"I used to be a policeman, Doc. I know about shock."

He nodded but looked at Spider, unconvinced. "Yeah. Sure. I'll be back in a minute."

Cavers reappeared after a moment, bearing Spider's screen, and handed it over. "Sorry," he said, "gotta go. Briefing."

Spider said before he left, "Really? You all carry on like nothing's happened?"

"Not out of choice, believe me, Spider." And with that, he was gone.

The medic returned after about half an hour, gave Spider an insanely sweet cup of steaming hot tea, and told him to sip it slowly, and keep himself rugged up. "And if you need anything, use your screen there to give us a shout, okay? Questions?" He clearly wanted to be gone.

Spider let him go. The ship continued groaning and heaving; Spider shuddered and shivered. One of the two other patients snored loudly and murmured obscenities. The other, by contrast, just lay there, her mouth wide open, taking loud, slow breaths. When Spider finished his tea, he tried to settle back on the bed and get comfortable, but couldn't. The bed was very narrow, more of a shelf, he thought, and hard. In any case, there was no prospect of sleep, not after a day like this one. Too many voices yapping away in the back of his mind — and too many of those voices were various versions of his *own* voice! He kept thinking of Soldier Spider, the way he'd looked in those reading glasses, tinkering with the causality weapon, so much like his own father. Spider wondered if he'd ever see his family or anybody ever again. If he'd ever find out who the hell killed Clea Fassbinder. He hadn't forgotten her. Everything, even all of this nonsense at the End of Time, was bound up with the Fassbinder matter, Spider could see that. But for her decision to go back and look for her own killer, he wouldn't be here right now. It did occur to him that as he became more a part of the furniture around here, and everyone got used to his presence, they might let up on that operational security thing, and give him access to Clea Fassbinder's file. A boy could dream, he thought.

He drifted off to sleep without ever becoming aware that he was doing so. Only when a bot in an apron woke him up to ask if he wanted something to eat did he realize he'd actually been asleep. He said no, he was fine, thanks, and the bot left, whirring back to the galley, whistling. Spider muttered and went back to the dark, dreamless sleep of the abyss.

CHAPTER 21

Almost immediately, someone was trying to wake him up. Spider did not take this well, until he saw it was Cavers, in full military kit, and Cavers told him, "Spider, power-output levels on the *Destiny* are crashing. Something's up. McMahon's people are prepping for something. We have to move now. You're with me." There was no further explanation offered. Cavers helped Spider get dressed, then dragged him to a nearby compartment where several tall figures stood around in what Spider took to be some kind of black EVA suits, going over checklists, loading gleaming rounds into weapon magazines, testing helmet subsystems.

A female technician who'd been assisting two of the others came over to talk to Spider. "Mr. Webb? Hi. Remember me? I'm Wendy. I'll be helping you get kitted up."

Bewildered, still half-asleep, Spider blinked a lot, very distracted by the sight of hardened military types and their weaponry. "I'm getting kitted up because...?"

Cavers came over. "Spider. You're on my assault team. Come on, we're leaving in ten."

Before he had time to formulate even simple thoughts like, "Assault team?" Wendy and two of the troopers cheerfully took command of Spider and helped him squeeze into a suit.

Cavers told him, "This is the suit the Skipper used to wear, Spider. Wear it well."

"The Skipper was a lot — ouch! — fitter than me," Spider managed as many hands operated straps, latches, clips and system connections — and it wasn't easy. There was a lot of squeezing, pushing, wincing and grunting to make it all fit. When they were done, Spider found he could breathe, but not easily. The hardest part to get used to was the weird smells inside the suit, the sense of constant pressure all over his body, yet a surprising freedom of movement. The helmet was a different matter: even before they finished latching it together under his chin, Spider panicked and insisted they take it off, and take it off *now!*

"Problem, Spider?" Cavers asked, checking the time.

"Helmet makes me feel like I'm suffocating. I can't do it."

"Spider, it's like this. You find a way to deal with the helmet, or you're off the team."

"What about Molly?" He wanted to collect her body.

"We'll do our best to find her, no worries. But our primary objective is capturing McMahon."

"So it's possible you won't get around to Molly, is what you're saying."

"Priorities, Spider. Move it or lose it."

Wendy helped him with the helmet, showed him how to make sure he had a good air supply, even if it did taste like burned plastic, and that helped him overcome the worst of the anxiety. It was like learning to breathe again. After a moment, sealed in, at least somewhat aware of how to use the interface projected onto the clear face of his helmet visor, Spider was about as ready as he was going to get.

Wendy helped with last-minute checks, certified him ready to go, handed him back his *Destiny* remote. Wendy had hacked this remote and made copies, he learned, and each member of the squad had one. This was the key to the whole plan, to get Dickhead to give him access to his ship. Without that remote, this entire operation could never take place. She wished him "good hunting", and, looking sicker by the moment, excused herself and ran off through a hatchway, a hand over her mouth.

He watched the troopers— "Time Marines", he'd been told to call them. There were five of them, including Cavers. Wendy had told him they were one man short, who was sick. These five, many of whom were probably sick, too, were on edge, revved up, ready to go, nervous. Two, he noticed, were using a set of rosary beads, and murmuring quietly. Spider asked if he'd be getting a gun; Cavers said they could only let him have a pistol, solely for defensive purposes. Spider said, "Sure, no worries," and tucked the proffered gun into a holster on his left hip.

Cavers went through a last-minute run-through with his troops, discussing the plan and all expected problems. He had a three-dimensional map of the *Destiny's* interior, and designated each of the soldiers to specific points of the ship. "Any questions?"

There was only one, from Spider. "Where would they be keeping Molly?"

Cavers indicated her likely location, and sketched in the best route to get there from where they would "land."

"Got it," Spider said, bouncing on his toes, fidgeting with the *Destiny* remote, and pronounced himself ready.

"All right, then," Soldier Spider said. "On my mark." The marines had their cloned remotes at the ready. "This includes you, too, Spider. Listen up. Okay, then. Mark!"

§ § §

The *Destiny*, when they arrived, was a mausoleum: crewmembers, some in groups, others off on their own, lay dead everywhere they looked. The time marines were too late. *Jonestown*, Spider thought, horrified to see it. Hundreds of bodies strewn about, as if they'd simply laid down and died, probably poisoned, and the poison was probably taken willingly. Cavers swore. Spider knew that if they'd just gone without him, they might have gotten here in time to stop it. He felt guilty, but mostly he simply felt an aching sadness. What had Dickhead told these people to make them do this? he wondered. The Jonestown victims had been told that their numerous and unstoppable enemies were coming to shut down their little paradise in the jungle. They had to die to prevent this. Dickhead, fourteen years older than Spider, certainly knew the Jonestown story. Had he always seen himself as a charismatic Jim Jones figure at the center of a little bit of paradise under siege from outside forces who'd never understand? Spider had often wondered what the hell went on in Dickhead's mind, but he had never expected anything quite like this, this silent horror. Then again, the way Dickhead went into raptures when he described the Vores, angels of destruction, burning down the universe for the greater good, he realized he only barely knew Dickhead, and that anything at all was possible. Spider suspected Dickhead had persuaded these poor buggers to take their lives by telling them he'd received transmissions from the Vores, telling him that the Final Secret of the Cosmos was now available, like a song you could download from the tubes.

Most compartments were open to space, fittings frozen solid and brittle. The silence as Cavers led the time marines through the ship — and it was a huge, spacious vessel — was oppressive, as if the ship itself was watching their every move. Spider, still getting used to the odd sounds and smells of the suit, asked Cavers, "Permission to look for Molly?"

"Take Mr. Raspa with you.

Raspa was tall and imposing. His equipment, as baffling as it was impressive, made him look twice the size of a regular human being. He told Spider, "Call me Ray."

"Spider."

They shook hands; Spider's gloved hand was almost lost within Ray's grip.

"One thing," Cavers said before they took off.

"Sir?" Ray said.

"Don't spare the stasers as you go."

Raspa grinned. "Sir, yes, sir!"

"There's still a chance Dickhead is aboard, waiting for us somewhere."

"Yes, sir," Raspa said.

"And godspeed." He met Spider's eyes for a moment, and in them Spider saw a glint of the same cold horror he himself felt at the scene before them, then looked away and started snapping orders at the rest of his troops. "Meet you back here in one hour. Wait five minutes. If we're not all back by then, head back home."

Soon Raspa and Spider were alone in the freezing dark, watching where they stepped to avoid tripping over bodies, their breathing loud inside their suits. "You okay, Spider?"

"Oh," he said, still weirded out by every single thing, "never better, mate."

"So which way?"

Spider had a graphic display lit up on the faceplate of his helmet, indicating where they were on the map of the ship; the path to Molly's likely location was marked out in red. He pointed. "Um," he said, turning this way and that, anxious to make sure he was reading the map the right way, "that way."

They set off, through cold, dark, airless compartments, their boots crunching tiny ice crystals, Raspa leading the way. Spider said, "Nice of Dickhead to leave the gravity on for us."

"He didn't. G like this is a property of the ship's structure."

"Oh," Spider said, looking around, trying to imagine the sort of physics that must be at work here. "Okay, then."

Before entering a new compartment, passageway or room, Raspa made Spider stand well back and fired a quick, silent burst from his staser rifle. Then Raspa would go in, check the area, and make sure it was safe to proceed. Spider asked what the staser was for. He thought it was a tool; Soldier Spider had wanted Spider to go and fetch him one.

Raspa said, "Freezes local time for a while. Anybody hiding in there in ghost mode? They're busted. Leaves 'em standing there like statues!" Spider nodded, impressed, but worried about what would happen when the freeze wore off. Not that it seemed to matter because, for all the shots Cavers used, none revealed anything other than a vast deathscape.

Spider was thinking about Dickhead. Two moves ahead of the game. "Bastard knew we were coming, he bloody knew it."

"Where would he go?" Raspa asked.

"He's only got a million other ships, remember?"

"Yeah." Raspa sighed.

"For some folks," Spider said, keeping his voice down as they crept through the dark, "there's no such thing as 'enough,' whatever it might be. Cars, troops, money, women, power, connections. You name it."

"Shh," Raspa said, so quietly Spider nearly didn't hear it. He stopped, locked up with sudden cold tension, listening hard despite the silence of vacuum and the noise of his suit, hair on the back of his neck standing straight up. His hand wrapped around the butt of his pistol. He felt exposed, useless: the time marines were covered in gear and armor and all manner of spooky protection; Spider, though wearing the same suit, did not have all of the same gear. Where Raspa would blend into whatever background he might be near, Spider would not. It was starting to occur to him, as he watched Raspa, that he might be in a lot of trouble. Raspa brought up the staser rifle, and fired three careful shots into the next area. They were in a large, open area, perhaps a dining room: there were plenty of tables, chairs, a serving counter, beverage dispensers, an inert media wall, rows of crew photos, ship insignia — and something that told Spider this was definitely Dickhead McMahon's operation: those annoying bloody motivational posters on every wall, huge, like Nazi propaganda, only with slogans like SERVICE; LOYALTY; SACRIFICE; LEADERSHIP; COURAGE; and DOMINATION. *"Such* a dickhead!" he muttered, chilled to the bone.

Nothing appeared out of ghost mode. Raspa waved his light around, trying to see hidden details, without finding anything.

"Strange," he said, moving around, peering at everything through his infra-red and night-vision visor. "There's nothing here. I was sure I'd heard—"

Spider was trying not to wet himself. How did these maniacs keep so bloody calm? he wondered. He certainly did not feel calm. He was terrified out of his mind. "How much farther to where they're holding Molly?"

"You know McMahon might have taken her body with him, right?"

Spider thought about what Soldier Spider had told him. It seemed to him, though, that Dickhead McMahon, prince among men, legend in his own lunchbox, would be more inclined to leave her dead body behind for Spider to find, a special, personalized message just for him. "No, she's here. Bet you anything."

"Just through here," Raspa said, indicating a door leading out of the dining area. "There's a corridor, some steps down—"

Spider told him to lead on, and found himself, despite the heated suit, rubbing his arms for warmth. That would be why he was shivering: because he was cold, right? You shiver when you're cold. He kept telling himself this, and wished Raspa would get a bloody move on!

At last they reached an area that reminded Spider of civilian police lockups: holding cells, meeting rooms, a control desk, and so forth. According to Spider's map, the second of the row of holding cells was Molly's last known address. Raspa got the door open, checked the room with his light, and paused, standing there, staring.

"Ray, what's the—"

Raspa waved him over and showed him.

Spider, doing his damndest not to panic, not to freak out, his stomach in painful knots, wanting only to get it the hell over with, show him her dead body already, show him the error of his ways, rub his face in his own mess—

Raspa shone his light around the room. Spider, seeing it all, thought he was going to be sick inside his helmet, and he had to sit down on the frozen floor, staring at nothing, numb with shock.

The timeship *Destiny* had a human crew of perhaps two hundred people, not counting Dickhead, who came and went, going about his business back in Spider's time, and traveling around the fleet. Spider had already seen most of those crewmembers, dead and frozen, on the way here. But in this cell, carefully stacked up like the piles of corpses he'd seen in grainy black-and-white documentary footage taken by Nazi filmmakers at Auschwitz during the war, were perhaps fifty more bodies. Were they Dickhead's personal executive staff, deserving of the great honor of such a dubious end? Or were they would-be rebels, and Dickhead needed to make an example of them? It was impossible to know. All Spider did know for sure, if Raspa's readings were accurate, was that Molly's body was in there with all of those others, their bare feet marbled and rimed with frost that glinted in the light.

"Oh, God, Molly," Spider managed to say, falling to his knees, staring at it all, taking in the full, horrifying extent of Dickhead's victory. This, Spider thought, was Zeropoint, the Dickhead way. This was the fate awaiting anyone who worked for him, who gave their lives to him to play with. It was more than monstrous, more than shocking. And Soldier Spider had persuaded him, a stupid time machine repairman, to get caught in the grinding mechanism of Dickhead's machine, entirely so that "the good guys" could come here, and see all this.

There was nothing else for it. Spider and Raspa set about trying to move all of those bodies into the passageway. It was heavy, fatiguing, disgusting work. One of these people, Spider told himself, fighting to keep his gorge down, was Molly. He had to find her.

§ § §

Raspa called Cavers and the rest of the marines, who joined them promptly; they reported finding no trace of Dickhead anywhere, and one of the ship's smallcraft was missing. Cavers said his team had also searched for little surprises Dickhead might have left for them to find the hard way: booby-traps, bombs, and so forth. As far as they could tell, the ship was clean. And, strangely, there was no sign of a Dickhead-led attack formation of other ships converging on this location. "So far, anyway. We're keeping an eye on the scopes," Cavers added.

Spider hardly heard a word of it. Raspa had stopped to listen to the boss, but he was still in that room, freezing despite his suit, trying to separate bodies. Many of them were frozen together, in huge, solid blocks. It took enormous effort and time to separate bodies enough to haul them out. Then there was the problem of what to do with them. Cavers, seeing that Spider would not stop, not now, and not ever, if it meant finding Molly, told his men to provide what help they could. Soon, with everyone helping, a neat line of frozen bodies began forming on the passageway floor. Spider checked each one, studying faces as best he could through the frost, trying to find Molly. It was, in many ways, even worse than separating the bodies themselves: up close, staring into those iced-up eyes, the full magnitude of what had happened here struck him like a great weight falling from the sky, again and again. At least at first. Then, after about twenty or thirty such bodies, he found he was starting to get used to it. Each new frozen face, while gruesome, stopped freaking him out quite so much. He wasn't sure whether to be horrified at himself or not, and got on with the job.

Molly was at the bottom of the pile. She, like the others, was frozen solid, her eyes shut. Squeezed shut, he noticed. Her face was drawn and lined in a way he had never seen before, and he noticed her shoulders looked wrong. Then he realized: her shoulders had dislocated.

Spider collapsed next to her, unable to speak, face buried in his shaking hands, his stomach heaving. The pain was unspeakable.

Cavers couldn't watch. The other marines sat down around Spider and Molly, and said nothing. They sat like that for a long while.

It was hard, Spider discovered, to prevent breaking Molly's hair when he tried to stroke it. When he regained his composure, at least a little, he found himself staring at her, his mind shot full of thoughts, memories — that first time she kissed him, surprising him greatly, considering she'd just been crying; the first time he'd seen her face by candlelight in a dingy little Italian restaurant in Nedlands, the way the light caught the highlights in her hair.

He managed a small smile, still staring at her in the torchlight. Something was wrong, though, he kept thinking. Molly didn't quite look like the rest of the bodies. Getting to his feet, he checked some of the other bodies, comparing the way their skin looked to the way Molly's looked.

"What?" He scraped a layer of crusted ice and frost from her face. "What does that look like to you?" he asked Raspa and the others. Everyone leaned in for a look.

"That's not right," Cavers said.

Spider checked her hands, her feet, and two of the marines checked the other bodies for comparison and reported back. Molly's feet and hands did not look like theirs. Once Spider scraped more frost away from Molly's body, he sat back, sniffling, and looked at her, tilting his head this way and that, his pulse quickening, but trying not to get his hopes up. "Is it just me," he said, "or does she not look frozen to you?"

Cavers hunched down next to Spider, and looked Molly over. With Spider's permission, he touched her face, her arms. He called the team medic, a no-nonsense female marine named Peel. She produced some diagnostic tools from her belt, and touched Molly's skin with the tips of each one, while watching tiny screens on her wrist. Spider thought he would explode if it took any longer. At length, Peel nodded at Cavers. "Stasis, sir."

"So she's not actually frozen?" Spider asked.

"She's not frozen, Spider," Cavers said.

"Is she... Is she...?" He couldn't say it.

Cavers glanced at Peel, who said, "Hard to say, Mr. Webb. It looks like she's in deep Level IV stasis — um, she's been stopped all the way down to the atomic level. Getting her back, well..." She glanced away.

"So she is alive?"

"I don't want to get your hopes up, sir."

Cavers said to her, "For God's sake, Peel."

Peel said, "I don't want to give Mr. Webb false hope, sir."

"How long," Spider asked, "can she stay like this?"

"Depends, sir," Peel said. "There's a certain amount of flux friction between the stasis field on one hand and standard background entropic activity on the other."

"Oh, shit," Spider muttered. "So you're saying, she could thaw out over time, kind of?"

"That's correct, sir, yes. And if she's not given the right treatment during that process..."

"So she could still die? Is that what you're—"

"Stasis is a rock in the stream of time," Peel tried to explain. "It's an affront to the natural order of things. The universe will do its best to overcome the stasis field. It's a question of whether the stasis is cancelled in one step, or whether it runs out over time. If the latter, Mr. Webb, different parts of your wife's physiology will start running again before other parts are ready. She—"

"I see," Spider said. He'd thought it would be something like that. "God. So how do we snap her out of it? Can you guys do that back on your ship? Have you got a 'thaw' setting on those staser rifles?"

Before Peel could answer, Cavers interrupted. "Spider. We have to go." With that, he assigned Raspa and Spider to carry Molly, and ordered his team back to base.

§   §   §

Spider stayed with Molly in the *Masada*'s sickbay. This was a compartment bigger than the one he'd occupied earlier: where that one only had room for three patients, this one could handle anything up to ten at once — though Spider noticed four of those beds were shut down, their monitoring screens dark. There were two busy scrubber-bots working over the walls and floor, humming softly. That aggressive antiseptic odor filled the air to a degree that was almost offensive, Spider thought. The doctor, the same guy Spider met before, not looking any better, told him the waste recycling system was up and running again, for now, but there was no predicting how long it might last before it crashed again. The doctor, Spider thought, looked like he'd been awake and under stress for so long he might just go crazy.

"And you know what's really funny?" the doctor said, wide-eyed, jumpy, fidgety, "I'm not even a real doctor. I'm a glorified nurse with a field promotion, ha-ha, ha-ha."

"Just tell me whether you can restore my wife, would you?" Molly occupied one of the operational beds. In this warmer environment, all trace of frost and ice had melted away, leaving Molly looking more or less fine — those dislocated shoulders notwithstanding — but very very still, like a three-dimensional photograph, a person caught between moments. It was an eerie thing to see, Spider commented. Something he never wanted to see again.

"We'll do our best, Mr. Webb. Best I can tell you right now."

Spider heard him, and heard within those words the real message: don't get your hopes up. He only had to look around, and think about what he'd seen of this ship earlier:

things were bad. There was very little available power. The EMP shot, so useful for taking out the causality weapon, had left them in trouble. Soldier Spider had told Spider that this was okay, and he should not feel bad about it. There had been a long meeting about it. The crew had reported that they could do a lot to harden critical systems, and that it should be possible to get things running after the shot, to some extent. It was better to shut down the weapon than have Soldier Spider — and potentially Spider himself — erased, leaving the *Masada* not only with bad internal damage, but with two baffling corpses as well.

So Spider settled in to wait, sitting next to Molly's bed around the clock, getting up only to hit the washroom and to eat whatever the ship's chef could scrape together. He slept lightly, uncomfortably, but would not be shifted from Molly's bedside. At one point he took up reading to her. He found a lot of reading material in that screen Soldier Spider had given him, and which Cavers had retrieved for him. Entire books and sets of books, thousands of different titles, occupied a small portion of the thing's enormous memory. There was *Pride and Prejudice*, he discovered, to his great surprise. It had been one of Molly's favorites, a book she read every couple of years. By the time he finished the final page, though, Molly was still locked in stasis, and the doctor, now feeling a little better after some badly needed sleep, had found nothing that might help, or which might mitigate the damage as the stasis field weakened.

"So we're screwed?" Spider asked, frustrated.

"I think we're at the limit of what we can do with this ship's resources. I'm sorry," the doctor said, meaning it.

"So that's it?"

The doctor was working a screen, and beamed something to Spider. "That's the specs for a treatment that will fix the problem, and provide the best chance for a full recovery."

"Looks like gibberish to me," Spider said, bitter, not seeing how it might help.

"Mr. Webb, Spider, listen to me. This is not advanced tech. It's not. It's something a well-equipped chrono-medicine lab in your time—"

"My time?" Spider stared at the doctor, starting to see what the doctor was saying. He knew, for example, that there was a state-of-the-art chronomed facility at the Queen Elizabeth II Medical Center, in Nedlands. "My God!"

"We can arrange a referral for your wife's case to go through DOTAS in your time, and that should facilitate the whole thing, and not cost you anything more than a hundred-dollar co-payment via Medicare."

Astonished, adrenaline blasting through his system, Spider stared in wonder at the doctor. "You little ripper!"

CHAPTER 22

Emergency Department, Queen Elizabeth II Medical Center. Queues for everything. Patients waiting for rooms stacked up five-high on what looked like shelving. Understaffed, overworked nurses hurtling about, frantic, exhausted. Phones ringing, alarms beeping, ambulances queued up outside, waiting for a delivery slot. Inside, kids freaked out on the latest street drugs; people who'd suffered unlikely home accidents; terrified parents nursing sick kids; and, standing around anywhere they could find a bit of space, poor buggers who in years past would have simply gone to see their local GP.

§ § §

Spider carried Molly inside where a keen-eyed male orderly placed her on a hospital hand-truck, saying "Well, obviously a wheelchair's no good to her, eh?" Spider had to agree.

"Stasis job?" asked the orderly.

"Oh yeah." replied Spider.

"Third one this week. Bloody time machines."

"Tell me about it."

The orderly wheeled Molly into a triage queue and handed Spider a light cotton blanket. "This could take a while."

Spider tried to spread the blanket over Molly as best he could — no easy feat considering she was more or less standing up.

Spider found it was difficult to see Molly like this, knowing he was responsible twice over. He resolved that if he ever got to become Soldier Spider, Warrior of the Far

Future, he would make damn sure he never ever used her like this again. "Right," he said, uneasy, "that's decided. Good."

With Molly was safely rugged up, Spider decided to call the shop. Malaria answered promptly. "Time Machines Repaired While-U-Wait, this is Malaria, can I help you?"

"Hi, Malaria, it's me," Spider said.

"Spider?" she said, "It's been twenty minutes. What's up?"

He managed a weary smile. "I'm at the QE II chrono-medicine facility."

"Are you okay?" she said.

"Everything's fine. I just wanted you to know that Dickhead might be out of the picture for the forseeable future," he said.

There was a moment's pause.

"Ooooookay," she said, wary.

"Any messages?" Spider asked.

"Street's been trying to reach you."

"No worries. I'll call her back."

"And Rutherford called about tonight."

The prospect of facing James Rutherford felt like one burden too many, and yet, he found himself saying, "Okay. I'll call him back, too." He rang off, dialed Iris' number, and left a message assuring her that all was at least reasonably well, nothing to worry unduly about, but he would appreciate it if she would meet him at the QE II Medical Center's chronomedicine facility.

At length, sometime after five p.m., Molly's name came up, and an overworked, middle-aged nurse from New Zealand gave Molly a brief examination. The nurse told Spider that Molly would be admitted, as soon as a bed could be organized in the chronomedicine unit, and that could take a few hours.

"Things are that busy?"

"School holidays, Mr. Webb. Teenage kids borrowing their parents' time machines. Mix in some booze and some dodgy drugs, guess what happens? Universe-devouring paradoxes are the bloody least of it, if you'll pardon me saying so."

Spider explained about his line of work, how he often had to fix — and clean — those very machines afterwards. The nurse nodded, understanding only too well, and squeezed his shoulder. She asked how Molly had wound up like this. Spider decided against telling her the truth, said he had no idea, that he had popped round to Molly's house to fix her toilet, and found her like that, on the ground next to her time machine.

The nurse nodded again, appeared to believe him, and said, "Yep, no worries."

A room for Molly became available sooner than expected, and soon Spider had to sit down with a clerk, providing Molly's details, insurance status, Medicare number and so forth.

By the time Iris turned up, Spider was sitting alone and depressed in the empty private room assigned to Molly. Molly had just been wheeled off for Stage One of her treatment. One of the nurses who'd taken Molly away told Spider she'd be gone for at least two hours, if he wanted to go off and get something to eat.

"Good grief," Iris said, after knocking on the open door, "you look like somebody shot your dog."

Spider looked up, surprised. "Hi, Iris. Thanks for coming."

"What's up?"

"Need a favor."

"How's your wife?"

"In treatment," he said, looking at the space in the room where Molly's bed had been.

"Right," she said.

"Stasis attack."

"Shit. She gonna be okay?"

"Should be. I got her here soon as I could."

She nodded. "So, eaten anything recently?"

"Oh, just, you know..." he said, thinking about some thin soup he'd eaten on the Masada a few hours earlier."

"Come on. Nothing you can do for her now."

It was true. Spider hated the idea of leaving, of not being here when they brought her back to the room. Then again, it also occurred to him, they could meet James Rutherford at that cafe in Crawley, listen to the poor bugger, then come right back. He heard Soldier Spider's voice telling him that James was trouble, that Spider was well-advised to leave James alone to self-destruct on his own, not to get caught up in it himself. It was good advice, Spider knew that. And yet, and yet... There was a chance James could lead him to Clea Fassbinder's murderer. And, of course, he was a mate. Charlie Stuart had been right. Mates help each other. If he could help James, even if it was just helping him get the care he needed, that was a worthwhile thing in itself, right?

With one last look around Molly's empty room, Spider told Iris, "Lead on."

§ § §

Once they were safely stuck in traffic, Iris asked him about his scruffy new look, and remarked that she'd never seen anybody grow that much beard in just a few hours.

"I've been a busy boy," he said.

"So tell me."

He told her.

When he finished, bringing her up to the present moment, she said, amazed, "So basically you're saying McMahon went all Jonestown at the end?"

Spider nodded. "The *Destiny* was his flagship, crewed by his very own cult, and they were all dead. We brought a few of the bodies back to the *Masada* for examination, and yeah, poisoned. It wasn't the infamous purple punch, but near enough. Just... unimaginable horror, really."

Iris said nothing for a while. The sound of rain beating on the windshield, and the electric wipers swinging back and forth, back and forth, gently squeegeeing the glass.

"And what about McMahon himself? You say there was no trace of him anywhere?"

"I think he knew what was coming, had a plan in place, and executed it. All in the name of the Final Secret of the Cosmos, of course. Just him and his handpicked senior staff, murderers all."

"Why would he leave your ex-wife alive?" Iris asked. Spider had thought about that, but was no nearer an answer. "Beats me. If I run into him again, I'll have to ask." In fact, there was one possibility, and it chilled him to contemplate it: what if Dickhead had left her alive because he knew she'd be so damaged, so broken, that she would never again be the Molly he had always known, and always wanted back. What if he'd left her alive because that would be worse than killing her? Worse for her but, most important, worse for *him* — seeing her like that, and knowing it was all his fault. *That'll teach you to go betraying your master, Spider*, he imagined Dickhead telling him.

Iris listened to him wax on about his dreadful, wretched guilt, then she said, "But it's not your fault."

Spider nodded. Cavers had tried to impress this upon him before sending him home. "Dickhead and his minions did this, Spider. They're the ones who snatched her, and they're the ones who hurt her. He wants you to blame yourself, so don't. Don't give the rat bastard the satisfaction."

It was a hard lesson to learn. He was pretty sure that if Molly ever did speak to him again, she would tell him it absolutely was his fault. "You should have said no when they first told you about it, you should have just refused!" she would say, and she'd be right.

As the traffic continued to move at a snail's pace, Iris remembered to tell Spider that she had a possible lead on the murder of his other future self, the one who'd gone and camped out in Spider's capsule at The Lucky Happy Moon Motel that night, intending to save Spider's life.

"Our tech forensics people, frankly, pulled a bloody miracle out of thin air and managed to extract enough data from that surveillance tape to get a brief — and I mean really brief — image of the killer." She popped her watchtop open and worked through the interface, pulling up an image, and showed it to him. "She look familiar to you?"

He leaned over and peered at the image. There wasn't a lot of detail, she was right about that, but he recognized that face. "Dickhead's personal assistant. A robot."

Iris hadn't been expecting that. "You're kidding me."

"Iris, I'm too wiped to lie right now. Believe me."

She was peering at the image now. "A robot? They have robots that look like that?"

"Oh, it's a land of fucking wonders, Iris. You've got no idea."

She nodded, surprised. "Any thoughts why this, um, this killer robot — I cannot believe I just said that — why this killer robot wanted to kill you?"

"Thought it was me. Well, it was me, obviously, but, um. It's difficult. I wouldn't be surprised to learn the idea was to wipe out my far-future self, Soldier Spider, the guy I go on to become, Dickhead's great nemesis, nice and early. Or something. Who the hell knows? Dickhead had all kinds of wacky schemes going."

"Did you ever find out about the 'Vores?'"

"Oh yeah."

"Should I be worried?"

He wasn't sure. "At this point, maybe. Maybe not. Dunno." Neither Soldier Spider nor Dickhead had given him any kind of timeline. The Vores might be thousands of years away from the present, or they could turn up, munching the ground out from him next Tuesday. He didn't know, and, the way he felt right now, didn't want to know. It was a battle for another time, he thought.

To change the subject, he said, "I've been thinking a lot."

"What about?"

"Free will."

"Free will?"

"Yeah," he said, trying not to fidget, a weird feeling in his head. "I reckon free will is bullshit."

"You need to get some sleep, Spider."

"No, no, I feel okay, more or less."

"Free will." she said, shaking her head.

"It's an illusion. That's all it is. Everything is already sorted out, every decision, every possibility, it's all determined, scripted, whatever."

Iris was looking at him as if she was worried. "Where'd all this come from?"

"I've been to the End of bloody Time, Iris. From that perspective, everything is done and settled. Basically, everything that could happen has happened. It's all mapped out, documented, diagrammed, written up in great big books, and ignored."

"You're a crazy bastard, you know that, Spider?"

"Maybe not crazy enough," he said.

Iris was still struggling for traction on the conversation. "You think everything is predetermined? Is that it? But what about—"

"No. You just think you have free will."

"So, according to you," Iris said, looking bewildered, "a guy who kills his wife was always going to kill her. She was always going to die."

"From his point of view, he doesn't know that, and neither does she, but yeah. She was always a goner, so to speak."

"There is no way I can accept this," she said. "It's intolerable. It robs individual people of moral agency. According to you nobody chooses to do anything; they're just following a script. That means nobody's responsible for anything."

"I said, free will is an illusion. We think we've got moral agency, we think we make choices. It's a perfect illusion. It just depends on your point of view."

"It's a bloody pathway to madness, I reckon," Iris said.

"I dunno," he said. "Right now, sitting here, thinking about everything, I think it makes a lot of sense. Kinda, anyway."

"Think you'll find that's just an illusion," she said, and flashed a tiny smile.

§   §   §

The Cafe Fuego at Matilda Bay, across Hackett Drive from the sprawling campus of the University of Western Australia, and only a few kilometers from the QE II Medical Center, was a favorite haunt of students and academics alike. Offering an unmatched view across the great gulf of the swollen Swan River to the luminous towers of central

Perth, it looked — and smelled — warm and inviting, all picturesque brass fittings, and dark polished woodwork.

They found a spot, not too far from the café, paid a fortune to the roaming ticket droid, and got out. Iris was snug in her belted raincoat; Spider, less prepared, felt the cold evening winds slicing through him, and he wished he'd brought a decent coat.

The sublime aroma of good, hot coffee hit them even before they walked through the doors. In some ways, Spider thought, it'd be great if James didn't show. It would be nice, after his recent harrowing adventures at the End of Time — to say nothing of the concentrated misery of the QE II Emergency Department — to just sit somewhere peaceful.

A voice called from the darkness. "Spider!"

Iris looked at Spider. "Was that you?"

Spider, his hopes sinking, started searching around. "You might as well show your self. Come on! Haven't got all night."

Another Spider emerged from the darkness beyond the lights of the café. "Thought you'd never get here," he said, hands deep in the pockets of a heavy jacket.

"Shit," Spider said, shaking his head, pissed off. "And what do you want?"

"Much as I'm loath to say so, Spider," the new Spider said, "we need to talk."

"We're meeting James Rutherford in a few minutes. You'll have to make it brief, whatever it is." Already, though, Spider had a very bad feeling about what this future self would tell him.

"James isn't coming." The other Spider, who, now he stood in the light from the café, looked no older than Present Spider, but did sport a scraggly beard, long hair needing a wash, and conveyed an air of fatigue and depression. He checked his watch. "Yeah. Right now, in fact, Electra is stabbing him. He'll bleed out in a few minutes." He reported all this with a lack of affect Spider found chilling.

"And you know this because...?" Iris said to him, not buying it.

"I know it because it's kind of my fault."

"Your fault?" Spider said. "I take it, when you were me, you resorted to time travel to try and save James's life? Only it turned out..."

"That my interceding like that more or less made everything worse, yeah," Near Future Spider said, bitter and sad.

Iris was watching the two Spiders. To Near Future Spider, she said, "A man is dying right now, yes?"

"Yes, Iris," he said. "And there's sweet bugger all you can do about it. Trust me, I spent months trying."

"Even though Soldier Spider told you to leave James the hell alone, that he was trouble, and you could even get yourself seriously hurt or killed?"

"He told you that, too, and here you are, waiting for the guy."

"Hey, I thought if I brought backup—"

Iris turned to Spider. "That's the favor you wanted? You wanted backup?"

"It occurred to me things might go pear-shaped," Spider said to her.

"Things did go pear-shaped," Near Future Spider said. "I was in hospital for three weeks. Thirty stitches!"

"Shit," Spider said.

Iris was on the phone, calling her partner, Aboulela. She asked Spider for James Rutherford's address, which both Spiders gave her, and she relayed that to Aboulela. "Get over there right now. I'll be there ASAP."

"You're already too late," Near Future Spider said, again with that chilling flat tone.

"We could use the time machine you used to come and visit us, couldn't we?"

"Sure," Near Future Spider said. "That's how the whole thing got started."

"I can't just let a man be murdered!" Iris told him. "Let's go. Where's your machine?"

"Across the road."

Spider said, "His daughter kills him? Electra? That daughter?"

Iris was pushing Near Future Spider to take them to his time machine, but he called back over his shoulder. "Yeah. Turns out she's the one who's trouble."

"But she's, what? Nineteen?"

"She's been tormenting James for years. He couldn't take it, so tonight he tried to kill her out of desperation, but—"

"She got to him first?"

They'd reached the road. The UWA campus spread out across the road. In a parking area, under sodium lights, Spider saw where Near Future Spider had parked the shop van, with an old Boron II on a trailer behind it. He could only assume the Boron belonged to a customer who had no idea what was being done with it.

They waited for a gap in traffic and ran across the road, Iris dragging Near Future Spider like an unwilling suspect. Iris's phone rang. "Street," she said, then, "Oh, Ali, right. Listen, I'm commandeering a time machine — what? What? You are fucking kidding me, you are absolutely fucking kidding me! He said that? Well, yes, Spider is helping me. No, he's not a suspect, as far as I'm aware — no, wait! Wait, listen to me. Ali! Oh, shit!" she said, "He hung up on me! Can you believe that, he bloody hung up on me!" She dialed again, but got nothing. She left a colorful message, then hung up, screaming in frustration.

"Trouble?" Spider asked, guts tense, knowing exactly what was wrong.

Iris went to the passenger door of the van. She called the Spiders over. "Get in!" Near Future Spider climbed up into the driver's seat, and opened the passenger door for Iris, who hauled herself up into the shotgun seat. Present Spider made himself comfortable in the back, squeezed in amongst racks of tools and spare parts. Iris ordered Near Future Spider to take them to Rutherford's place right now.

"It won't work, Iris," he tried to tell her, as he started the van and got it moving. "All we'll end up doing is make everything worse."

"Just bloody well drive! God!"

CHAPTER 23

Near Future Spider drove, or tried to drive. The roads were jammed with traffic: cars, scooters and bikes; no one was sticking to the marked lanes; progress was slow. Rain drummed on the roof of the van and spattered against the windscreen. Iris swore a very great deal. She got on the phone again, and anonymously arranged an ambulance crew to go out to Rutherford's place, saying she was a neighbor and she heard "some scary shit" from his place. She told Spider, when he asked, that they would send the first available ambulance, but it could be a while. Swearing, Iris tore off her phone patch, screwed it up into bits and flung it out the window into the rain.

"It's something, though," Spider said, trying to be helpful.

Iris turned in her seat and shot him a hard look. He shut up and sat back in his seat amongst the tools. It was bad enough that Iris couldn't get her squad to act on her information about Rutherford because of him, he thought. What was, in some ways, even worse was the sheer bloody-minded wretchedness of the modern health system, with its underfunded ambulance service. "First available ambulance!" she muttered.

Then, still steamed, she leaned around her seat to look at him. "And guess what? If it does turn out that a man has been killed in Rutherford's apartment, I'm to regard you — presumably both of you — as "people of interest", and bring you all in for questioning."

Spider tried to protest, "But I..."

"You said yourself," she said to Near Future Spider, "that it's partly your fault!"

He nodded. "That's true. The thing is, the thing you have to remember, though, is that Rutherford was gonna die tonight no matter what. The man was fated to be killed sometime tonight, regardless. That's what drove me crazy. I know about time travel. I know about history. History pushes back against attempted changes — unless you make your push at exactly the right point. You can't just go in anywhere in the timeline and try to change things. You have to know the right point, or it just doesn't work, and you end up with a big mess. But there I was, trying it anyway, trying to save the poor bastard. He didn't deserve to die! Nobody deserves to die. Sure, he had an affair with that bloody Clea Fassbinder woman, and sure that led his wife to get the best possible revenge a woman could arrange, killing herself like that. How could I not want to try and stop it happening? Plus, he's a mate, right? You can't let down a mate. It's not on. You have to do what you can."

Spider said, "How did James's wife kill herself?"

"Oh, mate. You've got to see it for yourself. She made a video of it, and had it posted to him."

"She what?"

They were inching their way through the canyon of St. George's Terrace, immense office towers looming either side of the road. "She uploaded the video to a service called Snuff.com. Somehow it ended up on an XVD posted to him. He didn't know what it was. There was no return address. And this is a truly broken man at this point. His life's in ruins — and we know what that's like, right? So, one night, drunk out of his mind, his daughter off somewhere with her useless boyfriend, he puts on the disc, and gets the shock of his life."

"God," Spider said, horrified. He had not known any of this. James had never gone into any detail about Sky's death. That she had chosen to kill herself to get back at her husband for his affair struck Spider as breathtakingly cruel. He could not imagine a degree of cruelty like that, and he'd seen some of the dreadful things people were prepared to do to people they hated.

Iris, settled down a little, asked, "How did she do it?"

Near Future Spider glanced at her. He hesitated. "Self-immolation. Out in the bush somewhere."

Spider was speechless. Iris shook her head.

Near Future Spider said, "Big on the dramatic gesture, was Sky Rutherford."

This, Spider was thinking, explained a lot about James's recent behavior. "So did he kill Clea?"

"Our late and unlamented far future self told us he didn't, right?" Near Future Spider said.

"I took it as more neither confirming nor denying, all that operational security bullshit."

"Well, the good news—"

Iris interrupted him. "It seems to me, and sorry for interrupting, that we need more of a plan than we currently seem to have."

Spider agreed. "Well, yes. Obviously. We can't just turn up at James's place and run through exactly the same things he's already tried. We need something new."

Near Future Spider, staring out at the teeming traffic and the rain, said, "Oh, I don't know. All that experience made me the man I am today!" He was joking, but it was hard to tell. Iris shook her head.

She said, "So what *you're* saying, Spider — er, no, I mean you, Spider, not, oh God, you..." She looked back and forth between the two Spiders, sighed, took a calming breath, and pointed at Near Future Spider. "What you're saying, is that a straightforward frontal approach is no good. History keeps repeating itself. James's murder and so forth is not the place to try and change things."

"Yes," he said, "that is the gist of it. The crazy bastards in that apartment have been stewing along for years, trying to keep this awful secret, but James is the one who's in danger of cracking first. Electra can't have that. James knows she's scheming. Someone has to take the first step."

"Sounds like they bloody deserve each other," Iris commented.

"What if we went back to the night of Clea Fassbinder's murder?" Spider said, thinking about it all. "It's only six years ago."

Iris said, "Section Ten sanctions. You do not mess with those guys. Sometimes you hear rumors, like somehow they've got time-hacking gear from the future, and that's what they're using here, to lock down the entire event-sequence of the Fassbinder murder, across every universe, the whole manifold." She shuddered, thinking about it.

"And this is just because Clea was a Zeropoint agent?" Spider asked.

Near Future Spider nodded, "Yeah. Section Ten would have their own investigation going. Or so they would have you believe, anyway."

Near Future Spider said, "And before you ask, no, James's death is not Section Ten shenanigans. It's strictly domestic."

Iris thought about all this, staring out the window. Spider, too. He said, "That just leaves the night Sky Rutherford killed herself."

"Except we don't know exactly when or where that happened."

"Yeah, but think," Spider said, "you, Spider, said there's an XVD, a video she made of the event."

Near Future Spider brightened up slightly. "Oh. Metadata in the file headers!"

Spider pulled out the screen Soldier Spider had given him, and looked up Snuff.com. "I'm just running a search for Sky's video. Hang on. Oh, wait. I have to register before I can search. Shit, they want my credit details."

"You prepared to say bye-bye to all your money, your identity, everything you hold near and dear?" Near Future Spider asked. "I mean, I thought of trying that, too, but I couldn't get the site to work. Every time it came up it flooded my screen with hostile malware, just about ate me alive!"

"It's playing nice with me, so far," he said, thinking about where this screen came from. "It still wants my details. Screw it, what the hell. I can always start over, and it's not like I've got much identity to steal, anyway." He entered his details, the system gobbled them up, and replied that he was now officially a member of "the most secretly visited site on the tubes — everyone does it, but no one admits it!" The flickering preview videos were distracting, and horrifying, enough. Spider tried to concentrate on the job, even as bits of footage kept coming at him showing people, often young people, about to be cut up, or shot, or operated on without anesthetic, or hit by out-of-control cars, or—

"Holy shit, this is vile," Spider said, and started looking for anything by Sky Rutherford. It turned out that Sky was quite the video artist, had been involved in several videos posted here — he wondered if James knew anything about this side of her — and, ah yes, here was her suicide video. "Got it!"

"How bad is it?" Iris asked, turning in her seat to look back at Spider. He sat hunched forward, the screen in his lap glowing and flickering, lighting up his face as he watched.

Spider paused the playback and looked up at Iris. "It's... hard to describe, at least so far. She's just sitting there, on a picnic blanket, in the middle of nowhere, looks like out in the bush somewhere. All red dirt, huge sunset skies, scruffy spinifex bushes here and there. Not a single landmark, point of reference, terrain feature, road sign, nothing. It's eerie. Recognizably the Australian bush, but nowhere at all."

"Shit," Near Future Spider said. "It's like she knew people would try something like this, try and find her."

Iris agreed. "No luck on the metadata?"

Spider was back watching the playback. Sky was sitting there on her blanket, reading a letter she'd written to James. Her hands did not shake; her voice never wavered. She was not visibly upset, nor did she raise her voice, or break down in shuddering sobbing tears. She read it with great, terrifying poise, like it was nothing. Her voice was mild, a little deep and smoky. She was, he thought, at once both very attractive, and also the most frightening thing he'd seen in years. She laid it all out very clearly: she was doing this to punish James. It was all very clinical and karmic in her view. You screw me over, I screw you over, only worse. She told him it might as well be his own hand killing her. His actions had led to this moment, she said. At the end, she paused, looked up at the camera, hesitated, her mouth tense, and for a moment she did look vulnerable, like a woman who knew she was about to die in extreme pain. Blinking a few times, she stared back at the camera, and said, her voice cracking slightly, "I love you, James." Then she picked up the one-liter can of petrol she had with her — Spider imagined she must have paid a small fortune for that quantity of fuel — and began, very systematically, applying it to her hair, face, arms and legs, clothes (front and back), the blanket around her, until she was done.

"Oh, God," Spider said, watching her reach, in the fading golden sunset light, for the plastic disposable lighter she had with her. "Oh my God..."

"Spider?"

"There she goes. I can't watch," he said, still watching, staring, as blue and yellow flames quickly wrapped themselves around her. Even as her clothes, her hair, her skin, everything went up, she kept staring into the unblinking camera's eye. It took, Spider thought, hours for her to start screaming. It was inhuman that someone could subject themselves to that and not scream, and when she did start, her voice almost lost amid the roar of the fire, it was heartbreaking. Spider watched on, wiping his eyes, unable to stop, for some reason needing to watch. He thought of Molly locked in stasis and buried in a freezer with dozens of corpses; he thought of Soldier Spider, deliberately blowing himself to pieces for reasons Spider could still only guess at, and hoped never to find out the hard way. He thought of Dickhead, talking his faithful servants to death that last day on the *Destiny*, motivating them to give up their mortal lives for the sake of the Final Secret of the Cosmos. He could see it, hear it, now. He thought, watching Sky Rutherford burn, curled up in a fetal position now, what someone with her awesome self-possession would have made of Dickhead, and he of her. He thought Dickhead would find her iron will and discipline irresistible.

"Spider!" It was Iris.

He jumped, startled, the screen slipping from his lap and tumbling to the floor, lighting up the darkness in the rear of the van. "God, Iris! What is it?" He bent forward and picked it up, but this time when he looked at it — a barely recognizable human form made of charcoal, wreathed in fire and thick smoke in the gathering dark — he looked at it differently. He stopped the playback, and then kept staring at the initial freezeframe image of Sky Rutherford, close-up, frowning intensely, adjusting the camera's lens. He felt cold and strange, his mind whirling about no central point, at once here in the back of this old van, and yet also still lost somewhere at the End of Time, the stink of smoke and burning composite materials thick in his nostrils. "Time lag," he said, absently.

"Spider, are you okay? You—"

He folded up the screen and put it back in his pocket. "People who time travel a lot, they build up a consciousness differential between their home and all the places they've been, and the more they jaunt about, the more the differential builds up, and starts messing with your head, and you start feeling not quite tethered to the here and now. Got it a fair bit back when I was a copper..." He trailed off, remembering what it had been like as he followed Sharp and his mates all throughout time.

"Spider, mate," Near Future Spider called out. "Get a bloody grip!"

"It's like," Spider went on, "kinda like the first time you get drunk. A bit out-of-body, looking at yourself, and you think, 'not looking too flash!'"

Iris said to Near Future Spider, "You know anything about this?"

"Yeah, but I'm over it now. Happened to me ages ago. It'll pass in a while, couple of days. I'd say that video did his head in, basically, plus everything else."

Iris said to Spider, "Can you hear me, Spider?"

He looked at her and smiled a little. "I'm not deaf, Iris, just a little timed out, so to speak." His tone of voice was light and dreamy, but in his head, Sky burned on, over and over. He suspected he'd be seeing her burn for the rest of his life. It was the first time he'd ever seen, albeit on video, someone take their own life. That she had been so determined, so cold and focused on the task, was the thing he kept coming back to, thinking about it, trying to imagine his way into her mind, trying to grasp that level of fury, but could not. It was frightening because it was so inhuman.

He heard Iris asking Near Future Spider how much further it was to Rutherford's place, and heard him tell her not that far.

Right, he told himself, his voice seeming to echo and echo in the cavernous, flaming darkness in his head, *time to snap out of it. Nearly there. Have to be on the ball, ready for trouble.* He remembered Soldier Spider telling him that he stood only a 14 percent chance of surviving tonight. Fourteen percent. These were not good odds. It got his attention, at least a little. He said, very deliberately, like a drunk trying not to sound drunk, "There was no time or date-stamp on the video. By the way."

Iris glanced at him, sorry for him, but also more than a little annoyed at him spacing out — timing out — on her, just now. "So we need the disc itself," she said.

Near Future Spider agreed. "Now how do we get the disc without Electra killing us?"

"How much of a threat is she likely to be?" she asked him.

"In my experience," he said, indicating a spot on his torso near his kidneys, "she can be quite a handful. Depends, though. In some versions she tops herself after doing her dad. Hard to say. Won't know 'till we get there."

"Lovely family," Iris commented.

"Yeah, and to think if only James had just kept his wick dry when he was with Clea bloody Fassbinder. If he'd just left her be, treated her like a professional—"

Spider, in the back, piped up, "Yeah, but she was pretty much obsessed with finding out how she died back here."

"Yeah, that's right," Near Future Spider said. "I'd forgotten that bit. Seems like bloody ages ago I did all that."

Iris said, "It's extremely difficult, I have to say, from my perspective, to imagine what this 'End of Time' might be like, let alone being there, and then back here."

"Not much to see," Spider said. "Blackness upon blackness. The ultimate void. Kind of scary."

"Sounds like something out of Lovecraft, home of the Elder Gods, dancing madly to the insane tootlings of their servitors," Iris said.

"Yeah," Spider said. "Like that, but worse."

"You all right, Spider?"

"I will be. We nearly there?"

Near Future Spider said, "Few minutes, give or take. You up for it, or am I going in again? Please note, by the way, there is only one correct answer to this question."

Spider heard the tone in his voice. "Yeah, yeah. I'm going in. It'll only take a couple of minutes, right?"

"Oh, absolutely," Near Future Spider said. "The times Electra got me, she got me within three minutes of stepping through the door."

"Shit," Spider said, trying to focus.

By the time they located the high-end apartment complex in East Perth where the Rutherfords lived their dismal lives, Spider was feeling a little better. He'd had a window open, and, like a dog, had been sticking his face out into the cold, rainswept wind. While he was now a little soggy, he did feel markedly more anchored to the present moment.

Iris said to Near Future Spider as they peered out at the apartment complex, "You coming with us or what?"

He winced. "I feel like I really should, but I'm just…" He shrugged. "I'm kinda 'been there, done that', you know?"

"Don't be such a sissy," Spider said with a ridiculous cheerfulness that inspired no confidence in his comrades. "Someone's got to watch our backs."

"I wonder if the ambulance guys have been yet?" Iris said, and produced a folding compact umbrella from one of her raincoat pockets. She opened the door, jumped down, and popped the umbrella. The rain hitting it was very loud. Spider heaved open the van's side door and joined her.

Near Future Spider was peering up at the huge apartment towers. "I have got *such* a bad feeling about this."

Spider made chicken-clucking noises. Near Future Spider muttered back that he was not afraid. He was just tired.

Iris said, "Mate, you should be afraid."

In the end, he got out and joined them, all huddling under Iris's umbrella as they scuttled up towards the gated entrance. Iris got them through the entrance's security system. Near Future Spider commented that when he was trying this, he had to wait for people coming and going and duck in behind them before the door closed again.

Once inside, they took in the lobby, all very high-end resort-type décor, high atrium ceiling, vast expanses of polished marble flooring and expensive hand-woven rugs. Spider commented that even the air smelled exclusive. He asked Near Future Spider about Molly, if she was okay in his time. Near Future Spider, not looking at him, said, too brightly, "Oh yes, she's fine, just fine. Thanks for asking." Spider felt cold and dismal, thinking about it, the prospect awaiting him.

Near Future Spider was taking in the luxurious lobby. He said that he always felt like he was lowering the tone somewhat just being there, and here he was again, same feeling. "Spent a lot of time here, sitting around, trying out the lounges, talking to anybody I could get to talk to me, trying to get some inside info on the Rutherfords. One thing I learned was that James Rutherford, once he was home from the office, never left the apartment if he could help it. Daughter Electra, by contrast, maintained a lively social life, parties, nightclubs, you name it. She and her idiot boyfriend, 'The Beat', he calls himself, have been talking about starting up a band.

"The other thing, and this one was useful, was that the Rutherfords are *dirty*."

"Dirty as in corrupt?" Iris asked, as they made their way to one of the elevator lobbies.

"No, the other. They live in filth. Especially the daughter. It's pretty disgusting up there. There's a big push on amongst the other residents to get them the hell out of the complex."

Spider, thinking about James, about times they'd gotten together on Friday nights for drinks or whatever, tried to remember if he'd ever known James Rutherford, in person, to be less than fresh. It was a stunning thing to learn about the man. "Really?"

They arrived at the glassed-in elevator lobby, which required another security pass. Iris, armed with her Police Emergency Access card, got them inside and into an elevator. Soon they were zooming upward at worrying speeds. While Near Future Spider stared at the display above the door indicating the floor number, Spider stared and stared at the mirrored walls of the car. In every direction, stretching away to infinity, images of himself. He looked rough and pale, not unlike the way James had looked the last time Spider had seen him. Spider wondered if he, too, was a broken man after everything he'd been through lately. Then it occurred to him, as he decided his near future self was smart in concentrating on the floor number display, that if you are capable of asking yourself such a question, you're probably not too far gone just yet. Even so, seeing these armies of Spiders all around him was too much, too resonant.

The elevator stopped at the floor they wanted. They got out, and made their way along the passageway. It was quiet, Spider noticed. It freaked him out a little. What? Was everyone out tonight? Was the entire complex holding its breath, waiting to see what Spider and his team would find at the Rutherfords'? At the end of the broad, polished marble corridor, a floor-to-ceiling window provided a view out into the dark night. Rain pounded against the glass.

Near Future Spider was saying, "Now, listen up. Step one is finding and neutralizing Electra."

"What do you recommend?" Spider asked him.

Iris said, "I've got a stun-gun, if that's any help."

"You wouldn't have an actual, you know, real gun, would you?"

Iris glanced at him. "Not on me, no. Rules. I'm supposedly off-duty, remember."

Spider had one other question on his mind. "I'm a little concerned about the whole 'crime scene' thing here."

Iris said, "In what way?"

"We've got two copies of me here, all set to go barging into James's apartment, no doubt shedding hairs and skin flakes and leaving footprints in the carpet, and all the rest of it."

Near Future Spider said, "Unavoidable. But if we can stop Sky killing herself..."

Spider saw his point. "Then this whole business never happens."

Near Future Spider said, "Well, it does, of course. It's just, there'll be one timeline..."

Spider saw his point. "Where everything works out." He was still thinking about what Soldier Spider told him, that he had only a small chance of surviving tonight.

"Right," Near Future Spider said.

"Okay," he said, anxious.

"This looks like the place," Iris said. "God," she added. "You were right," she said to Near Future Spider, wrinkling her nose. "The smell!"

Spider, who had never been here before, was similarly shocked. "That is nasty."

"Wait'll you get inside," Near Future Spider said.

Iris banged on the door. "James Rutherford!" There was no response. She tried again. Spider joined in, calling, "James! It's Spider! You okay?"

As they waited for a response, the door behind them opened. Spider and Iris both gasped, startled, and spun around. A severe-looking elderly woman, her silvering hair pulled back in a rock-like bun, dressed in expensive and tasteful sitting-around-at-home-spying-on-neighbors-wear, leaned out around her door. "Are you the police?"

"Yes," Iris said, trying on her best public-relations smile, warm but not gleeful, reassuring but not patronizing, and flashed her ID. "Have you heard something?"

The woman glanced back and forth along the passageway, and said, confiding in Iris, just-us-women-together, that the Rutherfords had been incredibly loud lately, as in the past few days. Constant raging arguments, things thrown and smashing against walls, the most appalling language, from that diabolical girl! Then, as of an hour or two ago, silence, just cryptic silence. "I think something might have happened."

"Something violent?" Iris said.

"I don't know," she said. "It's just not like them to be so quiet. It's a bit ominous, if you ask me."

"Can I take your statement later, if necessary, ma'am?"

"Oh," she said, "I don't know what I could tell you."

Iris worked out an arrangement with her, and all was well. Before they went back to the matter of the door, the woman added, "And please, please do something about that smell! My Donald gets these headaches all the time...?"

"We'll do our best, believe me," Iris said, smiling, and the woman smiled back and went back behind her door, listening, no doubt.

After a few more minutes they all agreed there was little further point in waiting for someone to answer James's door. Near Future Spider pointed out that most of his attempts started like this, too. "Once or twice Electra answered the door, covered in blood — and immediately had a go at me."

"Shit," Spider muttered, unsettled, tense and worried. It was good, in a way: stark fear helped anchor his consciousness in the here-and-now. He felt almost fully present in his own head.

Iris worked her lock-bypassing magic once more, and the door into the apartment swung open, revealing a seemingly living darkness, warm and fetid. She shook her head, glanced at the two Spiders, told them, "We just want the disc. That's it."

Spider noticed that nobody had tried to kill them just yet. A good sign, he thought.

Iris asked Near Future Spider where Electra might be if she wasn't dead. He told her, "Could be any bloody where. Once, she was even up in the ceiling crawlspace, and dropped down on me as I was leaving the bathroom. Practically shat myself."

"I think I've seen this movie," Spider said.

"Where is James likely to be?" she asked.

"Varies. Sometimes the living area, sometimes the main bedroom, sometimes slumped off the toilet, Elvis-mode."

"God," she said, covering her face, and led the way into the apartment.

Once inside, with the lights on, several things became obvious all at once: yes, household hygiene had sunk to the point of foulness. No one could see the floor; every step fell with a muted *crunch*; bugs scattered. Spider wondered how a man like James could live like this and still manage to convey the appearance, more or less, of cleanliness. When they found the laundry area, much of the mystery was solved: unlike the rest of the place, the laundry was clean, almost fetishistically so. He guessed that James was the one doing the cleaning in here.

Another thing that was obvious with the lights on: there were, as police would say, "signs of a struggle", even in the midst of all this stinking chaos. Iris indicated fresh blood-spatter on two of the walls near the couch, and smeared along the floor leading out of the room towards the bathroom.

Spider was distracted. Up on the huge media wall, stretching across the entire living area at the back, was Sky's suicide video, currently freeze-framed at the point where the flames first start to catch in her long, dark hair. Her eyes were staring out at them. The resolution, Spider could not help but notice, was amazing. He could see individual strands of hair; he could see the blue and the green in her eyes. There was a sense of immense fractal depth to the image, that he could zoom in and in and in endlessly, and there would always be more detail, coming closer and closer to Sky's burning flesh, so close he could just about feel the heat coming off her, the heat of revenge burning colder and harder than any mere fire.

Near Future Spider nudged him. "Electra got me several times while I was staring at that."

Iris had gone into the bathroom. She called to them. "Found the daughter. Shit."

They joined her. Like the laundry the bathroom had, until recently, also been fairly clean. Now there was blood on the floor, leading to the long, deep, tile-lined bathtub, full of still, dark water. Electra's pale knees stuck up out of the water, slumped to one side. Iris, careful where she put her feet, crouched and reached into the water, trying to feel a pulse in the girl's neck.

Electra's black eyes stared up from under the red-brown water, her black hair swirling around her face.

Near Future Spider stood by the door, on watch, listening.

"She's gone," she said. "Damn it all."

Near Future Spider edged away from the bathroom door to glance into the bath. "Yup. She's toast." Spider, watching him, even though he knew that Near Future Spider had been in this room, looking at this dead body, many times now, his lack of feeling was still chilling. He shivered, a little.

Iris was on the phone, shouting at people in Serious Police Tones, trying to organize her team. It appeared that now there was an actual body, they might be inclined to help — but that she was still under orders to bring Spider in for questioning. She hung up in great disgust and glared at both Spiders. She said, after a moment, to Near Future Spider, "So, are we safe now? If she's dead, we can't save her, so she can't go on to time-travel back here and kill us? Is that right?"

"I think so, yeah," Near Future Spider said, still visibly tense, "but who knows?"

Spider said, "Where's James?"

"I'm guessing the master bedroom," Near Future Spider said. "I'll show you." He led Iris back out, and added, "Just follow your nose!" Sure enough, at the end of another passageway, through an open doorway, the stench sharpening with every step, was the main bedroom, blood everywhere, even on the ceiling, and, in the center of the grim vista, the mortal remains of James Rutherford, in jeans and an old t-shirt. He lay, arms and legs spread out, as if placed there deliberately.

"Right, then," Iris said, looking about, taking photos and video with her watchtop, watching where she put her feet.

Spider, back out in the main living area, found himself facing the freeze-frame of Sky Rutherford once more, and he could feel himself falling into the image, practically smelling the burning petrol— *No*, he told himself. *Stop it. Think. We need the damn disc.* He turned away from the wall and started looking around. The room, like much of the rest of the house, was filthy from end to end, a mind-jolting contrast with the insanely thorough attitude to cleaning he remembered from the *Masada*.

That people, even broken people like James, could live like this beggared the imagination, yet he knew this was more common than was generally recognized. Even more or less healthy people sometimes wound up like this, and would swear and declare there was nothing wrong, nothing that a bit of "tidying up" wouldn't take care of. As it was, he wished he had a toxin protection suit. The sheer quantity of mold in here must be off the charts, and it was hard not to think of all those millions and billions of tiny spores drifting about, getting up his nose, getting in his mouth, his eyes.

The screen controlling the media wall was on the coffee table. It was the most logical place for such a thing, and it only meant relocating a stack of take-away food cartons, some old plates, coffee cups, and dismantling an impressive array of empty Zhujiang beer cans. The former copper in him felt dreadful about interfering with all this crime scene material, even though he was careful to take lots of photos before and after. Then again, exactly who would or could be prosecuted here? It was, most likely, a murder-suicide. There was no villain to catch and charge and prosecute. The entire thing left him with a bitter, hollow feeling, that it was all so pointless. From the point where James met Clea Fassbinder, the rest of the drama unfolded with grim inevitability: the daughter punishing the father, just as the wife had been bent on punishing him.

He glanced up at the image of Sky on the wall, looming over everything, presiding, like she still owned the place. He remembered her letter to James, the way she had laid the blame for the entire thing at his feet, told him that he was the one burning her, as if with his own hand. Not once, Spider realized, had she mentioned Electra. No fare-well, no "I love you", no "look after your old man". Noth-ing. She didn't rate a mention. Electra, he guessed, had seen this video, and probably had seen it a good many times. What must she have made of it, seeing her mother destroy herself without even a passing thought for her own daughter?

It gave him the creeps. The more he thought about this family, the more terrifying they became. And yet, he couldn't help but wonder, how many other families in this city were just the same, or maybe even worse? Surely the doom that came to the House of Rutherford was not unique. He remembered that much from his police days. There were no perfect, happy families — and he suspected the wide-spread use of time machines had only made things worse. Why had it never occurred to Sky Rutherford to go back in time, perhaps try to intercept Clea Fassbinder before she got to James, and have a quiet word with her. Watch out for James. He's trouble. Then again, he thought, Clea was looking for her death. Practically anybody would do, he supposed, once she'd taken care of her all-important mis-sion to keep the Kronos probe from blowing the cover of a clandestine Zeropoint operation in the 260th century.

He finished clearing crap from the screen, and felt him-self go weak inside. He sagged back on the filthy couch, staring at the shattered fragments of the disc. Releasing a great rush of breath, he shook his head. *You know what this means, right?* he asked himself, and he did know. It meant he would have to use the bloody Boron downstairs. He would have to come up here while James was still alive and ask him if he'd mind lending him the disc. How a conversation like that might go, he didn't want to think. Iris and Near Future Spider were still in the master bed-room. He got up, went and told them, trying not to look at James's body.

Near Future Spider was surprised. "The disc is broken? Really? Never seen that before."

"Off you shoot, then," Iris said, distracted by the crime scene, trying to figure out exactly how it must have hap-pened.

Spider went downstairs, through the lobby, and out into the wind and the rain, muttering under his breath. The Boron was still there, up on its trailer, ready to go. He hauled himself up onto the trailer, opened the driver's side door, and swung inside, closing the door behind him. The unit's interior smelled unpleasant, which was nothing new for a man in the time machine repair business, but it did make him stop for a moment, trying to figure out what that smell might be, and where it might be coming from. Habits, he thought.

So, to the controls. He got the machine powered up, checked the instruments, made sure he had green lights across the board, and went to dial in the destination time. Right now, the dashboard clock told him it was twenty-two minutes past ten p.m. He wondered if Molly was back from her treatment by now. *Now stop right there, he told himself. Concentrate. Stick to the task at hand.* He'd been told earlier that even at eight p.m. James was in the process of getting killed. He thought about this for a minute, trying to shake off a clinging sense of creepiness about the entire venture — *yes, all I care about right now is getting the damned disc, rather than trying to save James and Electra's lives* — and decided to drop in on Chez Rutherford at about six this evening. He set up the jump, checked once more that everything was working as it should, and hit the go button.

CHAPTER 24

All at once, it was much brighter outside; he winced at the glare, and started powering down the unit, and trying to think of just how he would go about talking to James about the disc, knowing what he knew about James's looming fate. Should he try and warn him about his impending death? Should he, in fact, try and take him off somewhere where Electra couldn't get him? Should he try and take Electra, instead, since she was the real problem? Had his near future self tried all these things and failed? That was the thing bugging Spider the most: that all these ideas had been tried, and succeeded only in making things worse, to say nothing of implicating himself into the crime scene. Go directly to Jail. Do not collect $200. Brood in jail about failing to stop Molly's torture.

Getting out of the Boron and down off its trailer, Spider found himself still getting rained on, still cold, still miserable, and full of doubts about his mission.

Right, then, he said to himself, glancing about, and looking up the central tower at James's floor. *All I have to do is go up to James and say, 'James, mate, listen, can't stop long, just passing by, no, don't straighten up, it's... okay. Yeah, anyway, look, would you mind lending me that disc with your late wife's suicide on it, please? Yes, that's the one. How do I know you've even got such a disc? Ah, well, you see...'* And here Spider stopped, cold rain pouring down his face, soaking his clothes, standing there in front of the complex, thinking about his situation. There was no way Spider could possibly know about the disc. James had, after all, never told him about it. It wasn't something he could have surmised after, say, accidentally stumbling on Sky's little video on Snuff.com the other day, as part of his normal relaxation time browsing among snuff movies. He shook his head, shivering in the cold, and went and stood under the entrance portico.

He would have to tell James that he'd come from the future, found the disc, but it was broken. Yes, he knew all about the video, and of course knew about Sky. Why had he come to visit James in the future? Since he had never been to James's place even once in all the time they'd known each other? Why had he been looking for the disc in the first place? What could the disc and its, er, content possibly contain that someone like Spider might need?

"Shit," Spider said, hating this entire situation. How could he possibly do this without letting James know that he would die tonight? What if even inadvertently letting him know about his fate somehow brought about that fate? Hadn't Near Future Spider warned him about that very thing?

Then, an idea: what if, Spider thought, all excited now, he could persuade James to leave the building? Then he could — no, wait. How would he get inside the apartment if James — and his keys — were not there? Electra could let him in, he thought for a moment. Hello, Electra, he could say. Is your dad about? No? Just missed him? Damn. What about? Well, as it happens, I'm looking for a disc your dad's got. I don't know what it's called, no. It's got a video on it, of your mum...

He shook his head, hating himself. Suppose, though, he could get them both to leave — but then, there's the problem of getting into the apartment without anybody there to open the door. He supposed he could try kicking in the door, but he knew that places like this had very solidly built doors. None of that hollow plywood crap you saw in cheap starter homes.

Suppose he set off the fire alarm? Get everybody running outside! Back to locked apartment door, though. He should have brought Iris with him. That had been the whole point of having Iris come along with him tonight in the first place. She might be helpful. "Idiot!"

So, go back to the present, get Iris, come back, try again? Once again, how do I know about the disc? How do I know to ask for it? Do I ask for it? Maybe I want something else, and James invites me in, offers some coffee, and while he goes off into the bowels of the apartment trying to find whatever it is, I stealthily swipe the disc? Seen that work in any number of movies and TV shows.

Yeah, right. "I need that bloody disc!" he said, anguished, thinking about everything he could fix if he could just stop Sky Rutherford killing herself — and that was assuming that something, anything, could in fact stop her going through with it. He'd seen her work. She was tough. Determined. Getting her to change her mind on a plan so well thought through would be more than hard.

He paced back and forth, thinking hard, rubbing his temples, as if to coax brilliant ideas to come out and play. Then, "I don't need the disc itself!" he said, wide-eyed with realization. "I just need..." Energized now, bouncing on his toes, unconcerned about being dripping wet, he knew what would do the trick. He just needed someone to let him in. He'd seen residents and visitors coming and going throughout this whole frustrating time; it was just a question, as Near Future Spider had told him, of waiting for someone and then slipping through behind them.

This took a while to come off. People coming and going suddenly became very shy about coming or going. Nobody at all used the main entrance. He thought about going downstairs into the underground parking garage — though he'd need to work the same magic there, as well, he realized. Damn it all!

Then, here came some guy, expensive suit under expensive raincoat, bearing designer umbrella, talking to someone on the phone. Spider shot him a nod and a smile, and the guy nodded back, indicated his phone patch, and rolled his eyes at Spider. Spider smiled again, understanding only too well what it was like when people called and just would not shut up or get off the line. The guy let him in.

Thank God, Spider thought, dripping on the polished marble. He squished his way to the elevator lobby, and stood there, again waiting for someone to help him out.

What he really needed, he knew, was a pizza delivery costume, preferably including a real, hot pizza, giving off very persuasive aromas that would convince anybody he was really there to deliver pizzas and was in a hurry. *Next time*, he told himself. *Next time.*

Eventually, someone came along and helped him out, and he made it into the elevator lobby. The ride up to James's floor was excruciating. The infinite Spiders reflected in the mirrors tormented him even more this second time. He watched the level indicator display, bouncing more on his toes, trying to keep at least reasonably calm, telling himself that when the doors opened he would not just run all the way to James's door. He would—

The car was stopping at another floor. "Good grief!" he said, and wanted to hit something. God, all he needed was this one piece of information, just one piece of info!

Well, he thought, *why not just phone the bastard and be done with it? G'day, James! Spider. Yeah. Hi. No, I haven't forgot about tonight. No worries. I just wanted to ask about...* Spider sagged against the wall of the elevator car, seeing how the rest of this would play out. *Yes, I just wanted to ask for very specific details about your wife's suicide. Which, of course, you've never told me much about, other than the simple fact that she did indeed top herself. Why do I want to know exactly when she did it? Why right now? Well, er, um...* Spider shook his head, frustrated.

The car stopped, the doors opened, and a middle-aged black woman, expensively dressed, stepped into the car. She gave him a polite smile, and concentrated on the level display. Spider thought her perfume was wonderful.

At length, he arrived on the correct floor. "Thank God!" He did his best not to run along the passageway. Passersby kept getting in his way, making him step around them. He had to keep a smile on his face, as if to say, *yes, I really belong here, I'm not an intruder, no, not at all, why do you ask? I'm just here to see my old buddy James Rutherford. Yes, you can smell his place from all the way back here, can't you?*

And there he was. The smell was bad. People inside were alive: he could hear a news show on the media wall, turned up loud. He knocked. Nothing happened. He held his breath. He knocked again, louder. He heard probably James's muffled voice shouting something, and then, he was guessing, Electra's voice, yelling back, which led to a very loud and hostile interchange. Spider was thinking, *oh no, don't say it all started because some poor bastard came to the door and they had a fight over who should get it? That wouldn't be right!* But he knew all kinds of stupid things led to people getting killed. He hadn't thought of this. Oh God!

Then he heard latches working, and then the door swung open a crack — releasing a great waft of landfill odor that nearly made him swoon and cough — and there was the delightful Electra Rutherford: shorter than he had expected, very post-goth, all shredded black lace combined with a fluorescent pink Fifties-style circle skirt, with layers and layers of shredded black petticoats, finished off with bright red Doc Marten boots. And in her hair, all manner of distracting flashing and blinking Christmas tree lights, or something like it, only they seemed to flash in time to something she was listening to on her watchtop. Her eyes were completely black, no whites showing, with extensive smudgy black mascara all around them. The effect was disgusting, and at first made him think she'd somehow put out her eyes.

"What?" she said, looking him up and down like he was something filthy she'd just stepped in.

And that did it for him. He was profoundly tired, felt like he'd been awake for days on end, still unsure that he was completely inside his own head, and, frankly, needed to take a dump sometime soon — and here he was, face to ghastly face with the infamous Electra Rutherford. He certainly had not intended saying what he now went and said, had in fact no way of knowing these words had been poised for delivery, as if waiting there, patiently, for weeks and weeks. Yet, the sheer bizarre sight of her in all her weird yet mundane reality, led him to say out loud the sort of thing which, if he had been more in his right frame of mind, he'd have kept to himself. This, however, was the strangest of strange times. He'd just seen this same person, dead by her own hand, submerged in a bathtub. He'd seen her father, slaughtered like a pig. It made him think of Clea Fassbinder. He said, "You really should have done a better job hiding Clea's body." And there it was, out and hanging in the air between them. He felt, in this moment of extreme weirdness, as if he could see the words, hanging there, jiggling a little, and he could quickly grab them and hide them away, and make it so that he'd never said such a stupid thing.

But they were not just hanging there, and he could not call them back. He had tipped the balance of time in a particular direction — and he felt like an idiot.

She first looked confused, then took a closer look at him, taking him in, this time examining him, sizing him up. *How much of a threat are you?* she seemed to be thinking. Her hideous black eyes narrowed. "What did you just say?"

"See," Spider said, "if it was me, and I was trying to hide a body, I'd stuff said body in a time machine, like you did, but just the one. I'd set the controls for, say, a thousand years in the future — or the past, but then again, you never know when some archeologist guy might do a dig on that site, and next thing you know you've got well-preserved human remains clearly belonging to the twenty-first century turning up in eleventh century dirt, right? So you send the body off to the future, never to be a problem for you ever again."

Electra stood there, staring and staring at this raving idiot going on and on before her. She said, "Who the fuck are you?"

"But no," he said. "No, you had to be a bit clever about it. It wasn't enough, was it, to just hide the body in a time machine? Your dad, probably, the great time machine engineer, famous in his field, told you about this neat trick you could do, more of an exploit really, hiding one time machine inside another time machine. Do it right, and nobody ever knows. The hidden time machine is buried away forever in its own little bubble universe. But that's only if you do it just right, and you, you stupid girl, you didn't do it just right, did you?"

She'd gone quite pale; the contrast with her eyes, hair and all that mascara was alarming. "Why don't you come inside, and we can talk about this quietly. What do you reckon?" She was glancing about behind Spider, to see if there were any neighbors listening.

Spider thought, *And here it is, the invitation.* Other versions of himself had been here, in similar circumstances, and they had gone inside, and come to horrible grief one way or another. He'd blown his secret: she knew he knew. He'd lost the game. Tension boiling and bubbling in his guts, staring at the full horror of her, he tried to decide what to do, but then—

James came up behind Electra. "Oh, hi, Spider." He looked stunned to see Spider standing there, and doubtless remembered the last time he'd seen Spider, and the state he'd been in when they parted company. Awkwardly, to cover embarrassment, not wanting to reveal anything in front of Electra, James went on, "I thought I heard your voice. Come on in, have a drink." It looked like James had already had five or six too many drinks. He stood there in old tracksuit pants and a grimy Linux conference t-shirt, a shambles of a man. *Just like I used to look*, Spider thought, with a shiver of recognition.

"James, hi, um, yeah," Spider said, at a loss, his entire plan in disarray, struggling to come up with a way back to what he was trying to achieve. He just had to ask James for the exact date Sky killed herself. Did he remember the date?

But here he was being swept into the dank apartment, James leading the way, and Electra behind him, close enough that he could smell her perfume, something offensively sweet and strong, like a candy store, only condensed and cold, mixing horribly with that vile landfill stench. She said, from behind him, a subtle tone in her voice he figured only he would notice, "Would you like something to drink, Mr. Webb?" She'd popped into the kitchen, he could hear her rummaging about in drawers full of clattering cutlery. He thought, getting scared now, *Oh shit, oh shit, oh shit! I've completely stuffed it up!*

And now here he was in the living area, his feet crunching on stuff on the floor, his eyes noticing small black things scuttling hither and yon with each footfall, and the smell, my God, the smell! He wanted to ask James, who looked, well, he looked too drunk to notice, probably, how he could live like this, but he couldn't quite do it. All too aware of Electra somewhere behind him, wishing he could put his back against the media wall behind him, and now James was clearing layers of crap from the couch so Spider could take a seat, kick back and relax.

Electra appeared with a can of Zhujiang beer, and offered to open it for him with her deeply scary long black fingernails. He said, no thanks, he was fine, and set it down on a few square centimeters of clear space on the coffee table. He could see the screen running the media center on the table where he "remembered" seeing it, in the future — or in one future, at least. He didn't know what was going to happen now. The other future, the one he'd already seen, would go on as it was supposed to, in another timeline. What happened in this timeline, however, was up for grabs, and here was Spider, without anyone to back him up, all alone and in massive, stupid trouble. He sat there, perched uncomfortably on the edge of the smelly couch, looking around. Electra popped into her bedroom for a bit, and then emerged again, equipped with a vintage Fifties-style handbag that, he realized, she probably got from the actual Fifties, and said, "Okay, Dad. Heading out to see The Beat. Back later. Be good now, you two..." She shot Spider a look that said, "You are so dead!" and flounced off to the door, stepped outside, and slammed the door behind her.

"Thank Christ she's gone!" James said, opening a new beer with shaking hands, and settling back into the couch, and, Spider noticed with creeping unease, appearing to blend into the couch, becoming a part of it. "Filthy fucking cow!" he said, staring across the room towards the front door. "Finally get a few moments' peace!" He helped himself to most of the can's contents in one go, drinking like a man in the desert dying of dehydration, like his life depended on it. Spider tried not to remember the sight of this man dead in his bed, a couple of hours from now.

"Kids, eh?" Spider said, hoping this remark was suitably bland, but also keeping an eye on that door, in case Electra came back unexpectedly.

"Kids?" James said, glancing at him. "Electra is no bloody kid, Spider. She's, I don't know, she's a fucking monster." The words of what he said sounded angry, but his delivery was all regretful sadness.

Spider decided to say nothing, and just let James talk. Sometimes it was the best thing to do.

"Heard you talking to her, before," James said. "How long have you known?"

"Not long," Spider said, doing his best to keep his comments brief, and to keep from blurting out, JAMES SHE'S GONNA KILL YOU, MAN! GET THE HELL OUT OF HERE NOW!

"It was all her idea. You wouldn't think a thirteen-year-old girl would sit around plotting murder, but there she was, working it all out, doing research out on the tubes, putting details together. She made it clear to me one night over dinner. I would help her with some of the technical details, because I had caused her mother..." He hesitated here. "Caused her mother to take her life."

Spider sympathized, but suspected time was short.

James went on. "She was right, of course. That was the point. I had brought about Sky's death. Here, look, this is..." He'd leaned forward and was starting to rummage among piles of crap on the coffee table near the media center control screen, and there it was, loose amid everything else, not in a protective case, just a loose XVD disc.

Spider stared at the disc in James's shaking hand. He forced himself to say, "What is it?"

James was staring at the disc, too, his face crumpling with anguish. "What is it? Here, let me show you." He placed the data side of the disc face-down onto the square reading surface of the screen, hit some controls, the nano-agents in the surface read the data, and then, replacing the TV news on the media wall, there was the by now familiar too-sharp, bottomless image of Sky Rutherford, at sunset, somewhere out in the bush, red dirt and dark blue sky, dazzling sunset light from the west carving sharp shadows across the ground, lighting her face as she read that letter, as she applied the petrol, with such care, not wasting a drop, and as she reached for the lighter—

Spider lunged forward and hit the stop button on the screen. "I think that's, God, that's more than enough, thanks."

James stared at the freeze-framed image up there, filling the entire wall of the apartment, so vivid it was like you could walk into that scene. He shook his head. "I watch it over and over, trying to understand, you know? How could she do it? How could she do something like that?" He was holding the disc again, staring at it, as if he might perceive some pattern in the glittering rainbow light that would explain his wife's actions. "She never said anything about this. Never said a word about Clea. I was the one who told her about Clea, did you know that? I felt so wretched over it, like I'd betrayed Sky in the worst way. I could have killed *my*self, but she was so calm about it, so understanding. She said she forgave me, it was behind us, she would forgive, but not forget, that's how she put it at the time. I couldn't believe it. How could she be so reasonable in the face of what I'd done?"

Spider shrugged, still trying to remain calm.

"And then one day she says she's going bush the next day, wants to get some shots of the desert and sunset, and I figure, fine, no problem. She was always heading off to work on her video projects. She'd always been an artist, mixed media, installations, you name it."

"My wife's the same," Spider said, chilled to think about the parallels here, but still keeping an eye on the door. Then he said, "So do you know where she went that day?"

But James was again staring at the disc, holding it in both his hands. "This is all I have of her, Spider, you know that?" He started trying to break the disc, as if he could tear it in half like an old-fashioned phone book.

Spider touched his arm. "You sure you want to do that?"

James glared at him, and snapped the disc in two, and he broke down, sobbing helplessly, even as he took the pieces of the disc and broke those, and then broke those pieces, making smaller and smaller fragments until he could do no more with just his hands, and he dropped the bits on the disc reading surface — where Spider had found them earlier.

Spider touched James's shoulder. "James," he said, feeling tense again, "I need to know if you remember the date that Sky... did that to herself. Do you know the date?"

He lifted his face from his hands. "The date? Why the fuck do you want to know the date? God, I don't know!"

Spider sagged back into the couch. "You must remember, James. It's the biggest thing that's happened in your life, your wife killing herself. You must remember!"

"I don't bloody remember, Spider. It was, God, it was six years ago! Six years! Do you remember stuff from six years ago?"

That was about when Spider met Dickhead, he was thinking. "Yeah, some things," Spider said. "Listen, what about, uh, you said that weekend she took her video gear out into the desert, right? Do you remember roughly when that was?" He figured he could work with a near-enough date, and refine it from there.

Sitting there, wretched, sprawled back into the couch, his arm over his eyes, breathing through his mouth, James tried to think. "Why'd you want to know, anyway?"

"It's complicated, James. I just... I can't say, but I just really need to know. It could help us both." The sight of Molly, her shoulders bent so horribly, when they pulled her out of that frozen tomb on the *Destiny*, loomed before him, filling his consciousness.

"I think it was, let me think, I don't know, sometime in March or April that year?"

"You can't get any closer? Think, James!"

James turned his head and looked at Spider. "Just what are you up to? You're trying to fix something, aren't you? You want to go back there."

"It'll help everyone, James. Please, just try."

"You think you can talk to her, is that it?"

"I've got some ideas, yes," Spider said, sure his time was running out.

James snorted. "She'll never listen to the likes of you. She never listened to anybody, not when it came to her art. Sky knew best, she always knew best, always had to have the last word." He stared at the fragments of the disc. "Always last word, Spider."

Spider was thinking. Sky's body had to have been found at some point after she did what she did. There would have been some kind of investigation by the local police of whatever the nearest major town was. How many suicide-by-self-immolation cases were there out in the bush back then? Probably not that many, he thought. "Anything at all you can remember, James. Anything."

"You look like you're in a bit of a hurry," James said.

"Not really," he said. "I just want to get on this."

"What do you know?"

"I—"

"What happens to us? What happens to me?"

"I. Can't. Say." He felt like shit.

"What happens to me, Spider?"

"James—"

"Am I dead, is that it?"

"Oh, God..."

"Is it that bloody Electra? Fuck. Listen, Spider, can you keep a secret?"

"Evidently not," Spider said, anxious, trying not to keep looking towards the door. "Why? What is it?"

"I have to kill her, Spider."

"Oh?" he said, trying to feign surprise and horror.

"She knows I want to go to the cops."

"Why haven't you?"

James sagged against the couch, anguished again. "I don't know. I'm scared of her. You ever been absolutely shit-scared of someone?"

He thought of Dickhead. "Oh yeah," he said, nodding, but wanting to fast-forward through this to what he needed to know.

"Things are bad when you find yourself planning the murder of your own child," James said, sad beyond measure, exhausted.

"Yeah," Spider said.

In the silence that followed, Spider heard rain against the windows, and faint scuttling sounds from somewhere nearby. James looked at him. "So."

Spider looked at James, and said, "I'm trying to save you," he said. "You just need to tell me everything you can about the day Sky died."

"I'm dead?" he said, curious, a little intrigued despite himself.

"Anything at all."

"When? Tonight? Is it tonight?"

"You could come with me, if you want. You might remember something later." He knew this was fruitless, and one of the many things his near future self had probably tried without success.

Then, to Spider's great surprise, the man who planned to kill his daughter later tonight, blurted out, "Oh, wait. She went to Southern Cross," he said. "She went to Southern Cross." James was surprised at himself. "I remember the police there calling me."

It wasn't the actual date, but it would do. He could work with it. "Thank you, mate. Thank you so much."

CHAPTER 25

It was tough leaving James that night. The man was a mess, and had been before Spider showed up. Spider felt awful. He had done (another) terrible thing: he'd left James with a sense of hope. He understood that if Spider succeeded in his mission, so much of the past six years might never occur. He might never find himself sitting there in filth, thinking about how to kill his daughter.

That hope was a heavy thing to carry, Spider found, as he turned his back on James's closing front door, and set off for the elevators.

Now for the hard part, he thought. Where was Electra? He knew she'd be around the place somewhere, waiting for him. God, he was stupid. Such an idiot move, letting the murderer know you were on to her. Sometimes, it didn't matter. It changed the dynamics of things, even made it more interesting, here and there, but in a situation like this, with no backup, no sidearm, no protection of any kind — and no reason Electra should let him live, he knew his best chance was to get out of this building, head straight for the Boron, and punch the hell out of here.

The elevators were slow. People shuffled on and shuffled off at different floors, chatting amongst themselves, people going about their lives, caught in their own dramas, maybe contemplating the use of time machines to solve their troubles. If he could offer them just one piece of advice, Spider thought, it would be to leave the bloody time machines alone. Who the hell thought it a good idea to let time machines become a mass-market item? Whose brainwave had that been? Maybe he should try to find out, go back in time and find that person — and kill him, or her, or them, and take care of the whole problem. Except, of course, that might not do it. The email from the future, the one that contained the attachment detailing just how to build working time machines, had landed in the inboxes of a great many engineers — electrical, electronic, software — all at once. No-one knew who had sent it. At first most of the recipients thought it was spam, and treated it as such. Not all, though, Spider knew, thinking about the dimensions of the problem.

He couldn't kill every single recipient of that email. He'd be caught in no time. Or someone would come back from the future and stop him killing anybody. Someone way up in the future felt it crucially important to start the proliferation of time travel sooner than it would have done otherwise. *That was the guy to kill,* Spider thought, realizing the difficulty of the problem as it gaped before him. You would as easily shut down the advent of chronotechnology as you would keep the world from learning the secret of the atom, and everything that entailed.

Feeling bleak, watching everything around him, Spider made his way across the beautiful lobby. *Electra,* he reminded himself, *is going to kill me.* He forced himself to focus, to come back to the here and bloody now. *Will she attack me while I'm safe in here, in the light, in front of people? No, she'd be lurking outside, in the gardens, taking advantage of the overcast sky, the lack of light, the weather.*

When he reached the main entrance, he peered out into the darkness, trying to spot the Boron on its trailer, but couldn't see it.

What if she's somehow broken into it and gone? he thought. He'd be stuck — at least until his earlier self, Near Future Spider, and Iris showed up with *their* Boron. Thinking about this crap made his head hurt. He edged forward, peered out into the darkness, trying to get his eyes adjusted.

There was nothing else for it. His heart pounding in his throat, hardly able to think straight, he set off, out into the open, making for the winding pathways that led through the expansive gardens, now picking up speed, glad he stayed on the pavement, and watching, all around him, for signs of extremely scary crazy young women in frightening clothes trying to catch him and gut him like a whale. He saw nothing other than all the things he expected to see: traffic, people coming and going, taxis. Then he was at the curb, near the taxi rank. Three taxis stood there, their drivers sitting at the controls, bored, reading things off their glowing screens, waiting for customers. The Boron, Spider saw, was just across that road. So close, so very close, he could almost taste it. He stood on the curb, waiting for a break in the traffic, freezing, shaking with the cold, trying to wrap himself in his flimsy jacket — there was the break he needed, and he darted out, dodged two cars and a gaggle of horn-honking scooter riders who yelled abuse at him, and there he was, climbing up on the trailer, fishing in his pocket for his keys, and for a moment he thought he'd lost them! Had he left them at James's apartment? Could they have fallen out while he sat on that horrible couch?

They were in his other pocket. *Thank God!* he thought, laughing madly, and fumbled with the keys, got the time machine's driver-side door open, took in that unpleasant smell again, but it was warm and dry, and he climbed in, pathetically grateful, slammed the door shut, and settled in at the controls, getting the unit ready to jump. The sooner he got out of here, the better he'd like it.

The Boron powered up, he had a complete array of green lights, the humming from the engine compartment sounded good, and it was time, at last, to go.

§ § §

The Temporal Positioning System on the dashboard indicated he was back in his present, only a moment after his departure. Right now, Iris and Near Future Spider were still up in James's apartment. Things were bad.

And, he noted, peering out the unit's windows, no sign of Electra. She must really have headed out for a night with her pretentious boyfriend, maybe to discuss setting up that band he'd heard about. Was that likely, though? She knew he was on to her. She had not looked happy about it. Just how devious could she be, if she put her mind to it? The thought gave him chills, but he also allowed for the possibility that his brain right now was so fried from all his recent adventures that he was seeing things that weren't there.

He popped the door, hefted himself out of his seat, aiming his leg for the trailer framework, muttering at the bloody rain again, and climbed back down to the ground—

Electra was waiting, soggy, idly fondling the remote for her Umbra, and, for one brief moment, she smiled at him. Then, before he could register shock, she was killing him. There was no preamble, no cocky, "I've got you now, Mr. Bond, now let me explain everything to you so you've got time to escape." None of that. She waited for him to hit the road, turn around, see she was there, and she lunged at him, pressing herself against him so it would look to passersby and bored taxi drivers like she was maybe very, very glad to see him, and she plunged the knife into him, hard, oh God, so hard, he could feel it, cold and hard and full of death, right there in his chest, he could feel his heart racing as he panicked, as he tried to react, his mind a blur; she was right there in his face, close enough to kiss him, so intimate, so warm, and yet so fetid, and sickly sweet, reeking of her home, of corruption and madness, a vision out of a bad horror movie, right there, not smiling, not laughing, just getting the damned job done, twisting the knife now — he cried out, feeling it against — was that a rib? Oh God.

The heat of his blood rushing out, away from him, leaving him, abandoning him to mortality, was its own special horror. He wished he could tell someone about it, wished he could talk to Molly one last time, even if it was only a one-way conversation, even if it was all just him standing there, telling her he was so fucking sorry, he thought it was the right thing to do, he should never have done it, never ever ever...

He was down, cold, sitting on the road, shivering, leaning against the wheel of the Boron's trailer, and she was crouching before him, watching him from behind those dreadful black eyes, pretending to help him. It was hard to hold his head up, and really why should he? He could see the lights from the apartment complex, and there were taxis, and cars, and Electra was down on her haunches, talking to him, telling him some damn thing, and he guessed, vaguely, that observers must imagine she was trying to help him, poor man. He tried to raise a hand, to wave for help, but his hand weighed — no kidding, this is true — about five tons! He couldn't lift it to, well, save his life.

So very cold, empty of blood but full of regret, he sat there, wishing she would go away, but she was waiting for him to go, to make sure he was gone, and couldn't get in a time machine later, and come back and get her in turn. He thought he heard her talking about cutting his throat, to get the job done faster, but then there was a strange, harsh, blatting sound, and someone calling his name,

"Spider!" He was limp, knowing he was leaving the world now, going the way of all flesh, and there was more of that harsh, blatting sound, and he heard, faintly, Electra cry out, and an arm whacked him in the face that he hardly felt, and something heavy collapsed and fell across his numb legs. He was so cold now that he was starting to feel just fine, thanks, and remembered, slightly, that this was bad.

A faint woman's voice was yelling something, he caught the word "ambulance".

Spider was gone.

CHAPTER 26

Four months later, and six years earlier, a tired man found a very determined woman out in the desert outside the country town of Southern Cross late one March afternoon. The woman, attractive, intense, full of purpose, had a lot of equipment with her, including a small but professional-looking video camera wirelessly linked to a high-end laptop. As the man strolled up to where she was spreading out a picnic rug — red and black tartan pattern, very nice — on the ground, he noted that she had a basket containing various items, including what he knew was a one-liter can of petrol, and a plastic disposable cigarette lighter.

It surprised him, as he came within speaking range, and particularly since he was not exactly creeping or tip-toeing along, that she appeared unaware of his approach. But that was her all over, wasn't it? he thought. Determined. Driven. This was Sky Rutherford in full flight, a woman on a mission, out to *make James pay*. Nothing, nothing at all, would deflect the bullet of her revenge from its path.

"G'day," Spider said to her, amiably enough.

She looked up, saw him, and stopped cold, genuinely surprised to see him — anyone — there. "Who the hell are you?"

Spider was gratified to see she was astonished. Someone had found her. How could anyone possibly have found her?

Spider, close enough now to take in the details of the scene, to appreciate the pattern on the blanket, to note the brand name on the petrol can — expensive! — and even to see the camera feed on the screen of her laptop — that was a very nice laptop she was prepared to abandon out here in the middle of nowhere, wished he could afford gear like this. This was a new laptop, state-of-the-art right now, easily three thousand dollars, more or less, and she was going to leave it behind. He knew she was crazy, but that was just *crazy*!

"My name's Spider," he said, sticking his hand out for her to shake. She declined, and kept about her preparations, checking the camera's focus and framing, going back and forth to make sure everything was just so, obsessively, Spider thought, as if composition actually mattered when you were making your very own snuff movie. "I'm a friend."

"How'd you find me?" she said, not looking at him, doing her best to ignore him as much as she could, but also not being particularly rude or hostile. In her mind nothing was going to stop her doing what she was going to do, so a guy like this, this grey-haired, bearded man who had that look about him of a man who had been fat and who had then lost a lot of weight in a hurry, a man who looked tired and worn out, who had a lot on his mind, wasn't about to change that.

"Asked around. Showed a photo of you around town. Talked to the local constabulary..." He didn't tell her that the constabulary in question were six years in the future from now. He had been right: the Southern Cross police had a file on Sky Rutherford's suicide. So much of the circumstances of it were so strange that they had mounted an investigation, discovered she was making a snuff movie of her own suicide, and had contacted James to tell him. Spider shook his head, trying to imagine the scene.

"Did James send you?"

"No, actually. He didn't. This is my idea."

"Your idea? How do you even know what I'm planning? I haven't told a soul about this."

"Time travel, Sky. Think about it."

She laughed. "Ooooh, you've time travelled back from the Future—" She emphasized the capital-F in "Future". "To save me! Good luck with that." She rummaged in a folder of printed documents in the back of her nearby SUV, and came back to the camera bearing a folded sheet of paper.

"That would be the letter you'll be reading?"

"This?" she asked, waving it before him. "You know about this?"

"I've seen the movie. Several times."

Unfazed, she said, "You're not worried about paradoxes and all that bullshit?"

"The universe takes care of everything. I wanted to ask you about that letter, though. If you don't mind."

She was a little amused, not even close to seeing Spider as a threat to her plans. "Ask away! I've got nothing to hide from a man who's seen my movie."

"No mention of your daughter."

This stopped her. "I beg your pardon?" She stopped and looked at him, astonished again, but this time actually disturbed, like he'd struck her with a huge fish. At last, he could see, he'd made some impact on her.

"Your daughter. Electra. Lovely girl. Tried to kill me a while ago. Did a damn good job of it, too. I was in surgery for almost twenty-four hours. Touch and go."

"Excuse me," she said, frowning, puzzled, but wary, no longer the unstoppable force of nature she had been. "I believe you have the wrong person here."

"No," he said, reaching into an inside pocket of his jacket, and pulling out a sheaf of large-format photo prints. "I believe I have exactly the right person. Here, see what you think, you're the photographer, right? Sorry about any composition issues..." He handed the pictures across to her.

Sky took one look at the top one — showing Electra submerged, but for her knees, in the tub, her unfathomable black eyes barely visible in the dark water — and laughed, and handed them back. "Nice try, but no banana."

He went to the next one in the series, this one showing James, butchered, on the marital bed. "Do you know this man?"

She laughed again, but not as much, and with a tone of doubt. "You are kidding. How'd you set these up? Who did the blood? It's very good."

"Your daughter was so destroyed by what you're doing here that she ended up killing James. He had been
planning to kill her, himself. He told me he planned to
do it later that night. They'd had years, Sky, of keeping
the secret of how they killed Clea Fassbinder — ah, you
recognize the name — yes, all of this stems from that.
And what you're doing now just adds to the fun for all
the family."

She took the photos from him, and went and sat on
the open tailgate of her SUV, out of the setting sun, flip-
ping through them, at first quickly, taking it all in, then
slowly, looking deep into each one, the way he had stared
deep into her video.

Spider said, "I've also got video, by the way."

By the time she put the photos down next to her, and
looked at him again, the sun had dropped below the ho-
rizon. Night was settling over the desert. Stars appeared,
one at a time, hard and bright. A faint breeze stirred the
red dust. It was quiet. Sky had said nothing to him. It
was worrying. At any moment he expected her to put
down the photos and tell him to fuck off and then go
about her original plan, though perhaps now with an
improvised message for poor troubled Electra. His repaired heart was booming hard, so loud he was sure Sky
would hear it. At last, weak electric light from inside her
car casting shadows across her face, she looked up at him,
now a different woman, with different, human eyes. "My
daughter did this?"

"I can show you the scar, where she got me," he said,
starting to unbutton his shirt.

She put a hand up. "No, it's..." She was lost for words
for a long moment. "I believe you. The look on your face.
You're not lying. You've seen... all this, haven't you?"

"You believe me?"

She had the photos in hand again, going from one to
the next, shaking her head, her lips pursed tight. "I do,
but... I always wondered about her, she was an odd kid.
We had a cat, once, Fifi. Pedigree. Persian. The most gor-
geous cat." She stared off into the western sky, saying
nothing, then went on, her voice lower, quiet, not looking

at him. "We could never prove that she'd done it, but we never got her any more pets. It was..."

"In your letter," Spider said, leaning against the back of the car, "you tell James that it's his hand setting you alight, that you're only doing what you're doing because he made you do it."

She stared at him, uncomfortable, nowhere to hide, fidgeting with the letter, and started reading it back. "Yeah," she said, weak, her resolve shattered.

"My point, Sky, is that what you're doing, what you intended doing, you're basically setting your daughter on fire. She will go forth from seeing this movie of yours, and she will become what she becomes. She'll kill James. She'll do her damndest to kill me. And of course, she'll kill herself. And it will be just as if you did those things. You'll be killing your daughter. Do you see that?"

She said nothing for a long time. She looked again and again at the photos, particularly the ones showing Electra dead, submerged.

When Spider was able to sit down next to her on the tailgate of her car, and put his arm around her, and hold her while she got as close to crying as she would ever get, he said to her, at last, "You know, Sky, most people, in your situation, they'd get a divorce."

"I wanted to make him..."

"Go home. Call your lawyer. Do the grown-up thing."

She shot him a look, and pulled away slightly. "The grown-up thing?"

"Yes. Grow up. Sure, he had a stupid affair with the shiny woman from the future, so exotic, so fascinating, so much more interesting than his mere wife. Yes, he lied to you and betrayed you, and pretty much destroyed your family. I do not excuse that. All I'm suggesting is that you, at least, do the mature thing. Ditch him. Take the house. Have yourself a cheap and sleazy affair and make him insanely jealous. Just don't do this," he said, indicating the camera and the blanket and the can of petrol. "He's not worth it."

"But—"

Spider produced a business card. "Here. This woman's the best. I did some research, asked around, and lots of people recommended her. Phone her up."

She took the card. "Denise Ganley," she said, looking at it, sagging against him, shaking her head. "I think I've heard of her."

"Take him for everything," he said.

"I had it all planned out," she said, staring at her set-up.

"It was really something to see."

There was a long pause. She said, "You wouldn't..."

He popped his watchtop open, rummaged through the jumble of files he had in there, and brought it up. "You ready for this? It's pretty strong stuff."

She looked at him, and in her dark eyes he saw her true strangeness, a quality he had often seen in Molly's eyes when she was working on something, preoccupied with it. She said, smiling a little, keen to see her own handiwork, "Wouldn't miss it."

He shuddered, and hit play.

Epilogue

It was Spider's first day back at work — six years after talking Sky Rutherford out of killing herself, and five months after just barely surviving Electra Rutherford's attempt to kill him. That both of these things happened, at least in his memory, did not bother him greatly. Probably, he thought, they should. Timelines sprouted hither and yon from every decision point: everything that might happen did happen, somewhere and somewhen. He understood that, at least in theory.

In practice, of course, things were different. These days, Spider had come to realize during his convalescence, Sky Rutherford was a quietly famous director of independent films. She had done well out of divorcing James Rutherford. James, on the other hand, had not done so well. Spider had a brand new memory of James telling him four years ago that he wanted to take Holy Orders, become a priest, or possibly a monk, and he'd taken off for Rome. Two years ago, and without a word of contact in the intervening time, Spider heard through the grapevine that James had been murdered late one night in a Naples park known to be a haunt of gay male prostitutes. The shock of discovering this new memory, as Spider lay in his hospital bed recovering from surgery, was terrible. This, he told himself, is your doing, Spider. You told Sky to divorce him. It was a hard thing to accept.

The Rutherfords' daughter, Electra, had done no better, he learned. She had been found dead of a drug overdose with her boyfriend, "The Beat," in what police regarded as a lovers' suicide pact, shortly after the Rutherfords' divorce was finalized.

When Spider talked to Iris about Electra's attack on him, she looked blank for a moment, then informed him that the attack was "unsolved", and her Major Crime Squad were still looking into it. "Reluctantly," she added. The only description of his attacker, taken from a bored taxi driver across the road that night, was vague to the point of useless. To Spider, though, the description sounded only too familiar: it sounded like Dickhead McMahon's robot personal assistant, the same assistant who appeared to have had a crack at his original Future Self that night at Mrs. Ng's.

All of which was fascinating, of course, but Spider was quite sure it had been Electra who'd tried to kill him. That she and Dickhead's assistant looked a little alike had never occurred to him previously, but the more he thought about it, getting more confused by the moment, the more it haunted him.

Speaking of Dickhead McMahon, Megalomaniac Tyrant of the Far Future, one of the first items of correspondence Malaria handed him on his first day back at work was from his absent employer. And Dickhead was indeed absent. His wife Sarah phoned Spider at work one day, wanting to know if he, Spider, knew where Dickhead had gone. He didn't know what to tell her, the poor woman. Malaria told him Dickhead had not called, had not visited, had not sent any of his annoying memos and reports and forms that needed filling out all the time. Indeed, government fraud investigators were actively trying to find him. It seemed the Time Machines Repaired While-U-Wait business was in deep financial trouble. There was talk of receivership, administrators, bankruptcy, and worse still to come. Dickhead was wanted on charges of embezzlement, fraud, tax evasion, and much else.

Charlie and Malaria asked Spider, on that first day back, if they were going to lose their jobs because of "stupid bloody Dickhead". He said he hoped not. The fact was the time machine repair business was robust: there was no shortage of business. Turnover was good. It was just a question of figuring out where all the money was going. Forensic accountants were trying to sort out the mess. It might take years — but then, once they'd concluded their investigation, located the money, and with a bit of luck Dickhead himself, they planned to time travel back to when Dickhead was still around, and arrest him.

So, Spider thought as morning tea time approached, about this letter from Dickhead. It was highly unusual to receive an actual printed letter, on letterhead, from the likes of Dickhead. He was so in love with email, and phone calls, that the weight, the formality, of an actual letter filled Spider with deep foreboding. He turned it over and over in his hands. Expensive paper. Felt heavy, like there was more than one sheet of paper inside. He didn't want to open it. Malaria offered him a reviving coffee, if that might help. She also asked if that might be his, "You're fired!" letter.

"Hope not," he said, but had his doubts.

Spider was, in fact, surprised to find Dickhead still, apparently, alive somewhere. He thought for sure the bastard would go all the way with his Jim Jones/Jonestown tribute and kill himself. But then, of course, he would miss out on the Final Secret of the Cosmos, wouldn't he? Spider was sure it all made sense to Dickhead, regardless.

Then, while he was still thinking about whether he wanted to open Dickhead's letter, his phone went off. It was Molly.

"Hi, Moll, what's up?"

"Al, I can't log in to the toilet again."

"Can you wait 'til I get off at six?"

"Yeah," she said, a bit sullen, and went away. Spider was happy to help her. As far as Molly was concerned, her entire experience aboard Dickhead's flagship, including the torture, had never happened. In her memory she returned from Bangkok that day, and Spider picked her up, as previously arranged. He drove her back to her place, dropped her off, offered to help with her bags, she said "no, thanks," and that was that, other than pestering him to fix things, mow the lawn, work on her home network, and so forth. More recently, Molly had started experiencing strange nightmares, filled with hellish imagery. She tried to articulate these feelings and images through her sculpture. From the way these HyperFlesh creations were posed,

Spider could not help but notice, they were enduring the torture Molly herself, at least in this timeline, had not experienced, and did not remember. When he asked her why she was producing works like these — works that gave him the horrors — she said she wasn't sure, but it felt "cathartic", she said, to do them, like she was working through something. It also turned out she'd developed an unexpected case of arthritis in her shoulders, neck and spine. Spider could see in the stiff way she moved, sometimes, that it hurt, but said nothing, and did his best to provide positive, constructive feedback to her about her work. Already, she told him, there were "nibbles" — sales leads — from as far away as New York, London, and St. Petersburg. She was going places, he thought, and was pleased, in an abstractly guilty way. He still remembered what had happened to her as a result of his choices, just as he still remembered Sky Rutherford on fire.

Which brought him back, at last, to Dickhead's letter. Made out to Mr. A. Webb, Head Technician, Time Machines Repaired While-U-Wait, Inverness Road, Malaga WA. There was nothing else for it, he thought. He was going to have to read it. He tore it open, peered inside — one sheet of heavy paper, lots of text, single-spaced, practically edge to edge. Subtle as ever, that was Dickhead, he thought.

The sending address was: "Timeship *Victory*, End of Time

"Dear Spider," it began. "Heard you were doing it a bit tough, thought I'd stop by to see how you were bearing up, and say a big hello! HELLO! (ha-ha)"

Spider sighed, a sour feeling collecting in his stomach, and read on.

"Very pleased to hear your lovely wife Molly is back to her former charming self. Please convey to her my best regards. It would be delightful to catch up with you two crazy lovebirds and have a drink or two. There's much to discuss! Things up here at this end of the universe are coming along a treat, just like I said they would, like clockwork, Spider, like clockwork!"

"I've got a really bad feeling about this," Spider said to himself, worried about reading further.

"For one thing," Dickhead went on, "We've finally smashed the last surviving stragglers from the *Masada*. I think they chose the name of their ship a little too well, you mark my words, Spider! Without your esteemed and wily future self to lead them, they collapsed in a heap. Couldn't organize themselves out of a wet paper bag! (ha-ha) So that's the end of them, and good riddance. They never saw what I could see, Spider. They never understood about the Final Secret. They thought I was kidding myself, oh yes they did, they really did. They told me I was delusional! Now who's laughing, eh, Spider?"

"Oh, God," Spider said, feeling ill, thinking about all the *Masadans* he'd met, who hung in there when everything seemed lost, like Cavers and Raspa and Peel and Wendy, all the rest. Soldier Spider couldn't have known that his death would undo all his good work, could he? Could he? The idea haunted him. But if Spider went on to become Soldier Spider, then he'd surely remember getting this letter from Dickhead announcing this great victory, this terrible collapse. Right? How could he kill himself, knowing it would lead to Dickhead's victory?

He slumped against the wall, staring into space, deeply troubled.

Dickhead wasn't finished. He said in his final paragraph, "I should also inform you, Spider, that you owe me a small favor."

"Oh, shit, here it comes," Spider said.

"To put matters bluntly, my friend, that stupid girl did actually kill you. You were dead. You died in the ambulance taking you to the hospital that night. You'd fallen off the perch, you were pining for the fjords, you were dead, Spider. Your heart was shredded, I believe the doctors said. *Shredded*. Think of it."

"Oh, no, no, no..."

"So I tweaked things a little, from up here. It was no problem. Done it before, probably do it again, doesn't hurt anybody. Anyway, we shifted a few threads about, jiggled things here and jaggled things there, and suddenly, no more shredded heart. You were still in bad shape, but they could, just barely, fix you up. It was the subtlest of things, Spider. It's amazing what you can do from here if there's no other bastards trying to interfere. (Ha-ha) So, I think you'd agree, my friend, that you owe me one, yes? Yes, I can see you nodding from here, I truly can. I kept thinking, Poor Spider. If he dies he'll never find out about the Final Secret. He'll go to his final rest unenlightened. And you are my best worker, Spider. I've always said that, and I've always had big things in mind for you, oh yes I have. I haven't forgotten, you mark my words. So, anyway, it's like this, Spider: I'll be in touch."

The letter fell from Spider's hands.

He spent the remaining portion of the afternoon out in the workshop, working on time machines, trying to forget, but could not. The work was strictly routine. Swap out busted component A, plug in new component B, reassemble and test. He brooded, thinking about Dickhead's letter, feeling the weight of the universe pressing him down. He was supposed to be finished with all that bullshit! he told himself. It was over! He'd got Molly back.

Charlie asked him how it felt to be back at work, and Spider had to fight back the urge to yell at the kid and tell him it was, maybe, not so good after all, you might say. Instead, he said, after a moment, "Just the same, you know."

That night, time to go, clear skies for once, a nice breeze wafting in from the ocean, Spider shut down the shop, locked up, went outside into the parking area and climbed into his bike. He pedaled out onto Inverness, looked both ways — and saw that damned Sony car just sitting there. The guy in the driver's seat looked kind of familiar, Spider thought. He sat there, looking at the guy in the car a moment, pissed off, and got out of the bike, let it fall over on the road with a clatter, and went over to have a quiet word with the driver—

But as soon as Spider got to within shouting distance, the car vanished, the driver flicking him a "be seeing you" salute he remembered only too well from ancient TV shows like *The Prisoner*. He stood there on the empty road, staring this way and that, and finally up at the doomed, unwelcoming stars. *The Vores*, he thought, seething, *can't get here fast enough*.

Our titles are available at major book stores and local independent resellers who support Science Fiction and Fantasy readers like you.

EDGE Science Fiction
and Fantasy Publishing

Tesseract Books

Dragon Moon Press

www.edgewebsite.com
www.dragonmoonpress.com

Our titles are available at major book stores and local independent resellers who support Science Fiction and Fantasy readers like you.

Dreams of the Sea by Élisabeth Vonarburg (tp) - ISBN: 978-1-895836-96-7
Dreams of the Sea by Élisabeth Vonarburg (hb) - ISBN: 978-1-895836-98-1

Eclipse by K. A. Bedford (tp) - ISBN: 978-1-894063-30-2
Elements of Fantasy: Magic edited by Dave A. Law
    & Valerie Griswold-Ford (tp) - ISBN: 978-1-8964063-96-8
Even The Stones by Marie Jakober (tp) - ISBN: 978-1-894063-18-0

Fires of the Kindred by Robin Skelton (tp) - ISBN: 978-0-88878-271-7
Firestorm of Dragons edited by Michele Acker & Kirk Dougal (tp)
    - ISBN: 978-1-896944-80-7
Forbidden Cargo by Rebecca Rowe (tp) - ISBN: 978-1-894063-16-6

Game of Perfection, A by Élisabeth Vonarburg (tp)
    - ISBN: 978-1-894063-32-6
Gaslight Grimoire: Dark Tales of Sherlock Holmes
    edited by Jeff Campbell & Charles Prepolec (pb)
    - ISBN: 978-1-8964063-17-3
Green Music by Ursula Pflug (tp) - ISBN: 978-1-895836-75-2
Green Music by Ursula Pflug (hb) - ISBN: 978-1-895836-77-6
Gryphon Highlord, The by Connie Ward (tp) - ISBN: 978-1-896944-38-8

Healer, The by Amber Hayward (tp) - ISBN: 978-1-895836-89-9
Healer, The by Amber Hayward (hb) - ISBN: 978-1-895836-91-2
Hounds of Ash and other tales of Fool Wolf, The by Greg Keyes (pb)
    - ISBN: 978-1-894063-09-8
Human Thing, The by Kathleen H. Nelson - (hb) - ISBN: 978-1-896944-03-6
Hydrogen Steel by K. A. Bedford (tp) - ISBN: 978-1-894063-20-3

i-ROBOT Poetry by Jason Christie (tp) - ISBN: 978-1-894063-24-1

Jackal Bird by Michael Barley (pb) - ISBN: 978-1-895836-07-3
Jackal Bird by Michael Barley (hb) - ISBN: 978-1-895836-11-0
JEMMA7729 by Phoebe Wray (tp) - ISBN: 978-1-894063-40-1

Keaen by Till Noever (tp) - ISBN: 978-1-894063-08-1
Keeper's Child by Leslie Davis (tp) - ISBN: 978-1-894063-01-2

Lachlei by M. H. Bonham (tp) - ISBN: 978-1-896944-69-2
Land/Space edited by Candas Jane Dorsey and Judy McCrosky (tp)
    - ISBN: 978-1-895836-90-5
Land/Space edited by Candas Jane Dorsey and Judy McCrosky (hb)
    - ISBN: 978-1-895836-92-9
Legacy of Morevi by Tee Morris (tp) - ISBN: 978-1-896944-29-6
Legends of the Serai by J.C. Hall - (tp) - ISBN: 978-1-896944-04-3
Longevity Thesis by Jennifer Rahn (tp) - ISBN: 978-1-896944-37-1
Lyskarion: The Song of the Wind by J.A. Cullum (tp)
    - ISBN: 978-1-894063-02-9

Machine Sex and other stories by Candas Jane Dorsey (tp)
    - ISBN: 978-0-88878-278-6
Maërlande Chronicles, The by Élisabeth Vonarburg (pb)
    - ISBN: 978-0-88878-294-6

Madman's Dance by Jana G.Oliver (pb) - ISBN: 978-1-896944-84-5
Magister's Mask, The by Deby Fredericks (tp) - ISBN: 978-1-896944-16-6
Moonfall by Heather Spears (pb) - ISBN: 978-0-88878-306-6
Morevi: The Chronicles of Rafe and Askana by Lisa Lee & Tee Morris
   - (tp) - ISBN: 978-1-896944-07-4

Not Your Father's Horseman by Valorie Griswold-Ford (tp)
   - ISBN: 978-1-896944-27-2

Of Wind and Sand by Sylvie Bérard (translated by Sheryl Curtis) (pb)
   - ISBN: 978-1-894063-19-7
On Spec: The First Five Years edited by On Spec (pb)
   - ISBN: 978-1-895836-08-0
On Spec: The First Five Years edited by On Spec (hb)
   - ISBN: 978-1-895836-12-7
Operation: Immortal Servitude by Tony Ruggerio (tp)
   - ISBN: 978-1-896944-56-2
Operation: Save the Innocent by Tony Ruggerio (tp)
   - ISBN: 978-1-896944-60-9
Orbital Burn by K. A. Bedford (tp) - ISBN: 978-1-894063-10-4
Orbital Burn by K. A. Bedford (hb) - ISBN: 978-1-894063-12-8

Pallahaxi Tide by Michael Coney (pb) - ISBN: 978-0-88878-293-9
Passion Play by Sean Stewart (pb) - ISBN: 978-0-88878-314-1
Petrified World (Determine Your Destiny #1) by Piotr Brynczka (pb)
   - ISBN: 978-1-894063-11-1
Plague Saint by Rita Donovan, The (tp) - ISBN: 978-1-895836-28-8
Plague Saint by Rita Donovan, The (hb) - ISBN: 978-1-895836-29-5
Pretenders by Lynda Williams (pb) - ISBN: 978-1-894063-13-5

Reluctant Voyagers by Élisabeth Vonarburg (pb) - ISBN: 978-1-895836-09-7
Reluctant Voyagers by Élisabeth Vonarburg (hb) - ISBN: 978-1-895836-15-8
Resisting Adonis by Timothy J. Anderson (tp) - ISBN: 978-1-895836-84-4
Resisting Adonis by Timothy J. Anderson (hb) - ISBN: 978-1-895836-83-7
Righteous Anger by Lynda Williams (tp) - ISBN: 897-1-894063-38-8

Shadebinder's Oath by Jeanette Cottrell - (tp) - ISBN: 978-1-896944-31-9
Silent City, The by Élisabeth Vonarburg (tp) - ISBN: 978-1-894063-07-4
Slow Engines of Time, The by Élisabeth Vonarburg (tp) - ISBN: 978-1-895836-30-1
Slow Engines of Time, The by Élisabeth Vonarburg (hb) - ISBN: 978-1-895836-31-8
Small Magics by Erik Buchanan (tp) - ISBN: 978-1-896944-38-8
Sojourn by Jana Oliver - (pb) - ISBN: 978-1-896944-30-2
Sorcerers of War by Kristan Proudman (pb) - ISBN: 978-1-896944-64-7
Stealing Magic by Tanya Huff (tp) - ISBN: 978-1-894063-34-0
Strange Attractors by Tom Henighan (pb) - ISBN: 978-0-88878-312-7
Sword Masters by Selina Rosen (tp) - ISBN: 978-1-896944-65-4

Taming, The by Heather Spears (pb) - ISBN: 978-1-895836-23-3
Taming, The by Heather Spears (hb) - ISBN: 978-1-895836-24-0
Teacher's Guide to Dragon's Fire, Wizard's Flame by Unwin & Mennenga - (pb)
   - ISBN: 978-1-896944-19-7
Ten Monkeys, Ten Minutes by Peter Watts (tp) - ISBN: 978-1-895836-74-5
Ten Monkeys, Ten Minutes by Peter Watts (hb) - ISBN: 978-1-895836-76-9

Tesseracts 1 edited by Judith Merril (pb) - ISBN: 978-0-88878-279-3

Tesseracts 2 edited by Phyllis Gotlieb & Douglas Barbour (pb)
  - ISBN: 978-0-88878-270-0

Tesseracts 3 edited by Candas Jane Dorsey & Gerry Truscott (pb)
  - ISBN: 978-0-88878-290-8

Tesseracts 4 edited by Lorna Toolis & Michael Skeet (pb)
  - ISBN: 978-0-88878-322-6

Tesseracts 5 edited by Robert Runté & Yves Maynard (pb)
  - ISBN: 978-1-895836-25-7

Tesseracts 5 edited by Robert Runté & Yves Maynard (hb)
  - ISBN: 978-1-895836-26-4

Tesseracts 6 edited by Robert J. Sawyer & Carolyn Clink (pb)
  - ISBN: 978-1-895836-32-5

Tesseracts 6 edited by Robert J. Sawyer & Carolyn Clink (hb)
  - ISBN: 978-1-895836-33-2

Tesseracts 7 edited by Paula Johanson & Jean-Louis Trudel (tp)
  - ISBN: 978-1-895836-58-5

Tesseracts 7 edited by Paula Johanson & Jean-Louis Trudel (hb)
  - ISBN: 978-1-895836-59-2

Tesseracts 8 edited by John Clute & Candas Jane Dorsey (tp)
  - ISBN: 978-1-895836-61-5

Tesseracts 8 edited by John Clute & Candas Jane Dorsey (hb)
  - ISBN: 978-1-895836-62-2

Tesseracts Nine edited by Nalo Hopkinson and Geoff Ryman (tp)
  - ISBN: 978-1-894063-26-5

Tesseracts Ten edited by Robert Charles Wilson and Edo van Belkom (tp)
  - ISBN: 978-1-894063-36-4

Tesseracts Eleven edited by Cory Doctorow and Holly Phillips (tp)
  - ISBN: 978-1-894063-03-6

Tesseracts Twelve edited by Claude Lalumière (pb) - ISBN: 978-1-894063-15-9

Tesseracts Q edited by Élisabeth Vonarburg & Jane Brierley (pb)
  - ISBN: 978-1-895836-21-9

Tesseracts Q edited by Élisabeth Vonarburg & Jane Brierley (hb)
  - ISBN: 978-1-895836-22-6

Throne Price by Lynda Williams and Alison Sinclair (tp)
  - ISBN: 978-1-894063-06-7

Time Machines Repaired Whie-U-Wait by K. A. Bedford (tp)
  - ISBN: 978-1-894063-42-5

Too Many Princes by Deby Fredricks (tp) - ISBN: 978-1-896944-36-4

Twilight of the Fifth Sun by David Sakmyster (tp)
  - ISBN: 978-1-896944-01-02

Virtual Evil by Jana Oliver (tp) - ISBN: 978-1-896944-76-0

Writers For Relief: An Anthology to Benefit the Bay Area Food Bank
  edited by Davey Beauchamp (pb) - ISBN: 978-1-896944-92-0